PHANTOM FIRE

PHANTOM FIRE

Phantom Fire

Michael Jace

Crow House Press

Contents

Prologue	4

MARKED · 9

1	Vermillion and Black	10
2	The Gentle Giant	19
3	Teacher	31
4	Bad Liars	42
5	Heartbeat	55
6	The Mark of the Phantom	70
7	Blood and Fire	82
8	Champion	97

WHAT LIES BENEATH · 123

9	The Scarlet Key	124
10	Eos	139
11	Sundown	151
12	Under the Mountain	163
13	Lost	173
14	Gilded Leaves	196

| 15 | Scoráneile | 208 |

PHANTOM'S EMBRACE 227

16	Burn	228
17	The Road of Giants	239
18	Blind Eyes	250
19	As Above	264
20	So Below	277
21	Pale Green	287
22	Rise and Fall	304
	Epilogue	316

Copyright © 2024 by Michael Jace

All rights reserved. No part of this book may be reproduced in any manner whatsoever without written permission except in the case of brief quotations embodied in critical articles and reviews.

First Printing, 2024

For Mom

Aspects of the Allmother	
Aspect	Domain
The Sovereign	Leadership, the Sun
The Warrior	Battle, the Forge
The Earth Mother	Nature
The Shapeshifter	Beasts, the Hunt
The Seeress	Divination, Time
The Witch	Magic, Trickery
The Faerie Queen	Revelry, the Moon
The Lover	Love, Lust
The Phantom	Life, Death, Rebirth

Prologue

Many had come and many had fallen. After the death of the king of Maecha, men and women gathered in Letha, capital city of the lush green country, to fight in the *bahvra*. The *bahvra* took place whenever the leader of Maecha died and was a year-long struggle between warriors to prove which one amongst them was the strongest fighter, and therefore, the rightful successor to the throne.

When Scáthan, the previous king of Maecha, passed away, his two daughters donned their armor and entered the *bahvra*. Aife and Branwyn were both masters of battle; trained in hand-to-hand combat from childhood, the sisters epitomized physical prowess. Although quite nearly equal in skill, Aife won more of their practice bouts than her sister, though many would agree that Branwyn was far more ferocious and intimidating in battle.

Upon entering the *bahvra*, Aife and Branwyn abstained from challenging each other for as long as they could manage, since a challenge meant a fight to the death. As the harvest season came to a close and competitors began to dwindle, however, Aife and Branwyn were forced to consider the possibility that they may soon have to do battle. One by one, competitors came to Letha to challenge one of the sisters and were inevitably slain.

The day came when Aife and Branwyn had defeated every other challenger in the *bahvra*. Knowing their battle was inescapable, Branwyn steeled herself as she submitted a formal challenge to her sister for their father's throne. Branwyn arrived at Aife's home and presented to her the collection of spoils, small family crests tied into loops of string, that she accumulated from her previous *bahvra* victories. Aife nodded solemnly as she amassed her smaller, but still quite respectable, collection of spoils and pooled them together with her sister's collection.

After the battle the next morning, the victor would claim the accrued spoils and become the next leader of Maecha.

Crowds gathered around the base of the great burial mound just outside Letha atop which all final *bahvra* challenges were fought as crows flocked to the nearby trees in anticipation of the bloodletting that was to come. As the sun rose over the distant hilltops and it was clear that dawn had come, Aife, in full leather plate armor and with her polished spear in her right hand, climbed the northern side of the mound. Branwyn, equipped with her own sharpened spear and her lighter armor, climbed the southern face of the mound. The two warrior-sisters met at the flattened top where they grasped arms in greeting before turning to walk to the edges of the hilltop.

Aife's eyes were full of sorrow behind her flaming red curls as she gazed upon her younger sister. Branwyn, knowing Aife was a slightly better fighter, was more nervous than saddened about the prospect of fighting her sister to the death. But she refused to show her fear and instead pasted a confident smirk onto her painted face. Sighing, Aife nodded and raised her spear to point across the gap. Branwyn released a long breath and brought the end of her own spear up.

Then it began.

Leather boots ghosted gracefully across the grass of the mound as the sisters sparred. Although Aife wanted nothing less than to fight her own flesh and blood, she did not falter. Branwyn fought with a fire that could not be doused, her blazing hair dancing around her face as she thrusted her spear at Aife over and over only to catch air or be parried away by a swipe of Aife's spear shaft with blinding speed.

What seemed like hours passed, and still, neither of the combatants wavered. There were no calls for respite. The sun was rising higher into the sky when the crows began to titter anxiously behind the amber leaves of the trees. They called out, their restless caws like the screams of the damned. Some of the spectators had gone back to their homes to rest, while the more resilient stayed on to witness the outcome and discover who the next ruler of their fair land would be.

When the sun was well on its way towards the center of the cerulean sky, Branwyn's energy had finally filtered out as her more ferocious fighting style took a more costly reserve of stamina to keep up. At last, when Branwyn threw one final weary slash of her spear in Aife's general direction, the elder sister easily disarmed her challenger, the spear flying from the mound. Defeated and utterly exhausted, Branwyn dropped to her knees and inclined her head to meet her sister's eyes in the morning light. The crowd and crows grew silent. The wind stopped rustling through the falling leaves. It was as if the whole countryside held its breath in that moment.

Slowly but purposefully, Aife closed the short distance. "Sister—" she whispered.

"Don't," Branwyn interrupted through labored breaths. "We both knew what we were doing when we began this *bahvra*. Now, do it. Finish me. Claim the throne."

Aife's spearhead didn't leave the ground. "Bran, I cannot do it."

Branwyn's eyes burned with anger. "Aife, you must! Do not don cowardice now! Put your spear into my chest and be done with it!"

Tears spilled from Aife's eyes as she shakily raised her spear to her sister's heart. Branwyn, with fierce determination, pressed her leather-bound chest against the spearhead. She felt the pressure of the steel point through her light armor, but it didn't pierce the skin.

"No!" Aife shouted as she thrust her weapon into the top of the burial mound.

"Aife - "

"No!" she repeated. "I will not kill my sister. You are my only family."

Branwyn shook her head. "Sister, you cannot claim the throne unless you kill me; you know that this is how it must be."

Aife was quiet for a moment. Finally, she whispered, "Not necessarily."

"What do you speak of?" Branwyn demanded.

"There is another option," Aife responded. Branwyn, confused, looked around as if trying to physically see what her sister was talking about.

"I am sorry, Bran," Aife said, her voice a ghost of a whisper. "I wish you would have won."

"What are you doing?" Branwyn asked as the crowd below began to grow restless. Then, she remembered. There was a way to claim victory in the final *bahvra* challenge other than through death, though it practically never happened. Although to lose the challenge that way meant you were forever dishonored.

"Aife," Branwyn said, rising wearily to her sore feet. "*No.* Do not do this to me."

"I do not have another choice," Aife said as she choked back her tears.

Branwyn let out an angry breath. "Either you kill me," she stated, "or I kill you." And with her last remaining threads of strength, Branwyn lunged at her sister.

Had Aife blinked, she would have not been quick enough. But Aife hooked her spear under her sister's arm and threw her sideways to the ground. She pressed her boot on top of Branwyn's back and rested the tip of her spear to the back of her neck.

"Branwyn of the Clan of Ulster," Aife pronounced loud enough for the people below to hear. "You are not worthy to perish by my spear this day."

A cruel murmur spread throughout the onlookers. With tears in her eyes, Branwyn struggled to fight back under the weight of her sister's boot before she could finish.

Although the words were bitter in her own mouth, Aife continued if only to spare the life of her sister. "You are hereby banished from the lands of Maecha. You must leave the green of this country and never set foot upon these hills again. Even should your life leave you, your remains shall never touch this land. Now, begone."

MARKED

1

Vermillion and Black

Eighteen years later

Vermillion and black were the colors of the Vallas family. As such, these were the colors that Castor bore for the festival of the summer solstice. A vermillion *chitos* was draped across his chest and over his left shoulder with a black leather belt tied around his center, leaving the rest of the garment to skirt down to just above his knees.

Alone in his private quarters, he gazed at his reflection in his polished bronze mirror. Dark curls brushed against his furrowed brow. His high cheekbones and pronounced jawline, he got from his father, though he was told he got his midnight eyes from his mother, who had died during his birth.

The sound of the festival below reminded him that he was required to at least make an appearance for the guests downstairs, though Castor dreaded parties. The only bright side of these things was that he was able to see his closest friend, Ophelia Patera, another noble from a neighboring province. Although they only really saw each other during the four seasonal festivals each year, they bonded over their shared dislike of the responsibilities of their nobility. They both especially detested the formality of holiday festivities.

PHANTOM FIRE | 11

Finally, he decided that he would rather be able to spend as much time with his friend as possible, even if it meant putting up with the other nobles of Odessa. Tossing the mirror to his bed, he strode out of his room and down the corridor to the grand staircase.

At the banister, he peered down to the foyer where some of the later guests were still spilling in. All the expected nobility must have already arrived and been let into the ballroom, as the guests below were clearly commoners of the city of Polara.

Ophelia must already be in the estate, he thought. With as much decorum as a noble who didn't care for his status could muster, Castor loafed down the stairs and into the ballroom.

Looking around the tall, decorative arches molded into the marble walls and through the thick white pillars that held up the second-floor balcony, Castor recognized several other nobles whom he knew and several whom he would rather like to avoid. The head of the Aren family, Asten, who saw over the Yrda province in the northeast, stood near the fountain in the center of the room chatting with Jessamine, the duchess of the Serene province which sat on Yrda's southern border. Helena and Beatrice, noblewomen from one of the southwestern settlements, were keeping to themselves against one of the walls, eyeing other guests with judgmental glances. A group of minor nobles were talking loudly with one another, already clearly drunk, near the far windows. Castor's father, the duke of the Anand province, stood wearing the vermillion mantle of the Vallas family near the columns of the western wall and was speaking with Karth Patera, duke of the Everell province and father of Ophelia.

Keeping his head down and squeezing through the other guests as discreetly as possible, Castor made his way to his father. Unfortunately, Asten Aren spotted him before he could arrive.

"Well, if it isn't the young Lord Vallas!" Asten Aren shouted, loud enough that many of the other guests' heads turned to look his way. "You missed the welcoming speech, you did. Decide you would finally grace us with your presence, did you now?" His eastern accent was a bit stronger than usual, probably due to the wine, Castor thought.

Castor sighed and straightened up as the other guests returned to their business. "I decided I did not want you to come all the way to the festival here in Anand only to be deprived of the light I bring whenever I walk into a room."

Asten let out a hearty laugh, his brown curls shaking around his chubby face. "Ah, and with the wit of his father, no less!" he slurred. "So, tell me," he said as he put his arm around Castor's shoulder. His breath stank of dark wine and his light green mantle carried a plethora of stains and the scent of sweat. This was one of the many nobles whom Castor would not have minded missing. "What do you think about Empress Dialaune's new law regarding the Maechan immigrants?"

If he was honest, Castor despised the current empress of Odessa. She was infamous for her contempt of Maecha, Odessa's northern neighbor, and it was clear her dislike came from unfounded stereotypes associated with the people who lived there. After all, Maecha and Odessa had had no real disputes in recent history if Castor's required history studies were to be believed. According to the empress, however, Maechans were all barbaric animals whose only desires were to murder and rape everyone in sight. This new law that Asten asked about was an edict making it illegal to house Maechans. The law also rewarded any Odessan who turned in a Maechan to the guards.

"What do *I* think?" Castor asked, feeling his temperature rise. "Personally, I think the law is a disgrace to Odessa," he said. "Obviously, the reasoning behind the law is based on racist propaganda that is continuously being spewed out by our incompetent - "

"Cas!"

He rounded at the sound of the familiar voice, turning his gaze away from narrowing eyes. A woman in an emerald-green *chitos* and cloth-of-gold belt stood nearby. Her soft, delicate features were famed and adored in her province of Everell, though Castor knew she was anything but soft.

"Ah, there you are, Ophelia," Castor said as the noblewoman approached. She wore an expression on her face that seemed to be a mix between incredulity and sternness. He received it whenever he was near treasonous talk in inappropriate places.

It was a common look.

"Good evening, Duke Aren," Ophelia said politely. "It is good to see you are well. Please send my best wishes to the rest of the Aren family." She grabbed Castor's arm and spun him around before either of them could continue their conversation.

"Goodbye, little beauty," Asten called out after her with waggling fingers. "My heart leaves with you!"

Ophelia shivered with disgust as she marched Castor to the door of the ballroom, squeezing through all of the nobles and commoners in her way. As they pushed through the ballroom door and into the nearly empty foyer, she said, "Where do we want to hide out this time?"

Castor thought about it. The gardens were beautiful this time of the year, but that usually meant that there would be more than a handful of guests milling about there. They could sneak upstairs, but then they would have to hide from the servants lest they be seen together; that could easily lead to some very racy and untrue rumors about the two of them.

"We could try the altar room," he suggested. "It normally stays quite empty during these things."

After Ophelia agreed to Castor's plan, they quietly stole into the altar room. As he assumed, the room was barren, save for the nine altars that lined the wall of the circular room and four stone benches that bordered the square fountain in the center of the room, the sprinkle of water echoing off the otherwise silent stone. The room was lit warmly by torches, their glow casting the shadows of the room's two new occupants into a gentle dance. Even when the altar room went through periods of relative disuse, there were *always* torches burning within.

This tradition of the burning torches was held throughout the country to honor the Sunfire in the land's capital city, Hale. If the stories were to be believed, the Sunfire was once a piece of the sun itself that fell to the earth and created the great chasm that the city was later built in and around. The flame from the Sunfire's impact all those years ago has been kept and guarded since its discovery, and the torches surrounding Castor now paid tribute to that impossible work.

"Our altar room is prettier than yours," Ophelia teased as she strode to plop down on one of the benches.

Castor did not usually spend much time in the altar room. He was not exactly very spiritual, but it wasn't as if he was entirely ignorant about the Allmother and the nine Aspects. The Allmother was the supposed creator of Serrae, and the nine Aspects were each a division of the Allmother who governed specific facets of the world. Most of the world was heavy with believers, except for one country far to the east of Odessa who favored their innovations over faith. Castor did not care much either way.

"So, have you talked to your father about it yet?" Ophelia asked as Castor sat back next to her.

"I, uh …" His voice trailed off as he suddenly became extremely fascinated with his fingernails.

"You are such a child," she remarked. "What's the worst that could happen if you asked him?"

"I could die."

Ophelia laughed. The familiar sound made Castor feel warm.

"Why don't you ask *your* father, then?" he countered, his voice echoing softly off the high walls.

"Because, while I hate being a noble as much as you do, I do not care to better myself at swordplay," she answered matter-of-factly.

"I just want to be trained by an actual soldier," Castor mused. "The weapons trainer here is fine and all, but he hasn't ever been in a real battle. I want to learn from someone who has actually done it, you know?"

"Tell your father that," Ophelia insisted.

Castor sighed but did not answer. As much as he yearned for the chance to escape his duties here in Polara, even if only for a year-long apprenticeship, a part of him feared the idea of such a drastic change to his everyday life.

PHANTOM FIRE | 15

After a brief silence, she went on. "I'm serious, Cas. You know you will never get to go to Endala if you don't just ask him. You have literally nothing to lose."

He sighed again. She was right, but he would obviously never tell her that, so he changed the subject. "Speaking of fathers, how is the situation with yours?" he asked as his eyes fell to a small cluster of burning candles. The orange of the dancing candlelight illuminated the altar of the Faerie Queen Aspect directly behind them. Apparently, a few of the partygoers had stopped by the altar room to pay tribute to the goddess of revelry before Castor and Ophelia had hidden away there.

Ophelia groaned and pulled at her dark curls in frustration. "IF HE TRIES TO MARRY ME OFF ONE MORE TIME - "

"So, it's going well," he said.

She scoffed. "I don't want to marry a noble, you know that," she said. "My father continues to set me up with other noblemen in our province, but they are all just so posh and snobby. Sometimes I wish I could just run away. Don't get me wrong, it is nice having all my wants and needs tended to at all times, but sometimes I wish I had the freedom to make my own choices with my life." She leaned back on her hands with a sigh. "Anyway, I've resorted to scaring off my suitors."

Castor snorted. "And how are you managing that?"

"It's not too difficult to act just mad or improper enough to frighten most away," she explained. "Though, if all else fails, there is this cushioned chair in the study, and if you sit in it just right, it makes a creak that sounds hauntingly reminiscent to a far - "

Castor burst into laughter before she could even finish, and Ophelia followed suit soon after. It was times like these when Castor was actually happy. The rest of his life was filled with the dull responsibilities of learning Odessan politics and making nice with other nobles to maintain good appearances. It was only when he was able to spend time with Ophelia, someone who actually understood his dislike of nobility, that he was able to enjoy himself.

Ophelia sat forward suddenly, a wild look on her face. "I'll make you a deal," she said, her tone serious.

16 | MICHAEL JACE

"This should be good," Castor muttered.

"If you ask your dad to go apprentice under the Spear Maiden in Endala, I will tell mine that I refuse to be set up with suitors anymore. It's time we took control of our own lives. I mean, by the Aspects, I have seen six and twenty summers! And am I wrong that this is your twenty-second?"

"Third," he corrected.

"All the more reason to do it!" she exclaimed as she sprang up from the bench. A minor draft swept in from somewhere that made gooseflesh rise on Castor's arms. Or maybe it wasn't the breeze that brought it on. "Come on! We have to go do this now - hurry, before I lose my nerve!"

"What? We *just* sat down, Ophelia."

"I don't care. Come on, let's *go!*"

Struck by Ophelia's outburst of courage, Castor stood and felt a nervous tingle of excitement flutter in his stomach. Ophelia just laughed as she tugged Castor along by the wrist through the altar room and out into the corridor.

As they burst into the ballroom, they saw that the festival was in full swing. Nearly every guest was entirely drunk on the endlessly flowing wines and ales. Maybe he would get lucky and his father would be so intoxicated that he'd actually agree to his idea.

They spotted their fathers leaning against each other near the fountain and laughing like the old friends they were. Ophelia and Castor grasped each other's hands tightly and nodded at each other before marching over to their fathers.

"Castor!" Karth exclaimed at the same time that Vasili, Castor's father, shouted, "Ophelia!"

"Hello, Karth," Castor responded at the same time that Ophelia said, "Hello there, Vasili."

"You go first," Ophelia said.

Castor nodded. "Father," he said through a shaky voice. Ophelia squeezed his hand, and his voice steadied. "I want to apprentice under the Spear Maiden in Endala at the turn of the season."

Vasili stopped swaying drunkenly as his eyebrows scrunched together in scrutiny.

Castor went on, adrenaline pumping through his veins. "It's only for a year," he added. "I think it will teach me - "

"Well, sure, m'boy!" Vasili chortled. "That sounds like a fantastic idea. You have really come along in your studies; it may do you some good to go out and get some real experience. Remind me again in the morning, and we can get all the details sorted."

A chill ran through Castor's blood as the hair rose on his arms. "T— Truly?" He looked from his father to Ophelia and back. "I mean - of course, Father. Thank you."

Castor's smile cracked his face as he squeezed Ophelia's hand, signaling her turn.

"Father," Ophelia announced, her voice like marble. "I do not want you to set me up with nobles anymore."

Karth's eyes narrowed.

"Also, I want to move away. I want to live on my own and - "

"What the hell are you talking about?" Karth nearly shouted. "You are a woman! Well, hardly even that. You have no idea how to survive on your own. You need a man to care and provide for you." Karth paused a moment, perhaps realizing the scene he was making. He cleared his throat and lowered his voice to continue. "You will be staying at our estate in Everell until you can settle down and get married to a suitable man. I will hear no more on this topic from you."

Castor couldn't believe what he was hearing. "That's horsesh - "

Ophelia discreetly stomped on Castor's foot. "Yes, Father," she said solemnly but obediently. Her grasp loosened in Castor's hand.

Their fathers waddled off together, leaving the two of them stranded by the fountain.

"Ophelia ..." Castor circled his arms around her as she buried her face in his neck. He thought she might cry, but after a brief silence, she just let out a long breath and straightened up. "Don't worry about me," she said. She had on a brave face, though Castor could tell she was hurting.

He gave her a meaningful look as they sat down at the fountain. He could not bring himself to show his excitement about his father's acceptance in the wake of his friend's rejection, so instead, they just sat and laughed at the other nobles while enjoying the flowing dark wine.

At some point in the evening when the wine had truly taken effect, Ophelia's mother, Neithe, emerged from the guest quarters where she typically stayed during the better part of these festivals. She always had some kind of excuse she'd give to any inquirers, though Ophelia had told Castor long ago that her mother just preferred the quiet.

Despite being a bit of a recluse, Neithe had a certain presence that could not be ignored whenever she entered a room. She stood tall and powerful, regal in her D'jadii-style *sh'kar* - a long, tight-fitting garment that left the arms and collar bare save for two silk straps that connected over shoulders. While her *sh'kar* was traditionally D'jadii formal wear, Neithe had it dyed emerald and trimmed with cloth-of-gold to match the Patera colors, bringing both of the cultures together in one beautiful piece. Her many dark braids cascaded down from the high knot on her head and halfway down the lengths of her toned legs that could have been cut straight from obsidian.

She had come to collect her husband and daughter for the evening.

They all retired to the guest quarters, leaving Castor with no one around he'd like to converse with, so he too followed the Patera's lead and went to his own bed.

Lounging in the candlelight alone, Castor let his mind wander as he tried to block out the far-off din of revelers below. His mind went to Ophelia and her father first, but that only made him angry for her. With a frustrated sigh, Castor guided his thoughts to a happier place—Endala and his future apprenticeship under the Spear Maiden. He fell asleep with a smile on his face, wondering what the next year would have in store for him.

2

The Gentle Giant

Across the Maechan border

The chill heralding the end of the season was apparent this time of the year in the village of Albainn. A cool breeze ghosted off the sea and around the trees. The leaves, yellowing from the beginning of the new season, swirled with the gentle wind and fluttered to the soft ground around the round stone and wooden buildings that populated the village. Amidst the crunch of the leaves and the lowing of aurochs, a rhythmic *clanging* sounded - metal striking against metal - that rang out like a harsh bell in the darkening woods.

Despite the brisk wind, sweat beaded on Aedan's brow as he struck the hammer against the glowing steel. The heat from the forge battled autumn's first breath all around the apprentice blacksmith - one second the swelter of the fire singed the hair on his arms, the next he would feel the cool of the ocean air on his seared skin.

Finally, the axe head was finished. He wiped his arm across his brow as he dropped the newly forged blade into the trough of water. The sound of red steel meeting cold water was music to Aedan's ears. It was the sound of a job completed. The sound of his hard work paying off through the creation of something new. This time, the sound was even more rewarding, since this creation was for his own use. The blacksmith he studied under finally allowed him to forge his own weapon in honor of his decision to fight in Albainn's annual competition.

The next day, Aedan would be combatting three other Albainn citizens for the chance to train under the legendary Spear Maiden in Odessa. It was Aedan's dream to learn how to fight from her, one of the most renowned warriors in Serrae. All he had to do was defeat the other combatants the next day and Albainn's ruling clan would fund his journey to Endala. He had the advantage of being bigger and stronger than the other three warriors, and he knew that he could easily take on two of them by himself. Bóina, the last warrior, was the only one he was actually worried about. She was small, much smaller than Aedan, though she was fast and wiry like an eel. He knew she fought with twin daggers, and if she got in close, he would definitely lose. He would have to make sure that he caught her with his axes before she could get to him.

The steel had cooled, so Aedan affixed it to a sturdy, slightly curved wooden shaft and began sharpening it. Once it was sharp enough to glide through flesh, he dropped back into an oaken chair and admired his handiwork. It was a tad heavy, but that wasn't a problem for the apprentice blacksmith. Aedan was bigger than most other men in his village; some of the other villagers would even joke that his mother would have had to have been part giantess to have had a child as big as him. Obviously, it was untrue; Aedan wasn't *that* big, though he did stand over most and could outmatch even more in contests of strength.

Aedan gazed out into the deepening night and decided that he should make his way back home to prepare dinner for when Fiona, his younger sister, made it back. He made sure to properly close down the forge before grabbing the haft of his new axe and heading out into the night. Instead of walking the direct path back to his home, he decided to take the longer route and let the brisk air cool his flame-heated skin.

On the walk back, Aedan passed out of the merchant quarter of Albainn and into the winding paths of the wooded quarter. Aedan loved this forested part of the village most. In the other three, most of the trees had been cut down to make room for buildings and the like; there in the wooded quarter, however, the small buildings were made around the trees instead. There were some shops here too that either were not prestigious enough for the merchant quarter or that had simply existed before the merchant quarter was even thought of. Aedan ambled by the rounded divination shop of Gladia, a very beautiful and skilled mystic, who was sitting outside her shop and smoking from a long pipe. She winked at him as he passed; he blushed and quickened his pace in response. He was not used to being shown interest so openly, as most were either intimidated by his great build or unimpressed by his surname.

Albainn was not so large a village, so it was not long before Aedan found himself in the domestic quarter. While there were homes spread about the entire village, most could be found there in the domestic quarter, including Aedan's. There was not much economic disparity in the fishing village; but the poorer citizens typically lived farther away from the center of town. Aedan's destination was on the outskirts.

When he arrived at the small, two-room home, he set his new axe aside and stretched his tired arms. He knew Fiona would be home soon, so he started a new batch of potato soup over the small fire in the hearth.

It was not too much longer before his sister pushed through the timeworn door and sat next to the fire. Aedan spooned some of the steaming soup into a wooden bowl and handed her a piece of stale bread.

"Did you find any new work today, Fi?" he asked her as he reclined back against the wall, already having had his fill of the bland soup.

"Just the usual," she muttered quietly as she took another sip of the hot soup.

Aedan cursed under his breath. "'The usual'? Fi, we talked about this."

She rolled her eyes and tucked a burgundy curl behind her freckled ear. "There isn't much else people will hire me for," she whispered.

Aedan felt his temperature rise as he tried not to think about all the men she might have been with that day, but it didn't really matter how he felt. He knew he did not make enough money alone for the both of them to survive. That was one of the main reasons he wanted to win the tournament the next day. After he was properly trained, he could enlist as a soldier in one of the larger settlements like Letha or Trícnoc. Soldiers made much more money than apprentice blacksmiths did.

She changed the subject. "Are you worried about tomorrow?"

"Of course I am," he said. "About Bóina, anyway. The other two are no problem, and they know it. I have fought with them before, and I always beat them. As long as I can take out Bóina, the others will forfeit."

"You want me to drop some belladonna in her breakfast?" Fiona asked. "That would make the fight a little easier tomorrow, I think."

Aedan laughed. "Well, yes; corpses typically do not put up much of a fight. But no, I do not want to cheat to win."

"Well, you'd better not die, Aedan," Fiona said, a motherly tone settling in. "The Spear Maiden is not worth that."

"Oh, come on, Fi. Obviously, I will forfeit if I'm about to lose."

She stared at him with accusatory eyes over the remains of her soup, but she did not mention any more on the topic. It was already growing late, and Aedan needed a good night's rest if he was going to stand a chance against Bóina, so when Fiona finished the last of the potato soup, she slid into the other room of the house and left Aedan alone.

The next morning, Aedan hoped that he was not going to need a good night's rest after all, seeing as he did not get one. His nerves were too wild. He could not help but think how bad it would be for Fiona if he did not win. He had to win. For her.

He ate a chunk of the old bread for breakfast and threw on a green tunic. He strapped hardened leather to his forearms and over his knees and slung his two homemade shoulder straps across his back to hold his axes. Only the axe he'd forged the night before was meant for battle; the other was a regular woodcutter's axe, though he figured it would get the job done just as well.

He tore off another piece of the bread and left it on the wooden offering plate that sat close to the wall near the hearth as he whispered

PHANTOM FIRE | 23

a prayer to the Allmother and her Warrior Aspect for victory. Fiona sometimes gave him a hard time for his faith in the Allmother. "How could you believe in someone who would put us through what we've been through?" she would say. But Aedan believed that the Allmother purposely put those challenges in front of them so that they could become tougher and more resilient. If they had soft, easy lives, how could they have learned to be strong anyway?

With his axes securely strapped to his back and with the favor of the Warrior Aspect, he hiked into the forest. Not too far away from Albainn was a beautiful, natural clearing in the woods. A winding stream fed by a hidden lake in the mountains trickled through the clearing, cutting it into two halves of lush green grass dotted here and there with bloody glories, those alabaster flowers whose wide, crimson-tipped petals appeared to have been carefully dipped in blood. The chill of the morning made Aedan shiver as he approached the meadow in which the battle would take place.

Some had already gathered in the clearing to watch, but the only other combatant who had arrived before Aedan was none other than Bóina. She stood alone near the stream and stretched her compact muscles. A sling of throwing knives wrapped diagonally across her torso, though Aedan was not too worried about those. While he was quite a bit larger than most, he had excellent reflexes. What concerned him more hung about her sides in leather sheathes. The two daggers there were quite a bit longer than the throwing knives - longer than most daggers actually. Bóina had them specially made to compensate for her lack of reach.

Aedan, being the kind and good-natured lad he was, decided to go chat with her before the skirmish.

"Hail, Bóina," Aedan greeted as he approached her.

Her eyes focused on him warily as she slowly stopped stretching her arms out. "Hail to you, friend," she responded. She untied a strap of cloth from around her arm and used it to pull her cascading black hair away from her neck.

"Do not worry; I am not here to get an early start on the bloodshed," Aedan said with a laugh as he noticed her trepidation. "I just thought we could stretch together before the fight. Is that all right?"

She still seemed a bit guarded, but she nodded and began slowly pulling at one of her ankles to loosen her leg. Aedan followed suit.

"I'm not going to take it easy on you," she said finally. "This has been my dream for years now - to go apprentice under the Spear Maiden."

"I did not think you would," Aedan said as he switched legs. "Nor is it what I would want. If you are the better fighter, then you deserve to go." He meant it, too. He would not want to win solely because someone took pity on his situation at home and his status in the village.

Her expression softened then as she pulled her elbow over her head. "Do you remember when we were kids, and we went on that hunting trip together?" she asked after a moment of silence.

"How could I forget? I couldn't bring myself to kill the doe," Aedan laughed. He had almost forgotten about it, actually. It was well over a decade before when he had turned ten and been allowed by his caretakers to go on a hunting party with two others his age. Bóina was one of them. Aedan remembered pulling back the drawstring of his bow, but not being able to let his arrow fly. "You did it for me," he said.

She smiled then. "Aedan Ó Bháird, the gentle giant," she teased.

He chuckled again. "I hope you know I've grown up since then."

"Like I said, I will not be taking it easy on you."

They continued stretching in silence. More of Albainn's villagers slowly crept in as the sun edged over the treetops surrounding the meadow. Some of them spread out blankets on the greenery to recline on while others wrestled or brawled for fun. The tournament was a very popular event for the village; there would be at least half of the population attending the affair, Aedan guessed, though usually there were more.

Shortly after, Aedan noticed the other two competitors had already arrived. There they stood talking by the edge of the tree line dressed for battle. The older one, Haig, carried a heavy broadsword across his equally broad shoulders. The other, Dian, was younger than Aedan and would be his first target. Dian's weapon of choice was the bow, and he was an exceptional shot. Aedan knew if he was too focused on another of the combatants, Dian could easily pick them all off. He would have to close in fast and trust in his reflexes to dodge any arrows that came his way, he thought as he finished stretching.

It didn't feel like long before the combatants each took their places equidistant from one another, the stream's gentle flow the only sound in Aedan's ears. His strong hands were itching to unsling his axes. Dian's fingers brushed the feathers of the arrows sticking from the quiver around his waist. Haig had one foot in front of the other, ready to sprint. Bóina's eyes were alert and focused.

The ruling clan's matriarch finally strode forward and announced the names of the combatants and each of the clans they belonged to. She did not speak much; after all, words did not hold as much power in Maecha as did prowess in battle. The elderly woman nodded to each of the four when she was finished, wished them all luck, and backed away to the crowd.

Aedan closed his eyes and took a deep breath. The breeze stopped rustling through the trees, the stream's trickle froze, the crowd's quiet murmur ceased. Time seemed to come to a complete standstill.

I need this, he pleaded to the Warrior Aspect of the Allmother. *Bless me with your strength, your speed, your skill, I beg of you. This opportunity is too important for me to squander. Please, Warrior. Please be with me on this day.*

He exhaled and opened his eyes.

"Fight!" the ruling clan leader called out over the clearing.

Aedan's axes were in his hands before the word finished escaping her lips. His legs were already propelling him towards the thin archer who had originally been targeting Bóina. Without missing a beat, Dian whipped his nocked arrow towards Aedan and let it loose. Expecting just that, Aedan sidestepped it without breaking his gait. As Dian reached for another arrow, Aedan stole a glance at the others.

Bóina and Haig were already at each other's throats. While Haig had the slower weapon, he was surprisingly quick. A good fighter himself, he knew to keep the knife-wielder at a distance, but not *too* much of a distance, lest she reach for her throwing knives instead.

Glad he needn't worry about the others for the moment, he turned his attention back to Dian just in time to drop into a roll to dodge another shot. As he came up from the grass, he threw his woodcutting axe at his opponent, who dropped an arrow and staggered away from the flying steel. That stagger gave Aedan enough time to close the gap and spring at the young man.

What was first terror on the archer's face quickly twisted to ferocity as Dian recovered. He whipped the wood of his bow across Aedan's jaw and lashed out with an arrow as he jumped to the side. The arrowhead sliced across Aedan's arm, but the blunt force of the bow hurt worse than the sting of the arrow. He did not have much time to process that, though, for as he recovered from the fall and rose, another arrow was already on its way, dead-on with his gaze. He threw his left arm up in front of his head just in time to feel a pain like forge flame blaze through his forearm. He used that fire as fuel as he took two large steps and swung his axe down at Dian's shoulder. The boy's freckled face filled with fear, and he raised his wooden bow in defense.

For the briefest of moments, the face of the doe from years ago flashed across Aedan's mind. His swing might have slowed had another, more familiar, face not followed the doe's directly after. The one he was fighting for. A terrifying roar escaped him as his axe crashed through the wood of the bow and down into the crook of Dian's neck. His lifeless body crumpled to the soft grass as Aedan tore the weapon from his chest.

A woman's cry came from the crowd somewhere followed by loud sobs. Elsewhere, there was cheering, for things were just starting to get interesting. Though to Aedan, everything was but a dull buzz in the background.

He snapped the arrow in his arm in half with a grunt and pulled the remaining end through the other side. Breathing through the pain, he bent to retrieve his woodcutting axe from where he'd thrown it and launched himself towards the remaining two. Bóina was on the defensive, using both daggers to deflect each of Haig's heavy blows. As Aedan got closer, however, he realized something. Bóina actually *wasn't* on the defensive. She was making Haig wear himself out lugging around that huge broadsword.

Bóina noticed Aedan's approach. She must have assumed Aedan would take Haig's side to take out the stronger opponent together, so as she slashed aside Haig's next swing, she deftly slid around his side and put her blade to his throat. Before she could finish him off, however, he called out his forfeiture in a weary voice.

Aedan slowed as Haig dropped to his hands and knees. Bóina removed herself from the man and closed the distance between herself and Aedan with a casual pace. She stopped just out of the reach of Aedan's axes.

"Well, would you look at that," she said as her eyes passed over him head to toe. "It appears as though I was wrong."

The adrenaline Aedan was feeling was starting to recede. "What do you mean?"

"I mean, it seems I will have to start calling you something other than 'the gentle giant'," she responded.

Confused, he looked down at himself and saw what she was referring to. His green tunic was black with Dian's blood.

He could not bring himself to think about that just yet. He would give honor to the young man when the battle was over. Before he let his adrenaline take over and send him lunging at the girl, however, he remembered that Bóina liked to tire out her opponent.

While that might have been a proper thought, he did not even have enough time to think of a countertactic as the girl had stepped to him and was driving her daggers towards his stomach. He fell backwards. Clearly, she was done with her previous tactic.

She spun in a whirl of steel, her daggers lashing against Aedan's now raised axes. He regained footing with a kind of speed he would later thank the Warrior for. They pushed back and forth, axes and daggers parrying each other away. Neither could gain a significant advantage against the other.

Not until Aedan got lucky and managed to knock away one of Bóina's daggers, but instead of that deterring her, she stepped in close and plunged her remaining dagger towards him. He managed to twist away from the blade before dropping an axe to thrust his open palm against her throat. She faltered back, choking and grasping her neck.

Before she could recover, Aedan shoved his boot into her chest, knocking her to the ground with such a great force he almost apologized. Still, he stood over her and swung his axe down. Still gasping, she unsheathed a throwing knife and lashed it across the fingers around the axe's haft as it came down. The axe sank into the grass just over her left shoulder.

He did not let her get back to her feet. Instead, he tackled her and felt the short throwing knife carve around his side in the movement. He did not worry about that just yet though. He would let himself feel that after.

He managed to get her wrists in his grip and hold them against the ground.

"Forfeit!" he snarled.

"You are going to have to kill me," she growled back.

He let out another roar as he brought his head down on hers, hearing an awful crunch.

Aedan's vision went white for a moment, but he recovered quickly. He pulled one of Bóina's throwing knives from the strap around her chest and drove it down just below her collarbone, and, with his palm on the pommel, he put his entire weight onto the blade, making it disappear completely within its owner.

The buzz in the background spiked in a clamorous crescendo.

Aedan pushed off the girl and rolled onto the grass next to her body. His breath was heavy, and his vision was still a little off from the collision. As he lay there, the buzz began to morph into a cheer. And then the realization hit him. He did it. He *won*. He was going to get to go apprentice under the Spear Maiden.

PHANTOM FIRE | 29

A sort of euphoria crept over him with that realization. He began to smile, and then chuckle, and then laugh as he lay there. Then the pain from his battle wounds slammed into him so his laughs were broken by intermittent gasps of hurting.

Suddenly, Fiona was at his side, tears staining her cheeks. He only sort of heard her congratulations and her worry over his injuries. The rush of victory was still the loudest thing in his ears. Others came to his side to help him stand. The ruling clan leader said something to him about his victory along with an assurance that he would be sent to Endala once his injuries were seen to so long as he promised to make Albainn proud with his accomplishments.

The rest of the day went by in a blur. His wounds were seen to by the best of the town's healers, and when all was said and done, the ruling clan made for him a victory feast to celebrate his skill in battle. They burned the bodies of Dian and Bóina and prayed to the Phantom Aspect of the Allmother to guide their brave souls to the Otherworld.

Finally, the ruling clan's matriarch stood and raised a drinking horn. "Aedan Ó Bháird was not alone on that field. The Warrior Aspect was watching over him today. The Warrior stood with him then, and she is here with us tonight, celebrating in the triumph of the strong. To the Warrior!"

"To the Warrior!" Aedan shouted.

"To the Warrior!" chorused the revelers.

Then, dancers broke out around the bonfire, and intoxicated men and women laughed and cheered and sang old and lively songs.

Fiona reached over and squeezed Aedan's non-bandaged hand. He met her gaze, and she smiled. He knew she was more relieved that he'd survived than anything else, and he squeezed her hand back. Though there did also seem to be a hint of worry in her eyes. He knew she wouldn't like being away from him for the next year, but what other option did they have? After this coming year of hard training, he would finally be able to make sure Fiona would never have to do her work again. They would finally be okay.

All my thanks, he thought in prayer. *All my thanks forever and ever.*

3

Teacher

The journey to Endala from the city of Polara in the Anand province took nearly two weeks by carriage. Castor was entirely exhausted from sitting down and was more than glad to stretch his legs when the carriage pulled up to the River Split.

A gruff man sat on a stool outside a lonely shack next to the water. He smoked from a short, tar-blackened pipe that would nearly disappear within his gray beard whenever he took a puff. A rowboat was tied to the dock that emerged from the shack. The man nodded at Castor as he hopped down from the black and vermillion carriage. Across the river, Castor could see the fishing village of Endala - just small dots of houses on the distant coast. If he looked north up the river, he could see a long, skinny island fraught with great trees. If he looked south, he saw only the great Undying Sea that connected all parts of the world.

Garrick, one of the guard escorts that rode with Castor, paid the man to row them across the river while the other stayed with the carriage. Garrick was an old knight of Polara whose fealty and friendship to Vasili Vallas had been a constant since before Castor's birth. Castor often wondered if Garrick thought of him as his own son (or grandson) since he had none of his own blood, and Castor naturally cared for the old man even if he did do *too good* of a job trying to protect him sometimes.

As they pushed across the wide, slow river, Garrick made sure to sit right next to Castor in the event that the boat suddenly capsized and the young lordling needed rescuing. Ignoring his guardsman's reminders to keep completely still, Castor found his gaze wandering north to the narrow island between the two larger pieces of land. Something about the way the wind swirled the fallen leaves or the way the crows in the trees called to each other just gave Castor a sense of uneasiness.

"Don't hold your gaze too long now, son," the boatman said. The suddenness of his voice shocked Castor out of his trance. "That's the Isle of the Sidhe, that is. If you look long enough, you may just see somethin' you don't want to see."

"The Sidhe?" Castor laughed. "You mean like faeries and elves? Don't tell me you believe in them."

"Ha!" A bit of spittle came out with his laugh. "Believe in them? I've *seen* them! You live close enough to a tear in the veil for long enough, you're bound to see and hear them."

"A tear in the veil?" Castor's escort asked. "What veil?"

"Well, the veil between this world and the Otherworld, of course." The man let out a gruff sound that sounded something like "city folk".

Castor, along with pretty much everyone else, had of course heard the tales of the Sidhe - faeries and elven creatures that lived in the Otherworld with the Allmother - though some people liked to believe that they could, on occasion, be seen in the real world, too. Castor wasn't so sure.

Yet still he couldn't keep from glancing over at the isle.

When they finally pulled up to the docks at Endala, Castor found himself a little surprised. The village was much smaller than he had imagined it to be. There were plenty of fishers out on small boats with large nets just off the shore, and just past the docks there seemed to be a fish market of sorts.

Garrick received directions to the training grounds from the ferryman, and off they went. The ferryman assured them that the training grounds weren't too far away. According to him, the grounds were apparently just outside of town on the northern end, near the shoreline - only an hour's walk, if they kept good pace.

The old knight carried a pack full of spare clothing, food, and supplies for Castor to keep once they arrived - which Castor was beginning to get nervous about now that they began to near it. He wondered what other types of people would apprentice under the Spear Maiden with him or if there would be any others at all for that matter. If there were, would he be better than them or would they all be far more talented? Sure, Castor had a weapons trainer back at his father's estate, but what if the other apprentices were already skilled soldiers that were just looking for a new challenge? Would he even stand a chance if he were asked to duel one of them? Would he be shunned for being such an embarrassment? Maybe they would send him back home in shame for being so useless.

"All right there, Lord Vallas?" Garrick asked. "You're lookin' a bit ill."

Castor released a breath he hadn't realized he'd been holding. "Just a bit anxious is all," he replied. "I will feel better once we're there."

"No matter," the knight replied. "You are a fine fighter already. You always bested me in practice duels, anyway." He laughed. "I am sure you will do splendidly."

Castor was not too eased by the attempt at comfort. While Garrick might have been an excellent swordsman in his prime, time had taken its toll, slowing his reflexes and atrophying his sword arm. "Well, thank you," Castor said all the same.

"We can always go back to Polara," said Garrick not for the first time since they'd left the estate. "There's no shame in focusing on your future as the leader of the Anand province."

Castor shook his head. "I appreciate your concern, Sir Garrick, but this is what I want to do."

Garrick nodded solemnly and continued onward.

Past the village of Endala was a forest. Not too thick, but enough so that there were sure to be dangerous animals about in its deeper reaches. Being so close to town, however, Castor only saw a few squirrels and rabbits - fat ones that seemed, like the trees around them, to be preparing for their autumnal dormancy.

They pressed on through the forest for a while before Castor thought he could see quite the sizeable longhouse through the trees. As they approached, he could hear someone talking on the other side of the building. When they came around, they saw two young men speaking between themselves casually. One was somewhat short and had the amber complexion and the large, round eyes of the Raajari people. The other was of great stature with layers of heavy muscle packed on who, with his fair skin and blond hair, Castor assumed was from Maecha.

Castor's escort handed him his pack, wished him luck, and, with a dramatic tear in his eye, reminded him that he would meet him on the Odessan shore when the apprenticeship was over before turning on his heel and making his way back through to Endala. Castor let out a shaky breath and approached the others.

The shorter one noticed him first. His dark eyes flitted to Castor, and one of his eyebrows raised with interest. He looked to be close to twenty years of age and quite slim. His midnight hair was cut as close to his scalp as possible. He wore garments strange to Castor - an extremely long tunic made from exquisite silks and a type of trousers that was tight around the waist and ankles yet loose around the legs. *They must be normal wear in Raaja,* Castor thought.

"Hello, there," Castor greeted, his voice quieter than intentional. He cleared his throat. "Is this the Spear Maiden's training grounds?"

The taller one turned to him then. He was a rather handsome fellow, close to Castor's own age, with a strong jaw covered with thick scruff. Soft green eyes glittered under his bushy eyebrows. His arms immediately folded over his chest, though his voice was friendly when he said, "You're in the right place. My name is Aedan Ó Bháird."

"I am Sai Ishaav," the other said.

"Castor Vallas," he responded with a polite smile. "Are you two also apprenticing here?"

PHANTOM FIRE | 35

Aedan nodded. "Sai says he got here nearly two weeks ago, and I arrived just three days ago. Cutting it close getting here on the day the apprenticeship starts, eh?" He smiled kindly.

Castor let out a breath of a laugh. "It was a long trip. Where is the Spear Maiden, anyway?"

"Sorry if I kept you waiting," a voice, heavy with sarcasm, echoed from around the trees.

Castor swore under his breath and, wincing, turned to face the voice.

A woman, tall and daunting, came to them pulling a deer carcass behind her by a rope. Her arms were bulging, corded with muscle. "Do not get your hopes up," she said in the common tongue. "This is for me. For the rest of your time here, you will be getting your own meals." She pulled the deer off to the side of the longhouse before stepping to them. She wore an undyed, sleeveless tunic tucked into worn breeches with basic footwraps only partially covering her dirt-encrusted toes. Her hair was a wildfire that blazed around her hawk-like facial features. Her strong hands sat on her hips as she silently sized them up. Either her gaze gave nothing away or she actually regarded the three of them as equals when it was overwhelmingly clear that this Aedan character was the strongest of the three by far.

"You will refer to me as Teacher. While you are here, when you are not participating in training, you are free to do as you wish and go where you wish. While you are participating in training, however, you will be present and do as I say. Although, if you wish to cease your training at any point, you are free to leave. If you walk into the house, your beds are on the left. My quarters are on the right, and they are absolutely off limits to the three of you. If I catch you there, you will be sent back to where you came from, though your return home will be quite difficult as I will have removed your kneecaps. Are the rules clear?"

They nodded nervously.

She nodded back. "Names?"

They introduced themselves.

She nodded again. "Payment?"

Fumbling, Castor reached into his pack and pulled out a sizeable sack of silver. When Teacher collected all three sacks, she said, "Your training starts tomorrow on the beach at sunrise." With that, she returned to her prey and began to prepare it.

✦ . ＋ . ✦ . ＋ . ✦

Aedan wasn't sure what to think of the two others he would be training with for the next year. There was Sai, the Raajari who had said he was sent there by his parents to learn an honorable trade as punishment for something he had done back home. He seemed nice enough though, Aedan supposed. Although, nagging at the back of his mind was the thought that his parents had sent Sai across the Undying Sea as a punishment; so, either his parents were incredibly disciplinary with loads of expendable wealth, or he had done something quite reprehensible indeed.

Then there was Castor, some nobleman from Odessa. He seemed friendly, but Aedan was not overly fond of Odessans, let alone Odessan *nobles*. After all, Odessans were quite open about their hatred of Maechans like Aedan, and word in Albainn was that Odessan nobles were making any law they could think of to keep Maechans from passing into Odessan territory. He hoped they could at least get along while they were here though. They were going to be stuck together for a whole year after all.

Aedan, along with the other two apprentices, already claimed one of the eight beds in the longhouse and put their belongings next to them. Teacher also informed them of where she kept her spare hunting equipment and fishing gear that was available for her apprentices to use for meals. As far as Aedan was concerned, he was set for the year.

There was only one issue.

When Aedan boarded the small trading vessel from Albainn, his sister apparently decided to stow away on the boat as well, which was *not* the original plan. The ruling clan of Albainn had promised to make sure Fiona was financially taken care of while Aedan was away; but Fiona had decided that she did not want to be that far from her brother. Obviously, she could not apprentice with Aedan; they were only given enough money for Aedan's apprenticeship. So, for the three days before Aedan's apprenticeship began, they searched for some way for Fiona to make money to survive on her own. They found a few leads, but nothing too promising. Since Teacher said they could do whatever they wanted until training started, Aedan decided to go back to Endala to check on her.

There seemed to be plenty of game on the island, even along the brief walk to the village. Aedan assumed it might have been because the locals seemed to eat mostly fish and eels and other sea creatures and therefore didn't pick the woods clean.

The breeze felt cool on Aedan's arms as he treaded through the thinning woods. Ahead, he could already see the outskirts of the village and hear the gulls screeching in the distance. Soon, he would hear the normal hustle-and-bustle sounds of the villagers as they went along with their everyday lives. Hopefully, someone would know where the only foreign, redheaded girl was. After all, he doubted there were too many visitors to the lonely village.

The sun was already more than halfway through the sky when he passed the first stone buildings, and he was reminded how full of life the village was despite the oncoming chill of autumn. Children chased one another down the paths giggling and screeching gleefully. Parents were hauling in their catches of the day, the smell of ocean heavy in the air. A nearby tavern was starting to pull in customers, and Aedan heard the comforting plucks of a lyre accompanied by a baritone voice echoing from the open door. If Aedan knew anything, it was that barkeeps knew everything about their town. He decided to ask there.

As Aedan crossed the floor of the tavern, the bard's song came to a close:

And as the warrior's wounds took their deadly toll,
She perched atop his shoulder to claim his very soul.

Lovely, Aedan thought as he leaned against the bar. The bard began another song as Aedan got the bartender's attention.

"Do you, by any chance, know where to find my sister? She's quite short, long red hair - "

"You mean that cute little Maechan girl?" the woman behind the bar replied as she scrubbed an empty mug. Aedan nodded. "She came in looking for work a few hours ago. I sent her off to Avelas's, though."

"Avelas," Aedan repeated. "Where is that?"

"Follow the path south to the well," she said, not looking up from her mug. "It's the house with the staff outside."

Aedan nodded and gave thanks as he quickened his pace through the village, excited that Fiona might have found work so quickly without him. The well was small, but he knew it must have gotten much use there in the small village. Aedan scanned the nearby buildings until he saw a wooden staff adorned with berries and herbs leaning against the front wall of one.

The door to the building was open, but he knocked nonetheless as he poked his head in.

"Ah, you must be Aedan," the elderly woman sitting behind an oaken counter said. "Please come in; Fiona has told me all about you."

He had to duck his head to fit through the doorway, but he managed to squeeze through. Shelves lined the walls stocked completely full with jars of dried herbs and seeds and liquids, dark and clear. "You know of me?" he asked.

"Of course," the woman said. "You are all your dear sister talks about. She is so proud and thankful for your sacrifice to come all the way here to train so the two of you could have a better life."

Aedan felt immediately embarrassed; he was not accustomed to praise in any form.

"She told me to expect you to show up eventually, and that I would know it was you because you wouldn't fit through my doorway." She laughed heartily.

He looked back at the door and blushed, absentmindedly pushing back his long tawny blond hair. "So, please do not take offense," he began, "but are you a witch?"

PHANTOM FIRE | 39

She laughed again. "No, dear boy, I am not a witch. Just a simple healer. Though my job might be a bit easier if I could weave skin together with magic rather than with thread."

A wave of relief washed over Aedan. Not so much for the fact that she was not a witch, but mostly because Fiona would be doing honest, safe work while he was off in training. Not only that, but he couldn't think of a better place for his sister to be safe than at a healer's hut.

"Where is she?" he asked. "May I see her?"

"I should think so," the woman said, "if you would but turn around."

Spinning, Aedan saw deep red hair framing a slightly dirty face. She was carrying a woven basket of wet clothing. A great smile split her face as he embraced her around the load.

"Where would you like me to dry these, Miss?" Fiona asked the woman.

"I told you that you can call me Avelas," the woman reminded kindly. "There is a stone by the garden. Thank you, dear."

Fiona bowed and motioned for Aedan to follow her.

"And stop bowing!" Avelas called as they stepped outside.

"Why are you not training?" Fiona asked him as she began laying out the few articles of clothing on the stone slab to dry in the sun.

"She just told us the rules and where things were," he said. "The actual training starts tomorrow at dawn."

"Dawn is *early*," Fiona said with a frown.

"Dawn *is* early," Aedan agreed, though he was excited just to get started. "So, you work for the healer then? Is Avelas paying you well?"

"Well," Fiona started as she made sure the dresses and wraps were as flat as possible on the stone, "she isn't technically paying me." Before Aedan could start, she went on. "She is letting me sleep here, and she is providing meals for me. All I have to do is take care of the more physically demanding labor and help cook."

"*You* are going to cook?" Aedan asked incredulously.

She punched him.

He laughed as he rubbed his shoulder. "Miss Avelas said she may even show me some of her healing techniques, which could be helpful for when you are a soldier and inevitably do something thoughtless and hurt yourself."

"What do you mean, *inevitably?*" Aedan questioned.

She gave him a hard look.

"Fair enough."

They talked for a short while longer before Aedan decided to make his way back to the training grounds. But before he went, Avelas gave him a chunk of warm bread and a large peach and informed him that he was welcome back any time.

A weight was off his chest as he passed through the darkening wood. His sister would be safe and her stomach full while they were here. He could focus on his training without needing to worry for her.

The training grounds were quiet, so Aedan went inside when he arrived for lack of a better idea.

He glanced to the right once he was inside and saw the light of a flickering fire glowing under the door to Teacher's quarters. Directly across from where he stood was a large, stone hearth with a small but warm flame burning within. In the center of the room sat a wide, circular table with a large wooden bowl in the middle where offerings to the Allmother were to be left. He dropped in his peach pit and a small bite of bread and sent up a quick thanks to the goddess for his sister's good fortune.

He felt eyes on him when he turned left towards the beds at the other end of the house. The other two apprentices turned their gazes away quickly - Sai's to a small book he was inking in and Castor's to a heavy volume.

Aedan decided to not let that bother him and instead pushed through the uncomfortable moment and went to sit on his bed.

"What are you reading?" he asked Castor.

Castor looked up at him over the tome and showed him the front cover. Aedan was too ashamed to admit he'd never learned to read, so he just nodded instead. Luckily, Castor said, "It's just an old book about politics and etiquette and other incredibly boring things. My father packed it for me. Apparently, he did not want me to forget how to be a proper noble while I was away." He rolled his eyes as he said it.

"You do not like being a noble?" Aedan questioned with innocence. He could not imagine how someone could dislike coin not being at the forefront of one's problems.

"I know I probably sound daft," Castor said, his Odessan accent rather endearing, "but having your entire life planned out for you has its drawbacks."

Aedan nodded, though he would still rather be rich than in poverty.

"What do you think our training is going to be like tomorrow morning?" Sai interjected as he set his book and quill down.

Aedan shrugged.

"Do you think she would have us sparring on the first day?" Castor asked. "I mean, I have had some weapons training, but ..." His gaze drifted to Aedan.

Aedan laughed. "Do not worry; I'll take it easy on you," he said grinning.

Sai and Castor both laughed along with him. They talked sparingly for the next few hours before sleep overtook them. Aedan rested much better knowing Fiona was safe and sound and with the idea that he may be able to get along with the other two apprentices after all.

4

Bad Liars

Castor spent most of the night worrying that he would not wake up on time and would be late for his first day of training. Luckily, the anxiety and insomnia made sure he was awake on time. His eyes were open before dawn when Teacher rose from her rest, although he feigned sleep while she whispered a prayer at the altar before going outside.

When the blue pre-morning light poured through the windows of the longhouse, Sai began to stir. It was then that Castor decided to get to the beach early. *If anything, it will show punctuality and willingness to learn,* he told himself. When he rose, the bed creaked under him. The previously stirring Sai sat bolt upright at the sound, fists at the ready.

Castor, midway through rising, froze. Sai's half-sleeping eyes stared unfocused in his direction.

"Sorry," Castor whispered, not knowing what else to do. Sai dropped back down like a rock, and Castor grabbed his clothes to dress himself away from the beds in an effort to respect the others' rest.

He quietly padded outside and availed himself of the washing trough next to the front door. Splashing the cold water over his face, he realized that it was actually sea water, the salty tang an unwelcome surprise on his lips. He tried to hurriedly dab the salt water out of his eyes with his sleeve while turning, though he managed to trip over his own foot and ungracefully descend to the cold, hard ground.

Eyes free of salt, he jumped back up and whipped his head around, praying Teacher had not seen what just happened. He sighed in relief when he saw no one. Hopefully, that would be his only blunder of the day.

He made his way to the beach, which was clearly visible from the longhouse and only a short walk away. When he arrived, he decided to remove his shoes to feel the sand between his toes. It was a strange but comforting feeling. He sat in the twilight and looked straight ahead at the Isle of the Sidhe which stretched out between his position and the land of Odessa.

He knew the old ferryman was mad, but he could not help but wonder ...

He stared long and hard at the isle until dawn was well on its way to sunrise, but he witnessed nothing of note. *As I expected*, he thought to himself.

"Good morning," a deep voice said. Before Castor could turn around, Aedan was already standing next to him. "May I join you?"

"O - Of course," Castor stammered, trying to reel back his surprise. *How is someone* that *big so silent on his feet?*

Aedan inhaled a deep breath, closing his eyes, before smiling peacefully and releasing it. "Are you nervous?" he asked, leaning back on his palms.

Castor looked away, back to the isle, and fidgeted with a lock of his black hair. "I think once we get started, my nerves will settle," he replied honestly.

Aedan nodded in response.

Castor could not think of anything else to talk about, so instead they just sat together in silence in the dawning light. The hush was not uncomfortable, though. The soft lapping of the waves, the gentle tittering of nesting birds, Aedan's rhythmic breathing - all of it melded into a peaceful ambiance. It might have even lulled Castor to sleep had

Sai not stumbled out of the longhouse looking entirely annoyed at the prospect of being awake at such an early hour.

"Good morning!" Aedan said with a cheerful voice as Sai approached them.

"No," Sai responded.

Aedan looked taken aback. "Bad morning?"

Sai nodded. "Back home in Raaja, no one wakes until midday, and even *that* is considered early for us." He rubbed his eyes and sleepily shuffled to where they sat.

Castor was shocked. Of course, with his nobility, he was forced to study the other lands and their cultures, but not much was known of Raaja. Castor learned of how the enormous country had been laid waste to by a volcano in its northern mountains many years before Castor was born in an event known as the Red Blight. He was told of how all the remaining survivors of the disaster had fled to its southernmost city, which had since grown into the most populous in all of Serrae. The only other thing Castor knew about the country was that it was filled with those who were obsessed with creating new technologies and discovering new sciences, though they were apparently reluctant to share their knowledge with other civilizations. "If you sleep that late, how do your people have time to get anything done?" he asked.

Sai chuckled drowsily. "My people have used sunstones to light our city at night for a very long time. We do most of our work during the dark hours when it is cooler."

Castor felt intrigued. "Sunstones? I have not heard of such things."

"Sometimes I forget that all your cities are like this village," Sai muttered. "Sunstones are pale green rocks that take in sunlight during the day and release it at night. We have the largest ones on towers to collect as much sunlight as possible during the light hours."

The Odessan noble suddenly felt like a peasant next to the man from Raaja. They could *light their city without fire*. Castor was jealous that these "sunstones" did not exist in his country.

"Incredible!" Aedan's voice boomed. "I would love to visit Raaja someday! You must tell me more of your land!"

PHANTOM FIRE | 45

Sai made a disgusted sound. "It is far too early for that," he said, yawning.

Aedan looked disappointed. "Perhaps over an ale after our training?"

"Raajari do not consume that which numbs our minds," Sai responded firmly.

The Maechan looked more surprised about this new information than the fact that they could make their city shine at night. "I ... I am at a loss for words," he replied finally. Then, he leaned closer to Castor and whispered, "Perhaps I will not be visiting Raaja after all."

Castor stifled a chuckle, and Sai rolled his eyes.

Just as the red sun peeked over the horizon, the Spear Maiden emerged from behind them. The three apprentices jumped up at her sudden arrival. Castor stood with his back straight and his hands clasped behind his back; Aedan stood with a wide stance and his arms crossed; Sai stood with his hands in hidden pockets in the sides of his loose, silky pants.

"For today, I will need to see where the three of you are physically, so I know what necessitates refining the most," Teacher said without introduction. "The first test is simple: Run until you can run no more. We will use the beach for this lesson, staying on the sand at all times. Let's go." And without any further notice, Teacher ran. The three apprentices shared a confused look momentarily before chasing after her down the beach.

Castor usually enjoyed running. He often jogged around the grounds of his father's estate. Jogging on *sand*, however, was a different story. He almost, on more than one occasion, twisted his ankle on the soft, uneven ground. Not only that, but it took so much more effort to run without a solid surface to push off from.

Not too long after they had started did Sai fall. Castor had heard his labored breaths behind him for some time before he heard him collapse. Teacher must have heard, too, for she called out, "Rest and meet us back where we started!"

They eventually turned about to run back. Castor was definitely feeling the painful claws of exhaustion ripping at his muscles and lungs. He should have stretched before, he cursed to himself.

He was surprised that Teacher ran with them. For some reason, he had pictured her sitting and silently judging their performance. He definitely felt respect blooming for his new master.

Aedan began to fall behind, too, before finally slowing to a crawl. Teacher laughed. "I wondered when the big one would give out," she said as if sharing a secret with him.

Castor smiled, and he decided then and there that he would at least make it back to where they started, no matter what.

At last, he could see the training grounds up ahead. He was hoping he would get a second wind around that time; but he had already *had* a second wind about ten minutes prior. His lungs burned, and his legs were exploding in agony. Pride and determination, however, pushed him harder and harder until he was side by side with Teacher.

He faintly heard her utter a simple, "Huh," which only spurred him on more. When he finally touched back where they began, he let himself stumble and roll side over side into the sand where he stayed gulping down breaths of air as though he might soon run out.

Teacher laughed loudly and happily. It was the kind of deep laugh that you feel in your bones – that infectious kind of laugh that convinces you to laugh along with it.

"Quite the show of stubbornness!" She dropped down onto the beach next to where Castor lay wheezing and patted him roughly on the chest. Sai, already having returned, sat nearby with a poorly disguised look of annoyance on his face.

"Is that good?" Castor managed to ask through labored breaths.

"'Good'?" Teacher asked, a smile in her voice. "Only the best warriors are stubborn!" She laughed again and added, "I have a feeling you will do great here, Vallas."

✦ . ✛ . ✦ . ✛ . ✦

After they had all properly recuperated from the run, Teacher let them be free to get breakfast, though they were to return as soon as possible for their next test. Aedan, coming from the fishing village of Albainn, decided to grab a rod and head to the beach for his breakfast, while Castor and Sai both went into the forest for theirs.

While catching his breakfast, Aedan couldn't help but let his thoughts wander back to the run on the beach. He was mildly upset that he had not been able to make it all the way back to the grounds while another of the apprentices had. He'd been certain beforehand that he had the advantage over the other two in combat, though now he was beginning to doubt.

Upon returning to the longhouse, Aedan properly cleaned and prepared what he caught and started a small fire in a nearby pit as Sai emerged from the trees with a rabbit in a small net, hanging from his grip.

"A trapper, eh?" Aedan asked as he positioned his catch on the spit over the flame.

"It's what I am best at actually," Sai responded. "I have always had a talent for building and setting traps." He prepared the hare on a table nearby before asking Aedan if he could use the fire as well, to which Aedan happily obliged.

When the fish was nearly cooked, Castor arrived, carrying an armful of blood-red apples. "I'll trade you an apple for a bit of that fish," he said, plopping down close to Aedan.

In Maecha, it was a common tradition for food to be shared, and Aedan respected that custom as much as any other. He accepted Castor's offer.

Castor tossed another apple to Sai as well. Perhaps Odessans' view of sharing meals was not so different from Maechans', Aedan thought. They ate quickly, though, to return to the beach as soon as they could.

When everyone had finished and returned to where Teacher stood on the shore, she began informing them of what kinds of training they could expect over the next year. There would be a lot of running and the like to build stamina. They would also be subject to strength training, which Aedan was much more confident about. And after a few months of conditioning, they would add weapons and combat training on to their usual routine.

"Do any of you have a specific weapon you are already proficient with, or one you wish to be proficient with?" Teacher inquired.

"I'm comfortable with an axe in each hand," Aedan replied first.

"The weapons trainer back home only ever taught me how to use a sword and shield," Castor answered, "though I do not think that suits me very well. I would be happy to try others out and find what feels best."

Teacher nodded and then looked to Sai, who shrugged, looking slightly embarrassed. "Combat knowledge is not as widespread in Raaja as it is here." His voice was quieter than usual. "I am afraid my only skills lie in trapping."

"Do not worry," Teacher reassured him. "You will learn proper ways to fight in the months to come."

Aedan thought he saw a look of annoyance flash over Sai's face when Teacher said "proper ways to fight", but maybe it was just his imagination.

When their breakfast had officially settled in their stomachs, they moved on to the boulder throw exercise - a self-explanatory exercise in which the apprentice must lift and toss a large rock. This was where Aedan shined. While he did not want to say it outright, he wanted to make sure the Odessan saw how strong he was since it was the Odessan who ran farther in the first exercise. He found he could not help but feel a bit competitive with the others.

Castor had a much harder time lifting the boulder and throwing it, and Sai could not even manage to pick it off the ground. Teacher was supportive of each apprentice's endeavor, encouraging Castor to lift higher and higher, and assuring Sai that he could simply roll the stone over itself until he built enough muscle to throw it properly.

The rest of the day, the apprentices' exercises continued. The other two tests that Teacher had for them were climbing trees and swimming in the ocean, both of which Sai excelled at. Aedan could climb trees without too much difficulty, but he didn't know how to swim very

PHANTOM FIRE | 49

well. Out of the four tests, Aedan was only the best in one of them. *One of them.* He wanted to not be frustrated that he was outmatched so easily by the others, but it was difficult. *It will be different when actual combat training begins,* he told himself.

So, the day came and went, and before too long, night was creeping in. The three apprentices sat around the fire; Teacher must have eaten somewhere else, for she already retired for the night. They talked, mostly about the training and how tired and sore each one was.

"I have a proposition for you," Castor said to Aedan over a tin mug of ale. Teacher had several barrels of the stuff stocked in the longhouse, which she decided to let the apprentices partake of after training.

Aedan looked over at him, pushing back his long, golden hair. "Oh? Tell me."

"What would you say if I asked you to teach me to hunt and fish as you do if I helped you learn to swim?"

"I ..." Aedan wanted to be offended that Castor had insinuated that he could not swim, but he also knew he needed help. He sighed. "You know, that sounds like a fair deal."

A smile spread over Castor's face, and his eyes twinkled in the firelight. "I was worried I'd have to live with only apples to eat for a whole year!" He chuckled warmly. "I am very grateful!"

Aedan laughed with him. "You needn't worry; I would have shared either way."

Castor smiled as he took a big swig from his mug. "Shall we start tomorrow, then?"

Aedan downed the rest of his ale. "You can accompany me when I go fish for breakfast, and I can teach you to shoot a bow for dinner," he suggested.

"And we can go swim right after training," Castor added. "If we are not too exhausted, that is."

"Agreed!" Aedan stuck his arm out to Castor, who took his hand and shook it firmly. Aedan faltered momentarily. "Is that how you do it in Odessa?" Aedan asked. When Castor looked confused, Aedan said, "Put out your hand again." When he did, Aedan grabbed Castor's forearm tightly. He could feel the lean muscle wrapped around the Odessan's arm under his callused fingertips. "That is how we do it where I am from."

Sai, who had been quiet for some time, chimed in. "How odd. In Raaja, we do no such thing. Instead, we clasp our hands and bow." He put his palms together and bowed his head. "In fact, respect for others' personal space is very important where I am from."

The three spoke for a while longer of each man's differing customs before they finally filed into their beds, exhaustion overtaking them.

✦. ✛ .✦. ✛ .✦

Aedan was good on his word the following morning. The two awoke early and quietly to allow their other comrade to continue sleeping, grabbing two fishing rods as they went to the beach.

"You will want to stay as quiet as possible," the Maechan whispered to the Odessan. "Fish scare easily, and if you are not careful, you can lose your breakfast with a few simple words spoken too loudly."

Castor nodded seriously, clamping his mouth tighter shut to make sure he didn't ruin the catch.

"Now, you will want to bait the hook," Aedan continued under his breath. He reached into a small, cloth pouch at his belt that Castor hadn't noticed before and produced several dead flies. Castor, not expecting anything of the sort, nearly exclaimed in surprise; he quickly reminded himself of the need to stay silent. Aedan gently speared several flies on the end of his hook. The care to which he took as he baited his hook was also a little surprising. Castor would not have expected someone so large to be able to be so gentle.

Misunderstanding Castor's expression, Aedan said, "I caught the flies yesterday and decided to try to keep a stock for fishing." He offered a few of the other insect corpses to Castor when he was finished. Castor took them, though not without a small amount of disgust, and mimicked Aedan's work on his own hook.

A broad smile spread over Aedan's face as he patted him on the back. "You are a born fisher!"

Castor smiled from ear to ear as they moved closer to the water. Aedan showed him the proper ways to cast a line and when it was appropriate to pull back on the rod. Towards the end of dawn, Castor managed to catch one small, fist-sized fish, while Aedan brought back three large trout.

"A commendable effort!" he said as they walked back to the firepit.

Castor laughed. "You're a bad liar."

Aedan only laughed back.

Shortly after starting the fire and preparing the fish, the two were joined by Sai and Teacher. When offered some of their catch, Sai sleepily obliged himself, though Teacher politely refused.

"We will be running far too much for me to accept your offer," she explained with a wry smile.

The three apprentices simultaneously stopped chewing and spared worried glances in one another's direction.

Teacher's smile never left her face. "I will see you on the beach when you are finished," she said as she rose and left them.

After a brief silence, Castor said, "I wonder if this is going to taste as good the second time."

"By the Aspects, I hope so," Aedan whispered as he stared apprehensively at the fish in his hands.

Teacher did not lie to them. They ran. And they ran. And they ran some more. Aedan's lungs were a forge flame, burning with a fire that could not be put out regardless of how many breaths of the cool air he gulped. His legs were in excruciating pain, his ankles were exhausted - even his toes hurt! And, no, the fish did *not* taste as good the second time around.

As the day went by, Teacher continued to put them through exercises that kept their hearts pounding. She gave them plenty of breaks to stay hydrated and one longer break in the afternoon for an early dinner. It was then that Aedan took Castor into the woods to help him learn the basics of hunting. Sai followed them into the trees as well, though he broke off on his own to check on several traps that he had apparently left out beforehand.

The two crept through the woods, both exhausted from the day, in search of something they could bring back for dinner.

"You will want to watch where you are stepping," Aedan advised. "Try to avoid any leaves or twigs if you can."

"Right," Castor said as he averted his gaze to the ground.

"But try to keep your eyes up so you can see your prey before it sees you," he whispered.

For a moment, Aedan thought he saw Castor give him an annoyed look, but maybe it was just his imagination. Time rolled by, and soon, they came upon a large rabbit sitting calmly in a patch of filtered sunlight. Aedan put his hand up to stop Castor and pointed at their potential meal. Castor's eyes went wide, and he nodded back. Aedan motioned for Castor to watch him before pulling an arrow from the small, leather quiver strapped around his waist that he had borrowed from the longhouse and knocking it against the wood of his bow. Castor followed along and drew back his bowstring.

Aedan's mouth tugged up at the corner as he shook his head quietly. He moved behind Castor and guided the Odessan's right hand back to rest against his cheek; Castor adjusted his aim accordingly. Aedan stepped back, and Castor let his arrow loose. It soared through the air and stuck right into the ground next to the rabbit, who hopped away in terror.

"Oh," Castor said, looking defeated.

"That was really close!" Aedan said in his most encouraging voice. "Rabbits are very small targets; I am impressed that you got so close on your first try."

Castor looked suspicious, but thanked him for his kind words nonetheless.

"No need to worry," Aedan said. "We can follow him, and you can keep trying until you get him."

Castor's stomach growled audibly. "Or," he began, "you could just get this one so we can eat sooner." He smiled sheepishly.

Aedan could not help but smile back. "As you wish."

✦ . ⁺ . ✦ . ⁺ . ✦

When they finished eating their rabbit back at camp, Teacher decided to let them have the rest of the day to themselves. Castor never felt relief as strong as in that moment. His *everything* was sore. Of course, he was still going to keep good on his promise to help Aedan with his swimming; but they decided to wait until later to work on that so Aedan could go back to town to visit his sister.

So, with his newfound freedom, Castor decided to go sit with Sai back at the beds in the longhouse.

"What are you writing in there?" he asked Sai by means to start conversation.

Sai had been sitting with a small bound book in his lap and a pristine black quill in his left hand. He had seemed to be quite engrossed in what he was writing and nearly flinched when Castor spoke as though he had not even heard him come in. "Oh," he said. "This is only a journal. My parents made me start keeping one these last few months as a way to keep my hands busy."

Castor nodded thoughtfully. "I see," he said. "Though your parents are not here now," he went on. "If you wanted to stop writing in it, I mean."

Sai shrugged. "I do not mind it much anymore. In fact, I think I have started to enjoy keeping it even."

"What do you write about?" Castor inquired. "If it is not too much to ask."

He shrugged again. "Just about things I do and think about."

After that, he went back to writing, and Castor decided to leave him be. Instead, he reclined back into his bed and closed his eyes for a quick nap before his swimming student returned.

And awoke seemingly as though he had only just closed his eyes. Aedan had gently shaken his shoulder. When Castor's eyes focused, he noticed Aedan looking entirely sheepish. "It's all right," Castor said groggily. "Are you ready to learn?"

Aedan responded with a nod and lowered his hand to help his swimming teacher rise. "I think I would just need to get the basic concept down before I would be comfortable practicing on my own," he said.

"Well then, we can work on it together until then," Castor responded with a friendly smile.

"You are a good man!" Aedan said as he clapped Castor's shoulder. And off they went to the beach where they slipped out of their outerwear and waded into the shallow waves.

For some reason, Castor noticed after some time in the water, Aedan just could *not float*. It came naturally to Castor, but no matter how much air the Maechan held in, he could not stay afloat without furiously kicking his feet and paddling his hands.

"I think if we can get you to float, then you will be able to swim much easier," he suggested. "Maybe if you just get comfortable with the feeling of floating, it will come easier to you."

Aedan nodded and followed Castor's instructions to lean back against him and bring his body to the surface of the water while Castor held him up. Little by little, Castor tried to separate himself from the other man without him noticing so that he would end up floating by himself.

Aedan eventually noticed that he was getting farther away from his instructor and splashed violently about before standing upright with a mixed look of terror, confusion, and mild anger on his stubbled face. Castor had to quickly explain his idea, and though Aedan said he understood his reasoning, Castor knew he would not be able to try that again.

For the rest of the next hour, they just focused on trying to get Aedan to float on his own (without too much success), though the waves *did* admittedly make things a little more difficult on occasion. When they finally emerged from the waters, Castor said, "You're getting much better! I think we'll have you swimming in no time."

Aedan shook his head with a smile. "You're a bad liar, too, you know?"

5

Heartbeat

Over the next few months, Avelas seemed to start trusting Fiona with more responsibilities in the healer's workspace. She was mostly assisting with basic treatments for smaller field injuries, since that *was* what typically drew in Avelas's customers after all. Fiona helped splint a woman's shin that had been fractured in an accident with one of the aurochs she tended, she learned how to brew a bitter tea for soothing most common illnesses, and she even considered herself an expert at bandaging wounds after all the experience she'd gotten during her time with Avelas. Overall, she was quite content with her job.

She definitely enjoyed when her older brother came to visit her, which was quite often; but she was having so much fun helping Avelas and learning how to make and administer medicine and emergency treatments that she occasionally forgot the original reason she had come to Endala. She hoped that when she and Aedan went back to Maecha that she would be able to get a job with a healer in whichever town they ended up in. She certainly didn't want to go back to Albainn - too many unpleasant memories - but other than that, she did not have much preference where they ended up.

During her down time from work, Fiona often wandered the outskirts of the forest. She did not dare to go too deep into the trees, though, for fear of the wild beasts that apparently lurked farther within, according to the locals. But there was one berry bush in particular that she regularly found herself trailing to that always seemed to have at least a few berries left, even this late in the year.

And lo and behold, as she passed the last few gently frosted trees that tried to block her path, she came upon the bush and saw several red berries dotted here and there, sharply contrasting against the thin white dusting of winter that seemed to cover everything in the forest. She felt her lips tugging up at the corner as she grabbed the first one she saw and let it burst between her teeth. As she reached for a second, she heard a strange sound a short distance away.

Instantly fearful of some mystery predator, she crouched down by the bush and tried to stay very still and quiet. Several seconds passed before she heard it again coming from the same direction. The fear began to recede as she realized the sound - a high-pitched *gii-gii* sound - seemed to be a noise of distress, though she admittedly had very little experience with animals. Still, she decided to investigate, although as quietly as possible.

The Maechan tip-toed around the bush and crept up behind a nearby tree, the *gii-gii* still occasionally coming from the other side. She felt around the ground near her and let her fingers close around a medium-sized stone. Slowly, she peeked around the side of the tree trunk and saw a bird, no longer than her forearm, lying on its back. It looked as though it was trying to right itself but couldn't.

Relief flooded over her as she realized she was not in danger after all. She dropped the stone and approached the bird carefully. When it noticed her, it began calling out louder and without pause. She lowered herself next to it and tried to calm it with gentle shushes and friendly words. When that didn't work, she almost gave up and went back from where she came; but she saw that the bird was trying to pull away one of its wings and that it was bent at an uncomfortable angle.

She felt the familiar tingle of excitement of being needed as she tore off a pale-yellow strip of cloth from the bottom of her skirt. "It's all right," she said in her most reassuring voice. "I am going to try to help you, but you need to be still for me."

The bird, not understanding the common tongue, did *not* in fact be still and instead began calling out even more frantically.

"No, bird," Fiona said softly. "I'm going to help fix your *wing*." She extended her left arm out straight and flapped it. Maybe the bird did not understand the common tongue, but it *might* understand visual interpretations, Fiona thought.

It did not.

Exasperated, she decided to just go for it. She scooped the bird's body gently into one hand, and when she went to grab the damaged wing, the bird screeched and bit her finger. She winced and let out a quiet string of Maechan curses that would have left many blushing, but she held her hands where they were nonetheless.

She let out a heavy breath and said, "I'm going to pretend you didn't do that," as she bent the bird's wing back to what looked like its original position. The bird screeched in pain when she moved it, its calls getting weaker and weaker as it realized no help was coming to save it from its red-haired torturer. She wrapped the torn cloth around the broken wing and the body to keep it from moving too much.

Still not understanding the situation—*even though* Fiona continued trying to inform it that it was going to be okay—the bird continued to bite and peck at her. "All right, you little bastard," she said, still in her soothing voice, "I am going to need you to please cut that shit out immediately so I can take you back and let Avelas have a look at you."

The bird drew blood from her palm in response.

"*I said please!*" she hissed through gritted teeth.

The bird's eyes went wide as it looked up at her quietly.

"Much better," she continued in her soothing voice. "You little bastard," she added lovingly.

Later, hours after she had arrived back at Avelas's home, the bird's wound had been treated more efficiently by a salve to rid it of possible infection and a more stable bind that would eventually and hopefully lead to the correction of the wing. Being the only healer in the village, Avelas had her share of treating animals here and there when necessary, and she seemed reasonably comfortable with treating the bird's injury.

"He's a sea falcon," Avelas explained once the bird had fallen asleep. "They're incredibly fast and can fly very long distances without needing to roost. I've heard they can also make good pets if they like you enough," she added.

Fiona showed her the battle wounds she received during the rescue. "The little bastard likes me as much as the plague," she muttered.

Avelas chuckled as they sat next to the fireplace in old wooden rocking chairs. "You are the one who saved him, though. He may end up sticking around once he realizes what you did for him." Her small brown eyes glittered in the firelight.

✦ . ✛ . .✦ . ✛ . .✦

Aedan was getting much better at swimming, Castor thought as the two were heading in one night. The chill of winter was beginning to set in, so the lessons were becoming marginally more difficult, but Aedan seemed to be quite resistant to the cold. That, and his pure determination to master swimming kept them at it.

Their training with the Spear Maiden had become a routine now. Though their muscles still ached as each day came to a close, they had grown accustomed to the pain. They were nearly finished with the body training portion of the year; any week now they would start training with weapons, Castor thought. He was definitely noticing some improvements to his physique, though. He had built an impressive amount of muscle since arriving in Endala, and his stamina had never been better. He still was not as imposing as Aedan, though admittedly it didn't matter how much more weight Castor put on - he would have to grow an extra foot taller to even compare.

So, they made their way back to their beds where they dried off and went to bed, the weariness of their long day seeping deep into their bones.

✦ . ✛ . .✦ . ✛ . .✦

PHANTOM FIRE | 59

It was some time in the depths of night when Castor woke with a start, though he did not know why. The moon still gleamed outside the window like an ethereal silver disc. He was sitting straight up in bed, and as he looked around the room, he noticed Aedan and Sai were also sitting up groggily.

Before anyone could comment, he heard it.

Thud-thud

A very, *very* distant sound, though strangely clear. Castor wondered if he was the only one of the three who heard it.

"What is that?" Aedan asked quietly.

At least it isn't just me, Castor thought.

Thud-thud

The three were silent as they stared from one to another. "Should," Sai began, "should we go see if there is anything outside?"

Castor definitely did *not* want to do that.

"It wouldn't hurt to look," Aedan said. "After all, it seems like whatever's making that sound is a good distance away." He pushed his hair back away from his eyes.

Castor reluctantly agreed, and the three stood and quietly tiptoed through the house careful not to wake Teacher who seemed to still be sleeping. Passively, he wondered why only the three of them suddenly woke while the home's fourth occupant was undisturbed, but he kept the thought to himself.

Thud-thud

It was louder outside, but not enough to cause any immediate worry. They looked around carefully, trying to see if they could discover the source but to no avail. The *thudding* continued, but it never sounded as if it were moving closer or farther away. Then, Castor raised his gaze across the waves, his eyes falling on the Isle of the Sidhe.

"Shit," Castor said.

"What is it?" Sai asked. He followed Castor's stare. "You think it comes from the island?"

"It would make sense," Aedan supplied quietly. He sounded almost as nervous as Castor felt. "The Sidhe are very mysterious. We should probably leave them be. You do not want to get trapped in the Otherworld, do you?"

"What is this nonsense?" Sai argued. "The *Sidhe*? Faeries and spirits and the like? Do not tell me you believe in them."

"Of course I do!" Aedan argued back. "The Sidhe live in the Otherworld with the Allmother." His tone suggested that the statement was fact rather than belief. "I have heard plenty of stories of humans being taken away by the faeries to the Otherworld never to be seen again, and the locals here have told me that the veil between worlds is thin on that island." His large green eyes were wide with only a tinge of panic.

"Exactly," Sai said. "That's all they were. *Stories*." He turned to Castor. "Shall we go investigate?"

"You - You want to swim across the river to the island?" Castor asked quietly. He was definitely more worried about the haunted island than the swim itself, but he wasn't going to say that.

Thud-thud

All three of them exchanged glances again.

Castor sighed. "Why not?"

Aedan nearly growled as he ran his fingers through his hair in frustration. "Fine. If you two are going, then I'm coming, too. I cannot leave you to yourselves if you come across something dangerous."

Sai rolled his eyes. "Then come."

Castor was beyond nervous, verging on terrified. The tide was up, and the river was flowing faster than usual. They ended up trekking north a short distance so they wouldn't have to fight the current as much as they swam across.

The water was *freezing*. The apprentices were wearing next to nothing to help them swim, and Castor knew that when they made it to the other side, drying off would probably be an issue. But Castor was much more worried about Aedan's ability to swim across. Sure, he had been noticeably improving, but it was a long swim to the island. Not to mention, the current was picking up in strength as they made their way across.

Before long, Castor noticed Aedan struggling.

"Are you all right?" he called out to the Maechan.

Aedan looked frustrated, though Castor assumed it was aimed at himself. "I do not think I can make it all the way across," he said finally as he slowed.

"Then turn back!" Sai shouted as he continued forward with ease. "No need to slow us down!"

Castor noticed a brief emotion flash over Aedan's face, though it was gone before it could be given a name. Without another word, Aedan turned back, though he still seemed as if he were having a hard time with the ordeal.

Castor bit his lip. "Are you sure you are all right?" he yelled out.

Aedan did not respond. Either the big man could not hear him, or he did not care to answer.

Torn, Castor turned and continued towards the island. About halfway across, the current really picked up. He had to fight to stay in control, though he made sure not to fight too hard lest he used up all his energy. The current was bad enough, but the bitter cold made the swim much more unbearable. His limbs were numbing already, each stroke proving more and more difficult.

He managed a glance behind him to check on Aedan's progress back, but he was nowhere to be seen. *Maybe it is just too dark to see him*, Castor thought to himself as dread hovered over him, threatening to descend.

It was at that moment that something large and slippery brushed against Castor's left foot. That was when the panic dove down, crashing into him with such a wrecking force that it was all he could do to keep breathing. He paddled his arms and legs like none had done before. He shot past the Raajari, his limbs fueled by a terrible fire. He crossed the rest of the river in record time, rolling up onto the sandy beach of the Isle of the Sidhe. He lay there on his back, trying to catch his breath which had escaped him sometime during the panicked swim.

When sanity edged its way back into Castor's mind, he jumped up and scanned the river, trying to find any sign of Aedan. He could not see him *anywhere.*

"What the hell was that about?" Sai asked breathily as he crawled onto the shore.

"Did you see Aedan?" he asked. "I don't see him."

"Wh - What?" Sai breathed. "Yeah, I saw him get back to the other side; do not worry yourself about it."

Sai's words did nothing to assuage him, but he frustratingly didn't know what else he could really do about it at the moment. What if Aedan really *had* made it back across like Sai suggested? It wouldn't do any good to make a big deal about it then, would it? And if, Aspects forbid, he *hadn't* made it back, what could Castor really do at this point?

"I am sure he is fine," Sai said as he stood up, shivering from the cold water.

Castor worried at his lip, but he knew there was nothing that could be done regardless. "All right," he said finally.

Thud-thud

The two young men stopped in their tracks. The sound was much, *much* louder here.

"So, it is definitely coming from somewhere here," Sai said.

"Great," Castor muttered, still hoping Aedan had made it back all right.

Then, Sai suggested continuing their search, to which Castor had no reason to disagree.

The crows that usually populated the trees were nowhere to be seen as they trudged through the forested island. In fact, there was no sign of life at all aside from the loud thumping that echoed through the trees.

"What if it is some huge, terrifying monster that is just waiting to kill us?" Castor hissed under his breath.

"That thought *did* cross my mind," Sai whispered back. "If it is, we should just defeat it and bring its head back to Teacher to prove how much we have improved under her tutelage."

PHANTOM FIRE | 63

Castor nearly snapped. "What? Kill the unknown beast? With what weapons, I might ask? You might not have noticed that we are practically bare, not to mention completely unarmed." He gestured vaguely to himself. "And how do you propose we bring the beast's head back to Teacher when we barely got here ourselves without drowning?"

Sai waved his hand dismissively. "You worry too much. Try coming up with solutions instead of problems." He continued picking his way through the trees, the moonlight his only guide.

Castor felt something inside him break then. "Here is a solution," he said as calmly as he could. "How about I check this side of the island and you check *that* side of the island?" He was trying to control his breathing, but it wasn't working too well.

"Good idea," Sai said, apparently not noticing Castor's tone. "We can meet back at this tree in one hour." And he was off, quietly breezing through the trees.

Castor stared incredulously at the spot Sai had been standing in. What was even *with* him anyway? He made a disgusted sound in the back of his throat and trudged along nevertheless.

Thud-thud

Some time went by, and the moon stayed where it was in the sky. In fact, it seemed to be in the same place it was when they left the longhouse earlier that night. He shrugged it off as he walked, running his fingers through his hair. His *dry* hair. *How the hell is my hair already dry?* It usually took his thick, black locks much longer to completely dry out. He also noticed that it was actually quite warm there in the forest somehow. *When did that happen?* Last he was paying attention, he was shivering. Now all of a sudden -

A child's giggle interrupted his thoughts.

He immediately froze, every inch of his body on full alert. Gooseflesh rose on his arms despite the mysterious warmth.

Thud-thud

Castor's heart was beating so hard he was sure it would give him away. He stood there in silence for several more minutes before he heard the rustle of leaves behind him. He turned about-face, but nothing was there. *Probably just a rabbit,* he told himself. But his heart didn't slow.

He turned back to continue on his way when he heard the unmistakable sound of footsteps approaching close behind him.

He didn't even turn around; he just ran.

The salty tang of sweat stung his lips as he blundered through the forest. He thought he could still hear the footsteps behind him, so he never slowed. It wasn't long before his bare foot caught the gnarled knot of a tree root. He fell, rolling side over side before sliding to a stop in a small clearing of the forest.

He rose up, slowly, onto his hands and knees. His breaths came out hard. His foot was definitely going to need some serious time to recover, some objective part of his mind thought briefly. He twisted and turned to see every tree around him - as far as he could tell, he was alone. He must have outrun whatever was chasing him.

Thud-thud

The beating sound had grown in intensity, he noticed. He could actually feel the rhythmic tremors in the rich soil beneath his hands. Whatever this was *couldn't* be some kind of beast, could it?

As he scanned the trees around him once again, he noticed something he had not noticed before when he'd been too panicked to pay attention. A low mound of some sort covered in grass sat on the other side of the clearing, and if he concentrated, he thought he could feel some sort of ... *pull* from that direction.

He struggled up to his feet and found he could walk fine enough on his right foot, so long as he did not put any weight on the toes. *Definitely broken*, he thought. He followed the strange feeling towards the mound, walking carefully and limping and cursing dramatically whenever he accidentally put pressure on the wrong spot.

When he reached the mound, he noticed it was actually stone underneath the grass. Odd, swirled carvings were etched into the rock

PHANTOM FIRE | 65

with grass growing out of the cracks. He touched his hand to the stone gently.

Thud-thud

He tore his hand away. It was as if the rock itself was thrumming like it had some sort of heartbeat or something.

He heard a rustle behind the darkness of the trees off to his left. He eyed the direction carefully, but after several minutes, nothing happened. So, he began walking around the mound, inspecting all the strange marks that were carved into it. Who would have carved all this?

The Sidhe, a small, rebellious part of his mind thought.

He continued walking around it until he made one full circle, but standing in the place he started was a single black crow. Its feathery down shimmered in the light of the moon; its eyes like tiny stars shining back at Castor. They stood there, staring at each other in silence until the crow hopped along farther around the mound. It turned its head back to Castor.

Slowly, Castor followed the bird. It would hop along several steps before turning around to make sure Castor was still there. Soon enough, they made a second rotation around the mound. And as they came back to where they started, the crow flew up to the top of the mound and sat down. Castor almost followed it up there until he noticed another crow was standing where the first had stood. It hopped along around the mound as the first had before turning to look at Castor with its beady little eyes.

Castor looked back at the first crow on top of the mound and back at the second. One questionable decision later, and he was following the second crow around the mound. Just like the first, he made his third trek around. When they finished, the second crow flew up next to the first and sat.

Instinctively, Castor turned back and saw a third crow on the ground. A small part of him was getting a little tired of this game. *What if I am just following these birds around this stupid hill like a mad person?* he thought.

Thud-thud

But this crow didn't lead Castor around the mound. Instead, it hopped partway up the hill and stopped in the center of a huge, spiraling carving where it pecked the stone three times. Each strike against the ancient rock echoed deep into the forest like a hollow drum.

Confused, Castor looked around, waiting for something to happen. When he looked back at the crow, he saw it had flown up to join the other two. He looked back to the ground, but there was no fourth crow that had taken the third's place. He was about to plop down on the side of the mound, thinking he had wasted his time when he noticed that there was a perfect doorway that led down into the mound right in front of him as if it had always been there.

"What the - "

"Castor!" Sai's voice rang out, filled with a kind of terror he had never heard before. "Castor! Help me!"

Castor jumped at the sudden scream for help, his head whipping around; he couldn't identify the direction Sai's voice came from.

"Please, Castor!" The man's scream was filled with pain and horror. "It hurts! I need - "

Castor would never find out what he needed. The air was filled with a long, bloodcurdling scream followed by complete and utter silence.

Every hair on Castor's arms stood on end. He stared into the trees waiting for something to move or make any sort of sound. Time stretched on for what seemed like an eternity before he managed to turn back to the doorway.

Crows covered every inch of the mound - there were hundreds of them, wing-to-wing, beak-to-tailfeather, an ocean of black flooded over the mound. All of a sudden, they started screaming. Castor fell backwards on his hands away from the screeching birds. He scrambled back on his palms until he felt a cold clammy hand grip his bare shoulder.

He sprang to his feet, refusing to turn around and ignoring the pain in his foot as he sprinted down into the hole in the mound.

PHANTOM FIRE | 67

The path was steep. Very steep. Castor ran and ran through the darkness only partly worried he would eventually run into a wall, but he did not.

As he continued in the darkness, he vaguely realized that the smell had changed. What was deep, wet earth slowly changed to a sweet, flowery aroma. Up ahead, he saw a dim, blue-hued light showing an upward bend in the path.

Confused, he slowed to a walk. *How could there be light this far underground?* he thought to himself, finally calming down enough to have a coherent thought. His breath was heavy as he moved to the bottom of the incline. When he looked up, he saw an exit from the tunnel. Though, instead of nighttime, it seemed to be twilight out there, the sky a dark, heavy blue. *Odd how the path up was so short when the path down had seemed so long.*

Castor moved up warily. The earth beneath his feet turned to smooth, overlapping tree roots. His bare feet had trouble at first accommodating the uneven ground, but he quickly got the hang of it.

Finally, he emerged from the tunnel, but where he emerged *to*, he could not say.

Thud-thud

He was in an enormous clearing. Trees, ten times as tall as normal trees stood in the distance. An enormous lake stretched out off to his left, the water as still and clear as glass. Dark red flower petals flittered down from the dark sky. There was no moon or sun above him, only strange flowing green lights, almost like rivers of light in the sky. He heard no wind, no rustle of leaves, only his breath echoed in his ears as he stood there in the strange land.

Suddenly, he saw something move in the trees up ahead. It was as tall as the trees themselves - a stag. Antlers like a hundred curved spears rose out from two spots on the enormous beast's head with leafy vines looping from point to point. It moved with a gentle grace. Castor stared in awe as the deer, easily several hundred feet tall, casually strode out of the trees, glanced at Castor with six eyes like burning stars, and walked back into the forest.

Before he could react, the surface of the lake rippled. He moved to stand on the edge of the stony outcropping that trailed a few feet past the water's edge and saw two koi fish with scaly bodies as long as the stag was tall. Their eyes shown as the stag's had, like twinkling silver stars, and their tail fins shimmered and flowed behind them as they swam around each other in the endless depths of the lake. He felt their preternatural gaze on him, and he didn't know if he should feel uncomfortable or honored or terrified.

Then he heard it. A cawing both like the crows on the mound and also unlike them. He turned back towards the mound he came out of. Far off in the sky flew a colossal crow, silhouetted in the flowing lights above it.

Thud-thud

Pulled by something deep inside, Castor raced to the top of the mound. The crow turned and began flying straight towards him. His blood turned to ice as fear nearly overtook him, but he stood his ground. As it approached, faster and faster, Castor realized that it was not one large crow after all - it was actually hundreds upon hundreds of crows flying together in synchronization in the shape of one. They lowered, eye-level with Castor.

Then, they were on him - shooting past him like screaming arrows of darkness. He covered his face as he felt their wings brush his skin on their way past him. The caws were deafening. He felt like there was no end to the murder, though eventually it was indeed over. He glanced back and opened his eyes, but the crows were nowhere in sight. When he turned to face forward again, he saw a woman standing on the mound with him.

Thud-thud

And suddenly he realized that the mysterious sound was coming from *her*.

"Castor Vallas," she intoned. Her voice was beautiful and terrifying at the same time, like the birth of spring and the death of autumn combined into one. Her hair was black as the night sky tied back in nine long braids. Her poreless skin was as fair as a full moon, but her eyes and lips were the dark crimson color of blood. She stood several heads taller than Castor himself and her frame was nearly skeletal, though not grotesquely so. She wore a simple black gown adorned at the shoulders and hem with shining black crow feathers.

"Um," said Castor eloquently.

She smiled, her teeth perfectly white pearls in her red mouth.

"Who—who are you?" Castor's voice was barely a whisper.

"I have been called by many names." Her voice resonated through his body like an inner thunder. "Though you would know me as the Allmother."

6

The Mark of the Phantom

"You - You're the Allmother?" Castor was so dumbfounded he couldn't even bring himself to move. How did you act when in the presence of an actual goddess anyway? He suddenly became aware of his hands and was unsure what to do with them at the moment.

"I am." She turned to face the lake and sat down, her palms on the ground behind her as she reclined and gazed out at the water. "I am what your people call the Phantom Aspect of the Allmother. The bearer of all children, the heartbeat that flows throughout all life, and the harvester of souls." She gently patted the maroon petals on the carved stone of the mound next to her. "Sit with me, if you like."

"Oh," Castor said. "Yes, o— of course." He moved next to her and sat. As he chanced a glance over to the goddess, he saw her gazing out over the clear waters. For a moment, under the strange shimmering lights above, he thought he could see *through* the Phantom's flesh to the grinning skull beneath. He looked away and found himself sweating and trying to control his uneven breaths.

"Be at peace," she said, her powerful voice cutting through the air like a sword. And he suddenly was. He felt as calm as if he were sitting with Ophelia Patera, not the goddess of life and death.

She was quiet for some time, so Castor said, "What is this place?"

The Phantom sighed and closed her eyes peacefully. "This is my home. This is what your kind calls the Otherworld."

He nodded thoughtfully. "Why am I here?"

She turned to him, her braids shifting around the feathers at her shoulders. "You tell me."

He cast his mind back. "My fellow apprentices and I woke in the middle of the night because we heard a strange sound in the distance. We followed it across the water to the Isle of Sidhe, though one of us turned back before getting all the way across. I separated from my other companion in the forest on the island and found a mound in the stone. I heard him screaming out in pain before I passed through the doorway in the mound that led here ..." He thought for a moment before asking, "Are they all right?"

She nodded and turned back to the water. "Your companions are sound asleep in their beds; do not fret for them. You have yet to find your answer, though."

Castor looked at her in confusion.

"You told me *how* you came to be in my home, but not *why*."

He furrowed his brow as he thought. "I guess I don't know. I only know that I am here."

She smiled. "You are here because you are here. I feel that is reason enough to be here, do you not?" He did not say anything. "Often in life, you will find there is no reason for happenings. Things happen because they just do. Worrying over the reason behind them is fruitless." Her words gave him a sense of ease.

"If I am here in the Otherworld, does that mean ..."

She laughed then. "You are but a visitor in my home," she explained. "You are alive and well, I assure you."

Castor breathed a sigh of relief. "If I am only visiting, does that mean I must leave?"

She laughed again, a warm sound. Castor smiled along. "Yes, you must return to your own realm." Castor felt a tinge of sadness. He rather liked the strange land. "Though before you do, I would like to bestow upon you a gift, if you like."

"A gift?"

"My mark," she said.

"Your - Your mark?"

She nodded. "It will grant you great power. Bear in mind, however, that it may just change your fate."

"For the better or for the worse?" he asked tentatively.

"That," she said gently, "is up to you."

He thought for a moment. "Why would you give me your mark?"

"Perhaps because you are the only one of the three who heard me who was able to find me," she said. "Perhaps because it has been many ages since someone has piqued my interest as you have. Or perhaps there is no reason. Perhaps I am offering you my mark simply because I am."

"Is there a price I must pay?" Castor inquired.

"My mark is a *gift*," she repeated. "Though all power comes with prices that must be paid. You must be ready to accept the consequences of what you do with the mark and what paths it leads you down. Will you accept my gift?"

He worried over what these "consequences" might be, but if he was honest with himself, it wouldn't really matter. He knew what he was going to say.

"I accept."

The Phantom Aspect of the Allmother rose to her feet, and Castor followed. They faced each other, and Castor suddenly felt a strange feeling. A feeling like he'd had one too many wines. Or maybe like he'd stood up too quickly and had begun to feel faint.

No, he thought briefly. *No, it's not either of those things.* The edges of his vision began to spot with darkness. *I think I'm - I think this is a dream.* He felt his heartbeat pounding in his chest, a very *real* feeling.

"There is no going back once you accept this mark," she said, her voice breaking him out of his racing thoughts. "I will ask one more time. Will you accept my gift?"

"Yes," Castor said immediately. "Yes, I accept your gift." His voice in his ears sounded thick - far off and muffled.

The Phantom must have still heard him, for she smiled and raised one of her hands to place on the left side of his chest. "Brace yourself." Her words were the only things that still sounded real in this fading land of magic and gods.

Before Castor could ask why he needed to brace, his flesh under her palm lit like a fire, searing his skin in burning agony.

Castor sat upright in bed, grasping his chest and gasping for air, the fading afterimage of a grinning skull branded into his vision.

The room was dark save for the glow of the moon through the open window. Aedan and Sai were fast asleep in their beds, the former snoring loud enough to wake the village of Endala, Castor mused absentmindedly.

He pulled the collar of his tunic down and saw that it was entirely unmarked - no scorch marks or wounds of any kind. Pressing a tentative finger to it, he found it cool to the touch.

When his breathing finally began to slow back down, he relaxed back on his cot. *What an intense dream*, he thought. He looked back to the other two in the room to assure himself that they *were* in fact there and breathing. Satisfied, he rested his head and wiped the sweat from his temple.

He sighed quietly and closed his eyes. For the rest of the night, his dreams were plagued by giant woodland beasts, the laughter of the Sidhe, and the sparkling eyes of a thousand crows.

"Today is going to be a little different than usual," Teacher told the three of them that next morning outside under the frosted trees. "I have seen great progress in all of you since you arrived here three months ago, and I am very proud of each of you." She smiled at them like a satisfied parent might have, Aedan thought. "I think it is time we begin the basics of weapons training. Do any of you believe you are not ready to move on?"

Aedan was more than ready. "No, Teacher," he said fervently, echoed by his two peers shortly after.

"Good. Now, as I understand it, Aedan you prefer to do combat with two hand axes. Does that still hold true?"

Aedan nodded, smiling wide. He could not keep his excitement hidden any longer. *At last,* they were going to be getting to the real stuff!

"Excellent. Keep in mind that while a good warrior is proficient with one combat style, a great warrior is skilled in many. If you wish to learn proper ways to utilize other weapons during your training, you need only ask." Then, she turned to Sai. "You, if I recall correctly, stated you were a capable trapper. While trapping is a useful talent when it comes to hunting, I think we can all agree that it will not help you much in a fight," she said with a well-meaning nod. "Are there any weapons you would like to learn first? If what you choose does not turn out to suit you, worry not. You may take as long as you need to find what you like."

"You have close to the same build as a warrior from my village," Aedan said helpfully when he noticed Sai's hesitation. "She used two daggers and was undoubtedly one of the deadliest fighters I have ever seen. Perhaps you might like using knives?"

Sai shrugged noncommittally. "I suppose I can start there."

Teacher nodded. "And you, Vallas. You said you were trained to use a sword and shield by your weapons trainer at your estate? Though if my memory serves me right, you stated you did not much care for that style. Do you have an idea of where you would like to start?"

Aedan watched Castor as he scratched his head thoughtfully. As Aedan examined him, he thought he saw something different about him. Maybe the sunlight caught Castor's eyes strangely, but for a second, it almost looked as though they had a crimson tint to them. He hadn't ever noticed that before.

"I think I will just stick with a sword and shield for now until I feel more comfortable to move on to something else," he said.

"As you like," she responded. "Come with me to gather the weapons you will be practicing with." She waved them over, and they followed their teacher back into the longhouse. Once inside, she moved the central table aside and bent to pull back at the corner of the heavy, brown rug to reveal a trap door Aedan had never even considered could have existed.

They were led down into the dark, wet earth on a creaking staircase. They stopped at the bottom, and for a brief moment, nothing happened. Then, with a crackle and a flash, a flame sprang to life at the head of a torch fashioned to the wall of the cellar. Castor and Sai started at the sudden light.

"Was that a flintleaf?" Aedan asked incredulously.

"What's a flintleaf?" Castor and Sai inquired simultaneously.

"Do they not grow in your homelands?" Aedan said, eyeing the others curiously. "They are the leaves of this common yellow plant, and if you pull one between your fingers, it makes a small flame. The flame lasts only for a moment, but they are incredibly useful for starting larger fires."

"The proper name for the plant is '*ignolia*'," Teacher informed them. "Though I have heard that some of the outlying villages of Maecha call them flintleaves as well."

Aedan's eyebrows perked up then. "Teacher, are you also from Maecha?"

Her back was to them, but Aedan saw her stiffen momentarily. Before he could question it, she said, "Yes, that is where I am from." Her voice had a hint of something Aedan had not heard from her before. Was that *sadness*? "Come now. Retrieve your weapons."

The now-lit room, Aedan saw, appeared to be the same length as the longhouse above—one, undivided room with weapons of all kinds imaginable lining the walls on oaken racks. Swords, spears, axes, daggers, staves, bows, claymores, rapiers, whips, iron claws, maces, flails, and many others decorated the cellar, filling Aedan's warrior heart with a silent glee.

After Aedan fingered the expert forge-work of the displayed axes for a few minutes, he gently cleared his throat and turned to Teacher. "Would it be all right if I used the ones that I brought with me?"

76 | MICHAEL JACE

"Of course," Teacher said, her demeanor back to normal. "The same goes for all of you. If you brought your own weapons and you would like to use them, you most certainly can."

Sai and Castor looked at each other and shrugged as they continued to pick through what was being offered. Apparently neither had brought their own as he had. He bowed his head quickly and left to recover his axes next to his bed. When he returned, Castor had decided on a fine double-edged sword with a blade only a little shorter than his arm and a small steel heater shield.

If I were to use a shield, Aedan thought, *it'd definitely have been a larger one to protect more of his body.* Though he supposed with great speed and finesse, the smaller heater shield could still be effective.

Sai had taken Aedan's recommendation, holding a dagger in each of his long-fingered hands. He was looking at them with a curious eye, examining the incredible sharpness of the edges.

When it was apparent that they were satisfied with their choices, they returned to the beach. For the rest of the day, Teacher instructed them on proper ways to carry and clean and sharpen their weapons. While Aedan supposed these were important things to know, he was just ready to start the actual combat training. Which is what he told Castor while they were deep in the chilly forest hunting for their dinner.

Since Teacher had decided to end the training early that day, there was still some sunlight through the trees, though not entirely too much. "I am ready to start the real training, too," Castor said quietly to Aedan as they crept around the underbrush, careful not to make too much noise. "Although, I am very out of practice," he added.

"As am I," Aedan said back honestly. "We can just train together until we are back in form - "

Suddenly, Castor threw his arm out sideways to stop him. Aedan, instantly on full alert, scanned the trees until he saw what Castor saw. A stag had appeared seemingly from thin air, and Aedan had completely missed it! He cursed under his breath for letting himself get so distracted.

PHANTOM FIRE | 77

He tapped Castor's shoulder and gestured for him to make the shot. He deserved it; he was the one who'd spotted the beast after all. Castor nodded seriously and pulled an arrow out of his quiver with a cautious hand.

Aedan watched him closely. His stance was good, much stronger than it was when they first hunted together. The muscles in his arms had grown substantially, too; the veins stood out like ropes under his skin in the cold, wintry air. Castor's gaze was intense, Aedan noticed. He was taking great care in ensuring his aim was sufficient. It was strange, but he thought he saw the colors of Castor's eyes slip into a deep red again as he focused on his target. It was gone when Aedan blinked, though. He must have just been imagining it.

A howling, human scream cut through the silence as Castor's arrow veered right, completely missing the stag who bolted at the sudden splitting cry.

"That sounded like Sai," Castor said before running towards the noise. Aedan followed as best as he could, which was difficult considering how fast Castor could run - even through underbrush, he was like wind over water.

They whipped through the trees, feeling the low-hanging branches scratch against their skin. Coming to an abrupt halt, Aedan nearly stumbled over Castor who had bent to his knees over a bleeding Sai.

"What happened? Are you all right?" When he was serious, Castor's voice was different, a small part of Aedan's mind thought. He didn't sound timid or fearful of the situation - his voice came out clear and commanding. *The voice of nobility*, he thought.

Sai was laying back against a tree trunk, his face twisted in pain. His hands gripped around his thigh where a large gash bled fiercely. Some type of bladed contraption sat nearby.

"I was setting a trap for a deer," he said through clenched teeth. "I accidentally tripped the wire and couldn't move out of the way fast enough."

"Avelas," Aedan breathed before Sai could go on. "We need to get you to Avelas. She is a healer in the village. Will you help me carry him?" he asked as he turned to Castor.

"Of course," Castor said. "Though we need to try and stop the bleeding if we can first." He pulled his tunic off over his head. Aedan noticed the muscles in his back and shoulders working as he tied it over the wound. "Hopefully that will hold until we get you to this Avelas woman," he said under his breath.

Aedan saw him shiver a little in the cold forest and almost offered him his own heavy tunic as Aedan was more accustomed to the cold than his southern-born friend, but Castor was already shouldering one of Sai's arms. Aedan wrapped the other around his shoulder and off they trudged, slowly but surely towards the village.

Fiona had been tending to the sea falcon, or Bas, as she had come to start calling him, in the back of the shop all afternoon and had not noticed at first when her brother and his fellow apprentices had come in. The bird was being incredibly stubborn as usual and was still more than happy to peck at her whenever she tried to feed him or clean his bandages. She did not understand why Bas was so ungrateful, but it wasn't going to stop her from constantly hovering over him and trying to make him better by any means necessary. He *was* her first patient after all. When it came to all of Avelas's other customers, sure, she let Fiona assist here and there, but Fiona was given full responsibility of the bird when he was brought in. Of course, she still guided Fiona when she had questions, but for the most part, Bas was her charge. And she took it seriously.

"By the Aspects, what happened?" she heard Avelas exclaim from the front room.

"A hunting trap was prematurely tripped," a breathy male voice said.

"Sorry to bother you with this, Avelas, but I did not know anyone else to go to," another voice said.

And at that, Fiona perked up. She knew that voice anywhere.

PHANTOM FIRE | 79

"I'll be right back," she whispered to the bird, who tried to bite her nose. She pushed into the front room.

"It is quite all right, dear," Avelas responded as Fiona entered behind her. "Set him down on my table over there." She pointed towards the southern wall against which a long, narrow table was pushed. On either end were two square tables which held scraps of cloth, a few bottles of alcohol, and a small variety of metal utensils.

"Aedan!" Fiona chirped when she saw him. Then her eyes fell to the bleeding boy he was half-carrying. She went to her brother's side and helped maneuver his friend onto the table. He was grunting and cursing under his breath a great deal the entire time.

"Will he be all right?" Aedan asked worriedly.

Avelas untied a heavy tunic from the man's leg and quickly went to work cleaning the mess. "Fiona, please escort your brother and his friend outside and return when you can to assist me," she muttered to her not unkindly.

Fiona pulled the other two boys outside after grabbing a soft quilted blanket and giving it to Aedan's shivering friend to cover himself with while they waited. She briefly explained that they needed to wait there and that she would return when she could, then rushed back inside.

Avelas's hands were smeared with vermillion when Fiona appeared at her side. "What do you need?"

"Already cleaned it," Avelas said to herself as if checking off a list, something Fiona recognized was a common thing when she was feeling under pressure. "Grab the rod from the hearth," she ordered.

Fiona retrieved the heated iron rod from the blazing hearth and handed it to Avelas who gave the man a gentle look. "Hello," she said sweetly. "My name is Avelas. What is your name?"

The man continued panting. He squinted his eyes open. "Sai," he breathed, clenching his fists tightly at his sides.

"It is nice to meet you, Sai," she responded, holding the orange-tipped rod in her hands nonchalantly. Fiona knew this trick. "Where do you hail from?"

"Ugh," he grunted through clenched teeth. "I am from R - "

Avelas pressed the iron onto his wound. He screamed. Fiona flinched slightly from his horrific howl, but Avelas steadfastly held the iron to his wound until it seared shut. The man - Sai - was completely flexed on the table, all of his muscles taut in agony. The acrid smell of burned flesh made Fiona wrinkle her nose.

"Grab the honey," Avelas said calmly. Fiona did as she was told, and Avelas splashed a healthy amount on the burn.

"Ahh-haha." Sai was still breathing hard, but he sounded like he was on the downhill of the pain. "Amazing," he said. "I have never felt pain like that before."

Fiona's eyebrows raised quizzically. "Is that a good thing?"

His dark eyes fell on her for the first time, and his expression dropped completely. "Oh, I - *Oh* - Er - Um - P - Pleasure to make your acquaintance."

His face was very amusing, Fiona thought. She smiled back.

"It's nice to meet you, too."

His face was torn in half by a smile.

Avelas rolled her eyes. "Anyway, the honey will help keep the wound from getting infected. Be sure to keep the wound clean and get as much rest as you can. For the time being, you may use the table until you feel well enough to move."

"I am grateful," Sai said. "I will return tomorrow with payment for your services."

Avelas inclined her head and exited into the room that Bas stayed in.

Sai's eager eyes returned to Fiona. "What may I call you?"

"I am Fiona Ó Bháird. And you are Sai?"

"Sai Ishaav," he said, his face still full of wonder. "Y - You healed me?"

Fiona's eyebrow quirked up again. "No, that was Avelas; she did all the work. I hardly helped."

"But you did," he said beaming. "You did."

Fiona smiled awkwardly and said, "I'll be right back; I'm just going to fetch Aedan and the other one." She smiled again and left to find Sai's fellow apprentices waiting impatiently on the other side of the front door.

"How is he?" Aedan asked, putting a large hand on her shoulder in a familiar way.

"He should be fine," she replied. "It was good you brought him to Avelas. I am still learning anatomy, but if I'm right, then that cut could have been much more serious if it was just a little to the left. Maybe even deadly."

"It is good we found him then," said the black-haired man, a wash of relief plain on his face.

Fiona nodded. "I'm Fiona, by the way," she interjected. "Fiona Ó Bháird."

"Oh, you're Aedan's sister!" the man said. "My name is Castor Vallas. I heard that he had a sister here, but it is good to finally meet you."

She smiled brightly. "It is good to meet you, as well." She saw the edge of Aedan's mouth curve up a little. "Come on in. I will put on some tea."

7

Blood and Fire

Teacher showed them proper ways to fight during the following weeks. Although maybe they did not learn to *fight* yet exactly, Castor thought. So far, they focused mostly on footwork and how to identify an opponent's weaknesses as quickly as possible. When they had chosen their weapons several weeks ago, Castor had felt a rush of excitement of finally being able to learn how to fight from a proper trainer. He supposed this other stuff was important too, but while Teacher might have commended him for his stubbornness, but being stubborn was not the same as being patient. And the more his impatience showed, the more mistakes he made during practice. And the more mistakes he made during practice, the more they had to practice. Maybe it was *his* fault they had not moved on to actual fighting yet?

No, probably not, Castor thought. It was undoubtedly because Teacher did not want to push Sai while he was recovering from his accident. That's what he told himself anyway.

Still, he pushed through several *more* weeks of exercise and footwork until finally they moved on to wrestling. Which was *not* using weapons, Castor groaned to himself.

"Wrestling is the most basic and primal form of fighting," Teacher explained, her hands folded behind her back and her feet shoulder-width apart. Her hair was tied back behind her head in a tight bun, her expression serious—as it always was when it came to training. "You may not always have your weapon with you when a threat appears. When and if that happens to you, you need to be capable of handling yourself without the assistance of iron and steel. Now. As always, I would like to see how good you are already so that I know where we need to focus to improve. Ó Bháird, step forward and ready yourself."

Aedan paled noticeably. Were they going to fight *Teacher?* Castor felt nauseous. Aedan was taller than Teacher, sure, and his muscles were also much larger than hers. Still. It was *Teacher.*

Aedan stepped forward.

Teacher tilted her head left and right cracking the bones underneath at a disturbingly high volume. Castor flinched with each pop. Her hands clapped in front of her, and she raised them openly before her gaze as she adjusted her footing. Aedan quickly tried to match Teacher's stance. Castor could see his hands shaking slightly.

"Begin," Teacher stated clearly.

Aedan lasted *maybe* fifteen seconds before Teacher had him pinned to the ground, his arm bent in an incredibly unpleasant way. He stubbornly tried to escape twice while Teacher held her grip firm, punishing his attempts with pain.

"You win," he grunted.

Teacher released her grip, and together they stood.

She patted his back in the rough way she always did. Castor was sure they all had a permanent bruise in the same spot on their backs where Teacher had shown her affection. "Stretch and come back," she said before turning to Castor.

His heartbeat quickened dramatically.

"Vallas, step forward and ready yourself."

He felt his stomach climb its way into his throat, but nevertheless, he stepped up. Teacher returned to the stance she assumed when she fought Aedan, and Castor copied her position as well as he could.

"Begin."

Teacher struck fast. Her left hand came around wide. Castor moved to block it, but it never connected. A surprise blow from her right hand to his ribs chastised his mistake. He huffed a painful breath of air before she swept his feet from underneath him. Slamming to the ground, he let out a groan. She was on him before he could recover. He tried to protect his face, but she quickly locked his arm and head in some kind of unpleasant hold. She squeezed once to show him how in control she was. Just trying to move an inch was incredibly painful. But then he remembered.

Only the best warriors are stubborn.

Grunting and cursing himself, he used his free hand to pull at her arm feebly. She quickly tightened her hold, a bolt of pain searing through him.

"Do you give up?" she asked in his ear.

He would have answered, but he did not want to use any unnecessary energy. Again, he pulled at her arm, and again, she tightened. He felt his heartbeat in his ears.

"*Do you give up?*" she repeated with more force though he could tell by her tone that she was smiling.

A series of impressions suddenly flashed by his mind's eye in an instant. A secret swim. A search through a forest. A murder of crows. A giant stag. A gift. A heartbeat.

It felt like the left half of his chest was on fire, like someone was holding a torch to his flesh. He yelled as he pulled her arm one last time. He felt a surge like fire pulse from the blaze on his chest through his arm and to his fingertips. A spark burst between his hand and Teacher's arm. He peeled her arm off him as easily as bending a sapling. He spun and shoved her, and what felt like tiny sparks crackled between his palms and her skin. She flew back with such a great force that Castor froze. Bouncing close to ten yards away, Teacher went rolling before coming to a stop. She was on her feet before Castor could blink, but she did not move once she stood.

No one moved in fact. Everyone was staring at him.

PHANTOM FIRE | 85

It was Teacher who spoke first. "What did you do?" She grabbed at her arm where Castor's fingers had gripped it. "And what is *that*? Are you on fire?" She jogged to him as he glanced down at his chest. Smoke was gently wafting through his tunic. He pulled it over his head and couldn't believe his eyes. A glowing mark like three spirals connected at the center burned on his chest; it was *hot*. He winced when he chanced a touch with his fingertip.

Aedan and Sai joined Teacher around him.

"What manner of sorcery is this?" Aedan looked at him with a fair amount of apprehension.

"I know of witches and their craft," Teacher said, "but I have never seen anything like this. What are you?"

Sai had a strange look on his face. "I have heard of the djinn that wander the Forsaken Lands of my country. They can appear human, though they have godlike strength and a mystical power over fire. I did not believe them to truly exist ..."

"No!" Castor shouted as he shook his head and took a step back from their crowd. "I'm human, just like you three."

"That's exactly what a djinn would say," Sai whispered.

"It's also what a human would say!" Castor shot back.

"Quiet," Teacher commanded. "It's fading." She grabbed Castor's shoulder, and they all stared as the light behind the spirals faded and faded before vanishing entirely without a trace. His skin appeared completely unscathed.

"His eyes are returned to normal, too," Aedan said, staring straight into them.

Castor had never felt more awkward and terrified at the same time. He reached and felt near his eyes. "What do you mean 'returned to normal'?"

Aedan looked over at Sai and Teacher with trepidation.

"They were red," said Sai. "Like blood."

Castor looked down at his unmarked chest as he tried to slow his breathing. *What are you?* What *was* he? Nothing like that had ever happened to him before. He searched his memories for some kind of clue.

"Is there something you have held back from telling us?" Teacher asked as she stared at his chest inquisitively.

He remembered the burning on his chest, and something clicked. All those images that had flashed through his mind right before he had thrown Teacher off him - they were not just some random impressions; they were *memories.*

"The Phantom ..." he whispered.

"What?" asked Sai.

Castor looked at them anxiously. "You're all going to think I am mad."

"I think you're running that risk either way," Sai muttered.

Aedan rolled his eyes. "You can tell us," he said reassuringly.

Castor sighed, but he found that once he started telling the story, the words just started spilling out of him. "I had a dream more than a month ago - or maybe it was more than a dream; I do not know. But in the dream, we were in the house here. The three of us apprentices woke all at the same time to a faint thumping sound in the distance. We followed it across the strait to the Isle of the Sidhe. We ... We got split up, and I stumbled across some sort of ancient mound in the ground with a door in its side. It went down for ages but eventually turned back up, and when I came out the other side, I was in another world. The *Otherworld* actually. It was ..." He paused briefly, unsure of how to even describe the Otherworld. He saw them looking at him expectantly, and he moved on. "And then out of nowhere, a woman appeared. She was *really* tall and terrifying and beautiful, and she told me that she was the Allmother. The Phantom Aspect, to be more specific - "

Sai scoffed. "What a load of - "

"Quiet!" Teacher said again. She nodded at Castor to continue, her eyes enraptured with every word he said.

PHANTOM FIRE | 87

"I remember ..." Castor's eyes searched as though trying to remember exactly what happened. "She told me she wanted to give me her mark."

The Allmother's words echoed in his mind. *It will grant you great power. Bear in mind, however, that it may just change your fate.*

He put his hand on his chest the way she had. "She touched me here," he said. "And it burned - it burned horribly, and then I woke up back in my bed here."

Teacher and Aedan had a mix of terror and fascination on their faces. "W - Why did you not say something sooner?" Aedan's voice was barely a whisper.

"I thought it was only a dream!" Castor retorted. "I woke up drenched in sweat and looked at my body, but there was nothing on it. I did not think more of it at the time; I just - I thought it was a dream," he repeated.

"So, what did you do exactly?" Sai asked. "It looked as though you had suddenly gained great strength."

"I don't think that's what it was," Teacher answered for him. "When he pulled my arm away, I didn't so much feel *pressure* from his pull than I felt a loss of strength to keep my grip. I felt some kind of shock from his hand, and then my arm just wouldn't hold on any longer." She looked hard at Castor. He felt naked under her scrutinizing gaze. "Do you think you can do it again?"

He shook his head, feeling embarrassed. "I don't know how I did it the first time."

"Wait," Aedan interrupted. "We don't even know how dangerous this is. The Phantom Aspect is the goddess of life, death, and rebirth. Her mark must be incredibly powerful; playing around with this kind of power might not be the best idea." He glanced worriedly at Castor.

Teacher looked from Aedan to Castor. She nodded finally. "You are right. It should be up to Castor if he wishes to use this gift." She looked at him with not a small amount of hope.

"No," he said. "No, I want to try. If it's true that the Allmother gave me this mark, it would be an insult to let it go to waste, right?" His eyes fell to palms. *Though all power comes with prices that must be paid. You must be ready to accept the consequences of what you do with the mark and what paths it leads you down.*

Teacher nodded with a smile of excitement on her face. "Shall we try now?" She looked to Aedan and Sai. "I am sure the two of you do not mind waiting to wrestle me again while Vallas and I see about this gift, no?"

They both immediately agreed.

She nodded, smiling. "Ready yourself," she said as she faced Castor.

"What are you going to - "

Before he could finish, Teacher feinted right before striking left. Stumbling back, Castor managed to dodge the swing. He put his hands up instinctively as he found his footing. But Teacher had more speed than Castor thought was humanly possible. She moved as though the fight was a dance to her. Castor tried to keep his defenses up, but she was too fluid to keep up with. When he finally tried to manage a strike of his own, she grabbed his arm and twisted it around until he cried out in pain. Aedan took an involuntary step forward.

Castor felt the fire rage again. Out of the corner of his eye, he saw the glow return to his chest.

"Hold it!" Teacher instructed. "Try to keep that energy without using it just yet."

Castor's arm screamed in agony, but he tried to focus on the burning pain of the mark instead. Still, the longer he tried to maintain the energy of the mark, the faster it faded. He pushed himself, flexing his body as tight as it could go, clenching his teeth, squinting his eyes - *anything* to keep it burning.

But it did nothing to help; the mark's light faded away as it had before - little by little until eventually winking out. He let out a breath he had not realized he had been holding, feeling his muscles relax. He felt a little faint. Teacher released him.

"Forgive me," he said, breathing hard and trying to focus his vision. "I think this is going to take some practice."

"Would you like to try again?" Teacher asked.

He was still seeing a few dark spots in his view. Actually, now that he thought about it, he was really exhausted. "I ... uh," he managed to say before the spots grew into a total darkness that overtook him.

I am grateful for everything you have done for me, Aedan prayed. *I thank you for keeping my sister and me warm and fed. Every day, I learn more and grow stronger, and I do it in your honor. Through you, anything is possible.* He stopped for a moment and sighed. He wanted to ask the Allmother why she gave her mark to *Castor*, who, while he was admittedly smart and handsome and was strong in his own way, was not a very spiritual person in the slightest, instead of giving it to himself who left offerings to her daily and prayed to her whenever he could. Aedan was clearly more religious and definitely had greater strength; he *deserved* to be blessed by an Aspect. Instead of saying that, he sighed again and prayed, *I only ask that you continue to watch over Fiona and keep her safe.*

He rose from the hearth in the longhouse and padded outside. Castor was napping back inside, resting from his earlier work with Teacher and his mark. Sai had disappeared off on a walk hours ago, a short time after Teacher had given them the rest of the day off training due to Castor's special circumstances. Teacher was sitting on the beach, looking calm and serene. She said she needed to meditate on all that had transpired that day. Aedan, who was the type who preferred the company of others to solitude, began the familiar trek to Endala to see his sister.

It was not long before he passed the tavern on the outskirts of the village. It was much quieter in Endala since the cold had finally settled in, Aedan noticed, although the tavern still pulled a small crowd. Aedan did not find this surprising; he himself would happily enjoy a mug during any time of the year.

He walked the usual route through the village paths down to the central well. Just as he was about to enter the square, he saw Avelas's door open. Expecting Fiona or Avelas, he was surprised to see that it was Sai who came out. He was turned, and, smiling, he said, "Until next time, my doe." The door closed behind him, and he left through another path back towards the longhouse apparently not noticing Aedan.

He shuffled over to the door, looking once over his shoulder back the way Sai left, still a little curious. As he raised his knuckles to the door, it opened.

"By the Nine!" Fiona half-yelled, stumbling back as she tried to catch her breath. "We've talked about this, Aedan! You cannot just suddenly appear places! That's how people die!"

Aedan, who had to duck his head and angle his shoulders to get through the door, supposed she probably had a point. "What are you doing today?" he asked her while patting her head lovingly with a large hand.

"I was actually just about to run to the market to pick up a few things for Avelas." She had a hand on her steadying chest and an empty pack strung over her shoulder. "I'll invite you along if you promise not to jump out at me again for a whole year."

As they paced through the frosted village, Aedan couldn't help but mention, "So. I saw Sai leaving Avelas's."

"Has he not brought it up with you?" Fiona inquired innocently. "He's been visiting me most days since he was hurt."

"Oh, so you have been giving him tips on how to take care of his wound then?"

Fiona's eyebrows creased as she gave him an odd look. "No, brother," she said. "I think he has taken a liking to me." Pink rose to her cheeks as she tucked a bit of her hair behind her ear. "I have come to enjoy his visits as well," she muttered under her breath.

Aedan looked at her incredulously. *Stop,* he told himself. *Be supportive.* He took a deep breath and then said, "I'll kill him - I mean, how fortunate for him. That you like him, I mean. That anyone would like him."

PHANTOM FIRE | 91

Fiona rolled her eyes and shoved him not unkindly. "Oh, quiet yourself," she said. "He seems like a good man, and he really seems to like me for *me*. Not for the reasons that the men in Albainn liked me," she added quietly.

Whenever that topic was brought up, Aedan had to truly fight to keep from screaming in fury. He hated that she had to go through that. That he was not able to feed them and keep them warm on his own. That she had to use her own *body* to provide for them. He pushed his hair back over his head and bit his lip to keep from letting out his true emotions.

"Forgive me. I only meant that Sai seems like a better person than most," she repeated. "Is there a legitimate argument you have as to why I should not let him pursue me?"

Aedan dug down deep inside him, searching for something he could say to express how uncomfortable he was with his sister *liking* someone without making it about himself. He sighed, defeated. "'My doe', huh?"

Fiona scoffed as she pulled him along to the store, but he could still see her smiling.

✦ . ⁺ . ✦ . ⁺ . ✦

It took Castor a few moments to collect himself when he woke mysteriously on his bed. But it all did come back. That dream with the Allmother - it was *real*. He really did meet her, and she really did give him her mark. And now he had some crazy power, though he wasn't actually even sure what the power *did* exactly. Sai had said he thought the gift gave him immense strength, but Castor agreed with Teacher. It didn't feel like he *overpowered* her, so much as it felt like Teacher's arm just *obeyed* what he wanted it to do. But what does that mean? Does the Phantom mark let him control people? Clearly, he was going to need to practice using and mastering his new gift. Not to mention that he had only managed to attempt to use it twice before he fell unconscious.

"You are awake," Aedan said as he suddenly appeared in the room, silent as ever, startling Castor not a small amount. "How do you feel?"

He padded over and sat on the edge of Castor's bed. Reaching gently, he touched the back of his hand to Castor's forehead.

"I feel fine," he responded. "Just a bit tired is all. Whatever that power is really takes a lot out of me."

A slight smile shown on his face briefly, but there was a hint of something else there, too, Castor thought. Was it annoyance? Aedan lowered his hand. "You should feel very proud of the gift the Allmother bestowed on you. I cannot imagine a higher honor."

"One thing I do not understand," Castor began as he pushed himself up into a sitting position, "is how you and Sai don't remember that night. If it wasn't a dream, then should you not also remember what happened?"

Aedan's brow furrowed. "Perhaps it was a dream," he said. "Perhaps the Allmother came to you in your dream to give you the gift."

Castor supposed that made sense.

"Or maybe she just stole our memories. Who could say?" said Aedan with a good-natured smile. Castor smiled and looked down at his hands. Then, Aedan added, "Do you want to practice using it some more now?"

Castor blew out a quick breath. "Oh, no, I think I need to take a break and go slowly with it from now on until I get used to the amount of energy it takes to use it."

Aedan nodded. "Best not to overdo it," he agreed, a tinge of disappointment on his tongue. "In that case, would you like to go with me to find dinner? I find I am quite in the mood to kill something."

Castor agreed, and, after getting properly dressed, he left with Aedan into the woods.

"To sate my curiosity," Castor began, "why is it you said you were in the mood to kill something?" Castor didn't bring a bow himself; he assumed Aedan would do all the hunting they needed. He followed him by his side, stepping quietly save for the soft crunch of frosted undergrowth. It smelled like winter outside, Castor thought. Like the season itself had muted the aromas of the forest and superimposed over it a vague scent of *cold*.

Aedan scoffed. "I think *Sai* is trying to *court* my *sister*." He said every word with not a small measure of distaste.

"Can you blame him?" Castor responded. "Your sister is a very beautiful girl. I am sure this is not the first time she has had a suitor, no?"

Aedan breathed a heavy breath through his nose. "Not a *real* suitor, no. People are not often interested in Ó Bháirds."

"What?" Castor sputtered. "How could you possibly mean that?"

Aedan gave him an odd look, which was soon replaced by one of recognition. "I sometimes forget that you are from Odessa. 'Ó Bháird' is not an actual family name," he explained. "That is the name given to those who no longer have a family to call their own. When a child's parents die or abandon them and they are taken in by an orphanage, they are given the name 'Ó Bháird'. People tend to look down on those of us who have no claim to a clan. We are often seen as *undesirable*, and it can be difficult to find work or a safe place to live, let alone to actually have a suitor."

"That ..." said Castor, nearly speechless. "That is one of the most ridiculous things I have ever heard." When Aedan said nothing in response, Castor pressed on for more information. "So, when did it happen?" he asked. "When you and Fiona lost your parents, I mean."

"I never knew mine," Aedan said. "I was left at the orphanage as an infant with apparently no explanation. Fiona came much later. She was seven years of age when she arrived at the orphanage."

"Oh," Castor said. Then something occurred to him. "Wait, what? Are you not siblings?"

A half smile curled on Aedan's lips. "In a manner of speaking, we are, yes - and we do call each other brother and sister. All Ó Bháirds call each other family since we have none other to claim. But no, Fiona and I share no blood with each other." Before Castor could respond, he added, "But there is more to family than merely common blood."

"I suppose I understand." Castor continued to walk side-by-side with Aedan until he suddenly threw his arm up to stop Castor's stride.

Castor looked at him, startled, before realizing he must have seen or heard something. Slowly they crept, with an arrow readied on Aedan's bow, between the trees. Then, Castor heard it, too. A rhythmic, *squelch*-ing sound over quieter, uneven breaths. As they came closer to the sounds, he heard a weak bleating.

"That's not right," Aedan whispered as he suddenly swept away in a jog towards the sound. Confused, Castor took a moment before chasing after him.

A short way away, they came upon a grisly scene - a young deer on the ground, two of its four feet sliced off at the ankle. Red entrails spilled out from a horribly long cut in its underbelly onto the white, frosted grass. A small figure - Sai - hunched over the still-breathing animal with a bloodied knife in his right hand. Castor noticed a contraption similar to the one that had injured Sai several weeks ago set up against a nearby tree.

"By the Aspects - what is going on?" Aedan managed to whisper, the bow and arrow falling from his hands.

"Hmm," Sai said in response. "It still needs work. It only managed to take her back two feet." He held up the two legs that ended in crimson stumps, the deer grunting weakly in answer. "It needs to activate faster to get all four." His eyes never left the gore.

"Did it ... Did your trap cut it open, too?" Castor stammered as he tried to find words.

"Hmm? Oh, no, of course not," Sai answered as he stuck the knife experimentally into some of the mess. "I did that after I found her here. I just wanted to see the inside of her." He moved some of the entrails around with the blade, uncovering more swollen, red organs. "Is it not wonderful how much we have inside of us?" he asked with a look of awe.

"This is not right," Castor heard Aedan whisper.

Castor was faintly aware of a smoldering heat, though he paid it no mind. Following his gut, he slowly walked to the other side of the animal and dropped down by its head. He rested his hand on its neck

PHANTOM FIRE | 95

and felt its weakening pulse under his palm. He felt so sorry for the poor animal - he just wanted to end its suffering.

Suddenly, heat burned through his body and out his fingertips; a near-silent crackle popped between his skin and the deer's. For the briefest moment, he was completely aware of every single part of the animal - he could sense each individual organ, every vein that wrapped throughout its muscle, all the blood that feebly pumped in and out of those veins, and its frail heartbeat. He focused on that heartbeat and let the heat flow through his fingertips. He could feel where the heart was, and he guided the heat to that specific spot. Only moments later, when he felt the heat encircle the deer's heart, did he let the fire consume it, snuffing it out. The deer breathed one last shaking breath before Castor felt it die.

"Oh," Sai said, sounding mildly upset. "This one did not last near as long as the others did."

"'The others'," Castor echoed as he stood on his feet, his knees feeling only a little like jelly. "Sai, this - whatever this is you are doing is just - completely morally reprehensible. I bid that you please cease this at once and never do this again to another animal. Killing an animal for food is one thing, but *this* ..." He gestured to the creature below. "This is just wrong." He started to feel faint as the heat receded into his chest before dissipating.

Sai stood up, looking defensive. "*This?*" questioned Sai as his grip tightened on the knife in his hand. "*This is science,*" he said. "I understand that no one in either of your countries comprehend the concept, but in my country, we learn how to perfect our tools to make them more efficient. And we do this largely through trials."

"I understand wanting to progress and advance," Castor said, a little irritated at Sai's condescending tone. "So, you were trying to make your trap more efficient, I get that. But when the deer did not die, why did you decide to cut it open and spill its entrails while it was still alive? What is the reason behind that?"

Sai scoffed, sounding disgusted. "You just don't understand science at all." He turned on his heel and stomped back through the woods without another word.

"I am not alone in thinking that, right?" Castor asked when Sai was well out of earshot. "This *is* really quite disturbing, no?" His eyes returned to the macabre view below them.

Aedan, who had not spoken since they had shown up, nodded. "There is something not right about him," he said. "And I know what you are going to say. That I'm only saying that because I do not like the idea of him courting my sister, but something just … feels wrong." He ran his fingers through his hair. "I need to learn more about him if I am to feel right about this," he added to himself. He shook his head as if manually clearing his thoughts. "That aside, you did something, didn't you? When you touched the deer, I heard a faint *pop*, and then it died. Not to mention that your eyes are also currently very red and not dark as they usually are. You used your mark again, didn't you?"

Castor, feeling the same fatigue as he had when he had first used his mark, nodded. "I think so. When I touched the deer, I could somehow …" He paused and searched for the right word. "*Sense* every part of it. And I just guided the fire from the mark through the deer's flesh and blood to its heart. Then, it died."

After a moment, Aedan blew out a breath. "We should tell Teacher. About *all* of this," he said. "Come. Let us return."

8

Champion

Despite being born in Maecha, a generally cooler climate, Fiona enjoyed the time of year when winter began to fade into spring. When the plants began to bud, and birds began to sing tittering morning melodies. When the frost melted, and the first hints of warm breezes crept in over the sea.

She sat there on the edge of the dock, her feet dangling over the water, relishing in the beginning of the new season. Her auburn hair billowed out behind her in the wind. Orange and golden rays of light beamed from the setting sun across the sea reflecting back like a thousand shimmering mirrors. The breaking of the waves beneath her were almost soothing in their hypnotic rhythm, the smell and taste of the salty air a welcome tang on her lips.

She felt a sharp, almost piercing, stab into her left shoulder, but she didn't flinch. She only looked over at Bas, who had perched there. The falcon had really taken a liking to her, just as Avelas had suggested he might. Fiona had been unsure for the longest time, but Avelas was right.

Fiona had thought - had been *looking forward to* the time when the ungrateful bird's injury would be healed enough to let him back out into the wild so as to save her from its incessant pecking and scratching, but when that time did come, she found that though he did often wander about the clouds, he always stayed near. For the last few weeks, he had been hunting entirely on his own but always returned to her shoulder when he had his fill. Fiona unexpectedly and a bit reluctantly found she was actually beginning to enjoy his near-constant company. It helped that the bird had warmed up to her enough to stop harassing her.

"Greetings!" came a familiar voice from behind her.

Fiona turned to see Sai approaching with a hand concealed behind his back. She hopped up gracefully and smiled. Bas's claws dug slightly deeper into her shoulder as he puffed his chest out, making himself seem larger.

Aedan had come to Fiona quite some time ago telling her about how he and his friend, Castor, had stumbled upon Sai in the forest testing out one of his new traps on a deer. She understood how that could have seemed unsettling the way Aedan had described it, but when Sai explained it to her, it didn't sound as bad as her brother had made it seem, who, she argued, was already disapproving of Sai for some brotherly reason.

"I went by the healer's, and she told me you liked to come sit at the docks here," he said, his dark eyes sparkling in the lowering sun. "Here." He brandished a small pink flower blossom from behind him. "I saw this on the way here, and it made me think of you."

Fiona felt herself blush as he combed aside her hair and placed it behind her ear.

"Beautiful," he said.

She had to admit, she didn't think of herself as one for romantic gestures, but the fact that there was this handsome boy who was taking an interest in her despite her surname outdid her distaste for them. "How sweet," she said. "Would you like to join me? The breeze is quite pleasant." Her smile was shy as she indicated the Sai-sized empty area next to her.

They sat on the edge of the dock next to each other, their hands mere inches apart. Neither spoke; they only listened to the waves slap against the shore behind them. Out of the corner of her eye, Fiona saw

Sai's hand moving closer to hers ever so slowly, almost unnoticeably so. Fiona, being the type of person she was, snagged his hand up in hers and squeezed it once.

He let out a breath of a laugh and squeezed her hand back gently. Their eyes met in the rosy light. "You always surprise me," said Sai quietly. "I have never met a woman quite like you."

Fiona flushed deeply.

Then he did something so surprising, Fiona did not know how to react.

He began to sing.

"My doe, my doe. This sunlight has cast you aglow, you know. My doe, my doe. To be without you is surely a woe, you know. My doe, my doe. For you I'd best any foe, you know. My doe, my doe. I'll follow wherever you go, you know. My doe, my doe."

She couldn't believe he would do something so humiliating like that, and even though his voice was a little off-key, she felt so touched.

"Though something has been troubling me of late," he said, his tone suddenly serious. His brow furrowed as he looked to the waters.

"What is it?" she asked, a shade of worry hovering over her.

"There are only a few months left of my apprenticeship here." He paused for a moment, but it wasn't hard for Fiona to tell where he was going.

"I admit I've thought about that as well," Fiona interrupted. It might not have been a pleasant conversation, but it was one she had already assumed she'd have to have at some point. "I am truly sorry, but I will be going with my brother back to Maecha when it is time. It is where I belong."

He nodded, though there was a strange look in his eye - a hint of sadness mixed with something else Fiona couldn't decipher. His nod assuaged her worry that he would be more upset with the news. She knew he wasn't happy of course - neither was she - but was there even another option?

"Maybe you could return to Maecha with us?" Fiona ventured, her voice slightly higher than normal.

A sad smile flashed across Sai's face as he said, "My family expects me to return to Raaja when my time here is done. But perhaps there will be a time when I can come to Maecha," he added, a new tone of hope in his voice. "Perhaps we can see each other again then."

A smile broke over Fiona's face. "Perhaps we can. Until then, let us just enjoy today."

✦ . ✦ . ✦ . ✦ . ✦

When Aedan and Castor had returned to Teacher those weeks ago and informed her of Sai's strange behavior, Teacher had chalked it up to Raaja being a strange country full of strange people, which, Aedan thought, was not good enough. Surely it was more than just that he was a little different, right? Castor had seemed to completely take Aedan's side at first; but after Teacher had given her response, Castor had fallen in line behind her it seemed. Aedan tried not to hold it against him, but it still irritated him that no one was as bothered by Sai as he was. Perhaps he was just making a bigger fuss about it than it actually was as Fiona had argued. Either way, he wanted more information and was determined to get it.

Investigative work, however, was proving more difficult than he originally thought it would be. Sai was not an open book by any means, and any probing question Aedan asked was shut down immediately. Aedan assumed Sai still held a small grudge for their reaction to his "experiment". He tried convincing Castor to ask Sai about his past, but the more he tried, the more exasperated Castor seemed to get. Maybe he was just blowing this out of proportion. *But then again*, Aedan thought, *maybe I'm not.*

He didn't blame Castor for growing annoyed with him. Castor was, after all, under more stress than he and Sai were. Since they all found out about his mark, Teacher had been keeping him late nearly every day, having him experiment with his power and trying to help him tame it. Some nights, they would be out even after Aedan and Sai went to bed.

But Castor was definitely showing signs of improvement. He was able to make the mark show a few times on his own without first administering pain, and he was getting to where he could call on its power four or five times before becoming too weary to continue.

All that aside, they had *finally* begun training with weapons. Aedan was not a boastful person, but it was clear that he was *by far* the greatest fighter of the three. Of course, he beat them all in wrestling (except Teacher), but Castor had had some weapons training already back at home, so he had been a little worried that Castor might have the advantage. But this was not the case. Castor, with his dulled training sword and shield, occasionally came close to landing a blow, but he just fought too defensively, Aedan thought, who had won all of their bouts.

He was slightly ashamed, though not too surprised, that he could never seem to triumph against Teacher. It was no wonder she was known as the "Spear Maiden" throughout Maecha. She was adept with every weapon she owned, but with a spear in hand ... Aedan had never felt such envy and admiration for another warrior's skill.

As they were collecting their weapons one day, Aedan saw Castor's hand hesitate over the practice sword he had used from the start. Aedan, with his two axes, paused and watched from the stairs as Castor reached past the sword and took hold of one of the few spears leaning against the wall.

"Oh?" Aedan said.

Castor whipped around, face red, apparently thinking Aedan had already returned to the surface. "I just ... thought I would try it," he said. Then, he sighed and said, "I see how incredible Teacher is with the spear, and I - I know I'll not ever be as proficient with it as she is, but I just - "

"No," Aedan said. "You should try it. Maybe you'll actually be able to land a blow on me with that extra reach." He smiled and winked at him.

A playful smile broke over Castor's face, his right eyebrow went up the way it usually did when Aedan teased him. "I guess we'll see."

In the sand, where they did nearly all their training, Castor and Aedan faced off against each other. Castor with a heater shield strapped to his forearm and his newly acquired spear gripped tight in his right hand, and of course Aedan with his usual dual axes. Sai and Teacher sparred nearby, Teacher's voice occasionally piping up to correct Sai's footwork or commend a good strike.

But Aedan couldn't focus on that right now. Castor had never beaten him before, but he had a look in his eyes that put Aedan a little on edge for some reason. And the way he held that spear - it was clear he had been keeping a close eye on Teacher's style.

Before he could wonder any more on the subject, Castor leapt forward with a sharp jab of his spear. Completely thrown off by this contrastingly aggressive style, Aedan stumbled back, barely managing to swipe the spear aside with his axes. Castor was too close now though; he had lost the advantage of the spear's longer reach -

And Castor thrust the butt of the spear out *hard* catching Aedan's stomach. He hacked out a hard breath as Castor pivoted back and followed up with a wide swing of his spear around towards Aedan's head. Finally coming to his senses, Aedan stepped in, out of danger from the dull blade, and swiped his axes sideways at Castor's ribs - but was stopped short by the shield which gracefully deflected both blows.

Castor hopped back and leveled his spear out in front of him, putting him far enough away to regain the advantage of reach. Aedan took the opportunity to catch his breath for a quick moment. He *really* had not expected Castor, an extremely defensive fighter, to initiate the fight, let alone sacrifice his distance advantage for a surprising blow like that. A half smile crept up to his lips as he realized that Castor might just be a decent sparring partner after all.

Aedan waited for Castor to make the first move; *clearly,* he was trying a new, more offensive style (much like Teacher's), so he guessed he would attempt to initiate again.

He was right. Castor stepped in, feinting low with the spear before attempting a strike to the head. Aedan saw it coming, remembering Teacher's often use of feinting when commencing a sparring match. He moved out of the way easily with one step and closed the remaining gap with a second and rammed his shoulder into Castor's open side. Castor fell to the ground with a low grunt, dropping the spear on the way. When his face rose to Aedan's, his axes were already raised to his gaze.

Castor sighed and let himself fall back into the sand; his eyes were closed but a sly smile cracked his face. He winked one eye open and said, "I landed a blow."

Aedan laughed. "And a fine one it was." He grabbed Castor's forearm and pulled him up, giving him a rough pat on the back after he was back on his feet.

"Again?" Castor asked. He retrieved the spear and gave it a little whirl around his hand. "I think I like this more than the sword."

"I admit it was quite the surprise," Aedan replied.

Castor looked over to where Teacher and Sai were, slowly going through specific strikes step by step. Aedan found himself smiling. He shook his head gently and said, "If you can reach even half her talent, you'll defeat me with ease. Or you could just use your mark on me. That would work, too."

Castor laughed. "That may be, but I would have to be able to touch you first. I cannot seem to make it work unless I'm touching skin. That aside, you know Teacher doesn't want me to use my mark during training. I have to at least give you a chance." He smiled mischievously.

"A *chance?*" Aedan roared with laughter. "You're a cheeky one, aren't you?"

"Haven't we met?"

Aedan felt something light in his stomach as he laughed. They returned to their starting positions and raised their weapons.

◆ . + . ◆ . + . ◆

After their dinner was the usual time when Teacher and Castor would practice mastering his gift from the Phantom Aspect. And this night was no different, Castor noticed. After their meals had finally settled in their stomachs, Teacher led him back down to the beach. They sat in the sand, side-by-side, facing the Isle of the Sidhe. Most nights they practiced conjuring the mark to his skin a few times, and during the periods in between calling on it, they discussed theories as to how it was used and what exactly the power even *was.*

"We know that the mark can be brought on most easily by pain and high emotions," Teacher said.

"I did make it flicker slightly by myself that one time, though, remember?" Castor supplied.

"Right," she responded. "So, eventually, you should be able to call on it on your own when you have practiced enough, don't you think?"

Castor nodded thoughtfully. "And it only works if I'm making skin-to-skin contact. It seems to work on people and animals, but not trees or stones."

"Which, as I have mentioned before, makes sense," Teacher said. "This is the mark of the Phantom, the goddess of life, death, and rebirth."

"Trees are alive," Castor added.

"True, but do you not think trees would fall under the territory of the Aspect of the Earth Mother?"

Castor looked back to the Isle, lit by silvery moonlight.

"When the mark is active," she began, "you say you can sense the target's entire body, down to their blood?"

Castor nodded. "That's what it felt like with the deer."

"And you made its heart cease beating?" Castor remained silent, knowing she was only using him to talk out her thoughts. "And with me, you were able to make me release my grip and throw me a great distance." They were quiet for a moment as she unconsciously scratched her collar with her dirty fingernails. "Perhaps your gift allows you to manipulate the flesh, blood, and bone of others?"

Despite seeing it happen and even *making* it happen, Castor still thought the idea was mad. How could *he* even be able to do that? It was almost too preposterous to even imagine.

Almost.

"That's all I can think it would be as well," he replied eventually. "It has been on my mind day and night, and still that is the only thing I could think it would be."

Teacher was silent, but Castor could sense a sort of hesitation about her as though she were holding something in. Feeling as though he was close enough to her after their months of training since he had first arrived in Endala, he pressed in. "Is there something you wish to tell me, Teacher?"

She let out a quick breath and gave him an incredulous smile. "You can already read me so well, eh?" She gave him a motherly ruffle of his dark, curly hair. Castor felt blood rush to his face as he grinned and looked away. "You are right in your assumption," she said looking back to the isle. "But I'll not tell you tonight. Tomorrow when the others are awake, I'll tell all of you. Now let us continue on to training." She stood and clapped the sand off her hands.

"Should I be worried?" Castor asked as he rose next to her.

She laughed. "It is not something you should fret over. I only think I may have discovered what I have been looking for all these years."

✦ . ✛ . ✦ . ✛ . ✦

Castor woke with a start that next morning. He had slept fitfully all night, unable to get Teacher's words from the night before out of his mind. Whatever she had to tell them must be important, he thought. And it must have something to do with his new power, too.

All the same, he made his way to the beach after splashing a few chilly handfuls of water onto his face. Teacher was already there, sitting with her legs crossed and eyes closed, basking in the warm morning light. He sat across from her silently and closed his eyes as well, enjoying the gentle spring breeze. It wasn't long before Aedan joined them, quiet as ever, followed shortly after by Sai, who coughed loudly, startling Castor into opening his eyes again.

"What are we doing today, Teacher?" Aedan asked, hardly able to keep the excitement from his voice. "Are we to continue our sparring?"

Teacher smiled mildly. "Perhaps after breakfast, but before anything else, there is something I would like to tell you about - the truth of my past." The three apprentices sat quietly and attentively, though Sai *did* rub his sleepy eyes, Castor saw. Teacher sighed and closed her eyes briefly. "As you all know, I am originally from the country of Maecha. I left nearly twenty years ago after the last *bahvra*."

"What is a *bahvra?*" Sai interrupted.

"It is the Maechan tradition of when clans compete to determine the next successor to the throne when a king or queen dies," Aedan spat out quickly, apparently annoyed at Sai's disruption.

Teacher nodded. "I left then, not of my own free will, but because I participated in the *bahvra* and was defeated."

Aedan's head quirked to the side, his back straightening slightly. "You were ... defeated? But then ... should you not be ..." His voice trailed off as his eyes scanned every inch of her.

"Typically, yes," Teacher responded. "To fail in the *bahvra* is to give your life in battle. I, however, was not seen as honorable enough to be given a warrior's death and was, therefore, banished from setting foot in my homeland again."

Castor struggled to find the words he wanted to say. "Wh - Who could possibly not see your honor?"

She smiled kindly at him, seeming appreciative of his words. "Aife Ulster."

Aedan perked up instantly. "*Aife Ulster?* As in, the *Queen of Maecha,* Aife Ulster? I cannot believe you actually did battle with *Queen Aife!*"

"I have done battle with Queen Aife more than I have done battle with any other." The three looked at her curiously but remained silent. "Aife and I trained together since we could wield our spears."

Aedan sucked in a breath, realization dawning on his face. "*You -* "

"Yes," she said. "Yes, I am Branwyn Ulster, the banished princess of Maecha."

Even Sai was stunned into silence. Admittedly, Castor had never heard the story of the banished princess, but it was astonishing news all the same. They sat there in silence, taking it all in. Until Aedan said, "Y - Your Highness, while this news is incredible, I do not understand why you are telling us this now." He fidgeted with his hands nervously.

The princess raised her hand and shook her head slightly. "Please, continue to refer to me as 'Teacher'. After all, Vallas here is also nobility, yet we do not call him 'Lord Vallas' as his subjects would."

Castor felt his face redden. "Yes, please do not do that," he said. He almost felt free out here away from any reminder of his pre-planned life back home.

"That aside," Teacher said, "I am no longer a princess of Maecha anyway, so that title is misplaced." When Aedan began to apologize, she waved away his concern. "Do not worry. To answer your original query, I am telling you who I am today because I also want to tell you how and why I have come to train warriors from across Serrae."

Castor leaned in slightly. What else could she possibly have to say that would be bigger news than the fact that she was high royalty?

"When I was banished from my home, I was lost and dejected." Her voice was solemn. "I caught a ship to Midoria and eventually found work with a mercenary company called the Sisters of Snow. For years, I fought bandit clans in the frozen Midorian mountains, guarded wealthy merchant caravans, did everything I was hired to do - was told to do. Over time, the leader of the Sisters, Jalla, saw my worth - unlike my sister," she added with a venomous tone. "The time came when Jalla decided to retire, and at that point I had worked for her company for almost half a decade and had grown to be her most trusted warrior, so she offered me her position to lead the Sisters." This part of the story, Castor already knew. So did many.

"I assumed the title of 'Spear Maiden' and led the Sisters of Snow to victory and glory in many battles of Midorian clan rivalry, in the Merchant Wars of Avarice, and in many conquests into the untamed wilderness of the Forsaken Lands of Raaja. Though after nearly a decade of making a name for myself, I began to wonder what my true purpose was. While I did grow fond of my fellow Sisters, I knew I didn't belong with them. I knew I'd never find true happiness again until I was back home in Maecha. I belonged there - I *belong* there," she corrected. She paused for a moment as though collecting herself, preparing for the crux of the conversation.

"You see, I do not believe my sister, Aife Ulster, should have the right to be queen. Admittedly, I may hold a grudge against her for dishonoring me the way she did; but it was in doing so that she showed her weakness. The Queen of Maecha should have the strength to defeat their enemies, and Aife does not have that strength. She has the *talent* to best any who challenge her, with no doubt, but she was too weak to give me the honorable death I deserved. *I,* however, do not have that weakness." Castor thought her words were a little more than treasonous, but given the fact that she no longer was a citizen of Maecha, he doubted she cared. "I came here to set up these training grounds. I used my reputation as the Spear Maiden to hopefully find and train a warrior who could best me in combat. I swore if I ever came across such a person, I would do everything in my power to convince them to help me."

In her brief pause, Castor said, "Help you in what way?"

She smiled at him. "Help me claim the throne that is rightfully mine. In Maecha, the reigning queen or king may be challenged for their position in which the challenger duels them to the death. If the challenger claims victory, they also claim the throne, as they have proven to be the strongest warrior of Maecha."

"Such a strange country," Sai muttered under his breath.

Teacher ignored him and continued. "I, however, know that I cannot best my sister in combat, leaving aside that I am forbidden to enter the country anyway. The only way for me to claim what is rightfully mine is to have someone be my champion and fight in my name."

"*That's* why you train warriors," Castor responded.

"Yes," she said. "As I said, I train people from across the world in hopes to find and train someone who can best me in combat. If someone can defeat me, then surely, they stand a chance against Aife. I understand that Aife is the better warrior between the two of us, but she does not have the inner strength required to be a good, fair queen. I believe I do. The question, however, is, Castor," she said, now looking directly at him, "do *you* think I do?"

"What? Me?" He looked to Aedan and Sai, but they seemed as confused as he felt. "Why does it matter what I think?"

"Because," she began, her face completely serious, "I want you to be my champion."

"You - You what?" His voice was almost a whisper; he wasn't sure he had heard her correctly.

"I want you to be my champion," she repeated. "If you are to be my champion and do battle with my sister in my name, however, you must believe, on your own accord, that I have what it takes to be the rightful queen. I do understand that you are not of Maecha and, therefore, do not have personal experience with Aife's rule, but you have known *me* for some time now. I will not take offense should you decline," she added.

Castor was too shocked to respond. "I do not dwell too much in politics myself," Aedan chimed in. "But there are some in Albainn where I am from who believe Queen Aife to be too soft."

After his words, Castor said, "But would Aedan not be the strongest warrior of us? I can hardly touch him when we spar," he said.

"But that is all it would take," Aedan whispered. "She wants you to do this for her because, with your blessing, all you would need to do is touch the Queen." He was speaking rationally, but he had a look on his face Castor couldn't quite decipher.

"Is that not a cheat?" Sai asked inquisitively. "Surely witchery is not allowed in your contest of warriors."

"It cannot be witchcraft," Teacher said. "Witchcraft requires tools and herbs and stones to perform. *This* - this is a gift from the goddess." Her eyes sparkled in rapture in the morning light. "You came to my home to train, Castor Vallas, and have since been chosen by the Phantom Aspect of the Allmother and granted a powerful blessing. I see this as a *sign*. You were meant to come here, to learn under my tutelage, and to be blessed by the Aspect of life and death. I cannot imagine why else this was meant to happen than for you to be my champion and help me claim what should have been mine long ago. What better than to have a champion marked by the Allmother herself? Surely all of Maecha will know who is meant to be their ruler with you by my side."

He searched and searched for the answer. Clearly, he was very fond of Teacher, but should he help dethrone another queen just for her? Although, if both Teacher and Aedan were right, then the country was in need of a stronger leader. *It will grant you great power. Bear in mind, however, that it may just change your fate.* The Allmother's words sang through him. This is what she must have meant, Castor thought. The Allmother must have given him this power so that he could help their country. Maybe this was his fate. He never wanted his fate to be ruling over the Anand province in Odessa, stuck as a nobleman for the rest of his life. Perhaps this is what it was supposed to be.

"How would this work?" he asked finally.

Teacher's eyes lit up like bonfires, her face cracked by a large, warm smile. "If you are to accept, you will have to journey to Letha, capital city of Maecha, to challenge my sister. It will be a long, difficult journey - one that you should not undertake lightly, and, as I am forbidden to set foot in Maecha, you would need to go without me. Once you defeat her, you would need to send word to Endala of your victory, so that I may make the journey there myself. Also," she added, looking slightly crestfallen, "you should know that should you win, you would not be able to return home. As a Queen's champion, you would need to stay by my side in Letha as a symbol of our power."

Castor was almost ashamed of his response, "I do not wish to rule - "

"You wouldn't!" Teacher said brightly. "Your status as a Queen's champion is only to defend her should the need arise. All of your needs would be taken care of; all you would need to do is be a living reminder of my right to rule."

So, he would perhaps be able to leave behind his old life after all.

"I do not know the way," Castor said quietly. "I doubt I could make it on my own. And, if I did accept, I would be leaving my father to find someone to take my place as his successor. He would disown me for discarding my responsibilities."

Teacher's face dropped a little. "As I said, I would understand should you decline. I know this is a lot to ask of another."

"Oh, I have dreamt for years of leaving behind my posh and proper life for one of adventure," Castor said, waving away her concern. "I only meant that I doubt I could receive aid using my family's resources to journey across a foreign land on my own after I do so."

"I would provide silver for a horse to get you to Argos in Odessa. From there is the safest passage through the Roinn Mountains; though you may need a guide through them, for which I will also be pleased to pay. Once you arrive in Trícnoc on the other side of the path, it is a direct route to Letha. You would only need to cross the Ebonflow once, and I believe you intuitive and skilled enough to be able to do that. I will also provide a map to help keep your way," she added.

A buzz of excitement shot through Castor as he thought about actually accepting her offer. Though he was admittedly still worried about getting there on his own. That would be a *long* journey to make by himself. His old friend Ophelia Patera *did* live in Argos, however. Perhaps he could convince her to abandon her duties as well and travel with him ... It was a long shot, but he wasn't sure what else he would do. He did not know many people he was close enough with to ask to accompany him. But how often would a chance like this come along?

He realized everyone was staring at him. "All right," he said, his heart racing. "All right, I will be your champion, Teacher."

✦ . +   . ✦ . +   . ✦

Castor was out practicing his mark with Teacher, and Sai was off with Fiona probably. So, Aedan sat sulking in the longhouse alone on his bed.

He hated being jealous of people, and Castor was so likeable and charming - it was difficult to think negatively of him. But Aedan felt deep inside that *he* was supposed to be the one to have met with the Allmother and been blessed and consequently been the champion to the lost princess of Maecha. How could someone so ... *small* be better fit for that job?

His thoughts of Castor's journey led to thinking of how the apprenticeship here was more than halfway over, and that he was going to need to come up with a plan for himself and his sister for what they would do afterwards. They originally had decided that, with a letter from the Spear Maiden, he could work as a soldier or as a guard for one of the larger cities in Maecha - her approval carried immense weight in his country. He decided he would bring it up with Fiona the next time he visited her so they could set a plan in stone.

Suddenly, something caught Aedan's eye. A rounded corner of something small and thin protruded from underneath Sai's pillow. Casually, he leaned over and pulled the straw pillow back revealing a black book smaller than Aedan's hand. Out of curiosity, he retrieved it and opened it. The markings inside were familiar enough that Aedan knew them to be of the common tongue, though he knew he would not be able to understand them no matter how hard he squinted. But still, he could tell some of the ink on the pages was quite fresh - it smudged slightly on his fingertip. *Sai must be writing in here regularly*, he thought. If that was true, then this was a great find! If only he could convince Castor to decipher it for him ...

As if on cue, the front door opened. Aedan hastily tucked the book back in its hiding spot and reclined back on his bed. Castor's light and happy voice drifted through the home followed by Teacher's rougher, more grizzled tones. They spoke unintelligibly for a moment before a door closed on the other side of the house. Seconds later, Castor appeared in their room.

"Oh!" he said. "I thought you would be out visiting Fiona." He smiled good-naturedly and plopped down on the edge of his own bed smelling of sun and sweat and fire.

Aedan just shook his head.

"Well, I was about to go for a swim to cool off," Castor went on. "If you would like to join me, you are welcome to." He began shucking off his damp clothes.

"Actually," Aedan said, "I know you have grown weary of me asking you to help with this, but I do need a favor from you."

Castor stopped, looking at him warily, his shirt halfway off. "Is this about Sai?"

Aedan nodded and quickly followed up with, "I swear to you that if you do this one thing for me, I will never mention the subject to you again."

He looked hard at Aedan for a long moment. Then, he sighed and pulled his shirt back down. "What do you need?"

Aedan clapped him on the shoulder and retrieved the black book. "I found this under his pillow. I think - "

Castor's eyes widened in recognition. "That's his journal! Whatever he wrote in there is private!" he hissed quietly, looking around as though Sai might just be hiding in the room somewhere.

Aedan felt a leap of hope. His *journal*! Surely there would be good information in there that would prove his feelings about Sai were not unfounded.

Before he could say anything, he saw a new, more curious, look move over the original one of panic on Castor's face. "What does it say anyway?"

Aedan opened his mouth and then shut it. He had forgotten that he still hadn't told anyone that he couldn't read. He felt his face flush. "I, uh … I don't know what it says. Being in the orphanage my whole life, I never learned to read." His voice was quiet, but thankfully, Castor did not let the silence last very long.

"Oh," he said. "That's what you want my help with."

Aedan nodded and looked at him pleadingly.

Castor looked to the front door again before snatching the book from his hands. "Fine, I will skim through it for you. Just watch at the window and tell me if you see him."

Smiling immensely, Aedan hopped up and stood by the window, keeping watch. He would occasionally turn his head over his shoulder to check for any wild facial expressions or some kind of hint of what was in there, but Castor was calm and silent, save for the systematic turning of pages.

Aedan stared out the window, his heart pumping furiously, waiting for any kind of news, until—

"*What the hell* …" Castor whispered.

Aedan spun around. "What? What is it?"

Castor had his hand over his mouth, his eyes wide with shock.

Aedan rushed to his side and looked down at the page. Still obviously not understanding any of the marks, he said, "What does it say? Am I right?"

Castor nodded almost imperceptibly. Continuing to cover his mouth with his hand, he said, "Sai killed his sister. That's why he was sent here. His parents wanted him to learn about honor and discipline or something. But," he paused momentarily as he read. "He tortured and murdered his younger sister." He flipped the pages back and forth as he spoke. Aedan sat back, aghast. "He *liked it.*" Castor whispered. "He goes on and on about ..." His voice trailed off as he continued to read. "About how she screamed for their parents who were away. About how she never stopped crying and asking him *why.*" Castor's voice shook as he spoke. Aedan's hands were white fists in his lap. "He found it to be *fun.*" His hands were trembling.

Finally, Aedan closed the book and held it there in Castor's shaking hands. They sat quietly, both too stunned and utterly horrified to say anything. After what seemed like an eternity, Aedan threw the journal back to Sai's bed. "I have to tell Fiona," he said. "She has to know who he is and what he is capable of." He turned to run out but stopped a few steps away. "I am sorry for asking you to read that, Castor," he said quietly. "I am in your debt. If there is ever something you require of me, name it, and it shall be yours."

As he turned to bolt out the door, Castor said, "Wait, I'll come with you."

And together they ran.

✦ . ＋ . ✦ . ＋ . ✦

Fiona had been having a lovely day with Sai. He had surprised her with a bundle of those pink flowers - he had called them *pastees* - that he seemed to bring with him every time he came to visit her. They each ate a peach together on the docks with their feet hanging off the edge over the gentle waves and the salty breeze in their hair. Later, right before he left, he stole a gentle peck on her cheek. His lips were soft against her skin, and she held her hand lightly against where he'd kissed her in heart-fluttering surprise. No one had ever kissed her like that before. With such youthful innocence and sincerity.

As she was sitting with Avelas by the hearth describing all the details of her time with him, a thunderous knock sounded on the small door, sending the two jumping up in sudden fright.

"Fiona! Are you in there?" a familiar, but panicked, deep voice bellowed on the other side.

"Aedan?" Fiona wondered aloud. She raced to the door and threw it open. There he was, her older brother, drenched in sweat, breathing heavily, and eyes as wide as she'd ever seen them. And his friend Castor, looking much less exhausted but just as terrified right beside him. "What is the matter with you? Are you being chased by a dragon?"

Through gulping breaths, he managed an exasperated sigh.

"Come in, dears," Avelas said, their worry spreading to her face as well. "Settle down with some tea by the fire."

"No time," Aedan breathed as he pulled Castor in the house behind him by the arm. "I know you told me to leave it alone, but I couldn't."

Fiona's eyes narrowed.

"I found his journal, Fi," Aedan said, his breathing slowing to a more normal pace.

"And you *read it*?" She could hear the furiousness in her tone and was momentarily pleased that she could even pull off furious with her voice that many described as youthful and soft. Before he could answer, it dawned on her. "Wait, no, you couldn't have - " Then, she gasped and leered at Castor. "*You*? I expected this from Aedan, but *you*?" The few times she had met the Odessan, she had really liked him. She couldn't believe he had let Aedan cajole him into doing something so invasive.

"Forgive us," said Castor. "But please listen to Aedan. Sai has not told you everything."

She wavered. If Aedan had come here ranting and raving about something like this alone, she mightn't have believed him. But Castor had always seemed so rational and practical. She sighed and motioned for Aedan to speak.

"In his journal, he talks about - " His voice broke off, and he looked to Castor pleadingly.

She saw mist in Castor's eyes as he finished for her brother. "He tortured and murdered his baby sister," he said. And then he told her details of what Sai had written in his private journal. Horrible things. Disgusting things. Inhuman things.

When Castor finished speaking, Fiona stayed standing motionless. There was nothing she could have thought of or told herself to prepare for what she had just been told. It just could not possibly be true, she thought. *Sai?* The boy who'd brushed a kiss ever so lightly upon her cheek earlier that day? Who'd brought her pink *pastees* every day he'd seen her? Who'd embarrassed himself with an adorable song about her?

It just didn't seem right. But there was conviction in Castor's eyes, and somehow, she knew he was not lying to her.

She took a trembling step backwards and was immediately swept up in Avelas's grasp. The healer guided her back to her chair by the fire with a cup of tea suddenly in her hands.

"There is no way you could have known, dear," Avelas said as she stroked her hair. "He had us all fooled."

"Forgive me, brother," Fiona said. "I should have listened to you. Your instinct was right; I should have stayed away from him." The shock had lessened and was replaced by disgust and horror for the feelings she'd had for him. She felt like she needed to physically wash herself to get the thought and feeling of him off of her.

"Don't apologize," Aedan said kneeling next to her. "I will make sure you never have to see him again. I'll talk to Teacher and get him sent back home to Raaja as soon as it is possible."

Fiona nodded. She just could not believe someone so sweet and sincere actually had the capacity to be such a monster. And here when she thought she was finally going to be able to be close with someone in a real way for once. Perhaps she was cursed, never to be pledged to another in love, to forever be a cast-aside. She closed her eyes and willed the tears not to come.

When Castor and Aedan had returned to the training grounds that day, they told Teacher of what they had discovered. She was furious. To kill another in fair combat was an honorable deed, but to torture an innocent child was another. Teacher flew into a rage; she nearly did away with Sai on the spot, but Castor, the most rational of the group at the time, stopped her. He convinced her to simply return him home, and she did, though Castor knew she was unsatisfied with that ending. Not a week later, Sai had been put on a boat and sent off without so much as a farewell.

It had been several months since he had been shipped back home, but his mark had been left on all of them. Somehow, just *knowing* that they had all shared a home with him for that time had left an evil cloud on the space. Sure, they all felt better with him gone in another country, but just knowing he was still out there somewhere was a little unnerving to say the least, Castor thought.

Nevertheless, they had a job to do. Castor was constantly practicing his gift and learning to use it in real-time combat situations. He felt he was really becoming more proficient with it; he could call the fire up several times before he would get too tired to continue. The hardest part was trying to lay a hand on Teacher during their sparring. She was just *so fast* - it was nearly impossible. At first, Teacher did not want him using his mark during weapons training because it wouldn't be fair; but afterwards, she decided it only made sense for him to practice doing both since that is how it would be in the real world. Only once did he manage to make skin-to-skin contact, though, but he was so caught up in the fight, he was not able to actually focus enough to make the fire do anything.

He did feel bad for Aedan who admittedly was not getting as much training as he was; Castor hoped it would not cause a divide between them. He had offered to practice sparring with him after the official training was over each day so that Aedan could get more time in, but

Castor was always so exhausted by then that he could hardly put up much of a fight.

It was after one of these duels that Teacher decided to join them for dinner by the fire. She was doing her best to explain the lay of the land in Maecha to help Castor understand the right path to take, drawing lines on a map to show the best courses of action. As time passed, she began teaching him of the different types of dangerous creatures that inhabited their country, and, to Castor's surprise, there were many he had either never heard of, or thought were complete myth. Like Odessa, they had wolves and boars and the like, but Maecha also had creatures like kelpies, murderous horse-like beasts, and the *bánánoch*, malevolent spirits that haunted places of great bloodshed. The more she spoke, the more Castor worried over his decision to go; he was not sure if he would be able to do this alone. He needed someone to go with him, and there was no guarantee that Ophelia would be an option.

Then, he noticed Aedan quietly focusing on the fire and felt a sudden pang of guilt. He and Teacher had been discussing his journey for so long, he was sure Aedan felt left out again. That's when it hit him.

"Aedan?" Castor said, feeling a weird sensation in his stomach.

Almost jumping as if startled out of a reverie, Aedan gave him a look as if to go on.

Castor hesitated. What was he doing? There was no way Aedan would agree to it. He had obligations with his sister already. He sighed. "Never mind."

Brow furrowed, Aedan said, "No, speak your mind."

They were both looking at him expectantly. He leaned back to look at the stars. "It is just that I am unsure if I can make this journey on my own. And to be honest, you are a *much* better warrior than I. I was only going to ask if you would want to accompany me for this journey." But before Aedan could respond, Castor added, "But then I remembered that you have your responsibility to your sister, so you do not need to - "

"Y - You actually want me to go with you?" Aedan said it so quietly and uncertainly, Castor thought he must have misheard him. The look of utter confusion on his face made Castor wonder if Aedan thought he did not hold him in such high esteem as he truly did.

"Of course!" Castor exclaimed. "I would very sincerely enjoy your companionship as well as appreciate your assistance with hunting and dealing with any threats that may cross us. But again, I understand that you will most likely want to return to Albainn with Fiona when the training is over."

"Actually, Fiona and I were planning to go to a larger city like Trícnoc or Letha after this." Aedan's face looked reddened as if the heat from the campfire had warmed his cheeks.

Castor felt a sudden leap of joy. "Do - Does that mean you will come with me?"

Aedan grinned, his eyes sparkling in the firelight. "I must speak with Fiona about it first, but I do not see why she would be against it."

Teacher, having been quiet for the exchange, smiled as well. "This is grand news! How about an ale to celebrate?"

The last weeks of the apprenticeship went by in a blur. Teacher was busy getting everything ready for their journey to Letha - doing everything from ensuring they had lightweight packs full of supplies to coordinating with the boatmaster in Endala to ensure the safe passage of the apprentices and two horses. *She really is taking care of everything,* Aedan thought.

He was just overjoyed to have been included at all, a small part of him thought. All of these incredible things were happening to Castor, and he had been feeling quite left out of it all up until Castor told him he wanted his help and company. He was not sure how much of that was true, but he was not going to push his luck by asking.

Fiona had been excited to go with Castor as well. She had actually taken a liking to him despite only seeing him a few times over the course of their apprenticeship. Aedan could also tell she was eager to leave Endala at all, probably to leave the memories behind, he assumed. Avelas had been grateful for her help and company as well and had told her she could return whenever she liked. She had also given Fiona a smaller pack of her own with a handwritten journal of poultices and remedies as well as a decent stock of herbs, which Aedan agreed would be of great assistance.

As for Castor, he had finally managed to successfully use his mark against Teacher. He had looked just so ecstatic about actually accomplishing it, Aedan would never forget that face he made. Castor still seemed somewhat anxious about the journey, but Aedan would occasionally catch Castor looking at him before letting out a heavy breath as though the reminder that he was not going alone was of great relief.

Time rushed by, and before he knew it, Aedan, Castor, and Fiona were on a small boat coasting to the mainland of Odessa. Teacher stood on the dock behind them, waving and sporadically calling out some last bits of advice, as a mother might have done, Aedan guessed with affection.

He sat back, leaning against the side of the boat and closed his eyes. He felt the cool gusts off the sea's waves ease the heat of the summer sun. A gull squawked overhead as he could hear the faint but lively conversation of Fiona and Castor on the other side of the boat. Aedan rocked with the gentle waves, and he smiled.

✦ . ✛ . ✦ . ✛ . ✦

As it turned out, stealing away on a rowboat had been easier than he had expected. He didn't plan on returning home anyway - not after *her*. He had hidden in the shadows for what had felt like an eternity, trapping all his meals in the forest and sleeping balanced on the boughs of trees outside the small fishing village. He watched as she performed her daily tasks. He watched as she helped heal injured villagers with her rough, worker's hands. He watched as that lumbering oaf came to visit her and tell her they were leaving with that *gifted* imbecile. They were making her go with them. She had told him before that she wanted him to go with her back to her country; he knew she didn't want them to leave him behind.

But still, he watched as they boarded their boat and sailed off to Odessa without him. It didn't matter, though. He was very resourceful. He would find a way to be with her again.

As the boat drifted farther and farther away, he sang, "My doe, my doe. This sunlight has cast you aglow, you know. My doe, my doe. To be without you is surely a woe, you know. My doe, my doe. For you I'd best any foe, you know. My doe, my doe. I'll follow wherever you go, you know. My doe, my doe."

WHAT LIES
BENEATH

9

The Scarlet Key

Castor hated being at sea. While Aedan and Fiona seemed to not mind it, if not *enjoy* it, the rocking of the waves always made him nauseous. He passed the time by getting to know Fiona better. She was very spritely and humorous, though her pet falcon did not seem to like him much. Fiona tried to assuage him by letting him know that the falcon - Bas - did not like *anyone* really. Though he did seem to like her a lot, Castor noticed not without a fair amount of envy.

When the boat finally docked at Odessa, they were met by several merchants with goods for Endala. Some of the sailors went to barter as Castor, Aedan, and Fiona stretched their legs on the shore. As Castor expected, there was also a guard from the Vallas estate waiting by a carriage done up in vermillion and black silks. Castor steeled himself for the next interaction.

"Lord Vallas!" Garrick called.

Castor leaned over to Aedan and Fiona and recommended they keep their hoods up and busy themselves for a moment to avoid being seen - it *was* illegal for Maechans to be caught in Odessa after all. And with their pale complexion and light hair colors, they were sure to raise some eyebrows. Aedan and Fiona left to collect their horses and give Castor a moment to talk with his guard.

"Lord Vallas," the guard said again with a small bow as he got closer. "It is good to see you are well. How was your apprenticeship?"

"It was fine," said Castor with a small sigh. He had forgotten how much he disliked the propriety that came with his status and how people treated him back home with all the "Lord"s and all the bowing. "I need you to deliver something for me," he said, trying to get straight to the point.

The guard looked confused. "Deliver? Is it not your noble self that I am supposed to be delivering?"

Castor smiled uneasily. "I am afraid not, Garrick." He swung his pack around and retrieved a handwritten letter sealed in an envelope and stamped with his family ring. "If you will, please deliver this note to my father on my behalf."

His confusion deepened. "But, my Lord, will you not be returning with me? Duke Vallas gave me very specific instructions."

"I understand," Castor said. "But no, I will not be returning with you. I will not be returning at all. This letter will explain everything to my father."

"But if you are not coming back home, then where are you going? Did your apprenticeship get an extension?"

Castor shook his head. "No, that's not it." He thought quietly for a moment on what he should tell the guard. He *did* like Garrick; Garrick had been a guard at the Vallas estate for as long as Castor could remember and had always been very kind to Castor. He smiled at Garrick sadly. "I have business in Maecha that I must attend to," he decided to say. "I am afraid that it will take a great deal of my time, and I may not be returning home for a very long time if ever."

Garrick's confusion gained a hint of ferocity. "*Maecha?* My Lord, what possible business could you have in *Maecha?* You know what the empress says about that land! And you are saying you may not return *at all?* Does this mean you are abandoning your duties as the future Duke of Anand?"

Castor sighed. "Yes, Garrick. The letter explains it more than I shall now, but yes, I am leaving behind my old life." He clapped a hand on the guard's shoulder and held it there reassuringly. He looked into the aging man's eyes and said, "You have been a wonderful guard for me these past twenty-four years. It was an honor to have known you, and I wish you happiness and greatness in the years to come."

The heat in Garrick's face seemed to sap away. Mist collected in his eyes, and his lower lip trembled. "My Lord?" he said. "Does this mean that, as of this moment now, you are no longer a nobleman of Odessa?"

Castor's brow furrowed. "I suppose so? Why do you as - "

The guard's great stature barreled into Castor in a heavy embrace. "IT WAS AN HONOR TO HAVE SERVED YOU, LORD VALLAS." He was sobbing openly, causing some of the nearby sailors and merchants to stare and making Castor only slightly uncomfortable. This was not the first time Garrick had made a dramatic scene with him; when Castor had left for Endala a year before, the guard had practically drawn the entire province's attention with his howling cries. Castor assumed the old man had come to think of him as a son or grandson in all the years he served their family. "PLEASE BE EXTREMELY CAREFUL WHILE YOU ARE OFF IN MAECHA," he wailed, still keeping Castor in the tightest bearhug he had ever received. "IF YOU DESIRE FOR ME TO ACCOMPANY YOU ON YOUR JOURNEY, YOU NEED ONLY ASK."

Castor tried to laugh, but found he had no air to. He patted the old guard on the back weakly. "Thank you," he tried to say, but it came out in the quietest of squeaks.

Garrick, apparently noticing Castor's lack of breath, suddenly pulled back from the embrace, but kept both of his shoulders in his large, rough hands.

Breathing finally, Castor said, "Your dauntless courage and loyalty does not surprise me, though it does bring me happiness to know you would come with me should I have asked." He casually felt his ribs through his hooded tunic to check if any had been broken. "But it is best that you return to the estate and continue your life there. Who knows what my father would do without you there to keep him out of trouble?"

The guard sniffed and wiped his face on his red sleeve. He nodded, though Castor could tell he was trying to stifle his tears. "Then I shall return with your letter," he said, finally at a normal volume. "Trust that I will not sleep until it reaches your father's hands."

"It is a two-week journey for you back to Anand; please sleep at some point," Castor said quietly as Garrick continued over him.

"I WILL NOT SLEEP," he yelled, startling Castor, "UNTIL IT REACHES YOUR FATHER'S HANDS." He enunciated each word clearly and carefully before turning and marching back to the carriage.

Castor smiled and shook his head. "Farewell, Garrick!"

The guard turned once more with tears in his eyes and called back his own farewell before stepping into the carriage and riding away.

A throat cleared nearby Castor's shoulder. He spun to see Aedan and Fiona standing there, the reins of their two horses held tightly in Fiona's hand. "That was quite the scene," said Fiona. "Is that man going to be all right?"

Castor laughed and rubbed his brow. "Probably not."

They had only two horses, so Aedan and Fiona shared one, a spotted gray rouncey with soft eyes named Bonedust. Castor rode the shorter, solid white rouncey named Sugarfoot. Being a nobleman, Castor was very accustomed to riding horseback and found Sugarfoot's gentle personality quite reminiscent of his own horses back at his estate. Fiona seemed to enjoy riding as well, documented by the enormous, excited grin on her face. Aedan, on the other hand, did *not* seem terribly fond of Bonedust's adventurous nature and was often heard cursing whenever the horse decided they were not moving fast enough. Both horses, however, seemed perfectly fine carrying the weight of their riders and their supplies, giving Castor a small amount of relief.

The group had about a month's worth of rations in their supplies if they were extremely careful, which should last them to Argos where they could resupply. Unfortunately, Argos was the only city along the mountainside that they would encounter, so they needed to make their rations last as long as possible, lest they had to hunt for their meals which would take away precious time from their journey. Though it was not as if they were on a specific timetable; Castor only felt he needed to get to Letha as soon as possible so as to keep Teacher from waiting. It was already going to be a long, arduous journey; there was no reason to prolong it if at all possible. Still, most of the food rations they had consisted of hardtack, a type of long-lasting bread that, in Castor's opinion, was not meant for human consumption, and bags of threpsiberries, small, red fruits that held a wide variety of nutrients, which Fiona seemed to love. With such a small variation in meals, Castor kept in mind that they may have to hunt for a few meals along the way.

Teacher was also sure to outfit them with weapons of their choice before they left. Aedan, of course, brought along the axe he forged himself along with a newer, shinier one from Teacher's collection. Alternatively, Castor chose one of the shorter spears with a head like a wickedly sharp cross and a light steel heater shield to protect his left side. They both brought simple, wooden bows and a healthy supply of arrows as well. Fiona, not by any means a warrior, was entirely unarmed - that is, unless counting her incredibly protective sea falcon who never let her leave his eyesight.

So, on they rode, with the Roinn Mountains on their left and the great Antesian Plains of Odessa on their right. They were currently making their way through the Tammel province, Castor noted. Somewhere, miles away, to the southeast of their location was the Anand province where sat the Vallas estate in the city of Polara where Garrick was headed. For a moment, Castor let himself feel wistful over his choice to leave home indefinitely before returning his focus to the journey ahead. When he did, he noticed a worried look on Aedan's face, who must have seen Castor's pining, but Castor gave him a smile and a quick shake of the head indicating not to fret over him.

Over the course of the first day of their journey, they never passed another person. Surely, one or two of the merchants who had met them at the docks was from Argos, though they were probably far behind, what with their greater load to transport. So, the three sat around their campfire and each ate a piece of filling hardtack along with two threpsiberries while Bas rested on the branch of a nearby tree.

"So," Fiona began, breaking the silence, "Aedan tells me that you met the Allmother, Castor. How was that?" She asked the question so easily, it almost surprised him.

"It was ... surreal," he replied, not quite finding the word he wanted to use. He stopped for a moment to gather his thoughts, then said, "You know, I never really put much thought or faith into the whole concept of the Allmother and the Aspects before the apprenticeship. I knew it was a huge thing for many people, of course, but it is difficult to put faith into what you cannot see, you know? Anyway, obviously I have since changed my mind on the subject. I still do not pray, per se, but I do try to recognize her Aspects in everyday things." He looked from Fiona to Aedan and back. "Forgive me; I only just realized you did not ask for any of that," he said, laughing and shaking his head at himself. He *did* have a knack for rambling at times. "But to answer your question, the Phantom was somehow very human and very *not* at the same time. She was like life and death mixed into one person, which, I understand is also not an incredibly helpful description." He paused again, trying to remember details of his experience in the Otherworld. "She just had this *presence* - wonderful and terrifying at once. She was very calm and kind. Very motherly," he added before running out of ways to describe her.

After a brief silence, Fiona said, "So, what you are telling us is that the *Allmother* ... is *motherly?*"

Aedan, who had been held in rapt attention by Castor's words, gave his sister a hard look, and Castor snorted. "Yes," said Castor. "Yes, I suppose that is what I am trying to tell you." He and Fiona laughed together while Aedan remained quiet.

"What else did you see?" he asked once they had calmed down. "In the Otherworld, I mean. Was it all bright lights and faeries with shining wings? What did it look like? Did you get to see any of the Sidhe?"

Castor took another small bite of hardtack and chewed thoughtfully. "I do not know if they were Sidhe or some other creature, but I saw great animals, taller than trees, with eyes like starlight."

"Aedan used to go to the temple in Albainn all the time to ask questions about the Allmother and the Sidhe," Fiona chimed in. "He is quite the expert on the subject."

Castor wondered why Aedan had never asked him about his time in the Otherworld before if that were true. Aedan blushed at her comment. "I claim no such thing," he said. "Though the high priestess in Albainn has received many visions of the Otherworld and told me that amongst the eldest and most noble of the Sidhe were the Tiarna Sí, giant intelligent beasts who protected their domain from any who dared infringe upon its absolute perfection."

"I would wager I happened to see them because they came to determine who had just stumbled into their home, then," Castor said.

Aedan nodded seriously. "What else did you see there?"

"Enormous trees wider and taller than any I could have imagined." He gestured to the tree Bas rested in. "Stack this tree upon itself ten times - they were taller still." Aedan and Fiona looked up as though trying to picture them. "Where there was no sun or moon, flowing streams of light shone in the sky before a million more stars than there are above us now. The cloudless sky gently rained down flower petals that cluttered the ground and skipped along the grass in the timid breeze. It was neither too warm nor too cold, and it was very quiet - not eerily so, but pleasantly."

Aedan sighed, and Castor saw him staring into the sky with a dream-like expression on his face.

"May I see it?" asked Fiona. "The mark, I mean," she added.

"Fiona!" Aedan scolded, snapping out of his reverie. "The mark is not some toy to be shown off for no reason! It takes a lot out of Castor to - "

"It is all right, Aedan," Castor said. "I should continue practicing summoning it anyway." He pulled his tunic off over his head while Fiona and Aedan stared and waited. He closed his eyes and focused.

PHANTOM FIRE | 131

With all the rehearsal he had done with Teacher, it was not too difficult to conjure it up anymore - *using* its power, on the other hand, was still very tiring. He dug down inside himself before soon finding the fire the Phantom had given him. He pulled it up and felt it burn on his chest where she had first touched him. Fiona and Aedan looked on in awe. There it was, Castor saw too, the mark like three spirals connected at the center glowing through his flesh like living flame.

Fiona moved over and reached a hand towards it. She paused an inch away and looked to Castor for permission, who nodded, before her finger grazed the edge of the fire.

What followed would have made a sailor blush as Fiona wrenched her hand away with a string of expletives and stuck her finger in her mouth.

"Forgive me," Castor said with an embarrassed smile. "I should have warned you that it was as hot as it looked."

"Do you feel it?" she asked him. "The whole time? I mean, does it actually *burn* you the whole time it is lit up like that?"

Castor looked down at it. "Yes," he said. "In the midst of a fight, I usually only barely notice it, but yes, it burns the entire time." And when she looked concerned, he added, "Not to worry; I practice holding it there as long as possible to get more accustomed to it."

Aedan looked from the mark to Fiona's hand back to the mark and then at his own hand.

"You want to touch it, too, don't you?" said Castor.

"Is that bad?" Aedan asked. "I feel like it is, but also, it is a *blessing* from the *Allmother*. How could I *not* want to touch it?" He scooted closer to Castor. "May I?"

Castor nodded and watched as Aedan's hand slowly crept towards him. He hesitated just before touching it and released a deep breath as if steeling himself. After a moment of stillness, his fingertips gently brushed Castor's skin. The mark flared under his touch, the flame glowing brighter and hotter than Castor had ever felt it before. Castor winced, and Aedan sucked air through his teeth as he held his fingertips against the blazing mark.

Finally, when neither could take it any longer, they pulled apart, and the mark faded away as Castor leaned back on his hands, breathing heavily.

"Did you see that?" Aedan asked. "The mark - "

"I *felt* it," Castor replied. "I do not think it has ever burned so intensely before." He touched a hand experimentally to his skin where the mark had been, but as usual, the spot had immediately returned to its normal temperature.

"Aww," said Fiona. "I think the mark likes you, big brother."

Castor felt his face flush, and Aedan said, "Or perhaps it *doesn't* like me." He looked from his reddened fingertips to Castor. "What do you think?"

"I do not know," Castor responded. "We should keep trying, though. If there is more to this mark than Teacher and I have already discovered, I would like to learn of it. Would you mind helping me practice sometimes, Aedan?"

A jolt of something hit Aedan as he sat up a little straighter. "Of course! I would love to help you learn more of your gift! Anything you need."

Castor smiled brightly, but the thought that there was still more to this gift than he had already ascertained nagged at the back of his mind. Why was the mark responding to Aedan's touch so intensely - or *at all* for that matter? Was it some meaningless side effect or was something actually going on? He was determined to find out soon. But for now, he needed rest more than anything. After several brief exchanges, the trio spread out their bedrolls, and Aedan decided to take the first watch while Castor and Fiona slept.

The night was quiet. Aedan sat with his back against the tree near the campfire stoically keeping watch for any manner of beast or man who may threaten his group, but no such tragedy befell them that night.

PHANTOM FIRE | 133

Instead, Aedan let his mind wander through all that had happened in those last few hours before his watch began.

First and foremost: the Otherworld and the Allmother. Before, he had refrained to ask Castor of his experience there mostly out of envy. Somehow, he thought, if he did not know the details, then he could make himself less jealous of Castor. After finally hearing about it, however, he did not feel less for Castor so much as feel full of wonder and excitement. When he had spoken to the high priestess of the temple in Albainn, she had told him of the visions she had had of the place - brief flashes of scenery or abstract colors and sounds - but Castor had actually *been there*. He had passed the veil that separates this world and the Other and had physically seen and experienced the Allmother's home. Aedan felt a deep sense of longing for the place, especially after Castor's descriptions. To have seen the Tiarna Sí wandering their domain and to actually be approached by the Allmother herself...

Clearly, Castor was special. There was no doubt in Aedan's mind. When he had first laid eyes on him, there had been something about him—some kind of *pull* that had made Aedan want to be closer to him, but he would never have guessed that Castor would be later chosen by the goddess of life and death and blessed with her mark. And for Castor to actually want *Aedan* to be around for his journey and to help him with the goddess's mark - it just left him completely bewildered.

And then what had happened when Aedan had touched Castor's mark? He admittedly had not been much a part of Castor's training with it before, or at all really, so he could not say if that was an unnatural occurrence or not. But Castor's reaction said that it was definitely something that had never happened before. Why had the fire blazed so strongly like it had then? Was Aedan actually special like Castor?

No, that is ridiculous, he told himself. He had not had any supernatural experiences like Castor had so there was no reason to believe that he had some mystical gift too. It was more probable that the fire only burned so hotly because it was trying to repel him, he thought self-loathingly as he slouched further against the tree.

When it was time for watch to change, he went to go wake one of them to take his place, but he stopped. They both looked so small and so innocent in their sleep. *Clearly*, he knew how much that was not true, but he just couldn't bring himself to disturb either of them. He had slept well the night before and had taken a nap on the boat as well. He could take another shift.

Castor and Fiona both had scolded Aedan for staying up all night while they slept, though secretly, Castor was thankful. Sleep had been difficult to hold on to the last few nights leading up to their journey, and it was nice to actually get a full night's rest.

They left early after a small bite of hardtack and a berry each. With their horses fully rested as well, they were making good time following the path at the foot of the mountain. Castor could tell Aedan would need rest soon and had mentally decided that he would make him at least get a few hours of shuteye when they stopped for lunch.

Several hours later, Castor saw up ahead and off to the right was a fair-sized copse of deep green trees split in two by a narrow stream. He relayed his idea to the others that they should stop there to give the rounceys a break and to fill their own stomachs.

Once underneath the edge of the shady grove, Castor told Aedan to rest his eyes for a while. "I will go out and see if there is any meat to be had here if you two will guard the supplies," he said. He left with a bow and quiver along with their water sacks to refill at the stream. He definitely was not as good of a hunter as Aedan was, but he *had* gotten better under his tutelage, he thought.

He crept quietly through the wooded thicket, careful not to step on any twigs or leaves as he went. He had made it all the way to the water without seeing so much as a hare. Disappointed, he stooped to fill the water sacks. As he tied the full sacks back to his belt, he heard Fiona in the distance—"Aedan!"—followed by a short scream.

Without thinking, Castor sprinted back the way he came. Dodging the dense trees and retrieving an arrow from his quiver, he came upon a scene that did not ease the racing of his heart. Four men had invaded

PHANTOM FIRE | 135

their camp while he was away. A fifth lay butchered nearby with deep axe wounds torn through his torso. A blood-spattered Aedan held two bloodier axes in each hand; his eyes were locked on Fiona who was being held on her knees with a knife to her throat by one of the surviving four men. Two others had bows aimed at Aedan, and the last stood near his fallen comrade with a dented, battered short sword.

"Drop your axes or the girl dies," the man with the knife ordered.

"If the girl dies," Aedan said, his voice rough and gritty, "you all die."

Something about the way he said it - like a caged beast almost - made the other men hesitate. Castor realized that the four rogues had not yet noticed his arrival and decided to use that to his advantage. He slipped through the trees as quickly as he could before coming out behind them.

He saw Aedan notice him and gave him a quick nod.

"All right," Aedan said lowering his axes slowly. "All right, we will give you whatever you want, just do not hurt us."

The man with the knife let out a short laugh. "That's what I thought." He leaned down closer to Fiona's ear and Castor heard him say, "Look at that. He gave up so easily for you. You should be proud. Go ahead and thank him for letting you survive."

Fiona scoffed, and Castor could just *feel* her roll her eyes at the statement. "Bas," she said instead.

"What did she say?" one of the bandits with a bow whispered to another who shrugged, confused.

"I said 'Bas'!" Fiona called.

"I still do not - " Before the man could finish, the sea falcon dove out of the sky at such incredible speed, no one had seen it coming. It tackled his face and neck and drove its beak and talons into all the soft spots it could find leaving him blinded and choking for air. The other two spun in surprise, and Castor took the opportunity. The mark was already burning under his shirt, so when he reached for and grabbed both of the men by the backs of their necks, he felt the spark of energy leave his fingertips and shoot through their bodies. With so much on the line, he did not stop to push the energy to any specific part of their body, like their hearts or their lungs, and instead just pumped the fire into their veins. He felt their blood boiling under their skin, and they were soon left twitching on the ground having been cooked from the inside out. The last man took one look at his friends and turned to run, but was stopped short by a very large, very angry Maechan with an axe in each hand.

The last bandit dropped his sword and fell to his knees. "I submit!" he cried. "Please don't kill me."

"Ha!" Aedan laughed. "And why shouldn't we? You and your companions were going to kill all three of us had you had your way."

The man's panicked breaths quickened. He looked over at the two Castor had used his mark on. "Wh - What did you do to them?" he whimpered.

Castor, feeling a high from the adrenaline of real combat and the fire coursing through his veins, pulled the collar of his tunic down to show his blazing mark. "I have been marked by the goddess of life and death, and what you saw me do to them is only a fraction of what I will do to anyone who harms my friends."

The man looked scared and confused, but he said, "All right, all right! Look, if you let me go, I will tell the rest of my group to let you pass through this path safely. There are many more of us who set up ambushes along the mountainside, but I can ensure your safe passage if you let me live."

Castor saw the outrage still plain on Aedan's face, but he liked the idea of a safe passage. "What do you think?" Castor asked them both.

Aedan looked at Castor incredulously, but Fiona said, "Take the deal!" When she saw her brother's exasperated expression, she added, "They did not hurt me, brother; I am fine. Please do not let vengeance command you. Let him go guarantee our safety."

Aedan, breathing vigorously, turned and threw his axes into the ground in front of him with a frustrated yell. He instantly spun back to the man and lifted him off his feet by the shirt. "I had better not see your slimy face ever again." He then menacingly brought the man's face closer to his and said, "And tell your *friends* what happened here -

tell them how these men were slaughtered for what they tried to do to my sister."

The man trembled as he answered. "Yes, I will." With one hand, he reached around and tore a patch off his sleeve. "Take this and another from - " His voice broke. "From one of the others. Fasten them to your horses and you will not be attacked again. Not by any of my clan."

Aedan nodded. "Though now that you have told us, there really is no point in releasing you now, is there?"

The man looked more frightened than Castor had ever seen someone look before. "No!" Fiona interjected. "Aedan, stop! He fulfilled his end of the bargain, now let him *go!*" she said, stomping her foot in frustration at the last word.

"Fortune seems to be favoring you today," Castor heard Aedan whisper before throwing the man to the ground. He fell, a rough tangle of limbs, before clambering up and running south through the trees without another word.

Castor looked at Aedan with apprehension. Castor had never noticed it before, but Aedan could be *scary* when it came to his sister. He was so gentle and kind usually that Castor hadn't expected it, but he saw that when Aedan's family was threatened, it brings out a protective, terrifying beast in him that was nearly impossible to stop.

Aedan turned on his heel and marched straight to Castor, who froze nervously. Aedan bent and enveloped him in a back-breaking embrace. "I am in your debt," he said. "You helped save my sister and myself, and I shall never forget that. You have my thanks and my axes, should the time come when they are needed again." He released him and gave him a single nod before turning to tend to Fiona.

Castor was glad Aedan was on his side.

✦ . ＋ . ✦ . ＋ . ✦

Hatvar was still shaking by the time he had made it to the small inn that night after his friends had all been murdered by those three travelers. He sat at a table with two others of his clan with a warm tankard of piss-flavored ale held firmly between his hands. Not able to take his eyes off the drink, he recounted the story of what happened.

"The Odessan said he had been 'marked by the goddess of life and death'," he told them. "I do not know if I believe *that*, but he had strange powers. He - " Hatvar choked on his words. "He *boiled* them alive from the *inside*." His voice was practically a whisper.

Suddenly, a woman was standing at the table, making Hatvar jump back in his seat. She looked completely innocuous - Hatvar had not even seen her in the inn in the first place. But there she appeared, clothed in the holed rags of a serf and with her wispy, limp hair hanging down over her shoulders almost completely concealing a small, faded tattoo of a simple red key under her right ear. "These people," she stated firmly. "The ones that you speak of. Describe them."

Hatvar, startled, described the three of them to the best of his abilities.

"Where were they headed?" she continued briskly.

Confused by the terse woman's curiosity, he eventually mumbled, "A - As we were coming upon them, we heard one of them mention Argos."

The woman nodded concisely. "My thanks," she said before silently leaving the inn.

Hatvar shook his head as if to clear it. He had had enough strangeness for one day. He pleadingly reminded his two friends to leave the three travelers alone before purchasing a room for the night and retiring for a sleepless night alone.

10

Eos

They stopped to hunt more than Aedan thought Castor would have allowed them to, but maybe Castor was getting as sick of hardtack as he was. Fiona was sure to let them know how much she disliked the bread as often as possible, too, so maybe he was doing it for her sake. Game was not too scarce along the mountainside, though it mostly consisted of goats and hares. What Aedan wouldn't do for a wild pig or a juicy slice of auroch steak right now, he thought while his stomach growled longingly.

Nevertheless, they galloped on. Some days seemed to drag on, but most of the time, Aedan was really enjoying himself. Being with Fiona without the responsibility of trying to make enough money to put food on the table was such a nice change of pace. And every day his adventure with Castor continued, the happier he noticed he was. This journey might just have been the best thing that had ever happened to him.

Aedan had been helping Castor practice his gift as they had planned, too. Back at Endala, Aedan had felt a little left out of the Phantom mark training, but now, knowing that Castor needed and wanted his help with his blessing from the Allmother herself - it filled Aedan with so much joy and excitement, it was hard for him to focus sometimes. Still, he tried. Nearly every night, they stayed up late together exercising

139

his power. Castor never hurt him with his power of course, but he was fortunate enough to feel the energy of the Phantom Aspect flow through him as Castor used it to move his arms or flex his fingers or wiggle his toes. It was a strange feeling, being unable to control your own body, but he trusted Castor. And he knew that if Castor was going to be able to defeat Queen Aife, he was going to need to practice as much as possible.

They still were not sure why the mark reacted to Aedan's touch as it did or even if it changed its effects in any way. Castor said the only difference was that he felt a more intense burning. He was still able to control Aedan's flesh and blood with ease when it burned extra brightly like that, but aside from the usual, neither knew what else to try doing with it when Aedan touched him. Though that didn't matter so much to Aedan. Sure, he was curious about why the mark burned as it did when he came into contact with it, but what really counted was that Castor was still able to use his power. Aedan respected Castor's prowess in combat, but the Phantom's gift was the only way he was going to have a chance of defeating Aife in battle.

Despite all the fun Aedan was having, he knew that it would only get more dangerous as they went along. Out in the countryside, they needn't worry about the law that made it illegal for Aedan and Fiona to simply exist on this side of the mountains, but Aedan knew that once they reached Argos, it very well may cause a problem. With their colors and complexion, it was very obvious they were not from Odessa, whose inhabitants tended to have light-to-medium brown skin and rarely had hair lighter than a dark earthy brown. He hoped their hoods would conceal their heritage well enough to deter unwanted attention while they made their way through town.

They wouldn't be staying too long in Argos anyway. Castor wanted to meet with a friend who lived there in town, but aside from that, they only needed to find someone to guide them through the mountain caves to get to Trícnoc on the other side. Hopefully, they would only have to stay one night in town to rest up before they entered the mountains, thought Aedan.

PHANTOM FIRE | 141

The days went by, and with each passing sunrise, they remained free of another bandit attack. That murdering scum must have at least gone through on his end to clear their path of his friends. Though Aedan still wished he could have exacted his vengeance on him for what they were going to do to Fiona had she not called down her falcon and distracted them long enough for Castor to get close enough to use his gift. That aside, Aedan had to admit that it was good to know they were safe.

When they finally came to see the city of Argos in the distance, Aedan's jaw dropped. "It - It's so big," he said quietly. To be fair, Aedan had only ever seen Albainn and Endala, so his frame of reference was not the most cultured; still, Argos was a *big* city. It was the capital city of the Everell province after all.

Argos was still off in the distance, but Aedan could still see the immense size of the place. Farms dotted the countryside around the central area of the city which was comprised of buildings and homes that grew taller and taller the closer they stood to the heart.

"And beautiful," Fiona whispered.

Castor smiled. "You should see Hale."

"What is that?" she asked.

"Hale is the capital of all of Odessa; it's where the castle is," Castor answered. "Hale is a multi-tiered city that sits in a massive crater where it's said that a tear from the Allmother fell to the earth. A red stone tower was raised in the center of the crater in honor of the flame that was left in the tear's wake - to this day, the residents of Hale all make use of the tower's religious services. Long bridges extend from each tier of the city out to the tower with gardens of flowers and fruits and ivies hanging between them. More people live there than Argos, too."

"How many live in Hale?" Fiona wondered.

Castor whistled low. "I believe around five hundred thousand. Though that includes those who live in Hale's Outer City - all the buildings that are outside of Hale's towering walls."

Aedan's mind raced. How could so many people live in one place? How could such a city even exist? Aedan could not even comprehend the size of that without seeing it for himself.

"Towns do not get so big in Maecha," said Fiona. "Many clans there prefer nomadic traditions, though there are still plenty who would rather settle down in one place as well."

"Was your village a part of one of these nomadic clans?" Castor asked as their horses trotted along.

"No," she said. "No, Albainn is a settlement of many different clans."

Castor nodded thoughtfully. "In Odessa, we have dukes and duchesses who rule each's own province under the empress. Is that how it is for your settlements as well?"

"Not exactly," said Fiona. "They have no official title such as 'duke' or 'duchess'. But each settlement does have a ruling clan, and the eldest woman of that clan, the matriarch, basically makes the laws for that city so long as they do not cross a law made by the ruling king or queen," she explained. "As for how the nomadic clans rule themselves, I do not know. They generally do not visit other settlements as they do not agree with those ways of life. I would assume that either their eldest or strongest member rules them, if I had to guess.

"While we are discussing rules," she went on, "why is it that Odessa has a law that outlaws our very existence?"

Castor made a disgusted sound. "*That* would be the work of Empress Dialaune," he said with not a small amount of distaste. "That woman is mad. For some reason, probably to gain favor from the more gullible half of our country, she believes that everyone from your country is out to harm every Odessan in some way or other, and she uses this hateful rhetoric to protect her status and keep the country focused on some nonexistent opposition while she passes laws in the shadows to increase her own wealth and power."

Fiona looked horrified. "That is completely insane. What have we ever done to Odessa? I thought our countries got along for the most part until we heard that that law was passed here."

"I knew it," Castor said decisively. "At the past few council meetings that all nobles must attend every year, Dialaune has been pushing the idea that Maecha is getting prepared to go to war against Odessa. She has been using the taxes collected from the provinces to build up her own personal army and navy to 'prepare for the war'."

"*What?*" Aedan was completely thrown. "No one - at least no one in Albainn - has any strong feelings towards Odessa, let alone wants to go to war with you!"

"We do not want that either!" Castor exclaimed. "Well, *I* do not want that, anyway. And there are several other nobles who also do not agree with Dialaune, but her word is law. She has all of us nobles as her council, but still, she can do whatever she wants to do. That aside, since I last heard, she had made no real plans of attack or anything of the like."

"That *was* over a year ago, though, right?" Fiona mentioned.

Castor was silent.

"When Branwyn is queen, we will tell her what is going on here," Aedan stated.

The other two nodded.

They had reached the first of the farms, and Aedan felt a sort of bittersweet joy that the first part of their journey was coming to a close. Bitter because the ride to Argos had been mostly an enjoyable way to spend time with his sister and Castor, but sweet because they were getting ever so close to being back in Maecha, his homeland. The only thing left standing in their way was the most difficult part - not getting arrested in Argos.

Through the farms, they began to pass through the outskirts of Argos, and Aedan assumed this was the area where the poorest of the city lived. The homes here were small, some quite dilapidated, and were made of simple, worn wood. The residents all wore similar ruddy brown and gray undyed rags, and though their faces were dirt-streaked from a hard day's work, they were bright with laughter as they chased young kids who laughed gleefully and ran ungracefully around trees and homes.

Aedan couldn't help but smile under his hood. These people re-minded him of his own home and childhood back in Albainn. His and

144 | MICHAEL JACE

Fiona's caretaker at the orphanage was a very kind woman who chased the two of them on many occasions while they ran and ran and ran in ignorant bliss of how little the rest of the world thought of their status. A small part of him envied the kids he saw now. To live so carelessly and with such happiness was a great blessing.

As they were nearing the edge of where the poor lived, Aedan noticed a man leaning against a building. The way his head was angled, it gave Aedan a perfect view of his neck, where he saw an odd tattoo right under his ear - a red key. Suddenly, the man jerked his head up and seemed to be scrutinizing Aedan and his fellow companions with a strange expression on his face. Aedan turned to look ahead of him for a moment, but when he turned back, the man had taken off down a nearby alleyway.

Shrugging it off, Aedan and Fiona continued to follow Castor out of the poorer section of the city and through the winding paths into the wealthier area. He was leading them to the estate that belonged to his friend—another noble, of course. He said her name was Ophelia, and he was wanting to see her one last time before he left Odessa for good. They were to split up when Castor gained audience with the noble so that they could go try to find a guide in a nearby pub Castor said he would point out when they neared their destination.

The people in this part of town were unlike any Aedan had seen before, except perhaps Castor when he had first met him - dressed in an odd sleeveless type of short robe that cut off above his knees and sandals that strapped halfway up his legs. The residents here were dressed similarly, though not the same richly red color Castor had worn before. He tried not to make eye contact with any of them as he passed by in the attempt of not drawing any unnecessary attention upon himself. Luckily, the people there seemed to keep to themselves; no one so much as gave them a second glance as they made their way to the towering estate up ahead.

Aedan had never seen such a glorious home before. A tall stone wall topped with curling wrought-iron designs wrapped around a wide, green yard. Through its iron gate, Aedan saw a beautiful flower garden that decorated the majority of the space separated by stone paths that led to a central opening in which sat an enormous three-tiered water fountain. The estate itself had four levels of hewn white rock and was wider than Teacher's longhouse. Majestic stone pillars held up an overhang over the first level providing shade from the beating sun.

Aedan was in awe. "*This* is your friend's home?"

Castor smiled. "Yes, this is House Patera. Beautiful, is it not?"

"To say the least," Fiona said in as much awe as her brother.

"I will speak with the guard here and see about talking with Ophelia for a moment before we go. There is no chance that news of my leave has gotten all the way here just yet, so there should be no issue for me. You two need to be on your guard, though," said Castor seriously. "If anyone asks anything about your heritage, just tell them one of your parents was Maechan-born; hopefully that will quell their interest. If I remember correctly, there is a hunter's pub down that path there just past the bridge." He pointed due north. "If you cannot find a suitable guide there, the barman should be able to point you to where we may find one. In any event, just wait in the pub, and I will join you when I am able. You have the money Teacher gave us, yes?"

Aedan nodded, patting the hidden sack beneath the chest of his tunic.

"Brilliant. Then I shall see you in a few hours." He clapped a hand on Aedan's shoulder and squeezed once familiarly. "Be safe."

Aedan returned the farewell and left the way Castor had directed. He turned back once to see Castor deftly hopping off Sugarfoot and approaching the guard who stood watch outside the gate. But then, Fiona led the horse around a house, and Castor was out of sight.

Breathing in a steeling breath, Aedan returned his gaze ahead of them. They traversed the winding street passing more and more of these large homes - though none could compare to Ophelia's home, Aedan thought. Still, each was bigger than Aedan could ever hope to one day own. Vines of ivy crawled through the street and snaked up the sides of the buildings around them in an effort to claim the city for themselves. Birds tittered away, calling their song to all who could hear.

146 | MICHAEL JACE

Aedan tried to keep his head down, but it was almost too beautiful to not let his eyes wander.

Eventually they came to the bridge and, upon crossing it, saw the hunter's pub Castor had mentioned. There was a sign hanging over the door, though Aedan was unable to decipher the words that curled around the painting of the full quiver that adorned the sign. They ushered Bonedust along to the entrance where they tied his reins. Fiona said she would stay with the horse and feed him while Aedan asked around for a guide. He nodded in response and quietly padded into the tavern.

Patrons were fairly scarce inside the place, probably due to the mid-afternoon hour, so Aedan traipsed straight to the barman who sat on a stool behind the bar discussing something quietly with a man sitting on the other side. Aedan pulled his hood a little farther down as he reached the bar.

"What can I do you for?" the barman asked, cutting off his conversation with the other patron. "You here for hunts or drinks?"

Confused, Aedan said, "Hunts?"

"Hunts," the man said. And when Aedan didn't respond, the barman motioned to a board near the door with a few squares of paper nailed into it. "Civilians come here to post requests for assistance in dealing with meddlesome critters and dangerous beasts giving willing hunters an opportunity to fill their pockets. There is also the occasional layabout hunter who wants nothing more than to come in and fill a seat for no other reason than to pretend they are doing any real work while they are not-so-secretly just getting drunk on ale in the middle of the day for the third time this week." The barman's eyes pierced into the other man's with accusation.

"You know you love me, Cyril," the man slurred. When the barman, Cyril, only continued to stare back, the hunter said, "Oh, *fine*, I will go look at the requests." He pushed away from the bar and sauntered over to the board.

Cyril watched him go with a mixture of affection and worry, and sighed. "He's going to get himself killed someday." Shaking his head as if snapping back to attention, he said, "Anyhow, you here for a drink or a hunt?"

"Actually," Aedan said, "I am looking for a guide who knows the Roinn Mountains well."

"The Roinn Mountains?" Cyril repeated. "That is dangerous territory. What takes you through that path?"

Aedan glanced back and saw that Fiona was still there patting Bonedust's neck lovingly. "I would rather keep that to myself if you do not mind."

"Oh, right, of course," Cyril said. "I meant no offense, m'lord." He put his thumb and pointer finger to his chin as he scanned the bar and thought. "There is always Perse and her husband, Janu. They are very skilled hunters, and if I remember correctly, they have taken many hunts in and around the mountains."

Aedan looked to where he gestured and saw two very athletic Odessans in very expensive-looking mail and leather, the woman with a scrap of paper in her hands as she spoke animatedly to the man. Before Aedan could ask how one goes about posting a request for help, Cyril said, "Though those two usually only take jobs with higher pay. How much were you looking to spend on this guide?"

Aedan subconsciously reached for his chest where the purse was hidden. "I can spend no more than sixty silver," he answered.

"Only sixty?" Cyril asked incredulously. "For a job like that, you should be offering at least three hundred. At *least*," he reiterated before blowing a breath past his lips. His eyes continued to wander the bar until he nearly jumped. "Oh! I always forget - you should go ask that one there." He pointed to the corner of the bar where a person sat, staring out the window indifferently with a small teacup in front of them.

"You think they will accept sixty silver?" Aedan inquired with a small amount of hope.

The barman shook his head. "I do not know for sure, but that one there is a *half-breed*," he said quietly with distaste.

Aedan was stunned by the suddenness of the man's change in temperament. "A what?"

Cyril gave him a confused look and whispered, "A half-breed! A cur! Half-human, half-Sidhe! Hardly anyone round here will hire them, so I'd wager they'd accept anything you offered them. Though I cannot recommend a half-breed to a patron, nor could I assure you their work would be of any fine quality. But," he went on, "if you are desperate enough, you may have to make do. My apologies for not being of more assistance, m'lord."

Half-Sidhe? Aedan thought with not a small amount of wonder. He thanked the barman profusely and strode to the corner of the room.

"Hail to you," Aedan said as he cautiously approached the half-Sidhe's table.

They turned to inspect who it was who came upon them. They had straight white, shoulder-length hair - striking for such a young age of what Aedan guessed was around twenty - with long, pointed ears poking through and the small, angular eyes of the Midorian people who lived to the north of Maecha across the sea. Their skin was paler than Aedan's and their eyes as green as pine. They wore a charcoal hood, though the hood itself was down, with a loose tunic and leggings of matching blacks and grays.

"Good afternoon," they said with a voice as soft as a butterfly's wing-beat. They took a sip of their tea without breaking eye contact. "You wonder if I would guide you through the mountains of Roinn, no?"

Aedan blushed as he responded. "I have only sixty silver to pay you with, and I understand now that that is far less than what it should be. But it is all I have." He nervously fiddled with his fingers.

"I accept," they said calmly and decisively. "I know what they say about me, but I swear to you that I am the finest choice for this request. My name is Eos."

Aedan felt a rush of relief flow over him. *That was much easier than expected,* he thought. "I am Aedan," he responded, purposely exempting his Maechan surname. While Aedan was excited at how quickly this Eos person accepted his apparently measly offer, he thought he should ask a few questions to ensure they really did know their way through the mountains. "Before we continue, I must ask, how is it I can trust that you know the Roinn well enough to guide us through?"

"You know part of my heritage lies with the Sidhe - the good barman was kind enough to announce it to the rest of his clientele when he told you," said Eos without malice. "The part of me that hails from the Otherworld can sense the natural ley lines below the earth. The magic of the underground knows where each tunnel of Roinn leads, and I know how to read them. With me, you can never be lost."

Aedan admittedly had no idea what any of that meant, but it sounded smart. "So," he responded slowly. "So, you are magic?"

The responding singsong chuckle was as pleasant as morning dew in spring. Eos looked at Aedan with an eye of curiosity and ... appreciation? "I do not know if I have ever considered it to be 'magic', but I do have a deeper connection with the natural world than do the people of this age and can sometimes ask of it to assist me in times of need."

Aedan wanted to know more with all of his heart, but he feared he may begin to sound childish should he continue to ask these kinds of questions. Instead, he nodded thoughtfully, trying to contain and mask his excitement. "I see," he said. "I suppose that could be quite helpful during our journey."

The corner of Eos's mouth twitched up slightly.

"There are two others with me; will that be of any issue?" Aedan continued quickly.

"Of course not," Eos answered. "Though do know that, while I am an archer of considerable skill, I may not be able to protect all three of you at all times."

"Oh, do not worry about that," Aedan said. "We are quite capable of defending ourselves. We only require your pathfinding."

Eos nodded with a serene smile. "Excellent. Do you plan to set off today?"

Unsure of the correct answer to that, Aedan made an executive decision. "Yes," he said. "When night falls. Is that agreeable?"

Eos nodded again. "The entrances to the caves are directly north from here. I will meet you there at dusk. I must go prepare." And

150 | MICHAEL JACE

without so much as a farewell, Eos was off - as silent on their feet as a leaf on a breeze.

Aedan could not believe his luck. He'd thought it would take at least an hour or two to find a guide, and not only had he found one much quicker, he'd actually found a guide who was part elven! *It must be fate!* Brimming with excitement, he rushed outside to tell Fiona the news.

But she was nowhere in sight.

Bonedust still stood nearby, but his caretaker had disappeared. "Fiona," said Aedan under his breath. He whipped his head around back and forth, but she was just *gone.* His excitement turned quickly to panic as he paced by the horse trying to think of what he should do. He *wanted* to go try to find her, but he knew nothing of this place. He also knew that Castor was expecting him to still be here when he finished his business. He clenched his jaw and fists as he agonized over what to do.

Surely, she would not just wander off, Aedan worried. *But if she were discovered and taken, would she not have cried out?*

Suddenly, a bird landed on the saddle of Bonedust - but it wasn't just *any* bird.

"Bas!" Aedan exclaimed as several passersby casted sideways glances his way before hurrying off with muddled whispers. "Where is Fiona?"

The falcon was clearly agitated - anxiously squawking and flapping its wings. Before Aedan could ask again, Bas lifted off the horse, smacking its wing against Aedan's head as it flew past him with a screech.

Aedan didn't even stop to think of what would happen when Castor arrived at the tavern expecting him to be there. He chased after the falcon.

11

Sundown

Castor watched Aedan and Fiona go for a few moments as they started towards the hunter's pub Castor had directed them to before eventually hopping off and guiding Sugarfoot to the guard that stood watch outside the estate's gate.

"Hello," Castor said to the man.

"Greetings, m'lord," the guard responded. Then, his face shifted as he recognized who he was talking to. "Lord Vallas! What an unexpected surprise! What brings you to Argos? Is Duke Vallas with you as well?"

"My apologies," Castor responded formally. "I sent a letter ahead of me to inform the Pateras of my coming, but I see that it must have been lost somewhere along the way." Twenty-four years of politics made lying come easily to the young lord. "And unfortunately, no, my father was not available to make the journey this time. But I am here to see Lady Ophelia Patera if she is entertaining guests at this hour."

"Of course!" the guard said. "I know the two of you are thick as thieves; I'm sure Lady Patera would not mind a visit with you. If you will follow me, Lord Vallas, I will show you to her."

"You have my gratitude," Castor responded with a polite smile.

As Castor was led through the gate into the massive garden, the guard called for a nearby servant to take Sugarfoot to the stables to be

152 | MICHAEL JACE

fed and groomed. They strode down a stone path lined with a variety of flowers of different colors and sizes, their intermingling aromas tickling Castor's senses. The splash and trickle of the central fountain nearly drowned out the sounds of everyday life outside the walls. Castor thought he could easily let himself get lost in this garden.

They pushed through, however, and hiked up the path to the front door of the estate where they entered through the large doors.

"If you like, you can sit in the foyer and await the Lady," the guard said motioning to a nearby cushioned seat. "I will send for her."

Castor nodded. "You have my thanks," he said. "Oh! And please do not inform her it is me who comes to see her. If you would, please tell her that it is a gentleman suitor here to confess his undying love for her."

The guard raised his eyebrows but said nothing else as he bowed and left to find the lady.

Castor sat back in the chair with a mischievous grin. He wondered what Ophelia was doing right then. Surely, she would have finished her studies for the day. Perhaps she was reading one of her favorite books. Or perhaps she was busy getting ready for a *real* suitor. Either way, minutes later, he was quite pleased with himself when he heard a distant but familiar voice call out, "Tell my suitor I am on my way; I just need to finish counting the teeth in my collection of bones from unborn children!"

The guard returned shortly thereafter and sighed when he saw Castor in the foyer grinning happily. "The Lady Patera will be here shortly," he said before giving a quick bow to Castor and exiting out the front door.

Minutes later, Castor heard footsteps approaching from the next room when the voice came out again, "Forgive me for taking so long, my Lord!" the woman called out. "I was just in the middle of trimming my ear hair when you arrived."

She came around the corner then and saw her "suitor" seated there, his face split in half by an enormous smile. Ophelia froze in surprise. She stood several inches taller than Castor himself, wearing a

PHANTOM FIRE | 153

beautifully long, floor-dusting gown in the colors of the Patera family
- gold and emerald. Dark golden hoops hung from her ears under her
hair, inky coils that danced around her head with every movement.

"I think you missed a spot," Castor said gesturing to her ear. "Though
I rather liked your ear hair how it was," he went on. "Long ear hair is a
sign of wisdom, so they say."

"Cas!" She ran to him, and he stood to meet her embrace. "What are
you doing here?" she asked as she pulled away while still keeping her
hands on his arms.

Castor smiled nervously. "Well," he began. "Perhaps we should go
for a walk, and I will tell you."

And so, they walked. As they entered into the garden, he told her
of Teacher and of Aedan. He told her of the first few days of training,
how nervous he had been and how intimidated he was of his fellow
apprentice. They sat by the fountain, and he told her of Sai and of
Fiona and how terrifying that had been for all of them. They moved
over to the stable to see Sugarfoot, and he told her of his dream of the
Otherworld and his visit with the Phantom and his subsequent mark.
They reclined under an apple tree, and he told her of Teacher's true
heritage and the favor she had asked of him. He told her of his decision
to abandon his duties as a lord for a quest to Letha to end the life of the
reigning queen.

When all was said and done, Ophelia breathed out a huge breath of
air. "So, what I am understanding is that you were housed with both a
Maechan with the body of a god *and* an insane, bloodthirsty murderer;
you met an actual Aspect, and she blessed you with her powers over
living things; and the banished princess of a foreign land has convinced
you to leave your home country forever and sent you on a quest to help
her claim her rightful throne. Did I miss anything?"

"Only that I could definitely beat you in a sparring match now."

"That is absolutely the least believable thing you have said to me all
day." She smiled at him, but Castor could tell it was a sad smile. "Is this
the last I will see of you, then?" she asked him quietly.

Castor sighed. "Teacher - er - Branwyn said that I must stay in Letha with her should I choose this path. I do not know if I will ever be able to return."

Ophelia looked back to her estate, her eyes trailing down the columns to the garden to the gate. "I envy your freedom," she said. "I wish I could just - "

"Come with us," Castor interrupted.

"What? No, I - "

"*Yes,* you can," he cut in. "I did it; and so can you." He stood up then and gestured to the northern mountains. "Imagine venturing across countries together! You do not want to be here anyway; imagine tossing aside all those responsibilities that I know you detest and just being able to be *free*. Free to do whatever it is you wish." He looked down at her with an expression of wonder and rebellion - but the tears in her eyes instantly quelled his enthusiasm. "Ophelia," he said as he kneeled down next to her.

"Aspects, I hate crying," she said wiping her face furiously.

"Why are you crying?"

She sniffed angrily and shoved away at a few coils of hair that had fallen forward and touched her face. "I cannot leave," she said. "I cannot do what you have done. I just cannot disappoint my father so greatly. He would never forgive me."

Castor sat back, feeling resigned but not overly surprised. When he had occasionally thought about asking Ophelia to accompany him, he had not had the highest of hopes. While Ophelia was as brave as they come, he knew her father just meant too much to her for her to be able to abandon her duties to her family. Still, it had been worth it to try.

"Tell me more of your year," Ophelia said, changing the subject.

Castor obliged as he leaned back against the apple tree.

They talked for some time as Ophelia sobered up, and soon, they were joking together again, though Castor tried not to think of it as the last time they would do so. It was only when two of the Patera family's servants, one old and one young, had come in through the side entrance carrying several baskets full of market goods that they stopped.

PHANTOM FIRE | 155

"Good afternoon!" Ophelia called out to them. Castor remembered how kind she always was to her servants, despising it when other nobles talked down to them. He recalled once when she had shouted at a minor noble for saying something degrading to her servants at a festival held here once. *They are better people than your slimy face could ever hope to be,* she had yelled at the man, causing her father to give her an hour-long lecture of proper decorum and etiquette. Castor smiled fondly at the memory.

She beckoned them over. "Come rest your feet for a moment," she called. They came and sat on the grass with Castor and Ophelia setting their baskets down next to them.

"Is that Lord Vallas?" the elder of the women said with a smile.

Castor smiled back at them. "Hello," he said. "I trust you two are faring well?"

"Lady Patera sees to it that we are well taken care of here," the younger one said with a grateful nod.

"I would expect no different," Castor replied. "So, what is the news around Argos lately?"

"Oh, nothing too exciting ever happens here," the elder said. "Though the market was rather abuzz today. Apparently, the city guards discovered a Maechan trespassing right down that road there!" She pointed down the path Castor had directed Aedan and Fiona towards.

"*What?*" Castor asked, jumping to his feet.

The other three flinched back at his sudden rise. "That is the word, my Lord," the elder continued. "They apparently have the Maechan in their custody and, according to our great Empress's law, should be getting her ready for execution at sundown."

"*Sundown?*" He vaguely heard the panic in his voice, but he couldn't care about that. Casting his eyes to the sky, he saw that the sun had already disappeared behind the walls surrounding the estate. It must be nearly sundown already, he thought. He looked at his friend desperately. He could not explain in front of the servants what this was all about, so he hoped Ophelia would be able to understand based off of all he had told her before. "Ophelia," was all he said.

She was already standing. "You do not need to ask," she said. She thanked her servants and wished them well before she chased Castor out of the gate without another thought.

"I will stay with Bonedust, here," Fiona told Aedan when they arrived at the hunter's pub. "He needs to eat, so go on in without me."

Her brother looked as if he were about to protest, but he went in nonetheless. Content at having a moment to herself for the first time in a month, Fiona gathered a handful of oats from a bag hanging on the side of the horse and held it to its mouth. It ate happily, and Fiona was only mildly afraid that it might accidentally chomp her outstretched hand. But when it was finished eating, she remained unscathed. When she reached for another handful, she was almost blown over by a sudden gust of wind. Laughing at her own clumsiness, she righted herself and grabbed more oats for Bonedust.

A few minutes passed before two men approached her. "Afternoon, miss," one of them said.

Noting their armor and the crests emblazoned on their overshirt, she assumed them to be city guards. Instantly cautious, Fiona reached up to pull her hood down a little farther just to be sure, but her hand found no hood to grab. *That gust of wind*, she thought, cursing herself for not paying more attention. She smiled nervously. "Hail ... Er ...Hello," she said, feeling her heartrate quicken. *Speak more like Castor*, she reminded herself. "What how can you do for you?" *What the* hell *was that?* she thought immediately after blurting out that completely nonsense sentence. *How about just try speaking like* any *person?* "I mean to say," she continued, trying to mimic Castor's accent and failing miserably, "what can I do for you?" Bas landed on her shoulder and puffed out his chest threateningly.

The two guards looked apprehensively at the bird for a moment before one said, "We were just going to ask if you would like us to show you around the city. You seem new here."

"Oh, no, that will not be necessary," Fiona said, breathing faster. "I live here," she added. "I have lived here for years." She pushed her long, red hair behind her back in a vain attempt to hide it.

The other guard looked curiously at Bonedust and all the packs hanging off his sides. "Is that so? Your rouncey looks to be carrying quite the load for a simple walk through the town."

Fiona looked worriedly to the horse then back to the guards. "Oh, I just - "

Then one of them interrupted her in a language she did not understand.

"What?" she responded immediately, and then almost slapped herself. They must be speaking the Odessan tongue. Fiona felt the blood drain from her face.

"I think you should let us show you around town," one of them said sternly in the common tongue again while resting a palm on the pommel of the sword on his hip.

Fiona bit her lip and looked inside the door of the pub, but Aedan was nowhere to be seen. "Can I just - "

"*Miss,*" he said, a darkness to his voice. "Try not to make a scene. We mean you no harm. Just come with us."

The edge to his words did nothing to soothe her anxiety. "All right," she said quietly, casting her eyes back to the door in a helpless attempt to see her brother. "All right; I will come with you." She patted the horse's neck and said with a shaky voice, "Stay here, Bonedust; be good while I am gone." Then, to Bas, she whispered, "Let Aedan know where I am."

"Let's *go,* miss," one of them said again, grabbing her elbow forcefully. Bas screeched once in response, but Fiona only waved him away. She didn't want the guards to take him, too.

And off they guided her. To show her around town.

✦ . ✝ . ✦ . ✝ . ✦

The cell they took her to was not the best, in Fiona's opinion. Dark, damp, and foul are some of the ways she could describe the barred room she was in. Small, cramped, and without comfort were a few more. At least, she was not sharing her cell with anyone else, she thought.

She had been sitting in there for what seemed like hours, but with no windows in sight, there was no way she could be sure. She only hoped Bas could guide Aedan to where she was. Or maybe Castor would be able to figure out what happened and know where she was being held based on time he had spent in this city in the past. But both of those things seemed more impossible every minute she spent holding her knees in the dark.

The two guards that had escorted her here were both in another room nearly out of earshot. She had heard others come in and leave as time progressed, but she never heard Aedan's voice amongst them. The only thing she was sure she did hear, however, was that she was to be put to death at sundown.

All her life, she was *less than*. Before her parents died, she lived in poverty with them, barely scraping by on her father's money from fishing. There were times when her mother sold her own body out to strangers to help make ends meet. Then, after they died, Fiona moved into the orphanage and inherited the name "Ó Bháird", which would prove to show her inferiority to any who knew her name. The name continued to curse her after she reached adulthood - no one wanted to give an *Ó Bháird girl* a decent job. So, she resorted to what she remembered her mother would sometimes do. She sold herself, and she hated every second of it. But finally, with the Spear Maiden's recommendation, Aedan would be able to make enough money for them to move away from Albainn, where all knew her name. She was going to be able to get a job doing something she actually *liked*. She even thought that, perhaps, with her experience with Avelas in Endala, she may be able to get a job as a healer wherever they settled. But even now, with that fantasy almost within her grasp, it was going to be taken away. By people who saw her as *less than*. It was almost fitting, she thought morbidly.

Suddenly, her thoughts were disrupted by two heavy thuds in the other room where the guards had been, their faint voices cut short. A sense of dread crept over her as she tried to huddle farther in the corner of the cell. But all was quiet. She sat there, every second dragging on for an eternity.

She heard someone scuffling around distantly, and then, for a moment, silence. Then, she heard the front door open.

"What the hell?" a feminine voice said. Fiona did not recognize it.

There were other voices, too, but they were too low for Fiona to hear. Footsteps approached. Fiona huddled closer to the walls.

"Fi!" an urgent voice whispered loudly.

There was only one person who called her that.

Fiona jumped up and ran to the barred doors of her cell. "Aedan!" she cried when she saw his giant form run to her. "Aedan, you found me!"

"Of course I did, Fi," he said, tears welling up in his eyes as he grabbed her hands through the rusted bars. "Bas showed me the way. But what happened to the guards?"

"What do you mean?" she asked.

It was then that she saw Castor behind him with a mixed look of relief and sickness. Another woman with the rich umber complexion Fiona associated with the country of D'jada far to the southeast of Maecha stood near Castor looking back the way they had come with an expression of stunned horror.

Aedan fumbled with a ring of long iron keys. "They - " He stopped short. "I think they have been murdered," he said quietly. "Did you hear anything while you were in here?"

"Not enough to know what was happening," she said, the dread she had been feeling before making a sudden reappearance. "Just get me out of here before anyone else shows up."

"I'm trying!" He sounded panicked.

Fiona was practically bouncing on her toes with anxiety by the time he found the right key. The door wrenched open with a hideously loud creak, making the D'jadii woman flinch.

Fiona fell into Aedan's rib-crushing embrace as soon as she was out.

"I am glad you are all right," Castor said.

"I am, too," Fiona responded after surviving her brother's hug. "Let us just leave this place before anyone sees I am missing."

"Or sees their friends' blood all over the floor," the other woman said with a flat voice, still staring down the hall.

"Let's go," Castor said as he turned to jog back the way he had come.

When they came to the front room, Fiona saw that the two guards were indeed very much dead. It was a grisly scene, but over the last year, Fiona had seen her fair share of blood and gore during her time with Avelas. Still, it was different seeing it on someone with no light in their eyes - on someone whom she could not help. Their throats had been cut and there were numerous stab wounds throughout both of their lifeless bodies with a nearly unbelievable amount of blood pooling from both victims.

But that was not the only disturbing thing in the room, Fiona noted. Scattered in the pools of blood were the petals of a certain flower. A certain *pink* flower.

She decided to let herself think over that later. When they burst through the door, a woman in a garb matching the two dead guards behind them stood, looking a bit stunned that four people suddenly erupted from the city dungeons, within arm's reach.

Everyone froze.

The guard's shocked eyes traced each of them and lingered bewilderedly on the D'jadii woman before noticing what was behind them. She moved one foot back and grabbed the hilt of the sword slung on her hip.

Before anyone could do anything else, Castor, in front of them all, touched his fingers to the guard's exposed neck. She crumpled immediately to the ground. Several passersby gasped, some clutching their chests as they stumbled back and some screaming for help.

"Go, just *go!*" Aedan boomed. He took Fiona's hand and tugged her along as he chased after Castor and the other woman who seemed to know her way through the city well (and who was a very quick runner for being in a long, dressing gown, Fiona thought).

They were definitely in the more unsightly part of town, Fiona noticed as she ran for her life. The buildings around them were nothing like those around the grand estate they had split from Castor at - these were all quite dilapidated and crawling with rats. The people that walked here were all dirty and smelled faintly of urine, though they seemed just as bewildered by their raucous exodus as anyone else. Only two of them - two men up ahead - did not have the same confused looks on their faces, though they let them pass without disrupting their run. A small part of Fiona's mind noticed each had a key tattooed on their necks.

Still they ran, Fiona too afraid to look behind them to see if they were being followed. She felt like her legs were going to explode, but still she ran - or more like *leapt* what with Aedan's pulling. They kept running and running and running until finally they came out the northern side of town with the crops of a farm ahead of them.

"Do you know where the caves are?" Castor called as they ran.

Fiona did not hear the other woman's response, but she slightly altered her course to the right. When they made it to the crops, they slowed and looked around. No one had followed them this far, Fiona noticed.

"They will find us," the woman said as she tried to push her hair back. "Someone must have seen which way we ran. They will send for us."

"We can go the rest of the way ourselves, Ophelia," Castor said to her.

Fiona almost slapped herself. *Of course, she was Ophelia.* During all the dread and panic, Fiona hadn't yet made that connection.

"You should go back to the estate," he continued. "You still have - "

"No, I cannot," she said angrily. "No, I cannot because all those people saw me! Everyone in Argos knows who I am, especially while I am in *this!*" She gestured to the beautiful green and gold dress she wore.

"They all saw me leave the dungeons and they saw me with you when you killed that guard and they saw me when we all ran - "

"I did not *kill* her," Castor objected quietly. "She was only unconscious."

"*Still!*" she nearly shouted. "There is no way I can go back now. Not after all of this." Her voice was frustrated and bitter.

"Forgive me," Aedan interrupted, "but we need to go. I do not mean to cross you, Lady, but my sister and I need to be gone from this land. If you can point us in the right direction - "

Ophelia slapped her hand to her forehead. "Of course; my apologies. I will show you the way." She turned, and in a hurried jog, continued towards the imposing mountains.

It was not long before the enormous opening of a cavern loomed before them like the jaws of a great stone beast. With the fallen sun, it was already nearly impossible to see into the mouth of the mountain, but they ran towards it nonetheless. When they passed through the entrance, Bas swooped down, the familiar feeling of his claws on Fiona's shoulder. Then, the softest voice stopped them in their tracks.

"Aedan," the voice said.

Skidding to a halt, they looked around until Fiona saw them. A white-haired person with pointed ears and hooded eyes stood innocuously by the entrance with an ornately carved oaken bow slung over their chest and a full quiver around their waist.

"Eos," Aedan answered, relief flooding his response. "Friends," he said to his three out-of-breath companions, "this is - "

"Introductions later," Castor said. "We are almost out of sight of Argos. Just a bit farther."

And into the darkness they ran.

12

Under the Mountain

The group of five came to a rest once they felt they'd gone a safe distance down into the tunnel. What had been a large opening of the cave had narrowed to a width that all five of them might have been able to just barely fit shoulder-to-shoulder. They had been stumbling through the dark until coming to a stop there where Eos had lit a torch using a flintleaf they had pulled from a bag attached to their belt.

Castor sat back against the cave wall, breathing hard, controlled breaths. Having been running on loose sand for the past year, he found that running on solid ground was much easier. Perhaps that was why Branwyn had them run on the beach, Castor thought briefly. The rest of the group seemed to be much more tired than he was, all of them except Eos hunched over and gulping air.

"Should I inquire as to why we were in such a hurry?" Eos asked nonchalantly.

"Long story," Aedan said through heavy breaths. "That aside, friends, this is Eos, our guide. Eos, this is Fiona, Castor, and Ophelia." He pointed to each as he named them and gave a smile to Eos when he finished. Castor felt his eyebrow raise, suddenly a little annoyed for some reason. Eos's eyes tracked each of them as they were introduced,

163

164 | MICHAEL JACE

though they seemed to linger on Ophelia for a moment longer, Castor noticed. *They probably recognize her as the Lady of Argos*, he thought.

"It is good to meet you, and we all appreciate your agreeing to guide us on this path," said Castor with a formal tone.

Eos nodded politely then gestured to Castor's spear and Aedan's axes. "I see some of you are outfitted for battle, though, if you do not mind my observation, I also see that you have not much supplies with you. This trek will take us no less than a week even should we make good time," they said. "Are you prepared for such a journey?"

Castor saw Fiona pale. "We forgot the horses ..." she said, sounding dejected. "They had all of our supplies on them."

"They did," Castor said. "But when Ophelia and I heard that a Maechan girl had been captured and was to be executed, we left the estate as fast as we could. Before we went to the city dungeon, we stopped by the hunter's pub to ensure that the rumor we heard was about you. When all we found was Bonedust waiting outside, I untied him and took as much of the supplies as I could carry with me." Castor gestured to the pack on his back. "About a week's supply of food for one person is all that was left, however."

Eos looked to him, a plain expression on their face. "There are four of you."

Castor blinked at Eos. "Right. Well, when we were running from the city guards, we did not have much time to stop and shop for supplies." He tried to keep the sarcasm from his voice, but, as usual, he found he could not help himself.

It did not seem to affect Eos at all, though Aedan gave Castor a hard look. "I do not think we should be telling our guide *too much*," he whispered quietly so Eos wouldn't hear.

"It is of no issue," Eos responded having apparently heard him anyway. *Those odd, long ears must be able to hear better than normal ones*, Castor thought a little irritably. "Being a pariah myself, I find it quite pleasant to be with a group who is also unwelcomed by society."

"We are *not* unwelcomed by society," Castor responded.

"Oh," Eos said casually. "So, these guards were chasing after you because of your model citizenry?"

"Look here - "

"*Anyway*," Ophelia interrupted, apparently noticing Castor's rising temper. "Eos, it does appear that we are ill prepared for this journey. Do you perhaps know if there is any sort of game here in the caves?"

"Some," Eos answered, looking at Ophelia with an unidentifiable expression on their face. When she looked back to Eos, they cast their eyes to the ground, away from her. "Though it is mostly rats and spiders, neither of which I would recommend unless you find yourselves desperate."

"Great," Ophelia said. "So, I am run out of my own city only to starve in a hole." Her voice was more bitter than usual.

"We have some hardtack and threpsiberries left," Castor offered.

Eos's emerald eyes lit up like the sun shining through a tree canopy. "Threpsiberries?" they asked. "Give me one, and none of you shall starve."

Castor seemed suspicious but pulled one from the pack and handed it to them anyway. Eos swapped the berry and the torch with Castor and squished the fruit in their now-empty palms.

Castor almost yelled. "What the hell - "

Eos held out their other hand to signal Castor to wait. They bent to the cave floor and let the delicious juice drip from their scarred archer's fingers. The liquid seeped into the earthen floor easily. Eos pressed their hand firmly over the spot with eyes closed and began to whisper something unintelligible. Castor looked to his other three companions confusedly, but they were all entranced by what was happening. Just before Castor was going to ask what was going on, a green sprig sprouted from the dirt under Eos's palm. The plant continued to grow and grow until a medium-sized threpsiberry bush stood right there completely defying the laws of nature.

"Oh, right," Aedan said as if remembering something. "Eos is one of the Sidhe."

"*What?*" Castor, Fiona, and Ophelia asked simultaneously.

Eos dusted their hands together as they admired their handiwork. Then, they noticed the others' expressions. "Only half," they supplied. "A full-blood Sidhe could not survive in this realm for very long before turning dark. Since I am also part human, I have no problem being here."

"Dark?" Aedan inquired, his intrigue of the Sidhe showing in his question. "What do you mean by that?"

"The Sidhe do not belong in this world," Eos explained as everyone else continued to collect themselves and gather threpsiberries off the new bush. "They can come here in spirit form for however long they may like to, but if there is a tear in the veil between our worlds, they can come through physically if the conditions are right. But being without the magic of their own realm makes them twisted and dark. Once the change begins, they soon forget who they were and become very unpredictable - usually dangerously so."

"Are there many tears in the veil?" Aedan asked.

"Only a few that I know of," Eos answered. "One lies under the Ebonpool which is what gives the water its strange color, another on a small island off the western coast of Odessa near Endala," Castor and Aedan exchanged a brief look, "one in the mountainous Yuki Isles near Midoria, and I do not mean to worry you, but I also know of the existence of one here in the Roinn Mountains. I am sure there are many more, but these are the only ones I personally know of."

"And why should that *not* worry us?" Castor asked.

"Because I know the paths," Eos said, not registering Castor's sarcasm, which irritated him further. "I can get you through the mountains without getting close to where the tear is. As I am able to sense the natural ley lines of the world, I can also sense where they are broken, and we shall not cross through a path where it is so."

Castor had no retort after that. They finished picking the bush bare in silence before Eos lit another torch and handed it to Aedan, who would be taking up the rear of the party, before setting off deeper into the mountains.

The cave was mostly tunnel, though it sometimes did open up into wider caverns. On several occasions, Castor could have sworn he'd seen something scurry away from the torchlight, but he was never able to get a good look at what was there before it merged with the shadows of the many stalagmites that spired out of the floor. Still, the hair on his arms stood on end every time he remembered that they were not alone.

They did not continue much farther on that day, for it was already late when they had arrived at the cave. They settled down in the next open chamber they found. They were low on sleeping supplies, so they used mostly one another for something soft to lay their heads on.

Two stayed awake at a time, one of them always being Eos, who said that their kind did not need sleep as much as full-blood humans. So, the full-blood humans took turns keeping watch with the half-elf. When it was Aedan's turn, he constantly bombarded Eos with questions about the Sidhe. Fiona talked at length about her apprenticeship with Avelas and had several inquiries regarding Sidhe healing techniques. Ophelia tried to talk with Eos about Argos, though they were not very chatty about their life there. Castor preferred silence.

The next couple of days were quiet. The caves were actually quite dull, thought Castor. Which he supposed was a good thing. He was not exactly sure what to expect down in the mountains, but he assumed it was probably better to have an easy, boring time, than to be constantly in danger.

Without having been asked, Eos would occasionally regale them with tall tales of the area. Of spiders as large as a house whose eggs held millions of hungry babies, of bloodthirsty creatures that swam in the deepest cave pools, of the lost city under the mountain where dark Sidhe lurked around every corner, of the fates of travelers who died there whose bodies were slowly enveloped by the stone, and of a hundred other horrifying things that made Castor want to be out of the mountains as fast as possible. The other three did not seem to mind the stories - Aedan even appeared to be enjoying them, Castor noticed with an eye roll.

They had just passed through another larger cavern with several branching paths while in the middle of Eos's story about spirits of the dead who wandered the ancient halls of the caves, when they were interrupted by a distant sound that echoed off the walls. A low, moaning sort of sound. Suddenly, every story Eos had told came back to Castor in a rush as gooseflesh rose on his arms.

"What is that?" Fiona whispered. Bas squawked uncomfortably.

They were all stopped in the tunnel, looking around, each growing more and more panicked, except for Eos, who stood with eyes closed as though concentrating.

"It is not human," they said. "I do not know what is ahead, but it is definitely not human."

"Great," Castor mumbled. "Can you tell if it is dangerous?"

Eos shook their head. "Whatever it is, it is not large."

The low moaning continued. It was distinctly feminine, Castor thought, though it was apparently not human. Eos began to walk forward again, and the rest of them followed close behind. With Aedan's help, Castor unlatched the spear from his back and held it in his hands - it comforted him to feel the familiar sturdiness of the weapon in his hands.

As they crept around a bend, the moaning got louder and louder until Castor could tell that whatever was making the sound was directly ahead of them. The wall on the right side of them was uneven and bent inwards awkwardly which concealed the side just past it from view.

The moaning - or crying? - was right on the other side of that bend; Castor could feel it. Eos drew their bow and silently hooked an arrow on its string. Together, the group sidled around the left side of the wall as they rounded the outcropping. The fear was so palpable, Castor could feel it in the air, like a thick, choking cloud of dread that weighed down on them as heavy as the stone above them.

It was a girl. Her arms still round with youth were wrapped around her bent knees as she sat on the ground, her matted hair draped over them like a greasy curtain. She was sobbing, her shoulders shaking with each breath. Her skin was scraped and scuffed and dirty with dried blood and cave dust. She wore only a tattered white dress, and in her left hand, she gripped a pale green strip of cloth, her knuckles white.

Castor reminded himself that she was not human. Though what else could she be?

"Name yourself," Eos commanded, their voice suddenly more authoritative. "What manner of creature are you?"

The girl cried even harder then. Her cries turned to wails as her arms dropped off her knees and hit the rock beneath her. She brought her head back as she howled, and the five companions jumped back against the wall. Her eyes were much too large for her face, and they were solid black. Bloodred tears streamed down her skin.

Before anyone could say anything, Eos loosed an arrow. It planted itself directly into the thing's chest, but her cries only worsened. The screams were getting so loud, they physically *hurt*. Castor could feel the sound like cold knives slicing through his body. Eos tried to grab another arrow, but the girl was suddenly rising to her feet and moving towards them.

As she moved, her limbs began to grow, extending out to longer than what any child's arms and legs ever should and with far too many joints. Her skin wrinkled and weathered and grayed with each passing second. The once seemingly young child was now ancient with grotesque, spidering limbs that bent at odd, broken angles and shuddered with every jerking movement.

Each step seemed like an eternity as the screams got louder and louder. It was agonizing. Castor could barely keep his eyes open as she lumbered closer and closer to them, her mouth agape at an awkward angle as though her jaw was hanging off its hinge.

He began to see his skin tearing at the sound - small cuts that grew along his arms. It would not be long before they would all be torn in half, he thought sickeningly. He needed to do something, but the force of her screams was just too much for him to focus clearly. Then, he felt a strong hand bracing itself on his shoulder. Aedan's hand.

Feeling a burst of courage, Castor thrust his spear deep into the thing's chest and shoved her body back against the other wall of the cave. But that didn't stop her. Her scream reached a crescendo, and Castor felt the ground rumble beneath him. Something grabbed him and threw him back the way they'd come as the ceiling caved in deafeningly right where he'd been standing, crushing the woman underneath and silencing her deadly wail.

When Castor regained his bearings, he saw he was on one side of the rocks with Aedan and Fiona, but Ophelia and Eos were nowhere to be seen.

When Castor stabbed the old lady into the wall and the ceiling began to cave in, Ophelia, feeling a surge of adrenaline, tackled Eos to the ground away from the tumbling rocks. They landed agonizingly, but Ophelia jumped back up just in time to see the way back becoming completely blocked off by earth and stone.

"Castor!" she cried out, pounding her bloody fists on the heavy rocks. That woman's screams had been so terrible, she hadn't even noticed that it had been literally *cutting* her flesh open. "Castor, can you hear me?" she yelled.

A muffled voice yelled back something that sounded like her name. Castor was alive.

With newfound energy, she began trying to move some of the rocks, but they were all too heavy. Eos was suddenly next to her, and they held their hand against the top of the cave-in for a moment. The boulder cracked under their palm, and they were able to clear a bit of it away, leaving a small hole to the other side.

"You are incredible," Ophelia said with a small amount of admiration. The hole in the boulder was not by any means large enough for anyone to crawl through, but she could at least see Castor and his two friends on the floor, propped up against the wall and breathing heavily.

"Cas!" cried Ophelia, flooded with relief.

"Ophelia!" he said back, sounding just as relieved. Though he looked awful; the woman's screams had sliced into him quite badly, too. A long gash ran all the way up the back of his forearm dripping blood like tears. "You are alive," said Castor as though reassuring himself that it was true.

PHANTOM FIRE | 171

"And what of Eos?" Aedan inquired.

"Eos," Ophelia echoed. "She - Er - He - Er - " She stopped, horrified, and looked back to the half-elf. She only just realized she wasn't sure what Eos preferred, and based on looks alone, Ophelia couldn't manage an accurate guess. Eos looked curious about her unasked question but only shrugged in response. "They are well, too," Ophelia answered.

"Is there any path we can take to join back with you?" Aedan called.

"Unfortunately, no," Eos replied through the hole. "But there is another path you can take. In the last chamber, there are several other tunnels. If you go back the way we came, turn right as you get back in the chamber and the first tunnel along the wall will also get through to the other side."

"That sounds easy enough," Fiona responded as she cradled a very stunned Bas in her arms.

"You must remember, though," Eos said. "That path will take you down a dark way. The ley lines there do not feel ... *right*. Something is not right down that tunnel, but if you follow it through to the end, you shall emerge in Maecha."

"Is it a straight shot there?" Castor asked with a note of doubt in his tone.

Ophelia saw Eos concentrate silently for a minute. When they opened their eyes, they said, "It feels like there are other, straying paths, but only in some large cavern farther along."

"Well, what do we do when get to this large cavern?" Castor asked with a small amount of irritation entering his words.

Eos looked troubled. "I ... I do not know. It is the northernmost tunnel you want, but it is easy to lose one's sense of direction underground when you cannot read the magic of the earth."

"Which way is north?" Aedan asked.

Eos pointed north, making sure their hand was visible in the hole.

Aedan pointed the same way. "I think, if I keep pointing this way, and adjust as we walk and turn, I can keep us on the right track," he said to Castor and Fiona.

A look of apprehension flashed across Fiona's face as she began quickly bandaging up Castor's and Aedan's more severe cuts.

"Are you sure?" Castor asked him as he held out his arm for Fiona gratefully.

Aedan nodded. "I think so."

"I am sorry I cannot be of more assistance," Eos said then. "But you. You who have been touched by that which is Other." Castor looked up with a surprised expression. "The Other is stronger in you than I have ever seen in a mortal before. If you become lost, you may discover that you are able to find your way if you listen to the Other."

Castor looked entirely confused, but nodded anyway. "Make sure you get Ophelia to the other side safely," was all he said in return.

"I will," Eos answered. "She saved me from the rocks; I owe her my life."

Ophelia felt herself blush. She wanted to argue that Eos did *not* owe her their life, but Eos went on.

"Your path will take another two or three days longer than ours," they said. Eos retrieved a bundle of torches from their pack. "These will help you on your way, but they may not last if you use them carelessly. So, be swift," said Eos as they tossed down a small bag of flintleaves.

Ophelia moved to the hole to look once more at her closest friend.

"Forgive me for getting you dragged into all this," Castor said when he saw her.

She shook her head, cutting him off. "Apologize when you see me in Trícnoc," she said feeling the sting of unshed tears. "I will wait for you there."

He nodded as they turned to go back. "Be safe," he said finally.

And then the three strode back the way they'd come and around the bend, out of sight.

"Be safe," Ophelia whispered.

13

Lost

"You do not owe me your life," Ophelia said to Eos as they continued on their way. It had been eating at her since they had said so earlier. "Anyone would have pushed you out of the way of those rocks."

Eos smiled at her, though their expression visible from the flickering torchlight hinted at a deeper melancholy. "That you would say so shows your kindness is genuine."

"Do people truly treat you so harshly?" she asked. Ophelia of course knew that there were many negative stereotypes about people like Eos, but being separated from the common folk by her status distanced her from the actuality of the inhospitality shown to them.

"It is unnecessary to dwell on that here and now," they responded, their face hidden by their long white hair. Ophelia felt a pit of sympathy dig its way into her chest. "Do you sometimes have issues being of mixed race as well?" they asked innocently.

Ophelia was quite surprised by the question. She had never considered how the similarities of their heritages did not draw similar reactions from others. Her father was an Odessan and her mother, whose looks she had inherited, had come from D'jada. "I cannot say that I have. Though the people of Odessa are much more familiar with the people of D'jada," she said. "Perhaps they only fear that which they do not know. And since they outnumber you, their fear is easily altered into contempt."

Eos looked thoughtful. "You are as insightful as you are kind, Lady Patera," they said finally.

Ophelia blushed. "You do not have to call me that," she said. "Please, call me Ophelia."

"Ophelia," Eos echoed, a strange tone to their voice as though they delighted in the sound of it on their lips. Ophelia found she liked the sound of her name on their lips, too. She smiled, feeling warmth in her cheeks.

Aedan was only a little concerned. They had lost their guide and only had vague directions on how to pass through the mountains on their own. Not to mention the path they were to take was apparently "dark" according to Eos, and the ley lines did not feel right to them either. All he could think about was Eos telling them about the veil tear in the mountains - that *had* to be what made the ley lines feel off to them, right?

Castor was in charge of defending them should the need arise. He kept his spear at the ready, and Aedan was sure he was prepared to summon his mark at any moment. Fiona was in charge of the torch, holding it out so that Aedan could point them in the right direction as they went along. So far, he felt like he was doing a good job at keeping them on track, adjusting his point as they came around bends, though that might have been because the tunnels were nearly always a straight path. It was strange; in his mind, he had pictured the caves of the Roinn to be much more complex than simple tunnels that opened up to the occasional cavern, though he was glad to be wrong.

They spoke sparingly, worried that any noise might garner some unwanted attention from whatever may lurk around the stalagmites. Still, Castor would occasionally give Aedan an odd look - almost as though he wanted to say something but decided against it. Finally, Aedan prodded.

"What is it?" he whispered to him causing Fiona to start at the sudden sound.

Blush crept into Castor's firelit cheeks. "I just ... I just wanted to thank you," he said finally.

"Thank me?"

With his free hand, Castor gestured behind them vaguely. "For saving me," he explained. "From the cave-in."

Aedan could not help but laugh, the cachinnation echoing off the solid walls. Castor flinched back, and Fiona whipped around with her torch causing Bas to screech in protest. Aedan tried to feel sorry for frightening them, but he just couldn't. "*You* wanted to thank *me?*" he said when he began to be able to control his breath. "You already saved my sister *and* me on our journey to Argos, *and* you saved us just a moment ago when that woman almost screamed at us to death. Not to mention you also invited us on your journey at all. *Also*, not to mention that you are my closest friend, so there is no fathomable reason why I would not have pulled you away from there regardless." He clapped a hand on Castor's shoulder, who looked quite stunned at all that he had just said.

"That is very touching," Fiona said through gritted teeth, "but can we just try *not* to cause another cave-in?"

Aedan felt blood rush to his face as he gave Castor a meaningful smile and squeezed his shoulder once more before they continued on their way.

They slept when they could, choosing to do so in larger caverns as much as possible so they could situate themselves as far out of the way as they could from the walkways lest someone or some*thing* stumble upon them. They slept in shifts as well as in total darkness to save on precious torchlight. Whoever's shift it was though, was sure to keep a flintleaf ready in case they heard something and needed to light a torch to see.

Aedan knew he was a very imposing person, knew his size could be terrifying to some, but sitting in the complete darkness of the mountains made him feel smaller and weaker than he ever had. At night, he sat against the wall with an axe in one hand and a flintleaf in the other, ready to strike it and drop it on the ready torch below to provide enough light to fight whatever came upon them. Each sound in the caves echoed throughout them all - a light, steady drip of water sounding from somewhere was enough to set him on edge. He tried not to imagine other sounds, but occasionally he would think he heard the scuttle of something with more than two legs clacking through a tunnel or a quiet, unintelligible whispering in the distance. Still, he remained stoically poised with his axe and leaf, ready to face anything that may come.

He only knew that when it was his turn to sleep, he had more trouble than ever. Sleep did not come easily when every sound, real or illusory, was a potential threat to their lives.

Sleep or no, time went on, and they continued moving through the tunnels at a quick, but comfortable pace. Thanks to Eos, they had plenty of threpsiberries to eat, and still some hardtack for substance, but their water rations were running worryingly low. The berries had juice in them at least but not enough to fully quench their thirst should they run out of water completely. While Aedan was busy worrying over that thought, the light from Fiona's torch suddenly went out as if it were extinguished instead of burning out on its own.

"What - " Aedan began but was shushed by Fiona before he could finish. Then, he saw it.

There was a bend up ahead, and Aedan saw it even though the torch was out. There was *light*.

But it wasn't sunlight. No, this light was an odd, blue color, deep as though the tunnel was underwater. But no, the light was too still for it to be water. Castor looked to Fiona and then Aedan and nodded. With his spear out and ready, he moved ahead of them and led the way.

They crept as quietly as they possibly could - even Bas helpfully kept his beak shut as they stole down the tunnel towards the mysterious light.

When they finally came around the corner, they saw it. An enormous cavern stretched out before them held up by natural stone pillars that rose hundreds of feet to the ceiling above them. They were on a cliff high above the cave floor and looking down into the main area of the cavern, Aedan saw a city unlike any he had ever dreamt of. A city made entirely of stone, seemingly carved straight from the cave itself, dominated the clearing. Some buildings rose up several stories, some stood isolated from the others, and at the very back, there was a *massive* façade carved straight into the stone wall with an equally massive set of stone doors that led inside. And off to the right of the city, a large waterfall splashed from above down into a large pool that glowed with the same cerulean light as the rest of the cavern.

The blue light they saw came from thousands of intertwining veins of some kind of luminescent ore that stretched throughout the walls and buildings of the city. The strange azure glow gave the city a sense of magic and mystery. It was mesmerizing.

"Whoa," Castor said. Bas squawked in agreement.

Snapping himself out of his sense of awe, Aedan looked at the direction he was pointing and saw only one tunnel close to where his finger indicated. The cave through which they needed to go sat down past the outskirts of the glowing city near the cascading waterfall. "That must be the tunnel we need," he said aloud.

"Wait," Fiona said. "Did Eos not tell us a story of a lost city in the Roinn?"

Aedan remembered then, and he nodded. "'Dark Sidhe lurk around every corner'," he recited.

"That was just a story, though, right?" Castor said hopefully. "They were just saying that to frighten us before; I am sure of it."

Aedan was not so sure. Looking out onto the city below, there was not a soul in sight. Whoever used to live here was long gone, Aedan suspected. Perhaps murdered by dark Sidhe, a small part of his mind thought. "Either way," he said, "we must continue onward. It will not do us any good to sit up here and worry. Eos said this was the path we must take - "

"Well then by all means, let us do whatever *Eos* says," Castor hissed. He began looking around the edge of the cliff they were on probably to see if there was a safe way down.

Aedan had noticed that since they'd met, Castor really seemed to have an aversion to the half-elf. "We *did* hire them to be our guide," retorted Aedan defensively. "Why do you dislike them so?"

"Because *you* - " Castor began before freezing. "Why do *you* like them so? You only just met!"

Aedan stepped back, stunned by the implication. "Just *what* are you insinuating?" he asked back, his voice rising. "I was, admittedly, interested in Eos's heritage; but that is all! I am not *fond* of Eos in any sort of way. I like - " But then his voice stopped short. He felt blood rush to his head so quickly, he almost fell over from dizziness.

"What?" Castor responded, his voice lowering.

Aedan found he had no air in his lungs nor the capability to speak whatsoever all of a sudden. Even if he could speak, Aedan realized he had no idea what he'd been about to say.

Castor stared at him quietly with a strange look in his eyes. Aedan fumbled for some way to finish the sentence he'd started, but he couldn't.

Fiona rolled her eyes then and walked forward. "As important as I'm sure this is, can we do this when we are *not* in a cave of death filled with creatures from another realm who most likely want nothing more than to make us their next meal? Priorities, gentlemen." She strode forward, shaking her head as she went.

Aedan released a gust of air he had not realized he had been holding and followed Fiona to the ledge.

"Look, there are stairs over there," she said. She pointed farther on down the cliff where there was indeed a set of stairs carved into the wall that led down to the cavern floor below. She gave each of them an amused but also somehow withering look before continuing down the path.

Aedan trailed behind her averting his eyes to the ground.

$\bigstar$. + . $\bigstar$. + . $\bigstar$

"What was that back there, anyway?" Ophelia asked Eos as they continued making good time on their path. "You said before that it was not human."

"The girl?" Eos responded. "She was not human. That was an example of a Sidhe turning dark from being without the magic of their normal environment - a banshee is what she is called."

"Oh, *that* was a banshee?" Ophelia had heard of the creatures before, but she had always heard that they were not dangerous themselves - that their wails only heralded the impending doom of someone, not literally ripped them apart. "She was much deadlier than any story I had ever been told," she said as she examined her cuts in the torchlight. Hers were mostly superficial, but she remembered the long gash that ran up Castor's arm. How much longer would they have survived her scream before they were all torn to pieces, she thought with a shiver.

"Are your injuries causing you any discomfort?" Eos stopped as they turned and looked her arms over in the waning light. They would have to light a new torch soon; Ophelia hoped Eos still had plenty left. "May I?" they asked as they gestured to her arms. She nodded and offered them out to the half-elf to inspect.

When they had started on their own path after the banshee had separated them from the rest of their group, Eos had tended to her wounds with a strange, thick liquid they had poured from a clay bottle that hung from a loop on their belt. There were several other bottles on the loop, and Ophelia wondered what they held. The medicine from the first, though, stopped her bleeding almost immediately when Eos applied it to the wounds.

Now that they were examining her wounds again, she was feeling much calmer than directly after being attacked by a terrifying Sidhe woman. She felt their hands as they traced gently over her scabbing cuts and listened to them mutter to themselves about how good they were healing. Their fingertips were callused from drawing a bowstring regularly, but their touch was extremely gentle. The care they took with her made gooseflesh rise on her skin, but Eos did not seem to notice.

When they were satisfied that Ophelia was healing appropriately, they offered her a polite smile before asking if she was ready to continue. She nodded and walked beside them as they went.

"So," Eos began, their voice careful, "why is it the Lady of Argos has left her city, if it is not too much to ask?"

Ophelia sighed. She told herself that she was upset with Castor for dragging her into this mess. Even though he had tried to apologize - and she *knew* he was sincere - she still felt a good deal of resentment inside herself. "That other Odessan?" she started. "He is my closest friend. He came to visit after not seeing each other for over a year, but he came with two friends I had never met. They were both Maechans, and, as I am sure you know, they were not supposed to be in Odessa for that. Anyway, when one of them was caught, we had to free them. Well, we were seen doing so, and we had to run." Ophelia cursed herself. She would not have gone with Castor had she known that the guards would have been murdered when they arrived. She only went with him because she thought she might have been able to use her position in the city to assuage the guards to let the Maechan go. Everything rapidly devolved after that.

"You begrudge your friend for this?" Eos asked with an innocent look.

Ophelia really wanted to say yes, but when they asked, she began to look deeper into her feelings. "I do not know how to feel," she said finally. She didn't know why, but she felt like she could open up to them. Maybe because none of the last few days had even felt *real* to her, so it almost didn't feel like she was even divulging her feelings to any real person at all. "I keep telling myself that I fault Cas for pulling me along with him, but ..."

Eos said nothing and just let her work through her words on her own.

"But honestly, I am not angry with him," she said with a long exhale. She took a heavy breath again as though admitting this was quite laboring - and to *her*, it was. "Honestly, I have never felt more alive than I have these last few days."

Eos beamed at her, their white teeth straight and beautiful framed in their lips.

"What?" she asked with a shy smile.

Eos shook their head, their tousled white hair revealing even more of their long, pointed ears. "I am glad you are enjoying yourself," was all they said.

Castor and Aedan had not said much since the cliff, but Fiona didn't mind. It was probably better that way, anyway, seeing as they were about to begin traipsing through an abandoned underground city that may or may not be filled with dark Sidhe. And if the dark Sidhe here were anything like that woman from before, Fiona thought it would be much better if they stayed silent.

Fiona led the way with her trusty falcon perched on her shoulder, the familiar sharpness of his talons giving her a sense of peace in the treacherous cave. She tried to stay on the peripheries of the city, hoping that the dangerous creatures stayed only near the heart so that they could skirt by the fringes without incident. She tried to keep her eyes on the tunnel on the other side of the cavern, but she could not help but gaze deeper, past the small stone buildings into the deep sapphire glow of the city.

As they went, she wondered who might have lived here and how long ago it was when they did. Before Eos, she had never heard of the lost city under the mountain or of anyone really who had ever tried to live here. Their own village, Albainn, nestled in a small nook between the western Roinn and the Undying Sea, but none of the people that she knew from Albainn ever ventured too deep into the mountains. Though she'd never heard of any entrance into the underground near Albainn reaching *this* depth.

Even from this distance, the cacophony of the waterfall masked the sounds of their feet, which was a relief. Although, as they got closer and closer to the waterfall and their exit, Fiona began to hear something other than the crashing water. Something soft and rhythmic. Flowy and melodic.

Fiona reached out a cautionary hand and gestured towards the sound. "Do you hear that?" she whispered.

They stopped and focused. Nodding, Aedan said, "It sounds like ..."

"Singing," he and Castor said together after which, they both looked at each other briefly before looking away.

Fiona rolled her eyes. "All in favor of not following the eerie singing voice into the city of evil faeries?"

They both nodded fervently.

"Good," she said. But before she could turn back around, Bas flew off her shoulder and after the mysterious song.

"Bas!" And without thinking, Fiona ran into the city.

She could barely keep up with him and almost lost him twice in the dim azure glow. Still, she ran, trying not to run into any of the barren buildings as she went, faintly noticing that the melody was drawing nearer and nearer. There were no words to the song, only a low feminine voice beautifully singing her mesmerizing tune. It echoed off the quiet buildings only competing for attention with the waterfall in the distance.

After turning down a different alleyway for the hundredth time, she finally did lose him. When she stopped suddenly, she was struck solidly in the back by what felt like a horse-drawn carriage. She yelped and crashed to the ground with a large lump of flesh on top of her.

"Sorry," said Aedan as he scrambled to get back up off of her. "I didn't know you were going to st - "

"Shh!" shushed Fiona manically as she regained her footing. Castor and Aedan looked panicked and ready for battle. She stood still and listened. But only the waterfall rang in her ears.

The song was gone.

Suddenly, she was hyperaware of the fact that they were deep in the haunted city, and that *something* was on the loose. And that it probably heard her when she had cried out moments before. And that it was probably on its way to come find them. And that whatever it was had Bas.

They were almost out, according to Eos. Only one more day of trudging through the endless tunnels and Ophelia would finally be able to breathe some fresh air again. Oh, how she missed fresh air. And the sun. And the trees. And the little birds that flew around and sang little melodies to each other.

Eos was not bad company to keep, though. The half-elf talked quite regularly to fill the silence and often about more scary stories and legends that they had heard. And Ophelia trusted their skill with a bow after they'd picked off several overgrown spiders that populated the caves over the course of their journey. Ophelia did not mind spiders usually, but she was used to the *normal* kind of spiders. The ones that silently scamper around the corners of her estate that could effortlessly be squished with a quick slap of the hand. *These* spiders, on the other hand, were easily the length of her forearm at the smallest. She had not yet seen one that was much bigger than that, but Eos happily informed her that they *do* in fact get *much* larger.

She hoped she would just be able to take their word for it.

Still, all the creepy stories they had been sharing was almost starting to get to her, though she would never admit it. Instead, she shared her own ghost story to add to Eos's many.

She told them of Ol' Maj who had fallen down the stairs and broken her neck in the Patera estate many years ago. Ol' Maj's pale ghost had been allegedly seen by many servants and residents of the estate floating down the hallways, her neck always bent at an odd angle. One servant even said that he tried to talk to Ol' Maj's spirit, and that when she had tried to respond, it only came out as hisses and croaks of pain. Ophelia herself had never seen Ol' Maj, but there were times when candles would light themselves or doors would be knocked on with no one on the other side.

Eos regaled her of the story of a village in the Yuki Isles near the country of Midoria. The village was small and the people friendly. They all worked hard every day and came home to their loving families. Then, one day, from a nearby tear in the veil came a woman. A woman with long white hair that dragged across the snow and with eyes of red like blood. Her feet left no prints in the fresh snows of the valley as she wandered around the outskirts of the village. Someone saw her and rushed to help the stranded woman, but when they got to her, she bit their neck with fangs like a snake. And then she disappeared, never to be seen again. The confused villager went back into town afterwards and went about their day, sure they had just had some wild dream. But when they went to sleep that night, something changed. They woke and did not remember who they were or who anyone else was. Only one thing mattered to them anymore. Blood. They went on a massacre, biting everyone in sight, killing some and turning others to become like themselves. By dawn, everyone in the village was dead.

"Wait," Ophelia said. "If everyone died, how do people know what happened?"

Eos chuckled. "It is just a story. Do not put so much weight on it."

They stopped then because they both suddenly noticed that the terrain had changed. They were no longer standing on solid ground but in mushy, slick mud. It was only a few inches deep, but it was enough to suck their feet down and make walking more difficult.

"Oh," Ophelia said with a look of distaste at the torchlit floor.

Still, they trudged on and into a wide cavern - the widest Ophelia had seen yet. She was just barely able to make out the tunnel on the other side of the opening past a multitude of spearing stalagmites. The thick, earthy smell of mud permeated the room.

Eos sighed, not looking too pleased about the prospect of crossing the cavern. They moved on nevertheless, but just a few paces in, the mud deepened to their shins. Each step was a battle from there, both of them helping the other with every move.

Then, the torch died out.

"For the love of - "

"It is all right," Eos soothed. "We still have a few more left. Let me find one and get it going."

Ophelia stood in the darkness slightly annoyed that neither of them had not noticed the torchlight getting low. She could hear Eos rustling around in their pack, but she heard another noise - distant, but definitely in the same room.

The sucking sound of a footstep in the mud.

An unnatural coldness seeped into Aedan's bones as they stood silently waiting for some sign of where the mysterious singer was. Aedan had not heard Bas's familiar screeches either. He hoped the bird was all right for Fiona's sake.

"My, my, my," a hissing voice echoed, deepening the iciness in Aedan's veins. "I hear a little mouse in my city. Do come out and play."

Aedan heard Fiona growl angrily under her breath, but he cast a warning look to her.

She shook her head at him and whispered, "I have a plan. You two hide in one of these buildings, and I will draw her here."

"We do not even know what she is!" Castor responded. "I do not think it is a good idea. We can just try to sneak up on her - "

He stopped as they heard something moving down a path a few buildings over. Whatever it was did not walk on two legs; the sound they heard was more of a *dragging* sound, like someone hauling an enormous burlap sack on the ground behind them. Aedan saw that the other two looked as terrified as he felt.

"I can *smell* you," the woman's voice taunted in a singsong voice.

"*Get inside!*" Fiona hissed at them, pointing to the broken door of a nearby building.

Aedan hated the plan, but he could not think of anything else on such short notice. He nodded at Castor, and they clamored through the small doorway and into what used to be someone's home by the looks of it. A long stone table with chairs to match dominated the center of the room. An empty hearth was in the back of the room that appeared to have not been used in many years. Everything was covered in a heavy layer of dust.

"I am here!" Fiona's voice roared from outside. Aedan felt adrenaline begin to rush through his arms as he gripped his axes with steely fervor.

"Oh, how brave!" the voice called back. "The mouse cannot wait to play!" The dragging sound quickened as it got closer and closer.

"Holy sh - " Fiona took several paces back, looking upwards at whatever had just rounded the corner. Aedan could hardly stand still, but he knew if he ran out now, the element of surprise would be broken.

"Now, now," the susurrating voice interrupted. "What kind of greeting is that to the queen of the city in which you are trespassing?"

"Wh - What are you?" Fiona breathed. The dragging sound slowly got closer to where Aedan and Castor stood - muscles tensed, ready to spring.

"Little mouse," the woman said. "I told you: I am the queen of this city. You would do well to remember that."

"Where is my falcon?" Fiona said in a voice that may have been meant to sound strong and demanding, but instead came out as small and scared.

"Oh, was that your pet? Well, it is mine now. You need not worry; it will not suffer. I cannot say the same for *you*."

Fiona grumbled something Aedan couldn't hear before he saw her stoop to gather and throw a good-sized stone down the alley. It connected with something.

"You *vile* little mouse! How dare you!" the voice sibilated. "You will regret - "

Fiona threw another stone.

The woman only screamed in pure fury before chasing down the alleyway. As soon as Aedan saw movement, he burst outside and swung both of his axes over his head and down in one fluid motion. They sank deep into something huge and scaled. Finally taking in what it was, he wrenched his axes back.

The thing cried out in a mixture of a scream and a hiss as it rounded on Aedan. Her face was nearly human, though it had some very snake-like characteristics - she had two slits instead of a nose and fangs that dripped with toxic venom. Her back was scaled, though she had human-shaped arms and shoulders, and she wore a golden bodice that covered her serpentine underbelly. Instead of legs, the creature had an *enormous* tail covered in deep, fiery red scales and appeared to be scarred from many battles. A glowing blue pendant hung delicately from her neck.

She lashed out with the back of her hand, *lifting* Aedan from the ground and throwing him down the alley, where he rolled several times before coming to a painful stop. He dropped his axes somewhere along the way, but he hopped back up, telling himself to feel the pain later and just focus on keeping Fiona and Castor safe.

But the snake-woman was slithering towards him. She was so fast, he hardly had time to raise his arms as she struck him again, this time into the solid side of a building. He didn't feel anything break, but he definitely could not just ignore the pain of that hit. He let out an injured moan as he struggled to push himself up.

He managed to get back to his feet in time to see Castor get a hand on the end of her tail where Aedan's axes cut into. His eyes flashed red as the cuts Aedan had made instantly grew to encompass the circumference of her tail, severing it from the rest of her with a sanguine spray.

She howled in agony and crawled away using her clawed hands to help pull her along. A trail of blood, black in the blue light of the city, followed her as she wriggled around the corner she came from. Castor and Fiona nodded at each other and Aedan and ran after the trail. Aedan gathered his axes and followed them, albeit a little more slowly.

✦ .   +   . ✦ .   +   . ✦

"Did you hear that?" Ophelia whispered anxiously. She was sure she had just heard the sound of someone else walking in the mud somewhere in the room.

Eos quickened their search for a torch without answering. Ophelia felt her hair rise on the back of her neck as though she was being watched. She cast her eyes around, but she only saw darkness.

188 | MICHAEL JACE

Another sucking step from the opposite direction sounded.

"*Eos*," Ophelia whispered urgently, gently tugging their shirt sleeve.

"Almost," was all they said. Suddenly, a crackle and a flash startled Ophelia, and then a torch was lit, its fire blazing up to illuminate their surroundings. They swiveled around wildly, trying to see what it was that was in the cavern with them. But nothing seemed out of the ordinary. Only a multitude of muddy stalagmites that stabbed out of the ground, their flickering shadows dancing like demons in the fire's light.

"I know I heard something," Ophelia said, mostly to herself. She stared long and hard in the direction the first sound had come from. The stalagmites were like a forest of stone, most of them in a conical shape, though one stood out to her—it was more rounded at the top and had two strange lumps below the tip. As she swept her gaze around, she saw more and more of those oddly shaped stalagmites. *Perhaps that is just how they grow here in these mountains,* she thought in an attempt to assuage her fears.

"Carry the torch, please," Eos said quietly. Ophelia grabbed it hastily as Eos removed the bow from their chest and kept an arrow ready in their hand. "Let us move onward," they said to her. "Be very cautious. Tell me if you see *anything* out of the ordinary."

Ophelia nodded obediently and watched every stalagmite with a keen eye, holding the torch like she usually would hold her rapier when in her fencing lessons. She had never used a torch as a weapon, but she was sure if she jabbed something in the face with it, it would be about as effective as her rapier at dissuading something from getting too close to her. Though she really did wish she had her sword with her now. She did not have the desire to be a soldier as Castor did, but she still felt safer when she was holding the hilt in her hand. Hopefully, when (and if) they got out of the mountains, she could purchase a blade from a smith in Trícnoc. But for now, she would make do with the torch if necessary.

PHANTOM FIRE | 189

She heard a step behind them. She whirled with the torch but saw nothing too strange. Though the tip of one of those odd-shaped stalagmites was sagging forward a little, dripping mud. She had not remembered any of them bent far enough forward for the mud to succumb to the gravity and actually fall off.

"Do you see something?" Eos whispered.

Ophelia kept quiet and continued to stare hard at the stalagmite. Something was familiar about the way it was shaped, but she just could not think of why. As she stared at it, wondering what was so familiar about it, the top part of it jerked up.

It was a *face*. It was not a stalagmite at all, but something *very* human-shaped covered completely in mud. The thick, brownish-black gunk flew back as the thing's head snapped up, spattering the wall behind it and seeping into empty eye sockets. The thing wrenched forward with awful jerking steps.

Ophelia couldn't even scream. Eos had seen it, too, and loosed an arrow at it. It pierced into the mud person with a sick sound like a knife stabbing into an overripe tomato. But it continued forward nonetheless.

"Go," Eos said.

Ophelia didn't need to be told twice. She went as fast as she could, though the mud pulled at her legs as though trying to pull her down and make her like one of *them*. She could hear the sound of arrows blasting past the wood of the bow behind her, but when she looked back, she saw it was futile. Whatever these things were did not seem to be bothered by Eos's arrows. They staggered towards them with their twitching, lurching movements.

Then, Ophelia tripped. Her foot had stepped on the edge of something solid but squishy under the mud, and now she was on her hands and knees over it, the torch still in her titan's grip with the flame sticking out over the mud.

The thing under her moved.

Something - a hand - snaked out and latched on to her shoulder. It pulled on her trying to bring her down to it, but her elbows were locked. Her breathing was panicked and her muscles frozen. She was too terrified to do anything but watch as the thing used her to pull itself up. A mud-covered face with eye sockets filled with the stuff broke the surface of the mud. Its jaw was completely missing with only a few of their top teeth jutting down like black daggers.

But it was not just the arm that was pulling her down. Ophelia swore she could feel the mud itself pulling her arms and legs down into it.

A booted foot came out of nowhere and swiped the pulling append-age clean off the mud person. Warm arms descended upon her and ripped her from the mud. She yelped in protest before seeing it was Eos. She thanked them silently, but now that the terror had faded, she still had a score to settle with that thing that tripped her and tried to bring her down with it.

She broke free of Eos's grasp and used her momentum to crush the mud person's skull under her sandals. Whatever they were, their bones weren't very sturdy, Ophelia thought. Still, they needed to move. More of those things were moving, coming out of the mud like the living dead rising from the ground. Luckily, they seemed quite slow. But there were still the ones in between them and the exit that they needed to worry about.

The mud people came at them from all sides from around stalagmites and from the creeping mud with arms that reached with spasming fin-gers. Eos and Ophelia swiped bow and torch through extending limbs as they went, cleaving a path through the gruesome cavern.

It somehow seemed like both an eternity and a single second at one time, but either way, they were finally on the other side. Ophelia whipped around with her torch and Eos with their bow, but in the light of the fire, there was nothing that stood out in the cavern. It was still filled with mud, and there were still stalagmites everywhere. But there were none of those *things* in sight. It was just a silent cavern.

Eos's soft whisper barely reached Ophelia's ears. "The mountains are more alive than I believed them to be."

PHANTOM FIRE | 191

Ophelia looked to her companion, and they both shared a shudder before running away from the room as fast as their legs could take them.

✦ . + . ✦ . + . ✦

Fiona felt a fire in her she had never felt before. Her muscles pumped with adrenaline as she led the way, chasing after the thick, viscous trail of blood left by the snake-woman. Later, she would wonder why she was leading the charge as she was the only one of the three without a weapon. But now, she only thought of Bas. And her fury made her braver than any blade could.

They tore past building after building following the winding path of blood before finally coming to an opening in front of the great stone doors that led deeper into the mountain. This area must have been a place of importance in times past, Fiona thought. The buildings were much larger and more-skillfully carved than others they had seen, and they were built in a semicircle away from the doors, leaving a huge clearing between them. The stone floor there was carved with intricate, flowing designs and symbols that seemed to hold some kind of significance, though Fiona could only wonder. A large stone basin sat in the middle of the area, the inside stained black.

Looking away, Fiona saw that the trail of blood ended near the doors. The woman seemed to have gathered two enormous claymores, both hewn from the same glowing ore that lit the city, and she rose up on what was left of her tail in a terrifying, imposing warning. But Fiona hardly noticed that at all. And roosted on a great pile of bones that cluttered the right side of the doors was Bas, sleeping peacefully.

He was still alive.

"Foolish humans," the woman said. "My lovely tail shall regrow in time, but your heads never will." She slowly began closing the gap between them, though Fiona could tell it pained her to move on her severed tail. "I shall rip the flesh from your body and suck the marrow from your bones. And when I am finished with you, you will be added to my collection of trespassers," she said. Fiona's eyes flashed towards the jumbled mess of bones.

Fiona had no time for the "queen" and her rambling. Gathering a fist-sized stone from the ground, Fiona launched it at her. The queen swatted the stone away with her sword, and with a roar, she coiled before lurching toward her.

But Aedan and Castor were there, each meeting the queen's blades with their own, deflecting each blow with perfect synchronization. Using the moment of distraction, Fiona darted past the woman and to the pile of bones where Bas slept.

"Bas!" she called as she got closer. "Bas, wake up!" She slid to where he stood and patted him gently on the head.

The sea falcon twitched away before opening his eyes and seeing his master's worried eyes on him. "Oh, thank the Allmother you are all right," Fiona sobbed as she held the bird to her chest.

Bas squawked in protest as he tried to escape her embrace. But Fiona held on for another moment anyway, welcoming the annoyed bites and pecks she had become so accustomed to receiving. Finally, she released him, and he puffed out his chest in aggravation.

Then, Fiona remembered the fight. "Bas, we need your help," she said as he took his place on her arm. And without another word, Fiona ran back to the fray, sure that Bas had understood what she meant.

As she rejoined Aedan and Castor, she sent out her falcon with a thrust of her arm. Aedan seemed not to be doing too well. He was moving slower than usual for some reason, Fiona noticed. Castor did not seem to have any problem keeping up with the glowing swords that struck all around as the queen slithered to and fro.

"Hey!" Fiona shouted, garnering the queen's attention for just a moment. But a moment was all Bas needed.

He swooped down with claws like daggers and dug them deep into the woman's eyes. She howled in agony as she violently swung her swords about. Castor moved to block one of the jerking blades only to have his spear wrenched from his grip. It landed near Fiona, but Castor seemed to have abandoned it as smoke began to filter through his tunic and his eyes changed to red.

PHANTOM FIRE | 193

The queen dropped a sword to swat the bird away from her face, but the damage had been done. What was once her eyes, was now a bloody mess of ravaged tissue. Bas flew back to Fiona's shoulder and all four of them kept absolutely still and quiet as the blinded serpentine queen hissed and sobbed.

Could they escape now? She could not see them, so perhaps they would be able to get away without injury, Fiona hoped.

Her hopes were quickly dashed, however, as their opponent, quick as lightning, gathered her fallen claymore and, in a sweeping motion, slashed both of the blades horizontally in front of her. Castor barely managed to evade it, falling flat on his stomach just in time for the azure blade to slice through the air. Aedan only succeeded in bringing his axes up to deflect the blow, but the force of it threw him back, far from the fight.

Fiona quickly retrieved Castor's spear as Bas flew off to sink his claws and beak into all the soft spots he could find on the scaled woman. Castor appeared to be trying to get close enough to use his mark, but he was kept at bay by the violent slicing of the swords. Seeing an opening, Fiona rushed in and thrusted Castor's spear deep into the queen's underarm.

She dropped the sword in that hand as she jerked the other down over her head. Fiona left the spear where it was as she dove out of the way in time for the claymore to bury itself in the carved stone right where she had been standing.

Castor managed to get into arm's reach and get a hand on the queen's tail while she was distracted. Fiona saw the red in his eyes deepen as the blood from the woman's severed tail began to roil and bubble as though it was being boiled.

She screamed and choked and shuddered, and Fiona took the opportunity to wrench Castor's spear free from its place and deliver a lethal blow to the woman's chest. Dropping her other sword, the queen's body spasmed vigorously as she slowly crumped down to the stone floor with one final hiss.

Fiona fell back to the ground on her hands with an exhausted breath.

Aedan approached them with a new limp and said, "I am quite tired of being thrown around." Then, he looked to the bloodied mess of the queen. "Good riddance."

"What *is* she, anyway?" Fiona asked no one in particular.

"I think that was a naga," Castor answered. "I have heard stories of them - snake-like beings who have the ability to charm animals with their song - but I never thought them to actually exist."

"Do you think she was the only one here?" Aedan wondered aloud.

The three of them looked between each other anxiously before silently agreeing to flee the city as quickly and as quietly as possible. Before they left, Fiona was sure to grab that glowing pendant from the queen's neck.

At the northern edge of the city, they came across another problem. One not so dangerous as a sword-wielding snake beast, but one just as harrowing. The tunnel that they had originally decided was the most northern was no longer alone. A second had appeared next to the first - or perhaps it had *always* been there, Fiona thought. She cast her mind's eye back, trying to remember how many tunnels she had seen before, but the nerves from the battle with the naga were clouding her thoughts.

"Perfect," Castor muttered as they stood in front of the two gaping paths. "Any idea which is more north?"

"Do *you?*" Aedan asked Castor suddenly.

"What?" he responded.

"Back at the cave-in when we were separated, Eos said you may be able to guide us through since you've been touched by the Allmother."

Hope sparked in Fiona's chest, though Castor looked worried and uncomfortable. Still, he agreed to try - probably for lack of options, Fiona thought.

He closed his eyes, his eyebrows furrowing in concentration.

Fiona looked to Aedan who was staring hard at Castor. Despite the trepidation she felt, Aedan did not seem as concerned. His gaze was more one of wonderment than one of worry. *He must really trust Castor,* Fiona thought to herself.

After a long silence, Fiona whispered, "How long is this supposed to take?"

"Left," Castor announced which brought a wide smile on Aedan's face.

"You're sure?" Fiona asked not unkindly.

He rubbed his brow wincing. "Not definite, but it does seem more *right.* Well, it's left, so not *right* right, but not wrong, just left. And right." The look on his face showed that he realized how little sense he was making. "In any case, if it turns out that I actually *don't* know what I am doing - which I still posit as the most likely case - we can just turn around and use the other."

It made sense to Fiona until Aedan chimed in with, "Unless it closes back up or moves or does whatever it is they apparently do when we aren't looking."

It was quiet for a moment until Fiona broke the silence with the idea that any decision is better than none. "Left it is!" She began marching into the left tunnel with the other two at her heels.

14

Gilded Leaves

After just one day under the Roinn Mountains, Ophelia could not help but wonder what it would be like to see the sun again. To feel its gentle embrace kissing her skin as its filtered rays penetrated the midday clouds. After an entire week underground, Ophelia thought she would go mad without it warming her bones.

But when she discovered that it was nighttime when they finally emerged from the mountains, she sighed with not a small amount of exasperation.

"What is it?" Eos asked.

Ophelia closed her eyes and felt the night breeze pass over her. "It is nothing," she responded finally. "I just miss the sun."

Eos smiled at her peacefully.

When Ophelia opened her eyes again, she plopped down on a large rock nearby taking in the scenery of the foreign land for the first time. Everything here was so ... *green*, Ophelia noticed. Of course, the trees and grass in Odessa were also green, but the green here just seemed so much deeper and so much more beautifully so. Rolling hills stretched out ahead, and Ophelia saw that quaint little houses dotted the sides of several to the north before opening up to a larger settlement. It was not as imposing as Argos was, Ophelia thought, but still respectable in size.

"That is Trícnoc," said Eos, answering her unspoken question as they joined Ophelia on the rock. "Second settlement to be established in the country of Maecha after Letha. And your destination."

"Right," Ophelia said, remembering. "They only hired you to get them to Trícnoc." She fidgeted with a lock of her hair. "Does that mean you are to return to Argos now?"

Eos inspected their hands with a sudden fascination. "I mean, I do not necessarily *need* to return to Argos. There is nothing there that ties me down."

Ophelia felt a little jump in her stomach. "I see."

Eos continued to examine their fingernails with scrutiny.

"So, if you did *not* return to Argos," Ophelia drew out slowly, "where do you think you might go?" She stared at the lock of hair between her fingers nervously.

Eos was quiet for what seemed like an eternity to Ophelia. "That is a good question," they responded finally. "Perhaps - "

Before they could finish, Ophelia noticed that two people were approaching them from the north. Ophelia and Eos both stood, and Eos gripped their bow firmly in their hand.

When the two strangers were close enough to see that Eos was armed, they put their hands in front of them in a show of peace. It was one man and one woman, and they were both dressed quite similarly - in the faded brown of the common folk. Each also had a small red key tattooed under their ears.

"Hail," the man said cautiously. "We mean you no harm, adventurers."

The woman nodded in agreement. "We received word of someone passing through the mountains. An Odessan. A man with eyes of red and a mark on his chest. He was seen traveling with two Maechans as well."

Ophelia's breath caught in her throat. What did they want with Castor? How did they hear about him?

"But we see now that neither of you fit that description," the man said. "We apologize for bothering you and wish you well on your way."

198 | MICHAEL JACE

They departed as suddenly as they arrived, leaving Ophelia and Eos alone in stunned silence.

"Is that something we should be worried about?" Ophelia asked the half-elf.

"Were they speaking of your friend?" Eos asked. Ophelia nodded. "Well, they were unarmed, and there were only two of them. I believe that your three companions would be able to handle themselves if those two *did* wish them harm."

Ophelia let out a small breath of air. *They did seem sincere,* she thought. Though still, something about them seemed off. What would happen when Castor *did* emerge from the mountains?

She shook off that thought. Eos was right - Castor would be able to handle himself if the need arose.

"I shall wait with you in Trícnoc until you are reunited with your companions," Eos said, breaking Ophelia away from her thoughts.

She felt the flutter return to her chest and smiled gratefully. "You have my thanks." But she couldn't help herself. "And after we are reunited? What will you do then?"

Eos smiled back at her. "I suppose we will see when that time comes."

◆ . + . ◆ . + . ◆

It was a good thing Fiona had decided to take that glowing necklace from the naga, Castor thought to himself when he fumbled in his pack for their last torch only to find he had miscounted and had just burnt out their last one. So, instead, they pressed on with Fiona and her sapphire glow to guide them.

Every step into the left tunnel made Castor doubt more and more of his choice. Back in the city cavern when he'd closed his eyes to try to sense the right path, he'd only barely felt the *wrongness* that the right tunnel brought. It was a sensation he wasn't sure he'd be able to describe later if asked, but he'd had to go with his instincts. Maybe once they were out safely - *if* they made it out safely - he would try to figure out more of this secondary ability.

After they had all gotten a few hours of rest following their fight with the naga, Aedan had seemed to be moving at a slower and slower pace as they went. When Castor and Fiona noticed him falling behind on more than one occasion, Castor asked him what was wrong.

"It is nothing," Aedan said, averting his gaze.

"It was the naga, wasn't it?" Fiona inquired. "She did hit you pretty hard a few times. Does it hurt to walk?"

"I am fine," he said firmly. "Let us just continue on already. I will keep up."

Castor and Fiona shared a look, but they said nothing more on the subject. When they began to push on through the tunnel, Castor wordlessly moved to Aedan's side, grabbed his arm, and put it over his shoulder. He held it there with one hand on Aedan's wrist and the other around his side to keep him stable. At first, he felt Aedan's muscles tighten, but they soon eased as Aedan allowed Castor to bear some of his weight.

Being this close to Aedan, feeling his heartbeat in his wrist, feeling the strong muscles of his body shift with each breath and every step, Castor could not help but let his mind drift back to their conversation on the cliffside over the underground city.

Just what *are you insinuating?* Aedan had said to him. *I am* not *fond of Eos in any sort of way. I like -*

And then he had abruptly cut himself off. *Who* was Aedan about to say? Castor knew what he *wanted* Aedan to have said, but he knew that was not the case. After all, Aedan had called Castor his "closest friend" - surely, he did not think of Castor in *that* way. Perhaps he almost said that he thought he may like Ophelia and thought that Castor may not approve. Or maybe with their year-long training with Teacher, maybe Aedan had deeper feelings for Branwyn herself - she *was* a princess, after all.

He closed his eyes and gently shook his head at himself. It was pointless to continue on with that line of thought. For all Castor knew, Aedan could have just been about to say that he liked venison. He sighed.

"Are you all right?" Aedan said quietly, his head turned towards him.

Castor looked up into his soft green eyes, and he saw Aedan's jaw tighten in the dim light.

"Yes," Castor answered after finding his breath. "Yes, I am all right."

Over the next few days, they trudged on without incident, except for a rather large spider that skittered out in front of Fiona causing her to string out a jumbled mess of screams and curses much to the startled enjoyment of her brother.

Finally, though, when the tunnel began to widen, they had hope they were nearing the end of the mountains. It was not until they saw the welcoming red light of a dawning sun splashed on the walls of the tunnel did they begin to run. Despite their exhaustion and their sore muscles, they bounded down the rest of the way and burst out of the dark underground once and for all.

"Oh, Maecha, I have missed you so much," Fiona said as she fell face-first into the plush grasses of her homeland. Bas took off with a screech and soared high into the sky, finally able to stretch his wings.

"Maecha," Aedan whispered with a look of deep love and longing in his eyes. "It is just as I remembered it. Beautiful."

"Yes, it is," Castor responded quietly before he looked away from his companion and out at the foreign land.

From this higher vantage point, Castor could see miles off into the distance. Dawn's glow cast the hills below in a beautiful palette of color and pierced the low-lying fog that hugged the ground. A clutter of buildings, which must have been Trícnoc, consumed a few of the hills to the north. And off in the distance to the west, nearing the horizon, Castor thought he could see the creeping edge of a lush green forest.

It really was breathtaking.

"Shall we go?" Aedan asked with a content smile.

"Yes, absolutely," Fiona said scrambling to get up. "I don't know about you, but I need a bath. Actually, I *do* know about you, and you both could use one, too," she added plainly.

They laughed, but she was right. Castor felt completely filthy. With a deep breath, they started on their way again. Though they did not get far before they were stopped by two individuals dressed in brown - a man and a woman - both with a matching tattoo of a key below their right ears.

Castor's hand automatically went to the spear on his back, and he saw Aedan's hands rest on the handles of his axes strapped to his waist out of the corner of his eye.

As they approached, something changed in their expressions, and one whispered to the other excitedly.

"Greetings!" the woman said, her face filled with a strange kind of awe. "My name is Igrid, and this is Teg."

The three of them shared equally confused looks.

"Is this normal in Maecha?" Castor whispered to Aedan.

Instead of answering, Aedan said, "Hail to you. Is there something you need?"

"Did you three happen to have come from Argos?" the man - Teg - asked. "And from the west before that?"

All three remained completely silent. Though Castor could tell he looked as shocked as he felt.

"I knew it!" Igrid exclaimed joyously. "So, is it true?" she asked Castor as she fidgeted with her hands nervously. "You have been marked by the Allmother, haven't you?"

"W - What? I - " Castor was so stunned he did not know how to respond.

Aedan drew an axe. "What do the two of you want?"

Fear mingled with their total awe for just a moment before Igrid said, "Please, do not be worried! We do not wish you any ills."

"We have heard of you, Marked One," Teg continued with his empty hands in front of him, palms-first. "We have been searching for someone like you for a very long time. Please, will you join us for the Scoráneile in a week's time?"

"The what now?" Fiona asked.

"Forgive us," Teg said. "It is a feast held in honor of the Marked One. Please, won't you come?"

"Feast?" Fiona said perking up.

All three of their stomachs rumbled simultaneously.

"Yes," Igrid went on. "A feast to celebrate the Allmother and all of her gifts. Surely, you have heard of it, Marked One?"

Castor just looked to Aedan and Fiona perplexed.

"Here," Teg said as he reached his hand out. In it was a folded scrap of parchment. Castor took it cautiously. "Directions are on here. We sincerely hope you will make it - it is in your honor after all."

"There would be no celebration without you there," Igrid added.

Castor nodded. "I shall think on it."

They smiled enormously. "You are ever so gracious, Marked One," Igrid said as she bowed. When she rose, she hesitated for a moment before saying, "If it is not too much trouble to ask - might we see the mark? Just to be sure."

They both looked so incredibly desperate, Castor sighed and indulged them. He pulled the collar of his tunic down to bare his chest and summoned the mark. The familiar pain of the fire burned on his chest. He winced a little, but he was mostly accustomed to it now. The mark appeared in a blaze as it flashed on his skin.

He thought they might faint. They reached out to touch him, but Aedan stepped in between them protectively. "That is enough," he said. "The ... er ... Marked One needs respite. We make for Trícnoc to rest from our journey."

"Oh, here!" Teg said enthusiastically, holding out a small, clinking sack. "This will pay for a room for a fortnight. Please, take it. It is the least we can do."

"Oh, no," Castor said, waving him away as he let the mark sink back under his skin. "We could not possibly take your money."

The woman was almost in tears. "I beg of you - just take it, Marked One! Please, use this money to stay safe until the Scoráneile. There is nothing we want more."

Fiona snatched the money from Teg's outstretched hand. Aedan looked at her incredulously, but she only shrugged in response.

Igrid and Teg bowed low to the ground. "We are forever in your debt, Marked One. We hope to see you in a week's time," said Teg.

"Farewell," Igrid said as they turned to go.

Once they had gotten out of earshot, Castor said, "What the hell was all that about? How did they even know about me?"

Aedan shrugged. "I do not know. We should be very careful while we stay in Trícnoc."

"Why?" Fiona asked. "They obviously do not want to hurt us. Also, *feast.*"

"Something other than hardtack and threpsiberries would be welcome," Castor mumbled.

Aedan sighed. "We can decide on it later. For now, let us make for town."

It had only been three days since Ophelia and Eos had been in Trícnoc when Castor and his two friends had arrived at the local inn. Ophelia had been so relieved to see they had all made it through relatively fine that she had literally jumped for joy at the sight of their dirt-streaked faces. They all exchanged exhausted embraces before they shared their stories of what each had faced in the dark of the mountains, including their experiences with the tattooed man and woman that had greeted both parties upon their flight from the underground. Eos seemed wary of their invitation having never heard of the Scoráneile feast, but Ophelia was of the same mind as Fiona - the two individuals seemed quite keen on Castor, almost as if they held him in some kind of reverence. She doubted they wished him any harm, and if they were going to provide them a feast, who was she to deny it?

When all the stories were told, Castor, Aedan, and Fiona left to purchase a room so that they could each take turns cleaning themselves up for the meal Ophelia promised to procure with the money she had acquired from selling her fine Odessan dress and expensive jewelry days before. The silks may have been a tad unclean, but the merchant did not seem to mind as he handed her a large sack of coins that she would use to pay for a room at the inn and food to keep her and Eos full over those three days as well as some light, breathable clothes to replace the regal gown.

Fiona reappeared first and stated that Castor and Aedan had promptly fell asleep as soon as they had gotten to their room so it would probably be some time before they rejoined them.

"In that case, how about you join me today?" Ophelia asked her. "In the Roinn Mountains, I realized how much I would need a weapon should I be continuing with you all on your journey. Would you like to accompany me?"

The Maechan girl looked slightly flustered by the invitation before stammering out her confirmation. "Yes, of course," she said, pushing some hair behind her ear.

Eos, who had been mostly quiet that morning, said, "Excellent. You should visit Maeve. She is a talented smith and owns her own shop on the west side of town. I can show you the way if you would like."

Ophelia perked up at Eos's melodic voice. "We would very much appreciate that," she said. "Will you be joining us as well?"

"No, no," they responded. "I wish to look into this Scoráneile matter - to see if any of the locals know of it."

A sudden memory prodded back into Ophelia's mind then. Eos never told her whether or not they were staying now that Ophelia was reunited with her friends. A bizarre longing sank into her chest as the thought passed through her mind.

"Good idea," Fiona said, breaking Ophelia from her reverie. "The more we can learn about those strange people, the better."

Ophelia nodded in agreement. "Then let us be off. I yearn to remember the feel of a hilt in my grip."

As they exited the inn, a bird swooped down to Fiona's shoulder where it obediently perched. Ophelia had of course noticed the sea falcon before, but now that they were not running for their lives, she could stand to be in a slight awe at the young girl's ability to befriend such a majestic predator.

Eos showed them across the village and to the smithy before bowing and disappearing amongst the small buildings and passersby.

"After you," Fiona said, ushering Ophelia into the wooden building. As they came in, the falcon took off again into the skies. "Do not mind him. He is only tired of being underground for so long. I do not think he has much desire to return indoors for some time." She smiled good-naturedly.

"Hail," a woman called out from the other end of the store. She was red of hair and green of eyes as were many Maechans, though her face was streaked with black lines of soot as though she had recently wiped her face with her hands unknowingly spreading the substance around.

"Hail," Fiona responded.

"Should you need anything, I will be around," the woman, presumably Maeve, supplied vaguely. The shop itself was lined with rows of display shelves, each carrying a different weapon. There were blades and bows and axes and spears and shields and arrows and many other lethal instruments Ophelia was unfamiliar with.

"How did you manage to tame him, anyway?" Ophelia asked as they began to browse the assorted weaponry. "Your falcon, I mean."

"Oh, Bas," Fiona said, shaking her head slightly with a smile. "I found him in the woods near Endala, injured. I helped nurse him back to health under the guidance of the healer I was working with then, and he has not left me since."

Ophelia felt a pang of envy. "That is amazing," she said instead. "Out of curiosity, why the name 'Bas'? An interesting name for a bird, no?"

"It's short for bastard," Fiona said plainly.

Ophelia snorted at the unexpected response. "How lovely," she replied through stifled laughter. "What made you decide on that name?"

"When I first found him, he pecked me. *A lot.* It was difficult to call him anything else after having only called him that for several weeks. I only thought I would shorten it to save on time."

Ophelia let her laughs spill out then, causing the storeowner to poke an inquisitive glance around to them for a moment before disappearing around another weapon rack.

"Well, then I believe that name suits him very well," she said finally when she was able to speak normally again.

"So, you are a noble like Castor?" Fiona began after several moments of silence.

Ophelia nodded as she fingered the delicate metalwork of a deadly-sharp cutlass. A beautiful curling pattern was carved into the flat of the blade from hilt to tip reminding her of the way smoke swirls in still air.

"You two are not what I would have pictured Odessan nobles to be like," she said, sounding somewhat careful in her choice of words.

"How do you mean?"

"I just mean to say that you seem very kind and fair to us Maechans, which is not what most of us would expect knowing the laws of your country."

Ophelia sighed but nodded understandingly. "It's a shame," she said quietly. "Many people from our land are very easily swayed by our empress's false declarations. She is venerated almost as a deity herself by many who will not believe that she could possibly lie for personal gain."

"Still," Fiona said, "it is good to know that it is not *all* Odessans that believe that way." She offered Ophelia a well-meaning smile, which she returned while feeling not a small amount of helplessness at the situation between the two countries. Despite her status as a noble, she really did not have much say in the political realm.

Then, a glint of sunlight off steel caught her attention. Near the end of the display shelf, there sat a gleaming rapier with a guard of gold sweepings that twirled around the grip beautifully. Ophelia rushed over to examine it more closely. Leaves were engraved along the guard and down the narrow blade on intricately carved vines. The steel itself was sharp enough that Ophelia felt she may cut herself just by looking at it. A scabbard of black and gold rested beside it. Ophelia let out a small breath as she took it all in.

"Would that not be difficult to - you know," Fiona interrupted as she mimed the act of beheading someone.

Ophelia laughed gently. "Well, yes, probably. Though if you stick enough holes in someone, it will not matter if they have their head or not, no?"

Suddenly, Maeve appeared beside them. "That was always my idea as well, lass," she said as she lifted the blade from the shelf. "Strength and power are worthy adversaries, it is true. But with speed and finesse," Maeve gave an invisible opponent several quick jabs with the rapier, "nothing will stand in your way." She bowed her head and presented the rapier to Ophelia who took it gingerly.

The Lady of Argos gave herself some distance from the others as she gave it a few practice swings and jabs. A smile spread across her face as the familiarity sank in. She really did miss having the hilt between her fingers.

"What price do you ask for such a beautiful blade?" Ophelia asked.

15

Scoráneile

Castor was not accustomed to the chill of Maecha. It was only the beginning of autumn, and it already felt like it could snow at any minute. When he had voiced that thought, Aedan had laughed and stated his own complaint of how excruciatingly hot he found Odessa to be in the summer. Though Castor knew that Aedan exuded heat as though he was his own sun, so it was no surprise that he did not like the southern heat.

Eos had found them relaxing at the inn about an hour before and had told them their plan to look around town for more information on those people and their mysterious feast. Seeming to understand their exhaustion and desire to take it easy, Eos asked if they knew anything else that might help them look around. Castor handed them the directions that the two people had given him, and Eos thanked him before disappearing outside. A part of Castor felt guilty for not going with them, but another part of him wondered why Eos was still sticking around and helping out. After all, they had only paid them to help them get through the mountains. Was it just sheer curiosity about the Scoráneile, or was there something else keeping them here?

Ophelia and Fiona returned later after sightseeing in the town, but they each returned with new weapons. Fiona carried a small, white-handled knife, which she said would mostly be used for medicinal

208

purposes, though Castor suspected she had also felt a little helpless back in the Roinn Mountains and wanted something she could carry around to protect herself with. Ophelia brought back a beautiful, golden rapier that she immediately challenged Castor to a duel with.

"Ophelia, I have not fenced in over a year," Castor rebutted. "And I do not even have a rapier of my own anyway."

"First of all, even if you had practiced fencing all year, I would still destroy you," she began playfully. "And secondly, fine, I will just find some sticks we can use. But I need a practice partner," she added pleadingly.

Castor sighed, his joints and muscles exhausted and sore from sleeping on stone for the last week. Then again, it had been a while since he had sparred with anyone. He nodded. "Alright, find some good sticks," he said.

They found a nice, flatter area on top of a hill outside of town and sparred for a while, after which Fiona and Aedan wanted to take turns as well. Ophelia was undoubtedly the queen of fencing out of the group. None of the other three stood a chance against her. She *did* try to help each of them at least. She explained the correct posture and footwork, how to correctly block, and when to lunge. Even with all her tips, though, she could not be defeated.

While Ophelia helped show Fiona her way to disarm an opponent, Aedan and Castor reclined in the grass and watched on. The chill of autumn had been somewhat unpleasant earlier, but with the sun high over them now, it was much more tolerable. That is not to mention that Castor was sitting so closely to Aedan that he could feel the body heat rolling off him.

They had been sitting in silence nearly the whole time the girls were practicing, but Castor had a burning question that he could not keep in any longer.

"Hey," he started, feeling a warm buzz behind his ribs.

Aedan turned to look at him curiously. His eyes sparkled in the sunlight, and wind tugged softly on his hair. "Yes?"

"When we were under the mountains, you told me that I was your closest friend ..." His voice trailed off in an unasked question.

"I meant it," Aedan said easily. "I did not have many friends back home, and when I came to Endala, you were the person that I always tried to be better than. You were the one that always challenged me to get stronger and faster - you even helped me learn how to swim. And then later, you also helped me with Sai's journal, even though I know it was against your beliefs to go through someone else's personal things. You are a very honorable man, and I look up to you as a good warrior and a good friend."

That was not at all what he had expected from Aedan - though it also was not what Castor was actually asking - still he was very touched. But before he could respond, Aedan said, "When I said that I look up to you, by the way, I did mean metaphorically. You are a bit on the shorter side."

"*Everyone* is on the shorter side compared to you," he responded as he playfully pushed him over on his side. Aedan recovered quickly with a deep chuckle and tackled Castor back, both of them rolling side over side down the steep end of the hill. Limbs were everywhere knocking each other roughly, and Castor was sure he had taken a hit from a rock or two in the leg on the way, though he and Aedan had managed to keep hold of each other the whole fall. When they finally came to a stop, Aedan was over Castor with his elbows on either side of his head and the rest of his body painfully pressed down on all Castor's new bruises, and their laughing dwindled to careful half-smiles. Their breaths were heavy, almost shaky, as neither dared moved.

Aedan's gaze bored into Castor's eyes with a strange kind of intensity that Castor had never seen from him before. His heart was pounding so furiously, he was sure Aedan could hear it. Aedan's soft hair fell past his face and tickled Castor's skin where it touched him. Their shirts had been rucked up on the way down, and where their bare stomachs touched was electricity. The heat fuming off Aedan's body was so close that Castor could hardly breathe, but when he did, he smelled damp grass and sweat and summer flowers and Aedan. There was something else Castor felt too - an acute sharpness in his chest, like a blade almost, softly flaying his skin apart.

Then, Aedan's eyes moved down to where Castor felt the odd pain. "Oh, the mark," he said as he moved himself off of Castor and next to him. "Did you mean to call it?"

Smoke was curling out of Castor's tunic. *The mark! That's what that pain was, of course!* Castor had no idea how he had not recognized it immediately. He pulled the top of his shirt down to reveal the blazing mark, its fire hotter and brighter than ever before. The fire of the mark always pained Castor, but it had become bearable the more Castor had beckoned it. But *this* flame was as though he had never grown accustomed to it. It burned like a fresh brand, so painfully that Castor winced as he tried to dismiss its power.

"No," Castor said honestly as he breathed through his teeth with effort. "No, I did not mean to summon it."

"Is it hurting you more than usual?" Aedan asked with a concerned tone to his husky voice.

Castor winced again and nodded. His eyes caught on a stray glint of sunlight on Aedan's lower lip, and Castor felt a tug in his stomach.

"Should ... Should we be worried?" Aedan asked hesitantly.

"No, the pain is starting to fade now," Castor responded as he pulled himself out of his distracting thoughts. They both watched as the flame of the mark died down to a dim ember before dousing itself completely. Aedan immediately put his hand to where the mark was.

"Your skin is cool," he said, not taking his eyes away from his hand.

Castor nodded. "It always is right after the mark fades."

For a long moment, his hand didn't move. Castor's heart thumped heavily underneath his touch. Time seemed to slow, almost to a stop, as they sat there unmoving.

Finally, though, Castor spoke. "We should probably return to the others," he said, his voice low. He cleared his throat and said more clearly, "They are likely wondering what happened."

"Of course," Aedan said, shaking his head as though clearing his mind. He stood and reached out a strong hand to help Castor to his feet, giving Castor's hand a firm squeeze before releasing it. And then they climbed back up the hill in silence.

✦ . + . ✦ . + . ✦

"Is everything all right?" Ophelia asked as they returned to the crest of the hill. She and Fiona seemed to have just finished a bout, and Aedan noticed that he and Castor had not actually been down there as long as it had felt.

"Yes," Aedan answered quickly. "Yes, we are all right. We just accidentally rolled down the side when we were wrestling."

Fiona's eyes narrowed suspiciously, but she did not speak. Ophelia, on the other hand, seemed slightly amused, though she tried to hide it.

"Well, *wrestling* aside, I have worked up quite the appetite," Ophelia said. "Are you three hungry? I'm buying."

The local tavern was actually part of the same building as the inn, and when they returned there for their meal, they found Eos. After they had all placed their orders with the kitchen staff, Aedan asked Eos how their search went.

"I found the house easily enough," they answered evenly. "I did not knock on the door nor check inside, but it seemed quiet - almost as if it were deserted."

"Perhaps no one was home at the time," Fiona offered.

"I thought of that," Eos returned. "Anyway, it is a larger home on the western outskirts of town. There were not any other houses around for some distance. The stable was empty, and I saw no servants milling about. Something about it just seemed *off*. Still, there is no evidence that this affair is a trap of some kind."

Aedan still felt suspicious about it. But Fiona did make a good point. The two outside the mountain, Teg and Igrid, seemed quite concerned for Castor's wellbeing. Surely, they did not mean them any harm.

"I think we should go," Castor said. "To the feast, I mean to say. If it is a trap, we should be able to handle ourselves. Those two did not seem like warriors by any means, and I can always summon the mark to help us. That aside, I honestly feel as though they did mean well, odd as they seemed to be. What do you all think?"

"I definitely think we should go," Fiona said.

"I do as well," Ophelia agreed.

"Wherever you go, you can trust that I will be at your side," Aedan said. "I am admittedly a bit wary of the ordeal, but should you choose to go, I will follow."

"Would it be all right if I accompanied you as well?" Eos asked. "As it turns out, I prefer your company to being alone in Argos." Aedan thought he saw Ophelia brighten when Eos spoke, but he may have just imagined it.

"Are you certain?" Castor asked. "We cannot afford to pay you to guide us through Maecha as well."

"I offer my services freely," Eos explained as they stole the quickest of glances to the Lady of Argos. "I can grow food in an instant so you shall never go hungry, and I am a skilled marksman should you have need for it."

Aedan wanted to accept Eos's proposal immediately, but he remembered Castor's words in the mountains. Castor had thought that Aedan was infatuated with them in some way, and it had been obvious Castor definitely did not approve of that thought. So, Aedan stayed quiet then so as not to offend Castor more.

Castor shook his head, and Aedan thought he was going to reject Eos's offer. "There is no need to justify your skills," Castor said. "Clearly, you are a very capable warrior and navigator - you managed to protect Ophelia all the way through the Roinn Mountains on your own. I believe I speak for us all when I say that you are definitely welcome to join us."

The rest of the group nodded emphatically, and Aedan felt his towering respect for Castor grow even more then.

So, together, they dined and turned in early for the night. Fiona and Ophelia shared one room, and Aedan and Castor took the other while Eos did whatever it was Eos did while everyone else slept.

As much as Aedan wanted to catch up on all the sleep that he had missed the last week, for some reason, he found it difficult to shut his eyes. Castor lay inches away in the bed on his side with his back turned, and he seemed to be fast asleep, so why was Aedan unable to do the same? *It must just be nerves,* he told himself. Their journey was halfway over, and soon, they would be challenging the *Queen of Maecha* to a fight to the death. He knew Castor was a skilled fighter with a powerful gift from the Allmother. He just hoped it would be enough.

It seemed like hours went by before he finally succumbed to slumber's embrace. Usually, he slept fitfully; whenever he dreamt, all he saw were those he cared about falling under iron and steel while he was too slow or too weak to help them. He dreamt of those bandits killing Fiona while he stared on helplessly unable to do anything to protect her. He dreamt of Castor fighting the queen and trying to get a hand on her before she cut him down.

But he found his mind at ease while he spent the hours dreaming in the inn that night. It held no evils or dangers, not even any heroic epics or last-minute rescues. No, Aedan dreamed only of a small cottage far away from the rest of the world. A small cottage next to the sea.

In the dream, he and Castor lay in the sand outside the cottage that dream-Aedan instinctively knew was the home they shared. For some reason, dream-Aedan didn't think the idea strange of he and Castor sharing a home together. Castor laughed, bringing the dream back into focus, and the sun shined a little brighter. The golden light dripped over Castor's olive skin and pooled around the both of them like honey. In the glittering gold, Aedan saw his hand reach out to Castor where it came to a gentle rest on his stubbled cheek. Castor's came up reflexively to cover Aedan's, and he closed his eyes with a small smile. Aedan's heart fell through his stomach at the sight, and he had the sudden urge to pull him closer. Aedan began to move, but as his did, his heartbeat quickened, and his dream quickly began to fade.

Sunlight - *real* sunlight - forced Aedan's eyes open for a moment, leaving his dawning consciousness with a distant yearning. He immediately closed his eyes back to chase the remnants of the dream, but it proved futile. Resigned to the fact that his dream was just a dream, he decided he should probably rise to check on the others.

But he found a strange weight on his body. Something foreign, but not uncomfortable, pressed into his shoulder and chest. He squinted his eyes open in the light, peered down, and his heart jumped when he saw that it was Castor. At some point in the night, he must have rolled over, and Aedan must have scooped him up with his arm. Castor was sound asleep in the crook of Aedan's shoulder with his hand rising and falling with Aedan's chest, and with Aedan's arm wrapped tight around his muscled side.

A strange fluttering spread through his chest and stomach as he gazed down at Castor's mess of black curls and craned his neck to see his sleeping face. He looked so quiet and peaceful as he lay there, his breaths slow and warm. He really was beautiful with his strong jaw and dimpled chin. He was even more beautiful when he was awake, Aedan thought with a small smile tugging at the corner of his mouth. His strength, his stubbornness, his strong sense of justice, his laugh, the sparkle in his eyes when he talked about the things he was fond of, the way he rubbed his eyes so dramatically when he was weary from a long day, the way his Odessan accent deepened whenever he would get frustrated, his bright smile that lit every room like the midday sun -

Aedan stopped and gaped at the ceiling. Realization flooded over him, as any remnants of sleep were briskly swept away. How was he so clueless to have not seen that his friendly admiration of Castor was actually much more than he'd ever imagined? How could he have *missed that?* He paused for a moment to marvel at the apparent limitlessness of his idiocy.

With everything so blatantly clear to him now, he wondered how Castor ever could have thought he was falling for anyone else.

He of course did not know how Castor felt about him, other than he seemed to respect him as a warrior and a friend, but beyond that, Aedan could only guess. He found it improbable, if not impossible, that anyone could ever think of him as more than that because of his surname, but that never seemed to bother Castor. Still, Aedan thought that he should not trouble his friend with his feelings - at least not until after they finished what they set out to do. It would not be wise to pile more onto Castor's plate than what he already had ahead of him. But he promised himself that when all was said and done, he would be honest with Castor about how he felt and accept whatever the outcome.

But for now, with the red rays of the morning sun creeping into the room, and with Castor sleeping softly in his arms, Aedan was quiet.

✦ ⋅ ⁺ ⋅✦⋅ ⁺ ⋅✦

When Castor finally stirred, Aedan quickly made the decision to pretend he was just waking up as well. The Odessan woke with a stretching yawn before realizing where he was. He sat up quickly and turned to see Aedan rubbing his eyes in false tiredness.

"I um," he started as he pushed himself out of the bed, the tops of his cheeks red in the sunlight. "Forgive me."

Aedan sat up then, too. "No, it's all right."

"I just, uh ..." He ran his hand through his hair nervously. "I did not mean to - "

Aedan stood then and took Castor's forearms in his hands. "Do not worry about it, Castor. I was not uncomfortable."

Castor seemed to relax then. They spoke sparingly after that before going down for breakfast. That day and the rest of the week went by surprisingly quickly. They all ate and drank and shared stories and sparred with each other. Castor even practiced with his mark most nights, which Aedan did not blame him for. When they had rolled down the hill that one day, his mark had come up on its own and was apparently more painful than usual. It was enough to stir up Castor's investigative side again.

That aside, those days following their arrival to Trícnoc had been a wonderful respite from their time in the mountains. And when the day of the Scoráneile had eventually come, Aedan was feeling not a small amount of anxiety about what was in store for them. Everyone else seemed all right with the idea of the affair, if not excited, but Aedan still had a sinking feeling that something wasn't right.

Nevertheless, that evening, the group cleaned up and tried to look as decent as possible for the occasion. Eos had some air about them that seemed to repel dirt or grime, so they were ready immediately. Ophelia showed Fiona a few ways nobles in Odessa arranged their hair, which always ended with Fiona laughing at herself because she just could not take herself seriously looking so elegant. She ended up deciding to keep her hair down as usual but with an ornate Maechan braid on the side.

Castor shaved his face as was apparently customary for Odessans even though Aedan thought he looked better with the facial hair that had been growing. Even so, Aedan decided to shave his face as well, mostly just to see what it would look like. He grimaced when he saw his reflection in the bronze mirror he held, but Castor tilted his head a little and smiled when he looked at him. So, Aedan wasn't too upset about it. Fiona then helped Aedan with his braids, which Aedan would have preferred to go without, but he begrudgingly agreed that they did make him look more presentable.

After all was said and done, they left to follow Eos to the house where the Scoráneile was to take place.

It was not as large as a typical manor house in Odessa, but it was still of respectable size. Unlike Eos's previous description, however, there seemed to be quite the large amount of people inside. There were at least fifteen horses in and around the nearby stable, and there was substantial firelight glowing from inside.

Steeling himself, Aedan led the group to the front door and knocked. It took longer than he would have suspected for the door to open. Igrid, the woman from before, stood on the other side in a hooded scarlet robe and beamed more brightly than Aedan had ever seen someone beam before.

"O Marked One, you did come!" she said, clapping her hands to her cheeks in surprise. "Everyone will be so excited to meet you! Please, follow me!" Then she seemed to notice they were all armed. "Oh, your weapons are not necessary here, Marked One. You can leave them by the door if you like."

"That is appreciated, but we will be keeping our belongings with us," Aedan said as he crossed his arms over his chest.

Igrid looked slightly taken aback by his words but bowed her head and said, "Very well. And the bird - "

"The bird stays, too," Fiona said with a tone of finality.

Igrid bowed her head again. "As you say. Please follow me to the ritual chamber."

"Ritual chamber?" Eos echoed.

"Of course," Igrid said as she turned to lead them into the house. The interior looked as though it was a shadow of a beautiful home. There was expensive furniture, a lovely chandelier, and an enormous bookcase full of tomes, but everything was covered in a layer of dust as though it was all here only for seeing, not using. *It's a house, not a home*, Aedan thought as his mind briefly flashed back to a small cottage by the sea. "The Scoráneile is a ritual that can only be performed on one of the four quarters of the year—"

"I thought you said it was a celebration," Aedan interrupted.

"It is both," Igrid said calmly. They walked down a long hallway before coming to a door at the end of it. "The Scoráneile is our attempt to open a doorway into the Otherworld. We try each quarter-turn of every year but have never been successful."

"Who is 'we'?" Ophelia asked. "And why do you want to go to the Otherworld? Is it too much to wait until after death?"

"All of your questions will be answered in due time," she responded as she opened the door and stepped in. "Mind your step," she added. The door led to a dark staircase that descended into the earth. Aedan found he had a difficult time making himself small enough to fit in the tiny stairway, but somehow, he found a way.

Now that they were surrounded by the dark, Aedan noticed it wasn't as totally dark as he had first suspected. A dim light was flickering from around a bend in the stairs farther down that was just barely illuminating the steps they were on, and there was a glowing blue light coming from behind him. He looked back and saw the naga's necklace shining around Fiona's neck - he'd almost forgotten she had even taken that.

They went down and around before emerging into a large cavern of earth and stone. The room was mostly circular with a gently sloping floor and a raised area on the far end like an extra tall dais with a stone ramp connecting it to the lower level. Torches lined the walls at regular intervals and a large bonfire burned in the center of the room. A grand table ran horizontally across the area before the bonfire and was decorated with fine silver plates and goblets and was overflowing with juicy meats and delectable fruits and savory vegetables. And milling about the cavern were around twenty people all dressed the same as Igrid in bloodred robes and shoes.

"Fellow members of the Scarlet Key!" Igrid called out to the cavern. Twenty faces turned to look at them. "Our honored guest has arrived. The Marked One is here!" She turned, gestured to Castor, and bowed. Castor, who Aedan assumed was used to being the center of attention due to his status, smiled and bowed politely.

Suddenly, they were swarmed by red robes, but Aedan made sure to keep his body in between theirs and Castor's. The Scarlet Key members' intermingled voices called out for blessings, for life advice, for a look at the mark, even for simple touches.

"Give him space!" Aedan thundered, becoming annoyed by the clamorous noise and reaching hands. The robed ones apologetically distanced themselves from their group a little, but their contained excitement alone was still almost too much for Aedan.

"We apologize," Igrid said as she bowed. "We have just been waiting for someone who has been touched by the Other for so long ..."

One of the robed ones removed their hood revealing a middle-aged man that none of the group had seen before. "Please sit at the banquet table," he said gesturing an open palm out to behind him. Let us eat before we begin the ritual."

Fiona excitedly pushed to the table before all the others and began stacking a silver plate with a variety of foods. The rest of the group was close behind her, and soon the entire table was packed with warm bodies reaching for food.

"May I ask a question?" Aedan inquired of Igrid, who sat across from him.

"Of course," she said. "This is Malus." She gestured to the man who sat beside her and across from Castor who had asked them all to sit just minutes ago. "He is the leader of the Scarlet Key faction in southern Maecha. He can answer any question you may have."

Malus was a strong, handsome man with a graying beard and piercing, hazel eyes. "Absolutely. I am sure you are wondering who we are?" His sentence ended with a question, though he was correct in his wondering.

Aedan nodded.

"I am not surprised you have not heard of us," Malus said as he took a large bite of a rabbit leg, taking nearly all the meat off in one go. "We are a quiet group, though there are many under our banner spread throughout the world. We are called the Scarlet Key, and we are a group who are wholly dedicated to the Allmother and her nine Aspects. We seek her out in every facet of life and constantly venture out into the world to find areas where we might be able to enter her home, the Otherworld.

"Over six hundred years ago, the founder of the Scarlet Key, Gian Ó Braonáin, discovered an ancient burial mound in the Elderglas Forest. In the mound, Gian saw carvings from ages past. These carvings told of the Allmother and her domain, but one spoke of a ritual to tear open the veil that separates this world and the Other."

"The Scoráneile," Aedan filled in.

Malus nodded with an approving smile. "Yes. But time had taken its toll on the ancient words, and several lines of the ritual were illegible. Still, Gian was determined to learn how to perform the Scoráneile, and soon, many were drawn to their cause. Word spread through whispers over the mountains and across the seas until people all over Serrae began to search for the *key* to the ritual that would open the worlds to each other and allow us to freely pass into the Allmother's domain. And thus, the Scarlet Key was born."

PHANTOM FIRE | 221

"And where does Castor ... er ... the Marked One fit into all this?" Aedan pressed. "His mark does not give him the power to open the veil."

"You have attempted this already?" Malus directed the question to Castor.

"Well, no," he admitted.

Malus nodded with a sly smile. "But you have been to the Other-world before, yes? Or did the Allmother visit you in this realm?"

"Neither," Castor answered. "She came to me in a dream. A very vivid dream, but a dream nonetheless."

"How very like her!" Igrid chimed in. "Truly, if you were in the Allmother's physical presence, you might not have survived it!"

"Yet you want to try?" Ophelia, who apparently had been listening, muttered sardonically.

"So, what do you want me to do when the ritual starts?" Castor inquired.

"You do not have to do anything!" Malus replied before motioning to the raised area of the room. "There is a circle up there in which you will stand when the ritual begins. Several of our members who are learned in the ways of the Witch Aspect will begin raising energy around you. We believe that by tapping into your energy - you who have been touched by the Allmother herself - we can create a door-way. We believe that you are the key we have been searching for all this time."

The idea of Castor being surrounded by a group of magic-users did nothing to quell Aedan's fears. But as long as Castor wanted to help, Aedan would stand by him.

Castor nodded. "You all have been very kind and generous to my friends and me," he said. "If this simple favor is all you ask in return, I would be pleased to accommodate you."

Malus clapped his hands excitedly. Igrid looked as though she might faint from sheer delight. "Excellent! We shall begin as soon as everyone has finished eating!"

So, they ate. Over the course of the banquet, several of the Scarlet Key members asked to see Castor's mark and for him to give them a demonstration of the powers it bestowed. He indulged them by touching one on the arm and forcing them to move their other arm without their own volition, which they were all too excited about.

He was also asked on multiple occasions to describe the Allmother, the Otherworld, and the Tiarna Sí - so many times in fact, that Aedan thought he could doubtless give someone the exact same description Castor used. He was honestly just tired of being on edge for so long and just longed to be back in the inn. He and Castor would probably share the room again -

"If everyone's bellies are full, we shall move on to the Scoráneile!" Malus called out, wrenching Aedan from his thoughts. "Marked One, if you will please follow me." He turned and strode up the ramp to the top of the dais trailed by Castor and nine robed Scarlet Key members.

Aedan moved to follow, but Igrid grabbed his arm gently. He turned to her as he fought back a sudden rage, but she shook her head with a polite smile. "Forgive me, but anyone else's energy may interfere with the ritual. Please wait here until the ceremony is complete." She gave him a reassuring smile, but Aedan did not feel reassured. He hoped this Scarlet Key cult was true in their intentions, but he just could not shake the feeling that something was wrong.

Still, he obeyed Igrid's behest and stayed near the bottom of the incline with his hands on the handles of his axes, though every step Castor took felt like a blade in his chest as his worry grew. Eos stood nearby, and Ophelia and Fiona were attentively watching as well. Aedan knew they would all be ready to assist if something were to happen.

Malus showed Castor where to stand, and he complied, staring out over all who stood below. The nine witches bowed to Castor and kneeled down in a large circle around him. Malus stood behind them all and paced back and forth as he began a long incantation in ancient Maechan. Some of the words were similar to the modern Maechan language, but Aedan couldn't be sure of anything that was being said.

As the leader spoke, the nine witches began to sway and chant in unison, and Aedan began to feel a change in the air - almost like the feeling during a storm when lightning could be felt before it struck. A cold swept into the room, but Aedan thought he could see sweat brimming on Castor's brow as if the heat were being sucked up to the dais above. Castor's hair was disturbed by a wind Aedan could not feel himself. His grip on his axes tightened, the muscles in his legs ready to run.

Malus continued speaking, his powerful voice echoing through the cavern as though the magic was carrying it to everyone's ears below. The witches' low voices began to rise, nearly drowning out Malus's own commanding words.

"Bring it forth!" the leader called out to Castor over the witches' chanting. "Summon forth the fire of your mark!"

Aedan looked to Igrid, but she was captivated by the scene above. He took the chance to take a few careful steps up the ramp. The witches continued their chant, and Malus stood silent with his arms raised out and his head tilted back. Aedan's ears popped in the pressure change of the air.

Taking a few more steps, Aedan cast a swift glance back to see Fiona watching him. He gave her a cautionary look, hoping that she would translate it to telling her to be careful and ready to run.

Just as he turned his head back to Castor, he saw something flash in Malus's hand, who had moved from his position near the back of the wall; he was approaching Castor from behind with a nearly exalted look on his face. Focusing his eyes through the nearly visible waves of energy, Aedan could just discern a black ritual knife in the Scarlet Key leader's grasp.

Aedan didn't even stop to think; he just ran.

His legs exploded in the sudden ferocity as he tore his way to the top of the chamber. No one seemed to notice him though as Malus raised the dagger in both hands over Castor's turned head.

Aedan felt all the air leave his lungs as he saw what was about to happen. He pulled out the axe he forged over a year ago in Albainn and threw it. The axe flew end over end, sailing far and true, burying itself deep into Malus's exposed side. At the same moment, a sleek arrow blasted the knife out of his hands. *So, Eos was ready to defend Castor as well,* Aedan noticed. He would have to thank them for that later.

Malus fell over twitching to the shrieking horror of all the cultists in the room. Castor turned and saw the grisly scene behind him, but before he could react, the nine witches simultaneously slammed their palms down to the stone, detonating all the built-up magical energy. A horrible blast of force blew Aedan off his feet and slammed him into the cavern wall, knocking the air out of his lungs.

He coughed furiously as he regained his footing and briefly took in everything that was going on around him. Several of the cultists had begun to flee, though many others brandished knives of their own, probably in an attempt to avenge their leader's death. Ophelia had already unsheathed her new rapier and was staring down three knife-wielding cultists, though she looked unafraid. Eos was raining arrows down on the witches above while watching their own back, and Fiona called out commands to Bas as she tried to keep her distance from a few pursuers.

Finally regaining his breath, Aedan called out, "Eos! Help Fiona and Ophelia!", as he rushed to Castor's side. Four of the witches lay still with arrows protruding from their vitals, and Castor just managed to get a hand on a fifth, causing them to collapse instantly. They made short work of the last few witches, whose magic took time and concentration to raise and direct - much more than it took for Aedan to swing his axe.

Castor turned to smile appreciatively at Aedan, though it was short-lived. His relieved expression instantly transformed to horror as his eyes focused on something behind Aedan. But before anything could be said or done, Aedan felt something he had never felt in his life. He was of course accustomed to scrapes and slices from growing up in Albainn and from his time as an apprentice blacksmith, and from sparring in Endala with Castor and Teacher, but this was different.

This was fire. White-hot liquid fire that melted into his back as the dagger stabbed between his ribs and through to his vitals. His breath caught in his throat as his knees buckled and his axe fell to the ground. His arms reached awkwardly around to the place on his back where the pain was, but black spots began to plague his vision. He fell to his knees and then to his side as he struggled to inhale just one breath of air. His chest tightened, and the heartbeat pounding in his ears sounded off.

Through his hazy sight, he saw that Castor was cradling his head in his arms as he lay there choking for air. He was saying something to him, but Aedan couldn't focus enough to discern what the words meant. He was too distracted by the strange sensation of water running down his back before he realized that it was his own lifeblood flowing out of him.

It was only then that Aedan knew he was going to die.

Some part of him remembered there was something he was supposed to tell Castor, but he couldn't quite recall the details anymore. He let the thought go as he looked up at the beautiful Odessan holding him. The flickering firelight reflected off the water in Castor's eyes, and Aedan couldn't help but smile. It was a weak smile, but it was all he could muster. He was just glad that at least his last moments were in Castor's arms.

Everything began to blur. The pain numbed. And then Aedan slipped into the darkness following the soothing song of a woman's voice.

PHANTOM'S
EMBRACE

16

Burn

Castor had just taken a witch down by causing their heart to stop beating with a touch of his hand when he turned and saw Aedan who had just rescued him from being sacrificed by the cult leader. His whole body felt the relief when he met eyes with Aedan. But then, Igrid was there. He supposed she had been approaching already, but it mattered not; she was there nonetheless, and neither Castor nor Aedan had seen her coming in time.

When he saw her arm plunge forward and Aedan's smile crack and break into a confused grimace, Castor thought he was the one who had been stabbed by the amount of pain he felt. He wished it would have been him anyway. Aedan didn't even *want* to come here, but he did because Castor wanted him to.

He took Aedan's head in his arms when he fell, forgetting all else. In that moment, it was only Castor, Aedan, and a growing pool of blood. With one arm cradling Aedan's head and the other gently stroking his cheek as he gasped for air, Castor felt the hot, anguished tears begin to fall from his eyes. And only when Aedan stopped moving did Castor notice that Igrid had been speaking the entire time.

"... only did what I had to do," she was saying through tears while kneeling on the ground. A long thin misericord lay nearby stained black in the firelight. "O Marked One, please forgive me. This man killed Malus ... He ruined the Scoráneile - "

Castor kissed Aedan's forehead and gently set him down as he stood. He hadn't called it, but his mark was burning furiously on his chest, the smoldering causing a hole to begin forming in the tunic over it. "*Stand. Up.*" His voice sounded distant in his own ears.

Igrid stood, her legs shaking. "Marked One, you understand, yes? You understand I only did what I had to do?"

Castor took two steps, closing the distance between them.

Tears filled Igrid's eyes. "Marked One - "

Her words were cut off as Castor's hand wrapped around her thin throat with enough force to knock her back several steps, but he kept his grip. Her fingers clawed at his as her eyes bulged in her head. The mark's fire flowed through his touch and into Igrid's weak body. Castor did not direct the fire to anywhere in particular or to do anything specifically; he just flooded her with its power. More and more poured into her until her skin began to tremble and expand. Then, in one awful violent moment, her body tore apart at every joint, exploding back and painting the cavern wall in vermillion.

Below, Eos, Ophelia, and Fiona finished off the last few cultists who had stayed behind to fight, but Castor didn't notice any of that. He didn't notice anything but how Aedan's large body somehow looked so small and frail all of a sudden. He gently pushed back a braid that had fallen over Aedan's bluish face as Fiona suddenly slid to her knees next to them. She whipped out a small book - the one Avelas had given her - from the pack on her waist and ripped open to find some specific page.

"Listen to me, Castor," she said with a tone of authority that was uncommon on her tongue. "I did not bring any of my supplies, but you can help him with your mark, can't you?" She sounded almost pleading in her words.

"I ... I don't know," Castor choked out. "I have never tried to use it for healing before."

"Just try!" she yelled, breaking Castor out of his shock. He nodded shakily. They turned Aedan on his side and quickly inspected the bloody wound. Looking back at her book, she said, "The knife must have punctured a lung." She pointed to a section of Aedan's torso. "You need to mend the cut on the inside, Castor. Can you do that?"

Castor said nothing. His mark was already running on high, and he was feeling the weariness of overusing it begin to seep into his bones. But it didn't matter how tired he was. He guided the fire through his touch down to where Fiona suggested the wound was. He sensed the fire licking around inside until it settled around a gash that probably should not have been there. He used his power to pull out all the blood from the organ before quickly stitching it up and searing it shut with the flames. He was beginning to see spots in his vision as he sat back and caught his breath. He was not so accustomed to using his mark for something so careful and precise.

"Did you do it?" Fiona sounded almost angry with him.

Castor nodded, unable to conjure up the energy to vocalize his affirmation. He vaguely felt Ophelia's hands on his shoulders behind him reassuringly.

Fiona looked back to her book urgently. "Why is he not breathing?" she asked herself as she flipped through the pages.

Then, Eos knelt down next to them. "With all this blood, I would suspect his heart was hit as well," they offered.

Fiona only looked back to Castor who was already putting his hands back on Aedan's skin. He forced the flames to go back into Aedan, and this time, he knew where to go. The fire shot straight to Aedan's heart, and Castor, with blood dripping from his nose from pushing himself so far, made Aedan's heart pump.

Aedan still wasn't breathing, so Castor went on, pumping Aedan's heart for him. Castor could vaguely hear Fiona's sobbing and pleading over the ringing in his own ears, but he continued his work. Time passed slower than Castor had ever experienced, but just before darkness took him, he saw Aedan take in a horrible, sharp breath with bloodshot eyes open wide.

Then, Castor fell.

✦ . ⁺ . ✦ . ⁺ . ✦

Castor had been asleep for over a day. Aedan had not moved from Castor's bed in the inn since they had placed him there after carrying him out of the cultists' house. He was breathing normally, Aedan saw, but he had not eaten or drunk anything since that night. Aedan had had no food either and only drank when forced to by Fiona or Ophelia. He only stayed at Castor's side, holding his hand tight in his own and willing him to recover.

For how powerful Castor was, his hand seemed so small in Aedan's, he thought as he traced the knuckles and veins with his fingertips. The limp hand in his was practically lifeless, he thought morbidly. Perhaps this was the cost of Aedan's life. The others had told him what Castor had done after Aedan had been stabbed. Perhaps this was how the Allmother kept the balance in the world. For Castor to pull Aedan back from the depths, he must offer himself to the abyss.

What a stupid man, Aedan thought angrily. What right did he have to trade his own life for Aedan's? How did he not understand how much more important he was to the world? At least how much more important he was than *Aedan*. Aedan was *nothing*. He was nobody special. But Castor ...

Then, his internal rage focused elsewhere. How dare the Phantom take Castor away from him? Castor was purely *good*. He was the epitome of justice and kindness and beauty and goodness, and the Allmother thought that *he* was an equal trade for *Aedan*? How could she make such a ridiculous mistake? She was supposed to be smarter than that - to be *better* than that, right? Surely, she must know that Castor's life far outweighed Aedan's own. And yet, she was trying to take him now?

Aedan squeezed Castor's hand even harder before a more rational thought passed his mind. The Phantom was not responsible for human decisions, and he was wrong to be so angry with her. *Forgive me, Phantom*, he prayed then, with his hands clasped around Castor's and pressed to his forehead. *Forgive me. I am sorry to have blamed you for this and for my anger at you. Of course, Castor would have done what he did -*

to have risked his life to save mine. That is who he is. That must be why you chose him to bless with your mark. He sighed solemnly. *I know that I have done nothing to deserve this, but please bring him back to me. If not for me, then for the world. He has so much left that he can do - so many more people that he would help, I just know it. Please, Phantom. I beg of you to please send him back to me. Please.*

He opened his eyes and dried the tears off his and Castor's hands. And there he stayed for the rest of the night. The others came in occasionally to check on him and on Castor's unchanging condition, but mostly Aedan sat there alone with him. As the night drew nearer, Fiona returned to ensure Aedan had some water and to kiss him gently on the head before leaving them there for the night.

Aedan had hardly slept the night before, but still, he tried to keep his eyes open to see any sign of Castor's return. His body demanded sleep, though, and before too many hours had passed, Aedan slumped over the bed, his hand still firmly wrapped around Castor's.

✦ . ✛ . ✦ . ✛ . ✦

Bright rays of morning sunshine forced Aedan's tired eyes open. He sat back up in his chair and blinked around the room, his mind foggy from restless sleep. He squinted around, trying to find something to focus his eyes on when he saw Castor's hand in his. Memories flooding back into him, he sighed and bent lower to place a soft kiss on the back of his hand.

When he came back up, he looked to Castor's face and saw him watching Aedan with straining eyes.

Aedan jumped out of the chair. "Castor!" he yelled, his voice shaking the floorboards. He tackled Castor in a heavy embrace despite the numerous pained sounds coming from him. "You're alive; thank the Phantom," he said through tears as he finally pulled back from him, though while still keeping his hands on his shoulders.

Castor grunted uncomfortably. "It appears to be that way, yes," he muttered.

PHANTOM FIRE | 233

Then, anger overtook Aedan. His grip changed from a firm grasp to a twisting pull on Castor's tunic. "What the hell were you thinking pushing yourself so far?" he shouted. "You could have killed yourself! You could have died, and it would have been for nothing! Can you not understand how ridiculous that is? How senseless of a reason to die for?" He heard the ferocity in his voice - saw Castor's flinch - but he could do nothing about it.

Castor's brow furrowed as he shifted slightly in the bed. His voice was barely a whisper as it cracked out of him. "You are *not* nothing."

Aedan's hands loosened on Castor's tunic, and his face softened as the anger melted away. Suddenly, he was pulling Castor to him and arching himself down to press his lips to Castor's. He hadn't meant to do it, but he also didn't stop himself. One of Aedan's hands pulled at the small of his lower back while the other gently caressed the back of his head. Castor's mouth parted under Aedan's, and for a moment, time stood still. Aedan forgot everything else in the world. Stars burst behind his closed eyes as he held one long kiss, savoring the softness of Castor's lips and the warmth of his closeness.

When he finally released Castor's mouth from his own, Aedan pressed his forehead to Castor's and held him there as tears welled in his eyes. Neither moved nor spoke; they only sat together and held each other.

"I am so sorry," Castor said eventually, his voice cracking. "I should have listened to you. We should have stayed away from those people. If I had just listened to you, you ... you wouldn't have - "

Aedan shushed him and stroked his cheek with his thumb. "Do not apologize. I am alive and you are alive and that is all that matters." He kissed him again and tasted the salty tears on his lips. Every kiss was an explosion of fire and light as Aedan sank deeper into the bed with Castor. He wrapped an arm under Castor's head and lay there next to him as close as they could manage. His fingertips traced Castor's brow, cheekbone, jaw, and mouth where Castor softly kissed them.

Something stirred in Aedan that he had never before felt so deeply - something soft and warm and good. A hint of a smile tugged at the corner of his mouth as he realized that this was really happening - that Castor felt for him the same way he did. It was unbelievable; Aedan nearly thought he was dreaming again. But no, he could definitely feel everything. This was no dream. He was there, wrapped up with Castor, and nothing in the world could keep them apart.

✦ . ✛ . ✦ . ✛ . ✦

Eos had spent that morning with Ophelia and Fiona discussing their travel plans after they informed Eos on where they were going and why.

"If we are journeying to Letha, we must first traverse the Elderglas Forest and cross the Ebonflow. After that, it is open hills and plains the rest of the way to the capital," Eos said. "Have either of you made this journey before?"

Fiona and Ophelia shook their heads in unison.

"Before this journey, I had not been outside of Albainn," Fiona said.

"And I have never even been to Maecha," said Ophelia.

A small smile played at Eos's lips. Perhaps one day they would be able to take Ophelia to everywhere she had not been. But that was a far-fetched thought, Eos told themselves. Sometimes it really did seem as though Ophelia might be fond of them, but humans were so much more difficult to read than the other creatures of Serrae.

"The Elderglas can be very dangerous," Eos explained, pulling themselves from their thoughts. "Though, since we will not need to tread too deeply into it, we should be able to get through without incident."

Fiona groaned. "*Why* would you say such a thing?" When Eos and Ophelia gave her confused looks, she went on. "'We should be able to get through without incident'," she mimicked. "You are practically begging for something to go wrong by saying that."

And so it was confirmed: humans were odd, Eos decided.

Fiona rolled her eyes and pushed her long hair from her face. "What kinds of things live in the Elderglas anyway?"

"In the less dense parts, like the part we will be going through, there are mainly just wolves and bears as far as predators go."

"And the denser parts?" Fiona prodded.

Eos sighed, knowing what they were going to say was probably going to cause Fiona fear and worry. "There are many things in the Elderglas Forest," Eos said. "Many things even I do not know of." Fiona stared on expectantly. Eos continued. "I know for certain that a great centaur tribe holds a sizeable portion of the northwest forest; while not necessarily evil, centaurs can be quite dangerous when they have been offended. As for throughout the forest, there are weres of many kinds as well as dark Sidhe who have lost their way."

"What are weres?" Ophelia asked curiously.

Again, Eos was struck by her beauty. Her numerous D'jadii curls fell about her head and face in such a way as though each was placed there intentionally to empower her natural allure. And her dark eyes were so large and innocent, Eos wanted to melt in them. Snapping back to reality, Eos cursed themselves, for elves were notorious for their fascination of pretty things. It was sometimes difficult for Eos to focus - and around Ophelia, it was a much more common occurrence.

"Weres are humans who can shapeshift into a specific animal," Eos explained. "They cannot always control their transformations and so have usually removed themselves from more populous areas. The Elderglas has become a haven to many of them."

"Back in Odessa, we have our fair share of dangerous forests as well," Ophelia added. "There is the Black Forest where no light can penetrate and the Whispering Wood where the dead are said to be reanimated."

Eos knew this already, but they decided to look intrigued anyway. Fiona, on the other hand, was actually intrigued. "You have a forest that brings people back to life?"

"Oh, no, not in the way you are thinking," Ophelia responded. "When the dead return to life there, it is not as they once were. They continue to rot and deteriorate, though they walk around with a hunger for flesh."

Fiona's excited expression quickly changed to horrified. "Well, that absolutely sounds like a place I will not be going to anytime soon."

Ophelia laughed. *A laugh like the water of a stream trickling off worn rocks*, thought Eos with a small smile. *Soft and pleasant.*

"It is likely just a ghost story," Ophelia said comfortingly. Though Eos, who had been to the Whispering Wood before, knew that it was much more than just a rumor.

In an attempt to get back to the original topic, Eos said, "As I said, however, we will just be going through the southern edge of the Elderglas. Should any danger arise, I am sure our group can take care of it."

"What do you know of the Ebonflow?" Fiona asked them.

"The Ebonflow can also be a dangerous place," they answered. "There is a tear in the veil between this world and the Other in the Ebonpool. Many Sidhe who fall through are carried down through the Ebonflow and become dark before they can they get back."

"So, that is why you said there were more dark Sidhe in the Elderglas," Fiona said. "The Ebonflow runs through the Elderglas in some places and is close enough in others that many probably wander straight into the forest before becoming lost."

Eos nodded. "And many also stay around the river. But I know of a bridge we can cross so we will not have to wade through its black waters. Still, we must be wary when we are there. There are many who use that bridge, and it would be wise if we were to pass by undetected."

Ophelia and Fiona agreed.

"The journey after that should be relatively simple," Eos went on. "Though, we would make much better time if we had horses."

Ophelia smiled sheepishly. "We have used all of our money to stay at this inn for as long as we have. We have none spare for horses."

"It is no matter," Eos comforted. "We will still get to Letha before winter comes - with or without horses."

With the plans solidified, Ophelia asked if the others would like to practice fencing with her. She needed to get her form back, she said. Eos agreed to help, and Fiona agreed to watch.

It was not until closer to midday when Aedan emerged from the inn. Something was different about him, Eos noticed. The big man had a sort of glow that shimmered about him and a smile painted on his face that looked somewhat permanent.

When Ophelia saw him, she dropped her practice stick immediately. "Please tell me you are smiling because Castor is awake?"

Looking a little lost in his own head, Aedan took a moment to reply. "For the most part, yes. And, yes, Castor is fine. Better than fine. He's great, actually."

Ophelia looked more relieved than Eos had ever seen. Without another word, she raced past them all into the inn to see her friend.

"He says he will be ready to travel by tomorrow, if we can just give him one more day of rest," Aedan told Eos and Fiona.

"Of course," Fiona said. "He brought you back - if he wanted to wait here for a year, I wouldn't argue." Then, Eos noticed Fiona suddenly scrutinizing her brother as though she saw the difference in him that Eos had seen.

"What are you doing? Stop that," Aedan told her.

"What happened with you two?" she asked him suspiciously as she promptly did *not* stop that.

Aedan looked surprised. "H - How do you mean?"

Her eyes squinted at him, and her lips pursed thoughtfully. They were quiet for a moment while she stared at him and he stared at anywhere else. Finally, she said, "You kissed, didn't you?"

"*How do you do that?*" Aedan almost yelled.

"Castor has his powers, and so do I," she responded easily. "How was it? Did you kiss him, or did he kiss you? What did he say afterwards?"

"Can I not just have this one thing to myself?" he exclaimed.

"Of course not," Fiona said to him as though he had just suggested she jump from the top of the Roinn. "It took you two long enough, anyway."

"What are you talking about?"

"The both of you are so obvious! I knew since Endala that you admired each other more than just friends do."

"*What?* You *knew?*" Aedan accused. "*I* did not even know until recently! Why did you not tell me before?"

Fiona threw her hands up in exasperation. "You are hopeless," she said with a sigh as she walked towards the inn.

Eos smiled at their interaction. A small part of them was envious of the siblings for having each other. Eos had grown up abandoned by their Sidhe father and left with their human mother who had not known the father's true identity until afterwards. Having the same prejudice as many others in Serrae, Eos's mother always treated them as an abomination; she could hardly bear to look at them most days. Eos ran from home before they were even grown and had lived mostly alone ever since. *It must be nice to have family who cares for you the way those two do for each other*, Eos thought.

Aedan marched over to Eos with a thunderous look in his eye, and the sight of the large man's coming stunned them out of their thoughts and made their heartrate quicken.

"Did *you* know, too?" Aedan interrogated with a pointed finger.

Eos put their palms up in surrender. They had originally thought that Aedan and Castor were already courting each other, if not already quite serious together, but Eos didn't think that this was the time to say that. Instead, they shook their head strategically, which seemed to garner the imposing Maechan's approval as he nodded and turned back towards the inn.

Eos released a small breath of air and tried to stifle a chuckle as they followed Aedan back inside. If nothing else, at least they would be entertained while they traveled with this group, Eos thought with a smile.

17 •

The Road of Giants

Castor longed to be out of the bed and back on his way to Letha finally, but he was still exhausted. His muscles ached despite not having exerted himself physically much in the last few days, and a splitting headache had set up a permanent residence behind his eyes since the night of the Scoráneile. Clearly, overusing his mark's power was not something he should do on a regular basis.

Still, there was not an ounce of him that regretted anything. If this pain and exhaustion was the only price he had to pay for Aedan to be alive and well, then what could there be to regret anyway?

That's not to mention that he and Aedan—

He shook his head and smiled at himself as he lay there in the bed. There was a light, airy feeling in his chest similar to the sensation of a coming sneeze, and no matter what he did, he could not believe that what had happened between the two of them had actually happened. They had been talking, arguing almost, and Aedan had seemed *so frus-trated* with him. What happened next would be something that Castor would remember for the rest of his life. That angry crease between Aedan's brows and the clench in his jaw and the straining muscles in his arms all at once just relaxed and faded away. And all of a sudden, Aedan was pulling him closer with those strong arms. And then they were kissing. Castor had been so stunned, that for a moment, he hadn't responded. But when the shock wore away, he remembered kissing him back and Aedan leaning into the kiss and him crawling into the bed next to him and intertwining their bodies and kissing and holding each other and Castor never wanting to let go.

In that moment just before Aedan had pulled him into their first kiss, there was a strange look in Aedan's wonderful green eyes that Castor had never before seen in someone's eyes when gazing upon him. It was not passion or lust or desire that filled his eyes - it was something else. Something much deeper and more beautiful than that.

Castor was lying in the bed with his eyes closed trying desperately to remember every tiny detail, every resplendent feeling, of that morning when Ophelia suddenly burst into the room.

"Thank the Nine," she said under her breath as she charged over to him and tackled him. "We were so worried about you," she said after pushing herself up to sit on the side of the bed. "How are you feeling?"

He knew she was asking about his aches and pains and about the mark's effect on him, but that was not what he was thinking about. "I've never been better," he said with an incredulous smile.

And at her surprised and confused expression, he told her what had happened between him and Aedan.

"Wait, so what you are saying is that you have been awake for several hours now, and I am only just now finding out about this because you couldn't stop kissing the messenger for ten seconds?"

"That seems to be the state of things, yes."

She laughed and stroked his hair like an older sister might. "Well, I am very happy for you," she said. "Both because you are alive and that you finally found someone who can tolerate you."

"Hey, *you* tolerate me."

"True, but in a much different way, apparently," she responded with a laugh. "So, apart from your sudden romantic tryst, how are you feeling?"

Castor grunted as he moved to sit upright. "Very tired. Sore. Unforgiving headache."

"But alive," Ophelia added optimistically.

"But alive," Castor echoed.

Fiona then came through the door followed shortly thereafter by Aedan and Eos. The Maechan girl gave Castor an appreciative smile and a gentle pat on the leg before Ophelia relayed Castor's pains to her. Fiona said she knew just the herb that would help, and Eos said they'd go with her to help find it. Ophelia gave Aedan and Castor a slightly amused smile before excusing herself.

Aedan stood awkwardly by the doorway with his hands clasped behind his back as he looked around the room as though he were fascinated by the plain woodwork. Red was high on his cheeks as his eyes focused anywhere but Castor.

"Would you like to sit with me?" Castor asked with a grin.

Aedan breathed out a relieved laugh as he moved to set himself on the side of the bed. He reached out and took Castor's hand in his and said, "Forgive me; I have never been in this situation with anyone before."

An incredulous look came upon Castor's face before he remembered what Aedan had told him some time ago. *When a child's parents die or abandon them and they are taken in by an orphanage, they are given the name "Ó Bháird". People tend to look down on those of us who have no claim to a clan. We are often seen as* undesirable, *and it can be difficult to find a job or a safe place to live, let alone to actually have a suitor.*

Castor still could not wrap his head around that. *How is it that anyone could look at Aedan and not find him fit for courting?* He shook his head. "You do not need to apologize."

Aedan scoffed. "Of course, I do! Here I am not knowing at all what I am doing with the most beautiful man Odessa has to offer next to me who is probably an expert at this."

Castor's head quirked to the side as his eyebrows scrunched together inquisitively. "An 'expert'?"

"Surely, someone like you has been with many people in his time," Aedan said dismissively. "I have never even kissed anyone until now."

242 | MICHAEL JACE

When Castor did not respond, Aedan looked at him, and the look on Castor's face must have made it click in his mind about how he sounded. He fell backwards onto the bed on top of Castor's lap and groaned loudly. "See, this is what I mean! I don't even know how to talk to you without being insulting!"

Castor just chuckled. "For the record, I have *not* been with *many* people." He reached out and turned Aedan's head to face him. "And I have *never* felt about anyone the way I have come to feel about you, Aedan Ó Bháird."

His green eyes looked full of yearning and disbelief as though he wanted so much for it to be true, but that he just could not make himself accept that it was. Castor decided he would just have to prove it to him, however long that may take. He bent and placed a kiss on Aedan's forehead as one of Aedan's hands reached around to bury itself in Castor's hair. He kissed Aedan again on the cheek and then on the jaw and then on the corner of his mouth before their lips came together and opened beneath each other in long, slow kisses that neither ever wanted to end.

It would be some time before either moved from that spot.

✦ . ＋ . ✦ . ＋ . ✦

Aedan had a dreamless sleep for the first time in a long time. When he woke the next morning just before dawn, for the briefest of moments he feared that the previous day had been naught but a dream. But when he finally forced himself to open his eyes, he was in the bed in the inn. And Castor was there with him with his head resting serenely on Aedan's chest. And Aedan closed his eyes again with a smile and thanked the Allmother that it was all still real.

He knew that dawn brought with it their need to leave Trícnoc and continue on their journey, but he just could not bring himself to wake Castor. If he craned his neck painfully enough, he could see Castor's face - high cheekbones, angular jaw, dimpled chin, and deep, olive complexion. Aedan sighed and wondered how and why someone this perfect could have liked him.

When the first rays of sunlight danced across the tops of the hills and through the window of their room, Castor stirred. It was slow at first - his brows furrowed at the new light, then the arm that was wrapped around Aedan shifted and moved up to rub his closed eyes, then a leg moved on top of Aedan's, and finally a yawn broke out before he finally squinted opened his dark eyes.

For a moment, he didn't move; he only stared squinting at the morning sun peaking over the hills. Then, Aedan felt him heave out a long breath as his hand moved up to trace around the muscle on Aedan's chest. With the arm wrapped around Castor, Aedan squeezed him in a one-armed embrace and kissed the top of his head, the curls tickling his nose.

"Must we?" Castor asked, his voice still rough from sleep.

Confused, Aedan said, "Must we what?"

"*Go*," Castor finished. "Must we leave this place and finish what we started?"

Aedan chuckled. "Not if you do not want to. Branwyn would understand, I am sure." He stroked his fingers through Castor's hair as he spoke.

"She probably would," Castor responded, his cheek still pressed to Aedan's chest. But then he sighed. "But I do not want to fail her. She did so much for me, I could not let her down like that."

"I know," Aedan answered. Castor's determination and loyalty were two reasons Aedan admired him in the first place. "But you are not going to be alone. Anywhere you go, I will follow you as long as you will let me. I will guard your back when there are dangerous eyes on it, and I will help you go forward when you feel as though to do so would be impossible. You will never be alone as long as I am still breathing."

Castor picked his head up and looked him in the eyes. His once midnight-black eyes seemed to be tinged with a dark, dark crimson in the morning light. When he used his powers, they would turn fully blood-red, but this was not so extreme - it was only a hint of the color that tinted his eyes now. Aedan briefly wondered if Castor's eyes would one day be consumed by the crimson color.

"Thank you," Castor said simply, but his gaze was serious. And before Aedan could explain that his thanks were unnecessary, Castor leaned in and silenced him with a kiss. Aedan would never get accustomed to that, he thought as he felt Castor's soft lips on his. No matter how many times it happened, it would always make his heart race. He pulled Castor into a deeper kiss, opening his mouth under Castor's, but then a knock on the door startled them out of it.

Castor rolled over with a sigh, sat up on the edge of the bed, and said, "Come in."

The door creaked open, and Fiona's red head popped through. "Good morning! The rest of us are ready to go, so when you two have finished defiling each other, we can begin to make tracks!"

Incredulous, Aedan opened his mouth to protest, but Fiona closed the door behind her before he could say anything. Her laughter echoed down the hallway, and Castor turned to look at him with an amused smile on his face.

"Forgive her," Aedan said with his palm on his face. "She does not know how to be civilized."

Castor laughed. "Don't worry; I think she's charming."

Aedan could not possibly see how, but he let Castor help him out of the bed. "How are you feeling?" he asked Castor. "Any better than yesterday?"

"Loads," Castor responded as he pulled a tunic over his head and strapped on his boots. "Still a little achy in some places, but mostly, I feel much better." He rubbed at his shoulder subconsciously as he spoke, but he smiled, lighting up the room and Aedan's world with its radiance. "And you?"

Aedan still felt a dull ache in his back where the knife had entered his body, but he knew it should be feeling much worse - and *would* be feeling much worse if not for Castor's magic. "Better than ever, thanks to you," he responded with a grateful smile.

They finished dressing and gathering their weapons before heading downstairs to find the rest of their company. Fiona, Eos, and Ophelia all

PHANTOM FIRE | 245

sat around a table with meals of meat and bread in front of them with two more in front of empty seats waiting for Aedan and Castor to eat.

After breakfast, when the day was well into morning, they all went to spend the rest of their remaining funds on supplies for their journey. Of course, Eos could make sure they never ran out of threpsiberries, but they all agreed they may want more than just that. So, instead of buying fruits that would soon rot, Ophelia suggested they purchase seeds from a local gardener that Eos could later grow when they were in need of food. Seeds were much lighter to carry *and* took up less space, Aedan thought. He noted with respect that not only could Ophelia poke a man full of holes before he could even draw a sword, but she was also quite bright.

So, with their packs full of seeds and hardtack bread, they were on their way out of Trícnoc and towards the Elderglas Forest. As they were leaving the town, Aedan cast one last glance at the place he may never see again, the place where he'd first kissed Castor, with a sad sort of longing.

But then, just there in the window of the inn, he thought he saw a familiar dark face, one he thought he would never see again - but when he refocused his eyes on the window, the face was gone. He laughed nervously to himself. It was probably just his imagination after all.

There was no way that Sai could have been in Trícnoc; he was all the way back in Raaja.

✦ . ✛ . ✦ . ✛ . ✦

All joking aside, Fiona was happy for her brother. It was about time he finally worked up the courage to do something about his feelings for Castor. Still, with them together and with Ophelia and Eos constantly making eyes at each other, she felt a little left out. She would always have Bas, though that obviously was not the same. Whenever he would swoop down from the skies to rest his wings, she would always give him some loving scratches.

Aside from the occasional bouts of loneliness and envy, Fiona really did enjoy being back in her home country. The rolling hills, the wild sheep whose white and gray coats could be spotted on even the farthest hills, even the crisp air there was familiar. Albainn itself was not built on hills as Trícnoc was, though there were still plenty of them nearer to the Roinn Mountains that blocked the village between them and the sea. Fiona breathed in that brisk, Maechan air with content as they trekked.

They were well on their way, several miles from Trícnoc, when they began to approach a steep slope that ran between two cliffs of grassy earth down into a great ravine. On the other side, nearly half a mile away, more cliffs rose up, towering over the bottom of the gorge.

"Whoa," Castor breathed as they all stopped to take in the view with awe.

"Giant's Ghyll," Eos said.

"I have heard of this place!" Aedan exclaimed. "They say when giants roamed the country, this was their road. They say the hoofs of their great horses wore this path down until it was a canyon."

"Truly?" Castor asked, intrigued.

"Or perhaps it was that river down there," Fiona muttered as she gestured to the waterway that ran all the way through the Ghyll.

Castor covered an embarrassed smile, and Aedan gave her a withering look. They all shared a laugh as they continued down the slope with care. Bas took off over the edge to get a look of things while they all helped each other climb down the steep slope.

Fiona was just as amazed by the view as everyone else seemed to be, but she could not help but notice when Castor would point out something to Aedan or when Eos would comment on something to Ophelia. She, of course, did not put any blame on any of them - she remembered how entranced she was when Sai began courting her back in Endala. She shuddered at the unpleasant memories that were brought back and returned her attention to the beautiful scenery. Someday, she promised herself, she would bring someone back here to show them this place.

They proceeded onwards after arriving at the bottom of the gorge. Looking left and right from the bottom was almost surreal. It was as though some huge, cylindrical thing had plowed through the earth for miles. The cliffs behind and in front of them were towering and imposing and they ran for farther than Fiona could see in either direction. She wondered how far the Giant's Ghyll actually went. Did it go all the way to west to where the Roinn Mountains curled north? Did it go all the way east to where Maecha ends and the Undying Sea begins? She wondered if she would ever get to travel to see where the Giant's Ghyll ends.

Crossing the stream was an easy task. They quickly found a shallower part of the water where the current was not too strong and only waist-deep on Fiona - the shortest of the group. Still, Aedan led the party through the water in case there were any unseen drops; being as tall as he was and the fact that he apparently knew how to swim now meant that he was the perfect leader for such an obstacle. She remembered their talk with Eos about crossing the Ebonflow and wondered what wading through those waters would be like.

As they continued on their way, they saw a small herd of aurochs about half a mile away on their left. While hunting just one down would be sure to fill up their food stocks beyond what they could carry, they had just bought all they could take with them before leaving Trícnoc. Surely, Fiona thought, they would see more aurochs again should their supplies dwindle far enough - those large bovine beasts were common enough in Maecha.

The other side of the Ghyll fortunately had a well-worn slope up to the top of the cliffs as well. While climbing up, Eos informed them that the Elderglas was only a short distance away from this side of the gorge and suggested they settle for camp under the cover of the forest's trees.

Fiona's legs were already dying. The sooner they could stop for camp, the happier she would be. She reminisced longingly about the month when they had horses, and sighed. Bonedust sure did make things easier. She wondered fleetingly if they might stumble across any wild horses and if they did, if it would be possible to tame them as well. Climbing up the slope of the cliff did nothing to ease the muscles in Fiona's legs, and she was more than grateful when they finally reached the top. Whoever she brought back to see this place with her next time

248 | MICHAEL JACE

would need to be strong enough to carry her up and down the cliffs, she decided wearily.

In the distance, probably a mile off, she saw the Elderglas. The great forest rose and fell with the hills stretching out all the way past the horizon to the north and the west. She would have been excited to see the destination where she would be able to stop and rest for the night had it not been for the dark clouds that rolled in and smothered the sun's light from the sky. When she thought about it, she was actually surprised they had gone so long in Maecha without it raining on them. Usually, the skies in this country were unforgiving with their drizzling torrents.

And so, the green country of Maecha did not disappoint her memories of the place. A cold, steady shower poured down on them, and Fiona was grateful for the mint she carried in her medicine bag that she could use for a nice, warm cup of tea later when they stopped for camp.

As long as the trip felt in the rain, they did eventually make it to the forest where they were mostly shielded from the water by the canopy overhead. Luckily, autumn had not yet taken the amber leaves from the forest. The trees the forest held, Fiona noticed, were *huge*. If their whole group held hands in a circle, they would probably be able to only encircle only the smallest of trunks. The roots and branches spiraled out in twisted, gnarled paths like broken, withered fingers.

They began unpacking once they found a reasonably flat and dry area. Aedan and Castor gathered up a few armfuls of wood from the surrounding area that seemed dry enough to burn, and Eos struck stones together to create a flame. Soon enough, their bones and rain-soaked clothes were warming around a fire. Fiona took advantage of the flame to warm a pot of mint tea to help ensure no one caught a sickness from the cold, wet weather.

Bas swooped down and nuzzled Fiona before flying back up onto one of the knotted tree limbs to rest. The rest of the evening was filled with idle chatter from members of the group as they told stories as well as the soft but constant patter of rain on the leaves above. It was not long before they were each curled up near the fire while Eos, who did not need the rest they all did, watched for danger.

Some hours later, Fiona, who had been sleeping peacefully, was suddenly being shaken awake by her brother. His brow was furrowed and there was an urgency in his eyes. He did not need to explain, though. When she focused her gaze elsewhere, she saw them. Six people dressed in the browns and ochers of the forest stood just outside of the fire's light.

18

Blind Eyes

Castor sat motionless as six armed strangers stood over them. Two held bows with readied arrows while the other four carried iron and steel. He knew if they tried to fight now, they would stand no chance. No one but Eos had their weapons on them, and Eos had the point of a spear pressed to their throat.

"What is your business in the Elderglas?" the woman holding the spear at Eos asked them.

"We are but travelers," Eos responded smoothly. "We come from Trícnoc and have business in Letha."

"What business?" another interrogated.

Eos looked back to Castor as though asking permission.

"Answer the question!" the first woman ordered, her knuckles white around the shaft of her weapon. "And do not lie."

"I have been given a task," Castor answered. "I am a champion on my way to challenge the queen of this land."

One of the strangers scoffed. "You? Challenge Queen Aife?"

"Quiet, Cecht," the first woman said. "It is his right as a - " Her voice cut off as she squinted at Castor. "You are not Maechan," she said.

"A champion need not be Maechan," Aedan inserted, his voice resolute.

250

She gave Aedan a look Castor could not interpret. "Perhaps not." Her hands relaxed on her spear. "What crest do you fight for?"

Castor looked at Aedan for an explanation, but Aedan answered. "He fights for Clan Ulster."

"Are you dim?" one of them asked with a laugh. "Clan Ulster? That is the Queen's clan."

Castor and Aedan shared a glance.

Then, the first woman's eyes rounded. "Branwyn," she whispered.

Castor nodded.

"Branwyn?" the man, Cecht, said incredulously. "You cannot mean the Queen's sister? The one she banished all those years ago?"

Castor nodded again. "I have trained under her for a year, and she chose me to be her champion to fight for her rightful place on the throne." The ambushers stood silently, unmoving.

"Will you let us pass?" Aedan asked eventually.

They all looked to the first woman. *She must be their leader,* Castor surmised. It looked as though her own thoughts were battling one another before she finally said, "No. No, you cannot pass through just yet."

"What do you plan to do with us?" Ophelia asked. Castor saw her hand inching towards her rapier on the ground a few feet away from her.

"You will come with us to speak with our matriarch. If she says you can pass, we will not stand in your way," the woman said.

"You are a nomadic clan," Fiona said.

The woman nodded as she lowered her spear from Eos's throat. "We are. And we are no danger to you if you come with us peacefully."

The five of them shared understanding glances. No one wanted to risk their lives if they could get through this without incident.

"We will come with you," Castor said as he stood.

The woman turned to two of the archers behind her and instructed them to run ahead and let the matriarch know they were bringing visitors. The two archers disappeared in the black of the forest, their footsteps silent. It was no wonder how they'd snuck up on them all so easily.

Castor and the rest of the group packed up their belongings and snuffed out their fire before following the woman off into the darkness.

For the majority of the time, the walk was quiet. It was also difficult given the lack of light to guide them. Either these people had incredible night vision, or they just really knew their way around the forest. There was just enough starlight trickling down through the trees that if Castor *really* tried, he could just make out large dark blobs that he assumed were trees. While the ones they followed seemed adept at traveling through the forest in the dark, Castor's group spent the entire excursion tripping over one another's feet and the gnarled roots that roped around the ground like giant snakes.

Suddenly, Castor heard Fiona mumble an "Oh" before the area was lit up with a sapphire gleam. "Forgot I had this," she said as she looped the naga's pendant over her head so that the stone rested around her navel. Their guide eyed it curiously but said nothing.

Ironically, it was not long after that that Castor thought he could see the flickering light of fire up ahead in the distance. As they approached, the woman stopped and turned to them. "You will conduct yourselves appropriately while in the presence of the matriarch," she said. "It is in your best interest if you do not show her any disrespect. You, champion, being from Odessa may not be accustomed to our way of life in this country; but you are still expected to abide by our customs."

"I understand," Castor said. He was truthfully not as nervous as some might have been in his situation. He was quite used to meeting powerful and important people from his life as a noble, and this did not feel much different.

The woman nodded as she returned to her previous gait. She guided them into a large camp, Castor saw. Many tents, perhaps over thirty, spread out around the many trees. There were only a few campfires out with a few of the clan members sitting around watching them suspiciously. *Most of them are probably asleep at this hour,* Castor thought. The tents seemed mostly structurally sound, at least against wind and rain, though they also looked as though they could be taken down quickly and easily. For a brief moment, Castor wondered what it would be like to not have a permanent home anywhere - to live constantly in motion, always moving from one place to another without settling down. Sure, he had generally enjoyed their journey since they had left Endala, but still, he did not think he would want to do it forever. A part of him longed for a soft, warm bed in a house he owned with someone he loved somewhere far away from the rest of the world where their only responsibilities were to each other.

He stole a sideways glance at Aedan. Maybe he would have that someday.

They were led to a tent seemingly like all the others if not slightly larger. "Wait here," the woman said as she pulled aside the tanned leather door and ducked through. Castor caught a glimpse of candle-light on the other side before the door swung back closed again.

They stayed silent as they exchanged awkward glances with each other and with the strangers around them. There were not many of them out and about - these must just be the ones keeping watch for the night.

It was not long before their guide's head poked through the door and told them that they could enter. On the other side of the door, a plethora of candles surrounded a cushion in the middle of the ground. Hanging on the far end of the tent was a family crest - a yellow shield with two black chevrons crossing its center and a knight's helm on top. A small fire burned in front of the crest, its smoke rising through a central hole in the top of the tent. The light of the fire nearly silhouetted a seated figure on the cushion, though the candles' flames were enough to give Castor an idea of what the person looked like.

It was a woman, older than Avelas had been. She was probably nearing a century or more in age if Castor had to guess. Her wrinkled skin hung heavily on her bones, leaving her face drooping but not without a touch of kindness. Hair as pale as the moon cascaded down, spilling around on the ground around her haphazardly, though still at a safe distance away from the circle of candles that encompassed her. She wore an ancient scrap of cloth that was probably once a brilliant shade of yellow over her eyes, concealing them all from her view. The robe that was draped over the rest of her pooled out behind her only barely hinting at her frail frame.

"Matriarch," the younger woman said. "I bring you five visitors. As I said, our hunting party found them camping in the southeastern edge of the forest."

The matriarch nodded her head slowly. "Thank you, Leana. You may go."

The younger woman started, a look of confusion - almost outrage - in her eyes. "Matriarch, you cannot mean for me to leave you alone with these strangers. I can stay - "

"That will be all, Leana," the matriarch said, her voice quiet but absolute. "I am not in any danger. If I have need of you, I will call."

Leana let out a breath of frustration through her nose before briefly bowing and leaving them alone with the old woman.

"Hail to you, travelers," the matriarch said once they were alone.

"Hail," they all responded politely.

"There is no need for you all to stand," she said. "Please sit."

The five moved to sit uncomfortably around the edge of the candles.

The matriarch nodded with a small smile when they had all gotten in place, almost as if she could *see* that they had, Castor thought curiously. Perhaps she could see through the cloth ...

"Please forgive my dear Leana for waking you all up and bringing you here," she said, her voice creaking. "She was only worried for our camp's safety. Though it may be clear to you and me that a small group of travelers would not bode much of a threat to an entire clan, my dear Leana is a worrier."

"It is no trouble, Matriarch," Aedan replied. "We are grateful for your kindness and hospitality."

Without missing a beat, the matriarch went on. "She tells me of your quest, to act as champion to dethrone Queen Aife and replace her with her banished sister. I can see that this is the truth."

Castor almost asked how she could see that it was the truth, but she raised a timeworn finger in his direction before the words could leave his mouth. "You are the champion, yes?"

Hesitantly, Castor looked around as if wondering if she was talking to him despite her gesture. "That is correct."

The matriarch quietly hummed a single note as though deeply considering something. "You have been to the deadlands, haven't you?"

"The deadlands?" Castor stuttered.

She nodded. "The land of the souls who have parted from this world. The home of their people," she said, inclining her head in Eos's direction. "The Otherworld."

Castor nodded back, then remembered she may not be able to see him. "Yes, though only in a dream."

A chuckle escaped her worn body. "A dream, you say? It appears as though it was more than just that." Before Castor could question her, she went on. "The Allmother has marked you, no? Which of the Nine laid their hands upon you?"

"It was the Phantom whom I met," Castor answered. Was she a witch? A seeress? How could she know all that she did?

"As I suspected," she said. She was quiet for a moment as she seemed to be thinking something over. Finally, she let out a breath, seeming satisfied about something and said, "Please forgive us for waking you and dragging you all here. We will not intrude on your mission any further. Feel free to rest here under our protection, though I would humbly ask that you please come speak with me before you continue on your way in the morning."

Aedan nodded emphatically. "Yes, Matriarch - " He paused as though seeking an answer to a hidden question.

"Mac Lellan," she answered. "I am the matriarch of Clan Mac Lellan."

They were shown to an area on the fringes of the camp where they were told they could rest, but as it happens, several of them were not really all that tired anymore. Castor and Aedan went off together, stating that they would stay within eyesight of the camp, but Fiona decided she would just stay and try to get some more sleep. Eos said they would keep watch as well, but Ophelia found she was also not so tired.

She silently moved away from Fiona and went to sit on the grass next to the half-elf.

"Are you not in need of more rest?" Eos asked with a small smile at her appearance.

She shrugged. "We slept for a while already," she said as she stared out into the dark forest. The trees here were really magnificent, she thought. She had never seen them grow to be so large. She supposed in other circumstances they might have even been somewhat ominous what with their gnarled reaching limbs, but with Eos nearby, she felt safe. "Morning should be here in a few hours anyway, right?"

Eos nodded. "There is still some time."

Silence grew between them then, and so Ophelia decided to break it if only to get to know more about them. "I know you lived in Argos, but where did you come from before then?"

Eos blew out a long breath. "I have lived in many places," they said. "I was born on one of the Yuki Isles near Midoria."

Ophelia sucked in her breath as she remembered a frightening story they had once told her. "You do not mean - "

They chuckled quietly. "No, I am not from the village from that legend. That village was allegedly on one of the islands to the north of where I am from."

Ophelia nodded. "Where else have you lived?"

"After I left home, I went to the Midorian mainland and lived off the land near one of the villages there. After a few years, I traveled across the country to the capital and found work helping tend the crops of one of the kinder farmers there. I stayed there for close to three decades until the old man passed away. Although he had no family around to take care of his land, the city would not allow me to continue working there, so I left. I stowed away on a trading vessel on its way to Letha in Maecha. The people there were nicer than in Midoria, but I still did not feel at home. I traveled from there to Loughur to Trícnoc, never really staying in one place for too long. I passed through the Roinn

PHANTOM FIRE | 257

Mountains and through Argos down to Hale, the capital. I lived on the streets there for some time before leaving and heading northeast to a village called Robary near where the Roinn meets the Undying Sea on the eastern coast of Odessa. I did not stay there long either, however. I soon left there and went back to Argos where I had been staying for almost a decade until I was hired by your company to bring you through the mountains. And you know the rest."

Ophelia sat wide-eyed at the explanation.

Eos noticed her surprised expression and said, "Where all have you lived?"

Ophelia blew out a short breath and said, "Oh, you know, I was born in Argos. And then when I was twenty-seven, I left home went on a mad journey with you and three others."

Eos giggled.

Ophelia had a burning question, though she hoped it was not too impolite to ask. "I do not mean this to be rude, so please do not take offense, but how old are you?"

For the first time since she had known them, Ophelia saw blush rise to Eos's pale cheeks. "I have been alive for seventy-two years," they said quietly. Their eyes stayed focused on the darkness of the trees.

"You look so young!" Ophelia exclaimed. "If any of my wishes come true, I hope it is that I can look as beautiful as you when I come to be that age."

Eos's head quirked to the side as she spoke. "You - "

Ophelia sucked in her breath, quickly feeling horror creep into her at the thought that she had accidentally insulted them. "I am so sorry; I meant no off - "

"You think I am beautiful?" Eos's voice was softer than Ophelia had ever heard it. She looked into their large, unnaturally green eyes, completely taken aback by the question.

She absolutely *did* think Eos was beautiful. Their complexion was so clear and fair and their hair and eyes so striking. "Of course I do," Ophelia responded quietly as she turned to face the forest, feeling heat behind her cheeks. She tugged at one of the coils of her hair nervously, spinning it around her finger.

When the quiet had gone on for longer than Ophelia could bear, she finally chanced a glance over at them out of the corner of her eye.

Mist had collected under the rims of the emeralds in Eos's eyes, she saw. "No one has ever said that to me before," Eos whispered as one of their hands absentmindedly tucked a lock of alabaster hair behind a pointed ear.

"I meant it," Ophelia said back, a flutter caught behind her ribs.

"I think you are beautiful, too," Eos blurted out as though they had only just remembered to tell her.

Ophelia let out a breath of laugh before she turned to look at them. They were still gazing out into the darkness, though red stained their face in a heavy flush.

She could not help herself. She leaned over and planted a soft, quick peck on their blushing cheek. Eos spun to face her in surprise as one of their hands crept up to their cheek. The surprise quickly turned to glee as Eos scooted close enough to her that their shoulders touched. And there they sat as they watched the darkness of the forest.

They did not stray too far from the lights of the camp on their walk that night, careful to make sure their calls for help would still be heard should they come across something dangerous. They had been walking for only a few minutes when Aedan had felt Castor's rough hand slip into his, their fingers intertwining as they walked together. It had made Aedan's heart jump for he had never held anyone's hand like that before. Something so simple, and yet it shot fire through his veins, all his nerves tingling.

They did not speak much as they went; they were mostly just enjoying their time apart from the rest of their group until Aedan saw a small area up ahead where a good deal of moonlight was shining through the canopy above. He angled their path in that direction, and when they came to the opening, they stopped.

PHANTOM FIRE | 259

Silver light shimmered down from the sky lightening the dark wood of the surrounding trees. A cool wind rustled through the leaves, and, while Aedan was accustomed to the chill of Maecha, Castor shivered.

Aedan pulled him to the base of a tree where there was a small nook between two of its roots that was just big enough to seat both of them if one of them sat partially on the other. They sat there together with Aedan's arms around Castor while they watched the moon hang beautifully in the sky high above them.

After a few minutes, Aedan began to smell smoke. He flinched, ready for some kind of danger, but Castor just said, "Do not worry; it's only the mark."

"Oh," Aedan said, suddenly feeling guilty for causing Castor pain just by holding him. "We can sit farther apart if you w - "

Castor laughed under his breath as he pulled one of Aedan's arms tighter around him. "No, I do not want that." He turned his head from the night sky to rest in the crook of Aedan's neck. He could feel Castor's warm, steady breath escaping onto his collarbone, and now it was *his* turn to shiver.

"I think I know why the mark does that when you're close," Castor said eventually, keeping his head nestled against Aedan. He could feel the vibrations of Castor's words in his bones as he spoke.

"Oh?"

Castor nodded, his hair brushing against Aedan's face with each movement. "I have been thinking about it since that night when we first set off, but I think I know now. See, back when we first discovered the mark, back with Teacher and then later with Sai and the deer, the mark came up on its own when I was feeling some strong emotion. Pain with Teacher and horror with Sai. But neither of those times, when the mark came on its own, did it burn as painfully as when we are together. And I think that it is because the way you make me feel is stronger than any other emotion I have ever felt before."

A smile crept over Aedan's face as he gently kissed the top of Castor's head.

"I think the mark has known something for a long time that I am only just starting to realize," Castor went on. Before he continued, he lifted his head to look Aedan in the eyes. Even with the penetrating moonlight, it was quite dark there under the tree, but Aedan could still make out Castor's features. His gaze was so serious, for a moment Aedan thought Castor was going to say something terrible. But he did not.

"I love you." His low voice was resolute.

Everything washed out of Aedan with Castor's words. Every fear, every doubt, every anxiety - every single negative thought Aedan had ever had disappeared into nothing. All he had left were those three words. They warmed every part of him that had been left cold by his past. They filled every empty space that had been left hollow. When Castor said what he said, for the first real time, Aedan believed him.

"I love you, too, Castor," Aedan whispered. He rubbed his thumb over Castor's cheekbone as the rest of his fingers curled around his jaw and into his dark mess of hair. Castor's eyes shimmered in the pale moon's light before he closed them and leaned into the most perfect kiss.

They stayed there in the nook of the tree with their arms wrapped around each other for the rest of the night.

Fiona couldn't sleep. She had been trying for what felt like hours, but she just could not manage to relax enough to actually fall asleep. When she had opened her eyes, she saw Eos and Ophelia leaning against each other at the edge of the light, but she didn't want to disturb them. So, instead, she went off on her own with only Bas to keep her company who perched on her shoulder and watched vigilantly. She walked around the margins of the camp giving a polite smile and nod to anyone she went by.

As she padded around the southern bend of the camp, Bas took off into the trees, probably in search of a midnight treat. Fiona sighed before she noticed a handful of pink flowers growing under a nearby tree lightened by the sapphire glow of her pendant. She stopped in her tracks and stared at them for a moment before eventually moving to them and sitting.

She plucked one from its roots and felt its soft petals between her thumb and finger while reminiscing about the time before she knew the horrible truths of her last and only suitor.

A sudden breaking of a twig alerted her to the fact that she was not alone. She whirled her head around and saw him.

Sai.

It was as if she had accidentally summoned him straight from her thoughts. He was standing on the edge of where her pendant's aura bled into the darkness looking as she had always remembered him.

She sucked in a breath ready to call for help, but Sai moved *fast.* He was suddenly on his knees next to her with his hand over her mouth, but his expression did not look angry or vengeful. He looked small and sad and helpless. He was filthy, Fiona saw absently. He was covered in dirt and grime, his hair had grown substantially, and he even had a light, patchy beard. He really had not been taking care of himself, she thought.

"Please, do not scream, my doe," he whispered, looking around frantically. "It is just me, do not be afraid."

My doe. The words that had once been sweet now were now tinged with something foreign and *wrong.*

Was he not *going to hurt her?* Slowly, she nodded, and he took his hand away. Where his hand had been, her face was now damp as though his hands had been clammy with sweat, though it smelled of something else Fiona couldn't name.

"Why are you here?" Fiona asked. He was supposed to be in *Raaja* after all. Thousands of miles away from Maecha.

"I am here because you wanted me to come with you," he said as though it were obvious. "You do remember, do you not? You wanted me to come see you in Maecha. That is what you said. And I know your brother and the other one do not approve of me, so I had to come when you were alone."

Does he think that I am all right with what he has done? Fiona thought wildly.

"You are happy to see me, yes?" he asked, his voice taking an almost warning tone.

Fiona saw the glint of two hilts protruding from behind his sides and swallowed thickly, feeling beads of sweat form under her hairline despite the chill.

"Sai, you cannot be here," she said as she inched away from him. She remembered how quickly he had just moved and knew that he would be able to catch her should she run. Sure, Bas would help her, but she was not sure where he was and if he could even get to her in time.

Confusion muddled his expression. "I came all the way here for *you*," he said. "Surely you cannot mean that."

She felt her mouth dry out. She could lie to him and tell him she still liked him, but then would he not still keep following her? And if he kept following her, there was a chance someone could be hurt. What if he hurt Aedan because she was too afraid to tell him she did not want to see him anymore? Surely, he could handle a bit of rejection.

"I do," Fiona said carefully. "I know what you did, Sai, and I cannot accept it. Please, Sai, go home. Go back to Raaja. Ask your family for forgiveness and - "

"*Go home*?" he asked incredulously. "I followed you halfway across Odessa, saved you from execution in Argos, braved the Roinn Mountains, and traveled through this land *for you*. And you want me to *go home*?" Despite his tone, his voice was still very quiet.

Fiona began to feel dizzy - almost nauseous. Still, she held her ground. "Yes, Sai. I am sorry that you thought I still wanted you to come, but I do not." She felt as though she had had one too many ales despite having had none. *What is wrong with me*, she thought briefly. "Please accept my apology and return home."

He stood up then, looking at her with an expression of immeasurable hurt. When he moved, there was a delay in Fiona's vision. She was suddenly very tired and was struggling to keep her eyes open. She vaguely remembered his hand being wet when he had cupped it over her nose and mouth. "What did you do to me?" she mumbled.

She saw him watching something in the camp, and when she turned to look, she noticed one of the nomads walking over to them. Feeling relief wash over her, she looked back to Sai, but he was gone.

"Are you all right, lass?" the man asked as he approached.

"I - " was all she was able to respond before she slipped into unconsciousness.

19

As Above

The next morning, Castor and Aedan joined the others back at camp. Everyone was already awake when they arrived, and they were all eating something steaming from wooden bowls.

"Boar stew," Ophelia supplied after swallowing a mouthful. "It is surprisingly just as good, if not better, than most things cooked back at Argos."

Castor's stomach rumbled at the smell of it.

"Did you all sleep all right?" Aedan asked as he sat on the grass next to Fiona who had one hand curled around the bowl of stew and the other massaging her temple.

Ophelia and Eos shared a brief glance before Ophelia responded. "I was not particularly tired anymore, so I stayed up with Eos." Castor noticed red staining her cheeks, and he squinted suspiciously. He would ask her about it later, he told himself.

"Fi?" Aedan asked.

She groaned and leaned against her brother's shoulder.

"She said she had a splitting headache this morning," Ophelia said. "One of the lookouts here saw her just outside of camp last night, and when he went to ask her if she was all right, she went out cold. He carried her back here and laid her down, but she slept the rest of the night," she said.

"Fi, are you all right? What happened?" Aedan asked, putting an arm around her. Castor could tell when his "big brother" voice was being used as it was now.

She groaned again. "I don't remember. All I remember is coming here and lying down. I do not even remember getting up to walk around," she said. "I am fine, though. Just feeling a little under the weather."

Castor could tell Aedan was not satisfied with her response, but he just nodded.

Shortly after, the woman from the night before, Leana, approached holding two more bowls of steaming boar stew. "Here you are," she said as she handed them to Castor and Aedan. "We have more, so please eat until you have filled yourselves." She turned to walk back from where she came but seemed to remember something and spun around to them. "The Matriarch wanted me to remind you two that she would like to speak with you before you set off again."

"Just the two of us?" Aedan asked gesturing to himself and Castor.

Leana nodded. "She will be waiting in her tent when you are ready, but there is no need to feel rushed. Take your time eating and see her when you are finished."

"Thank you," Castor said with a polite smile and nod. Leana nodded back and turned to walk away.

They spoke sparingly as they wolfed down their bowls of stew, thankful for something so filling and satisfying for once. Castor saw the worried looks Aedan gave his sister, but she was here and safe, so there was not much to worry about, he thought.

When they finished eating, Castor and Aedan made their way to the tent they had been brought to the night before. The person standing guard outside of it inclined their head to them and pulled back the curtain so that they could enter.

It was as it had been the previous night, Castor saw. A family crest, a fire, a ring of candles, and the seated Matriarch Mac Lellan with her eyes covered. This time, however, Leana was standing near the crest in the back with an unreadable expression on her face.

"You are ready to set out?" It was more of a statement than a question.

Castor nodded before silently cursing himself and saying, "Yes", out loud. "Yes, we are ready to continue on our path. Thank you again for the hospitality," he said.

She waved away his words as though his thanks were unnecessary. "Before you go, I would like to send you off with a few gifts that I hope will help you on your quest."

"Really," Aedan said, "you have done more than enough for us - "

"I do not recall giving you an option to decline," she went on. "If the goddess wills this, then we shall assist in what ways we can. First of all, traveling on foot can be long and tiresome if not outright dangerous at times. We will give unto you five horses who will carry you on your way to Letha. Do not worry about returning them; only promise that they will be well cared for wherever you end up."

Castor felt a wave of relief wash over him. *Horses.* Their months' long journey would be shortened a great deal from that gift alone.

"Another thing," she said. She gestured Leana to come forward. Leana was carrying something that was folded neatly in her arms. Was it ... a shirt?

"This is one of our most prized possessions," Matriarch Mac Lellan said. Leana handed it to Aedan who took it with a look of pure gratefulness in his eyes. "It may not look like it, but this armor will protect you from nearly everything."

Castor looked at it, squinting. It was the color of undyed linen, although it was made of something that had a strange rigid pattern to it. It seemed quite flexible in Aedan's hands as he felt it, Castor saw.

"What is it?" Castor asked.

"It is made of dragonskin," she answered. "Dragonskin cannot be penetrated save by dragons themselves. And do not worry about the fit; it will fit itself to its wearer no matter their size."

Aedan was staring at it with a look of such awe and amazement, but then it seemed as though something passed into his mind as the look broke off suddenly. "Wait, why are you giving this to me and not to Castor?"

The Matriarch smiled. "I have seen that you are his protector," she said. "You are his shield, and a good shield must stay standing. Wear this armor and protect him. You will do this, yes?"

Aedan nodded fervently. "I swear to it, Matriarch. I will put this gift to good use."

She smiled again and nodded before reaching into the folds of her robe. "A final gift before you go."

Castor reached out a hand to accept whatever was enclosed in her small fist. It was an iron disc the size of a coin with the Mac Lellan crest carved into one side.

"Should you ever need to find us again, know that you must only toss this into a fire," she said.

Intrigued, Castor wanted to know more, but he only nodded and said, "Thank you; I will."

As they turned to leave, the Matriarch added, "When you defeat Queen Aife, remember those of us who helped you."

✦ . ✛ . ✦ . ✛ . ✦

When Castor and Aedan emerged from the tent finally, Ophelia saw that Leana was leading them. Leana motioned for Ophelia and the others to come, and she saw that they were being showed to where the horses were kept. She unrestrained five of them and handed the reins of each horse to each rider.

"Ride safe," she said as the five of them mounted their horses after having packed their supplies on first. "Carry the Allmother close. We will await news from Letha of a new ruler if it comes to be." And with that, she turned back into the camp and left them with only the forest ahead of them.

So, off they went.

Traveling by horse was by far easier than traveling on foot, Ophelia thought. Sure, she had ridden horses before at her estate, and she had traveled by carriage before, but she had never actually traveled by horseback. She knew she would still be sore when they stopped to rest, but at least she did not have to actually *walk* across the whole country of Maecha.

The trees that whipped by were somehow much less ominous when she was flying by them instead of trudging across their mangled roots. She had to protect her face from scratching branches several times, but this was still much more preferable to going on foot, she thought.

They still had some time before they would be out of the forest, according to Eos. Two days at most on horseback. After that, they would have about five days before they reached the bridge at the Ebonflow, and then a little over a week before they would arrive in Letha.

Ophelia was already ready for Letha.

It was not as though she was not enjoying the journey so much as she just wanted to sleep in a safe, warm place again. Her mind stretched back to her cozy estate as they bumped along their path. She remembered the warming tea in the mornings, the beautiful flower garden, the hearth that always kept the drawing room so comfortable - she would often relax there when they were not entertaining guests, and it was left otherwise empty. For a while, when she had first began doing so, the servants would dote on her, trying to feed her or start the fire for her or take care of her in some way, but she would always politely refuse their insisting and instead tend the hearth herself while resting on the rug in front of it with a nice, heavy book. She sighed as she longed for that hearth.

Over the next couple days, they stopped occasionally for food as well as to give the horses a rest. They would chew on some hardtack, or Eos would plant a few seeds and use their Sidhe magic to make them produce food. They did not run into any trouble along the way - Ophelia guessed the horses' hoofbeats scared away most wildlife before they were even seen.

Before long, they were out of the Elderglas and back under the open sky. The terrain was roughly even and flat, though Eos assured them that, once past the Ebonflow, the hills would return.

Ophelia did not mind the cold as much as Castor seemed to. What bothered her most about Maecha was how cloudy it seemed to be most of the time. She was always one to enjoy the gentle kisses of the sun, regularly basking in it whenever she had a chance to at her estate. But with all of the overcast skies in this country, she was rarely blessed with its light and warmth. Still, there was something charming about Maecha. Perhaps it was how *green* everything was. It was such a deeper, more pleasurable green than anything Odessa had to offer, only coming close in the middle of spring when her country was brimming with life and growth. It was as though Maecha was perpetually in a state of mid-spring - always giving birth to new life, every flower and every tree as strong and beautiful as it ever could be.

How could all of these plants possibly be so green and beautiful in Maecha when there is *no sun*, she thought bitterly as she glared at the clouded sky.

Up ahead, she noticed their path sloping down into a narrow valley of sorts.

"We are approaching the Ebonflow," Eos announced as their horses trotted alongside each other. "Be wary of any onlookers near the river."

"Onlookers?" Fiona asked.

Eos nodded. "Humans do not often tread over the Ebonflow when they can avoid it. If we see anyone or anything, they will probably be Sidhe."

Recounting her only experiences with dark Sidhe, Ophelia agreed that they should be wary.

"Hopefully we can cross without any interference, though," Eos said.

They soon came upon it, and Ophelia saw firsthand why it was called the Ebonflow. The water was not blue nor green nor clear, but black as night. It was nearly sixty feet wide at this crossing, and it ran westward, seemingly calm at the surface, though Ophelia would bet that there were unseen undercurrents that were as deadly as the creatures that inhabited them.

The bridge was there too, though they came upon it from the west so Ophelia could see the stonework from the side. It was prob-ably beautiful when it was first erected, she thought. The white stone had cracked and weathered down to a graying mess overgrown with moss that flooded the intricate and worn carvings that swirled along the sides of the stone. Two large iron hoops stuck out from the walls of the bridge, rusted and ancient. Ophelia tilted her head and decided that despite its dilapidated, nearly decrepit looks, it still had a sort of mysterious charm or beauty to it that she could not deny.

She scoured her vision from the banks of the Ebonflow below up to the horizon, searching for any "onlookers" that could potentially be a danger to them, but she did not see anything. Still feeling watched, however, their horses guided them to the bridge where they stopped and dismounted from Eos's command.

"We do not want them to be frightened by anything while we are on their backs," they said. "They could throw us off into the river or jump in themselves with us still on them. Best to be careful."

The rest nodded as they each held the reins of their own horses and began to lead them across the bridge.

Ophelia felt gooseflesh rise on her arms and the hair on the back of her neck stand on end as they tried to cross as quietly as possible. All five of the group were scanning around them, looking for anything like that banshee they encountered in the Roinn those few weeks ago.

When they crossed over the arch of the bridge, Ophelia saw it.

It was as though it had always been there and had just shimmered into Ophelia's vision. A solid white cat sat at the end of the bridge, completely unmoving except for its tail that slowly waved back and forth behind it, curling at the end in the shape of a little hook. It was admittedly quite cute, Ophelia thought. It was very fluffy for a cat, its long hair and serene pose giving it a regal air.

Eos cursed under their breath.

"Sidhe?" Ophelia whispered.

Eos nodded in response. "Aedan, Fiona? Can you two please go tie the horses' reins to those iron hoops on the front of the bridge?" Never once did Eos take their eyes off the cat as they spoke. Wordlessly, the siblings did as they were asked and returned momentarily.

PHANTOM FIRE | 271

"Please let us pass," Eos called out to the mysterious cat as they halted in their tracks. "We only mean to travel to Letha. We mean you no offense or ill will."

The cat stared on quietly.

"Are you sure it is a Sidhe?" Castor whispered. "Maybe it is just a lost cat."

"I do not think a lost cat would be sitting at the end of a bridge like that," Ophelia muttered. It was no doubt odd the way it was just calmly waiting for them. A lost cat would definitely have fled at the sight of them.

"May we pass?" Eos asked, taking a few more steps forward. "Please," they added, almost pleadingly.

The cat began walking forward then, causing Eos to freeze in their stride. As the cat slowly, but purposefully, lounged forward, it changed. In a single fluid moment, the cat's back legs elongated and transformed into those of a human and its front legs into human arms and hands. He stood on his now-human legs and stretched out behind himself as his feline face morphed into something that looked much more human, though not entirely so. While the fur had seemingly vanished, he still had the curved mouth and the small, pink nose of a cat. His eyes were larger than normal as well with vertical black slits cutting through the abnormal gold irises. The hair that was left on the mysterious man's head was long and unnaturally white, pulled back into a single braid that hung over his right shoulder. He wore only a fluffy, white robe that seemed to be of some animal pelt as though the skin of the cat he had once been had expanded and tanned itself into a wearable cloak.

"Your pleas are tiresome." His voice was low though it carried across the bridge to them as though he were right next to them. He lazily padded to the side of the bridge where he then sat, crossing his legs and regarding them all with a look of disgust and boredom. His long, sharp claws drummed on the stone as he seemed to be deliberating on what he wanted to do with them.

All five of them were silent the entire time except for Fiona who had let out several choice curses when the cat man first transformed.

He hummed a bored, monotone note before saying, "How about we play a little game?"

Ophelia thought she could see Eos sweating. "Please, just let us through," they said. "We do not mean you any - "

He scoffed and rolled his eyes. "Did I not just tell you how very boring your pleas are? I will not ask again. If you win, I will let you pass."

"And if we do not win?" Eos ventured carefully.

He only smiled in response - a dangerous look for what had recently been a small cat.

Eos turned back to the rest of them. "He is a cait sith," they whispered.

"Is that a kind of dark Sidhe?" Aedan asked.

Eos shook their head. "No, he has not become dark yet. Cait siths are extremely powerful magic users said to be able to be mortally wounded nine times before actually dying. If I guessed, I would assume he is able to hold off the darkness much longer than other Sidhe."

"Do you know what kind of *game* he wants to play?" Castor asked.

Eos shook their head again. "It could be anything but be prepared for his magic. It will undoubtedly come into play during the game."

"Do we have another option?" Ophelia offered. "Perhaps another crossing somewhere?"

"Not for miles, unfortunately," they responded. "We would have to travel through miles and miles of the Elderglas before coming to another place that would be suitable to cross."

"Let's just play," Aedan said. "How bad could it be, really?"

Fiona groaned. "I cannot believe you just said that," she muttered.

Eos turned back to the cait sith. Nodding to him, they said, "Fine. It is a deal. If we win this game of yours, you let us pass."

The cait sith hopped off from his perch on the side of the bridge squealing in excitement. "Oh, this is going to be so much *fun!*" he cheered as he clapped his hands together. Ophelia noticed his slit pupils enlarge into wide circles like black saucers as he became more animated.

PHANTOM FIRE | 273

"So, what manner of game would you have us play?" Eos asked tentatively. Ophelia saw their finger brush the feathers of an arrow in the quiver around their waist.

"Oh, a *fun* one!" he exclaimed as he hopped nearer to them. "But only one of you gets to play at a time!" He hummed as he looked between the five of them deciding who to pick. "You first!" said the cait sith as he pointed a clawed finger at Fiona.

"*No*," Aedan said stepping forward. But as he advanced, he cried out in pain and fell to his knees, clutching his stomach in his arms. Castor reached for the spear slung on his back.

"*Tsk, tsk, tsk*," he tutted. "This is *my* game, and *I* decide who plays."

Fiona dropped to her knees next to Aedan with her arms around him. "I will play!" Fiona cried. "Just make this stop!"

The cait sith looked slightly bored at the scene, but eventually, Aedan breathed out a sigh of relief and managed to push himself back up.

"Are you all right?" Ophelia heard Castor whisper, and she saw Aedan nod back.

Fiona stepped forward and said, "What must I do?"

"It is simple! All you must do is answer my question. If you are correct, we move on."

"And if not?" Fiona asked.

As expected, the cait sith only smiled in response.

Fiona sighed. "Ask your question."

His pupils widened in ardor as he jumped and clapped his hands. "Oh, very good!" He began lazily pacing back and forth as he thought of a question to ask. "I am as light as air, but the longer you hold me, the harder it is to keep me. What am I?"

"W - What?" Fiona uttered. "That is - "

"Careful!" Eos snapped. "Speak only your answer."

"A game of riddles," Ophelia muttered.

The cait sith looked on, somehow both amused and impatient. As Fiona struggled with coming up with an answer, the cait sith moved to sit back upon the parapet of the bridge and began drumming his claws on the stone sending up pink sparks where they scraped against the ancient bridge. Suddenly, Ophelia began to feel as though they had just risen several thousand feet in elevation. The air seemed to thin, and it felt as if Ophelia lungs were not getting enough air in them.

She began breathing a little more heavily to try to compensate for it, and as she looked around, she saw that most everyone else, save Fiona, seemed to be having the same trouble. Aedan and Castor both had their hands pressed to their chests, and Eos's shoulders were rising and falling more rapidly.

Fiona glanced around and saw everyone else struggling to breathe normally and looked back at the cait sith. She opened her mouth with a mixed look of fear and fury before shutting it, probably remembering Eos's warning.

"Better make haste," the cait sith giggled. "I do not think your friends will last much longer."

As soon as the silky words left his mouth, the pressure in Ophelia's chest increased a hundred-fold. She doubled over, dropping to her hands and knees as she choked, unable to take in any air at all. The other three were also on the ground - not even gasping for air, just silently writhing.

Just as Ophelia began to see black spots pervade her vision, Fiona blurted out, "Breath! Breath is as light as air and is harder to hold the longer you keep it!"

A look of disappointment flashed across the cait sith's face. "Very well; that is correct." He looked into the distance as though thinking of what to do next, but Ophelia only barely noticed that as her sight went dark.

"*My friends!*" Fiona yelped.

"Oh, right, right," he responded. A wave of his hand sent more pink flashes of light cascading through the air.

Sweet, beautiful air swam back into Ophelia's lungs at once. Her chest was exploding in pain, and tears were streaming down her eyes as she tried to regain a semblance of composure. Eos's arms were around her suddenly though their breaths were just as severe. Together they stood and awaited the next riddle.

"You," the cait sith said, pointing his finger at Ophelia then. "I have been black, brown, blue, and green. I have a twin whom I've never seen. In hard times, I flow, but in good, I glow. What is my name, if you now know?"

Ophelia, completely unprepared to have been chosen, raced through the riddle over and over in her mind. *"I have a twin whom I've never seen"? What does that even mean?*

She heard a gasp to her left, and, turning, she saw Castor, Aedan, and Fiona clutching each other in frantic grips, blinking hard.

"Ophelia," Eos whispered as they hung on her shoulder, "I do not mean to frighten you, but I believe we have all gone blind now."

The cait sith chuckled. "And blind you will remain unless your dear friend answers correctly."

Ophelia felt her breath and heartrate quicken, though not due to lack of air this time. Her eyes searched the ground and the waters below as if searching for the answer to the riddle. *"In hard times, I flow"? A river? No, that doesn't glow.*

Then, she remembered the last riddle's answer was "breath" and that no one could breathe until Fiona answered it. Now, everyone was *blind,* so ...

"Eye!" she shouted, victorious. "Eyes are all different colors. It cannot see its twin eye, it cries in hard times, and shines in good times!"

The cait sith looked perturbed at her answer. "Fine, you win again."

Ophelia heard the sighs of relief as her friends' eyes danced around at their surroundings as though happy to see them again.

The cait sith scoffed. "This game is not as fun as I thought it would be. Your kind are usually more entertaining."

"Does that mean we win?" Eos asked. "Will you let us by?"

"I said I would let you by, and I will," the cait sith said. Though he had a sudden twinkle in his eye as though he knew something they did not. Ophelia felt her skin crawl as he smiled his cat-like smile. "But my *friend* never promised any such thing," he finished with a wink before shrinking back down into the shape of a cat and bounding north off the bridge.

"His friend?" Castor repeated.

"I have a feeling his friend is not *our* friend," Aedan muttered.

As soon as the words left his mouth, the bridge shook. There in front of them, on the side of the bridge, was a large, gnarled hand, big enough to hold half of their party in, wrapped around the parapet, hoisting the rest of itself up and over.

20

So Below

An enormous humanoid beast towered over them, easily twenty feet tall. Murky green skin hung loosely over its massive bone structure. It had a long, drooping nose that stretched past its warty chin. Its ears pointed back like Eos's, Aedan saw, though not in the elegant way theirs did. These ears were crooked and bent like bolts of lightning. Its arms were abnormally long, the knuckles dragging on the bridge as it stood upright. It wore tattered clothing only covering the necessary bits. The stench was dreadful.

"*That* is a dark Sidhe," Eos said as they took several steps back and nocked an arrow. "A river troll." They released the bowstring. As the arrow struck into the beast's hide, it let out an annoyed gruff before lumbering forward several steps and swinging a massive hand at the half-elf. Eos easily dodged away from it, yanking Ophelia back with them.

"At least it's slow," Castor said. He looked to Aedan, and they nodded at each other, the words unnecessary. With weapons in hand, they charged.

They wove in an out between the legs and swinging arms fluidly together as a team while the thing was assaulted by rapier and arrow and falcon from the front. Aedan and Castor met on the other side of the troll and simultaneously drove their steel into the beast's meaty calves. Aedan's axes seemed more effective than Castor's spear, as the troll went down to the knee on Aedan's side.

As Aedan wrenched his axes free from the rough hide, he noticed Ophelia take an opening from the front. She thrusted out with her rapier, piercing the troll's eye. With a roar, the troll retaliated with an unnaturally quick blow that sent Ophelia flying and rolling end over end before slamming into the stone pillar where the horses were tied. She lay unmoving there.

Seeing his friend hurt, Castor went into a silent rage as he leapt from the damaged leg up onto the troll's back and drove his spear deep into its ribs, hanging on by the shaft of his weapon. The troll shook violently in an attempt to get Castor off of it while a flurry of arrows pinned themselves into its neck and face. Still, it seemed mostly unbothered by the arrows, though it sure did not enjoy Aedan hacking away at its legs.

It spun, arms out, catching Aedan's shoulder and knocking him off his feet. Aedan regained his footing just in time to see the troll finally manage to throw Castor off and into the black waters below.

Time slowed. All that time at the inn waiting for Castor to wake up suddenly rushed back to Aedan. *No*, he thought. *I only just got you back.*

Fueled with a sudden burst of energy, Aedan ran to the parapet, but he could not see Castor below anywhere. He turned back, feeling menace in his eyes and dodged under another of the troll's violent swings. Coming up, he cleaved his axes into the beast's forearm and ran, dragging the steel up through its arm and out its shoulder.

The troll let out a monstrous roar, swinging at Aedan and missing again. He spun around to the side of the river troll and hacked out a chunk of stinking, rotting flesh. But as fast as Aedan had been, he was not quick enough to avoid being grabbed, dropping his axes as his arms were pressed down to his sides.

Aedan would never know if the troll was going to crush him in its hand or throw him into the river after Castor.

In that second, Fiona appeared, and with a jump, she pierced her healer's knife into the thing's wrist, and with her descent, severed the hand from its arm. It howled and held its stumped wrist in agony as Fiona helped free Aedan from the still-tight clutches of the troll's severed hand.

Once freed, Aedan regained his axes and scrambled over to the distracted beast delivering a crossing slash to the troll's exposed neck.

The howling ceased immediately and was replaced by a disgusting choking sound as the river troll lumbered around on its torn and hacked body, finally settling to lean against the low parapet. Its weight overpowered the ancient stone, and it crumbled, sending the troll down into the deadly Ebonflow.

It was darker and colder than anything Castor had ever experienced. Even the swim across the River Split from Teacher's training grounds to the Isle of the Sidhe was nowhere near this intense. He remembered falling and slapping the water hard, sinking beneath the surface and being caught up in a vicious undertow. The current took him as he fought to break the surface, slamming into unseen rocks as *things* slithered by him in the darkness.

He knew better than to try to fight the current itself, and instead he tried to swim diagonally up and to the side. The only problem with that was that he could not exactly tell *which way* was up and to the side.

The unforgiving Ebonflow took him anyway. He held his breath as long as he could, and only when it felt as if his eyes would burst from their sockets did he finally give up. He did not fight anymore. He breathed in unending gulps of excruciatingly painful water, his body spasming and convulsing with each terrible breath. Then, he was still.

Castor woke finally, coughing and vomiting up the black water of the Ebonflow as he pushed himself up to his hands and knees on the shore of the river, shaking uncontrollably. He collapsed back down to his side, unable to hold himself up any longer, and continued choking out the water inside of him.

Everything hurt. He felt the cold down to his bones as he shivered in the brisk air. His vision was blurred as he tried weakly to see where he was and if he was safe. He just could not believe he had managed to survive.

He heard a distant sound - a voice maybe? He tried opening his eyes to see who it was, but he had no strength in him to do so.

At some point, he felt hands on him, and he could hear familiar voices chattering away above him. Warmth encompassed him at once, though the cold was deeper than the heat could fix so quickly. He was lifted from the wet bank of the river and carried in the arms of someone who exuded so much body heat, he finally felt as though he would continue to survive. He curled up into the bared chest that held him and let himself slip into unconsciousness.

The next time Castor woke, he tried turning left and right but found his way blocked. When he finally opened his eyes, he saw a small campfire crackling in front of where he was sitting up at. Ophelia, Fiona, and Eos were sitting on the opposite side of the flames and were talking quietly amongst themselves. The sky above the plain was surprisingly clear for once and dark, lit by a waxing moon and a million twinkling stars.

His eyes traced from the sky to the horizon and down to his own self. He saw he was covered by a tunic that was not his. It smelled vaguely of sweat and fire. Then, he noticed that the reason he could not turn before was because he was being held up in a pair of long arms roped with muscle. Aedan's arms.

He sighed and rested his head back against Aedan's collarbone.

"How do you feel?" Aedan whispered in his ear.

Castor's throat and lungs still hurt, but he said, "Like I just drank death."

Castor felt Aedan chuckle against his back. His arms tightened around Castor, and his thumb traced small circles where it rested on the side of his arm. Castor smiled. "Are you not cold without your tunic?" he asked Aedan.

PHANTOM FIRE | 281

Aedan shook his head. "I grew up as an Ó Bháird, remember? There were many days I braved the cold without a shirt." Castor felt a pit in his stomach. "But do not worry; it is not so cold out tonight anyway."

If he had had the strength to, Castor might have made Aedan take back his tunic, but he sat there instead, too tired to move.

"You and I are going to need to stop dying if I am ever going to get a good night's rest again," Aedan said finally.

With a small, painful laugh, Castor mumbled, "Deal."

The rest of the group noticed he was awake then. Ophelia asked how he was, Eos commended him for surviving the river, and Fiona brought him a bowl of something steaming.

"Potato soup," she said as she patted his shoulder comfortingly.

Before Castor could even reach for the wooden spoon, Aedan snatched it up. Castor wanted to object, but he was too tired and sore to argue. As Aedan fed him, he asked, "So, where are we now?"

"Only an hour's walk away from the Ebonflow," Eos answered. "We wanted to get far enough away from it that we would feel safer from whatever the water carries."

Castor nodded and accepted a mouthful of soup from the spoon. Each swallow still pained his throat, and there was a deeper pain in his chest that he thought might never go away.

"And how far until Letha?" Castor asked as he managed to swallow.

"Probably close to nine days," Eos said.

"And then, all I have to do is fight the Queen," he muttered.

The rest of the group looked a bit unhappy about the concept, but it was Aedan who said, "You still do not have to if you do not want to. Branwyn would understand if you changed your mind."

Castor shook his head. "No, I made a promise, and I am going to keep it. I just need some rest first."

The others agreed, and after Castor finished as much of the soup as he could tolerate, he lay down in the grass next to Aedan, and they fell asleep.

All night, Castor was plagued by nightmares. In some, his friends were drowning, in others Aedan was drowning, but in most of them, it was Castor. He tossed and turned as he dreamt of suffocating under the black waters, caught in the dark current and unable to find the surface. Feeling his lungs explode in agony before finally choking on the defiled water.

Several times, Castor found himself sitting bolt upright sure that he had been drowning all over again only to find a worried Aedan next to him squeezing his hand in his. He would lie back down and curl into Aedan's large frame before trying to fall asleep again, knowing that it would probably happen again through the night.

When it was in the beginning stages of dawn, before the sun had managed to make a full appearance and was only just lightening the world enough to bring a vibrant blue hue to his environment, Castor decided he would live with the amount of sleep he got that night. Upon sitting up, a panic hit him. He slapped his hands down to his legs before, feeling a flush of relief to find the iron Mac Lellan coin there. It had not washed away in the river after all. He wasn't sure when or if he would even need to ever contact them again, but surely the seeress knew more than he did about his future.

Then, another panic hit him. His eyes roamed all around, but upon failing to find what he was looking for, he looked to Eos, the only other one awake at the time. "Good morning," he began.

"Did you get enough rest?" Eos asked, a concerned tone to their voice.

Castor laughed weakly. "No, but I will survive. I was only wondering about - "

"Your spear?" Eos finished. Castor nodded sheepishly. "When we were finally able to kill the troll, it fell into the river, but I managed to retrieve your spear before the troll took it to the water with it."

Castor sighed, relieved. "And no one else was hurt, right?" He tried to remember back to the fight, but it was all mostly a blur. Though everyone seemed healthy while they were sitting around the fire the night before.

Eos nodded. "Ophelia took a bad hit, but Fiona and I agreed that nothing was broken."

PHANTOM FIRE | 283

Castor felt a small hollow in his stomach. Aedan, Fiona, and Eos had all chosen to come with him on this journey, but Ophelia did not get to choose. Whether or not she was happy about her circumstances afterwards, she was still forced to come. So, any injury she sustained, any consequences she bore from this trip would forever weigh heavily on Castor's shoulders. At least she was not permanently harmed this time. Still, he would feel better once they made it to the capital where *he* was the only one in danger.

Eos noticed him shiver then and said, "Are you still cold from the river? You were dry when you went to rest."

Castor nodded. "I am not wet anymore, but I still feel a little cold. It is nothing to worry about, though. This country is far too cold for my liking anyway." He let out a breathy laugh. Eos looked skeptical, but they kept their comments to themselves.

Though, it was not as though Castor was cold all over; the cold seemed to come from his chest mostly. There was a dull ache somewhere behind his ribs, but that was probably just from inhaling all that black water. Something still seemed *off*, but Castor could not put his finger on just what that was.

He needed to pull himself together, though. He knew this next week would fly by, and he would be fighting the Queen of Maecha to the death before he knew it. The *Queen of Maecha* who was, according to Branwyn, an even better warrior than *she* was. How was Castor supposed to win this anyway? Surely, he would be slaughtered before he could even get close enough to lay a hand on her. How could Branwyn have made the mistake of assigning him her champion? No, how could the *Allmother* have made the mistake of trusting him with her gift?

He shook his head of those intrusive thoughts and thanked Eos for retrieving his spear before padding back over to lie down next to Aedan. He shut his eyes, willing himself to get just a few more minutes of sleep before they were to be on the move again.

✦ . ✛ . ✦ . ✛ . ✦

Over the next few days, as Castor began to feel better and better from his trip to the bottom of the Ebonflow, he began sparring with his comrades whenever they were stopped for the night. He needed to get back in the swing of things anyway. Of all things, however, it was his mark that was giving him the most trouble. It was noticeably easier than Castor thought it would be to refamiliarize himself with sparring against other people, though it seemed to take longer to summon his mark than usual.

He could still bring it up on command, but it did not burn so hot or so bright as it had before, nor would it come as quickly as it had used to. Still, he practiced. As frustrated as it made him, he could still use it, so he tried not to pay it much mind, instead just trying to summon it to have it ready earlier than usual.

He sparred with Aedan and Ophelia mostly. With their jarringly different fighting styles, Castor had to make use of different tactics and strategies for each, which he thought might be helpful when he fought Aife, whose fighting style he did not even know. Ophelia was unforgiving - her speed unmatched. Castor's muscles burned as he pushed them to move fast enough to block her volley of strikes.

Aedan, on the other hand, seemed to be taking it easier on him than he had back at Endala. Either that, or Castor was just improving beyond what Aedan had. Though, Castor assumed the first, which infuriated him to no end. Once Castor finally scolded Aedan for letting him win so easily, Aedan sighed, and Castor had a much more difficult time getting a hand on him. If he was going to train for a fight to the death with the strongest warrior in all of Maecha, he needed to train right.

Eos would occasionally step in to help him with his reflexes by fashioning blunt arrows they magicked from nearby wood and stone and shooting them at him. And then, just when Castor thought he was getting used to being able to guess where the next arrow would be shot so he could dodge accordingly, they changed the game. Castor had to spar with either Aedan or Ophelia *while* Eos shot their blunted arrows at him. That was the most difficult of all. Still, he did not let himself become frustrated when he lost. He knew he would need these skills if he was going to survive this duel.

Every night between the Ebonflow and Letha, they trained. Castor garnered more scrapes and bruises than he knew what to do with, though whenever they rested for the night, he summoned his mark to seal any wounds he had collected from training. But it was getting more and more difficult for him to use his mark for such precise details as sewing up a wound or making a bruise fade. While it troubled him deeply as to what was going on with him - perhaps just nerves? - he decided not to tell any of his friends. Not even Aedan. He didn't want them to worry more than they needed to. Still, it wasn't as though he couldn't use the mark at all. He could still summon it, only with more difficulty. If nothing else, at least that made him try harder with his spear and shield.

As much as Castor felt he was not ready, the day came when, standing atop the crest of a tall hill, he could see Letha in the distance. While not as large as Argos, it was certainly close. The city was still a distance away, but with the sun beginning to dip in the western sky, he could just make out the stretch of buildings pushing out towards them from a sizeable castle on the opposite side with the Undying Sea behind it reaching out past where eyes could see.

They had made it. Castor felt the impossibility of it, yet there he was. He had crossed two countries and had nearly died twice, but Letha was there in his sight. He had done it. Not alone, of course; there was not a chance that he would have possibly been able to get there without the help of his friends who were always watching his back. Even Eos, whose company Castor was growing to enjoy.

With a sigh, Castor tapped his heels against his horse to get it moving towards the capital.

The hills mostly leveled out here towards the sea, though there was one standalone hill just outside the city's limits, that Castor thought seemed a little out of place there in the plain. As they came closer, though, he saw that it was not a hill, but a burial mound. For some reason, it gave Castor the deepest sense of foreboding. Even after they passed it, he found himself looking back over his shoulder at the mound as though he were afraid it might just move.

For obvious reasons, it did not.

It was not long before the five weary travelers were traipsing through the city and towards the castle. They did not receive too many odd glances as they went - perhaps the capital sees many travelers, Castor guessed. It was not difficult to find a tavern as the light of the sun began to recede behind the hills - they just had to follow the sounds.

The White Raven sat somewhere between the center of town and the castle itself. A jaunty song bounced out of its open door accompanied by the upbeat synchronized clapping of an audience in rhythm with the lyrics. Castor cast one last look at the stone walls surrounding the castle before stepping into the tavern.

Fortunately, a room at the White Raven was not so expensive. They did not have much money left, so they gave the innkeeper what they had and gave them a small amount of their food supplies in exchange for a night there. But as they were only able to afford one room, they all had to crowd in together. As much as Castor protested, everyone else refused to take the bed, insisting that he needed more comfort than they did that night.

He could not make himself fight them too much, though. He knew very well that this might be the last night that he ever *got* to sleep, so he took the bed in the end. And as everyone settled down to rest, Castor closed his eyes to sleep for what could just be the final time.

21

Pale Green

Even with the mild comfort of the scratchy bed in the White Raven, Castor did not get much rest. When he did sleep, which was not often, he did not dream, and when he finally rose the next morning, he did not feel as rested as he thought he should for what he had planned for the day. Still, they gathered up their things and made for the castle after they all filled up on hardtack and Eos's magically grown vegetables.

It should have been colder there, Castor thought as they walked and guided their horses along, but with the packed buildings and crowded streets, there was a comforting warmth that the wilds of Maecha could not match. Castor decided then that he might as well start cherishing every detail of life should this be his last day.

He grabbed Aedan's free hand in his own and squeezed it, feeling the rough calluses on his palms and fingers and the heat that radiated from every part of Aedan's body. He knew, even should he die, he would remember that.

Still, he let his senses wander, taking in every aspect of that walk. Small birds chattered as they fluttered after one another; passersby spoke animatedly about their lives with their friends who listened intently; the smell of freshly baked bread permeated the area with its lovely aroma; the *clang* of metal on metal signified a blacksmith

288 | MICHAEL JACE

somewhere nearby; children chased after one another in fits of laughter as they played in this very normal day for them.

But this was not a normal day for everyone in the city.

Castor breathed in deeply and let it out, steeling himself as he approached the man standing guard in front of the two enormous wooden doors that served as what seemed like the only entrance into the wall.

"Who goes there?" the guard barked in the common tongue.

"My name is Castor of House Vallas, Lord of the province of Anand - " He stopped himself before he could finish the rest of his titles, as he was not technically a lord anymore, nor was he a protector of Odessa, as the remainder of his proclamation would have suggested.

"What business does a lord of Odessa have here in Letha?" the guard asked.

"I am here as a champion to challenge the Queen for the throne," he said, trying to put as much power and confidence in his voice as he could muster.

The guard looked thrown by what he said. Perhaps this does not happen very often, if ever, Castor assumed. "Y - You want to *challenge* Queen Aife? For which crest do you fight?"

"Clan Ulster," Castor answered firmly.

Seeming absolutely baffled, the guard said, "Clan *Ulster?*" He opened his mouth to say something else before the realization hit him, and he stopped, looking pale. "*Oh,*" he said. "Very well. You shall be granted an audience with the Queen so you may challenge her formally. Please wait."

He moved to the side of the great wooden doors where there was a smaller door that blended in with the side of one of the two towers that stood on either side of the great entrance and disappeared through it. He returned after a several minutes with an undecipherable look on his face. He did not say anything, so neither did Castor, though it was only moments later that one of the doors began to open.

PHANTOM FIRE | 289

"If you will come with me," the guard said as he marched past the door and behind the wall.

They followed him into a beautiful courtyard. The circular keep stood tall in the center of the area. It was easily taller than the Vallas estate was, though there was no denying that it was clearly made more for utility than aesthetic. The rounded stone wall rose high up above them dotted here and there with arched windows. It was beautiful in its own way, Castor supposed. If you liked stone prisons anyway.

Smaller structures lined the inside of the wall, Castor saw. There was a blacksmith there, reclining next to a cold forge taking a nap that seemed quite early in the day to Castor. A fletcher's workplace stood next to the smith's with piles of arrows littered about inside open walls. What appeared to be a stable was set into the wall near them on the right, and, to confirm that suspicion, several servants emerged to retrieve the five horses that Castor's group had brought in. They promised to clean them and feed them while they were there, and the group happily obliged.

Few others milled about there in the courtyard that Castor could see, though he did hear the familiar sound of wooden swords striking each other on the other side of the keep. Did they train soldiers here as well?

Castor's curiosity would be satiated as, surprisingly, it was *towards* that sound that the guard led them and not into the keep itself.

As they silently made their way around the imposing keep, Castor saw that he was slightly wrong in his assumption. It was not *soldiers* that were sparring with wooden swords, but children. Four of them, around the age of nine, Castor guessed, practiced their hand-to-hand combat skills against one another, under the watchful eyes of a circling woman who looked all too familiar.

But of course she looked familiar, Castor realized. She had the same chin, the same nose, the same scrutinous eyes, and the same blazing red hair. This was Branwyn's sister, Queen Aife.

"Wait here," the guard ordered as he approached the scene.

Castor watched as the man spoke quietly to Aife. Her eyes flitted to Castor, and he immediately felt his heart hit his stomach. Never before had he ever felt so nervous, except for when he was in the presence of the Allmother herself, of course. He did all he could to stand there looking as stoic and fearless as possible, though he wasn't sure how successful he was.

Eventually, the guard walked back past them without saying a word. Aife stood for a moment longer, watching the children spar before seeming to be satisfied and informing them that they should take a break and drink some water. Then, she turned to come towards Castor.

Despite all the similarities between her and her sister, Aife had a much different air about her than Branwyn did. Her eyes were kinder and her expression less severe, though she stood taller with wider shoulders. Hard muscle wrapped her bared arms. Despite her similarities to his Teacher, Castor knew what he set out to do.

"Hail," Aife said. Like a river, her voice was gentle and powerful at the same time. It was a kind, melodic voice, but it was clear that there was strength behind her words. As soon as she spoke, Aedan and Fiona dropped to a knee and bowed their heads. Castor almost followed their example, but something kept him standing. "My guard tells me an Odessan lord comes with important matters to discuss. What is it I can help you with?"

For some reason, Castor was expecting Queen Aife to remind him of the Empress of Odessa in some way. To have her anger, her indignation, her spite. Aife was different. She seemed... nice.

But before Castor could respond, she said, "Oh, please, you do not have to bow. I implore you to rise." Aedan and Fiona shared an awkward look before standing back to their feet. Seeming satisfied, Aife looked to Castor to go on.

"I am here to issue a challenge," Castor said, somehow managing to keep his voice steady. "A challenge for the throne."

A look of intrigue passed over Aife's passive demeanor. "Is that so?" She smiled, almost excitedly. "Forgive me for assuming, but you

PHANTOM FIRE | 291

appear not to be of this land. Pray tell, for which clan is it that you challenge me?"

Castor breathed out a shaky breath. "Yours, Your Majesty. I am the champion for Clan Ulster."

Aife's joy and amusement washed away immediately, replaced only by a dark glimmer of disbelief. "Bran ... Bran is alive?"

Castor nodded firmly. "Yes, Your Majesty. Branwyn is very much alive, and she sent me to claim the throne for her."

Expecting a thunderous response or even a frontal assault, Castor was surprised when Aife let out a boisterous laugh instead. He flinched at the sudden sound and stared on, confused.

When her cackles finally slowed, she whispered, "Bran's alive," to herself as though she still could not believe it. "Very well," she said, grinning. "Very well, I accept your challenge - " Her voice trailed off with an unspoken question.

"Vallas," Castor said. "Castor Vallas."

"Lord Vallas," she repeated, the smile still as large as ever. "I accept your challenge, Champion. I have only one favor to ask of you."

Taken aback, Castor said, "Oh ... Er ... Yes?"

"Please come into the keep with me. I want to hear all about Branwyn," she said. "We can schedule our duel in a week's time. Surely, you could use some proper rest before such a fight could be had fairly. Forgive me for saying so, but the five of you look dreadful. I think a week would give you enough time to properly prepare yourself, wouldn't you say?"

Absolutely stunned, Castor only nodded. "Yes, Your Majesty. A week would be sufficient; but we do not have the necessary money to fund our stay here for a week."

"Oh, forgive me if I was unclear. I would like you all to stay here in the castle. Your meals will be seen to, and you may rest as long as you wish."

The surprise evident on Castor's face was reflected in all of his friends' as he looked to them for assistance. After receiving none, he said, "Your graciousness and hospitality are unmatched. We would be pleased to accept your offer."

Her smile remained unchanged. "Excellent. Now, please come with me; I would love to hear more of your travels and of my sister."

The keep was incredible. Aedan was in awe for the entire tour. A giant spiraling staircase wound around the inside wall of the entire keep, connecting all the floors to a single spiral. The first floor was the throne room. Two thrones made of stone inlaid with branching veins of gold sat near the far wall on a raised platform three steps above the stone floor. Braziers each holding a blazing flame that shone on the two banners hung on the wall behind the throne. The banners showed the crest of Clan Ulster - a blue shield dotted with white stars and a severed wolf's head on top. And there on the wall, hanging between the two banners, was the largest, most monstrous skull Aedan had ever seen, but he had of course already known it would be there. It was the legendary skull of the Shiverscale, an ancient dragon with breath of ice that was said to have been the scourge of Midoria before coming to Letha where it was slain by Myth-King Tadh Ó Conor. *Whether the story is true or not, the dragon's skull* is *right there*, Aedan thought.

He looked to Castor, but Castor did not seem as thoroughly impressed by the keep as Aedan felt. *He must be used to buildings like this*, Aedan thought. And for a moment, Aedan let himself wonder what Castor's home must have been like before they moved on up the staircase.

The second floor was the drawing room. Comfortable, cushioned seating dotted the room all facing a centralized, low table where a pitcher of red wine sat surrounded by several goblets. When a visitor needed to speak to the Queen, they used the throne room. When the Queen was *entertaining* visitors, however, this is where they would come.

The third floor was what Queen Aife called the war room. A sturdy wooden desk dominated the center of the room with a map of Serrae unfurled across it. Aedan saw the stretches of each continent on it,

PHANTOM FIRE | 293

wishing he could read the scrawled handwriting just to know which country was which. For some reason it seemed as though most everything in the war room was covered in a fine layer of dust, as though nothing there had been used in some time.

The fourth floor was dedicated to the library. Bookcases lined the curved wall of that floor surrounding the aisles of bookcases that ran parallel to each other across the floor. There were more windows on that floor than any other to allow a greater allowance of daylight to penetrate the keep.

The fifth and final floor was the Queen's personal chambers, and they were not given a tour there.

Finally settling in the drawing room, with a goblet of wine in every hand, they talked. For someone who banished her own sister for being unworthy of dying in combat, Aife seemed to really want to know all about Branwyn and her life in Endala, Aedan noticed. He wondered why she must have thought her sister so dishonorable if she spoke of her now with such interest and love. Did the love Aife had for her sister really outweigh her ability to give her an honorable death?

Aedan thought briefly of the idea of being in her position. Would he have been able to give Fiona an honorable death? Or would he have banished her and forever cast dishonor on her name in order to save her life? He shook his head to himself. He was just glad he was not the one who had to make that decision.

Aife asked them about Branwyn and their time in Endala with her. Her eyes glowed with every detail they told her, small chuckles escaping whenever a random detail would come up about her, and she would say, "Just like Bran," with a small shake of her head.

After they finished telling her a brief account of their year in Endala, she said, "She really does loathe me still." She sighed sadly. "I suppose that is fair given what I did to her those twenty years ago." With a shake of her head, she changed the subject. "So, then she chose you to be her champion because you were the strongest warrior she had ever trained?"

"Well - " Castor started, but Aedan interrupted him.

"Yes, Your Majesty," he said quickly. "Yes, Castor was the strongest warrior she had ever trained." He saw Castor look at him oddly out of the corner of his eye, but Aedan did not want to give away Castor's power. Despite how kind Aife was, Castor was still going to battle her, and he needed every advantage he could get. Aedan knew, even though she seemed so sweet, that Aife was a dangerous warrior. She even defeated *Teacher* in fair combat. If Castor was going to win, his power would need to be a surprise.

She looked slightly skeptical, but then she shrugged. "Bran would have only sent you as her champion if she thought you could defeat me," she said matter-of-factly. "So, you have traveled all the way here without a ship? That must have been a long, terrible journey. It is a wonder you have all survived intact. I have heard the Roinn Mountains are most treacherous."

They all regaled her of their tales, though they seemed to catch on to Aedan's idea of concealing Castor's power; so, they left out the story of the Scoráneile and any detail that included the mark of the Phantom. Aife sat and listened, gasping at the terrifying parts and smiling at the nicer parts of each story. She was the perfect audience, Aedan thought with a strange smile. Strange only because he knew that he should not enjoy her company so much since they were sent there to kill her after all. Surely though, he thought, Castor could separate this friendliness with his duty.

Soon it was time for lunch, so they left the keep and followed Aife to one of the buildings that adorned the inner wall of the castle which turned out to be a dining hall with an adjoining kitchen. The servant quarters were also near this building, Aife informed them, should they need assistance during the week they would be staying there.

After lunch, Aife showed them to the guest quarters, which were on the direct opposite side of the wall that the servant quarters were on. While not near as incredible as the keep was, they were still nicer than anywhere Aedan had ever stayed. They were almost reminiscent of the inn in Trícnoc where they had stayed, except more luxurious and made from stone instead of wood. The bottom floor of the guest quarters was

PHANTOM FIRE | 295

a single, huge communal gathering room with cushioned seats around a table with a glowing hearth in the back. The top floor held the bedrooms, all quite similar with a large, comfortable-looking bed, a heavy wardrobe, and a wooden bathing tub lined with soft linens.

Aife informed them that servants would come by to help them with bathing should they request it and to let them know when meals would be prepared throughout each day as well as that should they need any more assistance, that they could simply go find one of the servants who roamed about the castle. Aedan had never experienced such luxury in his entire life. Nothing even came close to this amount of pampering; it almost made him uncomfortable. Still, a small part of him thought it would be nice to be taken care of for once.

After making a quiet comment on the appearance of their clothing, Aife let them know that she would have servants bring over selections of clothing that they could choose from to have tailored to each of them. At every turn, Aife was surprising Aedan with more kindness and generosity.

She left them alone then, saying she did not want to overwhelm them and thought they needed more rest. So, they sat in the gathering room on the first floor of the guest quarters in silence, all of them staring at one another in complete bafflement over the completely head-spinning morning they had just experienced.

"I think," Castor began finally, "I think I am going to go to bed. As you can imagine, I did not sleep very well last night, and I would like to rest if that is quite all right."

He stood with a smile and a nod at his friends before retreating up the stairs and out of sight. Aedan suddenly felt the weight of his weariness hit him as well and decided to follow Castor up.

Finding the only closed door amongst the bedrooms, Aedan knocked hesitantly.

"Come in," he heard Castor call out in a tired voice.

He pushed open the door, feeling red bloom in his cheeks. He saw Castor on the bed, sprawled out in all of his filthy clothes and with his

296 | MICHAEL JACE

shield still strapped to his arm. "I was too tired to do anything," Castor muttered when he saw who it was.

Aedan laughed under his breath. "Is it all right if I stay in this room, too?" he asked, scratching the stone wall with his fingernail as though fixing some invisible imperfection.

Castor lifted his head up, his brow knotted and an odd smile on his lips. "Was that not the plan already?"

Aedan breathed a sigh of relief. For some reason, he still felt like their relationship was not entirely real. But whenever Castor said anything to the contrary, it just reminded him how ridiculous he was being. He closed the door and went to help Castor remove his shield.

As Aife said, the tailors came with a grand assortment of clothing for Fiona and the others to choose from. Aedan and Castor were still asleep in their room, so Fiona, Ophelia, and Eos got first picks. Ophelia settled on a golden dress with brown and peach accents that complemented her skin tone wonderfully, Fiona saw. Eos looked uncomfortable with the idea of wearing anything so expensive and decided to politely decline their offer and instead keep their own black and gray clothes that Fiona admitted suited them more than anything the tailors had to offer.

Fiona on the other hand had difficulty deciding on what to choose when Ophelia mentioned that the pale green dress would accent her hair color well and really bring out her eyes. Blushing at actually being complimented for once, Fiona chose the green dress.

The tailors did their job of making the measurements to fit the clothing to them before they left with their duties, saying they would be back with the altered dresses as soon as possible, as well as with someone who would size Aedan and Castor once they were ready and able.

The rest of the day, Fiona spent feeding Bas treats and watching him fly around the high walls of the castle, seemingly happy with his new temporary home. Fiona loved watching him fly, oftentimes wishing that she herself had wings like his. Sometimes she found herself so desiring to be able to just fly away from all her problems. Oh, how she wished she were a bird. How easy life must be for them.

After dinner, Fiona was introduced to the servant who would be specifically in charge of assisting her with anything she needed. Aria was her name, and she was surprisingly close to Fiona in age. At first, she was very formal, though Fiona made sure to let her know that it was entirely unnecessary.

Old habits die hard, though, and Aria was constantly correcting herself. It was almost not even worth having her try to be informal if it was easier for her to keep calling her Miss all the time, Fiona thought. Over the next week, Fiona found herself enjoying Aria's near-constant company even more, though. Perhaps she was finally making a friend who would not run off and fall in love with her brother or be head over heels for a half-elf.

That week, they talked together for hours on end, each learning all about the other's life. Fiona tried to leave out the whole prostitution and murdering stalker bits, though. Just to keep the conversation light. Aria, on the other hand, was of Clan Sétanta, which was apparently the clan most loyal to Clan Ulster, having served them in the previous king's reign as well.

Being born into a clan whose main purpose was servitude was not necessarily an honorable one; although it was not as though she were an *Ó Bháird*, Fiona thought with a slight amount of bitterness. Still, Aria claimed to be happy with her life. She worked hard most days, but she held that Queen Aife was kind and generous and never made work or life difficult for her.

A part of Fiona briefly wondered why they were here to take the throne from such a nice queen before she remembered that being in charge of a country requires more than just being *nice*. Surely, they were doing the right thing in helping a stronger queen rise to power.

The morning before the day Castor was set to do battle with Aife, Fiona awoke to a surprise. There, on her bedside table, was a small wooden plate with a delectably creamy pastry sitting on top. She looked around for Aria, but she was nowhere in sight.

Fiona felt her stomach rumble at the sight of such a perfect little dessert and shrugged. She savored each delicious mouthful of the sweet pastry as she wondered absently why Aria had brought it to her without waking her. She would have to remember to ask Aria about it when she saw her later.

After she finished, she rose and slipped into her tailored, pale green dress and went downstairs.

Putting off the duel with Queen Aife for a week had given Castor even more time to mentally and physically prepare for the deed. Not to mention, it had given him the opportunity to get some much-needed rest, just as Aife had suggested. A part of him thought she was too kind to actually kill, but the other part of him knew that when they began the next day, she would not relent. He knew she was more skilled than Branwyn, and that he would need to give it his all if he were to survive.

The week had gone by in a blur, and suddenly, it was the day before the fight. Despite the extra week to prepare, Castor felt entirely unready.

Still, he did not feel as bad as Fiona did. She had apparently eaten some pastry that morning and had gotten violently ill shortly thereafter, and was now surrounded by a hovering Aedan and Aria who would not leave her side no matter how much she begged. Aria had insisted she did not remember leaving a pastry on her bedside table, and none of the other servants admitted to it either.

A healer came by to check on her, but they said she would recover soon and just needed water and rest, which sent a wave of relief over Castor and the others.

Castor guessed that one of the servants fancied her and tried to do something nice by giving her a pastry, but that it had been accidentally made poorly or with spoiled ingredients and now her suitor was too ashamed to admit to it.

Fiona repeatedly said that she would be fine, that she was only under the weather and needed some time to recover and rehydrate. After incessant pleading, Aedan finally left her side, though Aria remained to keep an eye on her and fetch her water and keep a cold cloth on her head.

"I hate when she gets sick," Aedan said once he and Castor were alone in their room that night. "I never know what to do."

"The healer said she would be fine," Castor said, resting his hand on Aedan's cheek comfortingly. "I think if there was something to worry about, the healer would have said so. She just needs to rest."

Aedan sighed. "You're right." He pulled off his clothes and settled down gently in the hot water of the bathing tub that their servants had brought up just before. He was so tall, he hardly fit in the thing himself, his long legs coming up to rest on the rim.

"Join me?" he asked. "The water is perfect."

Castor felt his head buzz with a nervousness that was very much different than the nerves he felt about fighting Aife the next day.

Without a verbal response, he gently shucked off his new, tailored doublet and linen trousers and slipped into the water, resting his back against Aedan's chest. Aedan was right, the water *was* perfect. Still freshly hot and swirling with flowers and perfumes, the bath soothed Castor down to his bones.

Aedan's arms came around him then, pulling him closer into him, while he placed slow, sensual kisses on Castor's neck and shoulders. Despite the heat of the water, Castor felt a chill shiver through his whole body. He leaned his head back against Aedan's shoulder, while Aedan slowly and gradually worked his way back from Castor's shoulder to his neck, to his ear, to his jaw, before finally turning Castor's head to kiss him on the lips.

They did not move from their bath for what felt like a long time - a long, wonderful time, before Castor stood up feeling the water run off his body and back into the tub which had at some point cooled significantly, he noticed absently. He reached a hand down to Aedan who took it and stood with him.

They dried each other off with linens before crawling into the bed next to each other. They had slept next to each other many times since they'd confessed their feelings for each other, but never before had they been this close.

Aedan's skin was even hotter than it had ever been, and Castor submerged himself in the heat, savoring every kiss, every touch. Their legs slid together while their hands began to explore each other. Aedan trembled under Castor's touch, and as he bent to kiss Aedan's neck, he felt the vibration of Aedan's voice mumbling in his throat.

"*Mó krii.*" The Maechan words slipped out of him seemingly without his volition.

Castor, not fluent in the language, leaned back with an inquisitive look. He briefly worried if he'd done something wrong.

Through heavy-lidded eyes, Aedan saw him and flushed more deeply than he already was, but he scooped Castor into an embrace and pressed his mouth over his hard and fast, surprising Castor into a soft laugh.

"In the common tongue, it means 'my heart' or 'my life', though that isn't quite enough to fully explain," Aedan began in a low voice as he held Castor's body tight to his, their eyes locked. "It is what we Maechans say only when we are speaking of and to our one person - the one who is *everything.*" Aedan's eyes were shining so brightly in the dim candlelight. "*You* are my heart, Castor. My life. My everything. *Mó krii.*"

Castor's mark burned, and he felt his muscles give way as he melted into Aedan then, both of them sinking deeper and deeper into the bed.

✦ . + . ✦ . + . ✦

Castor woke the next morning feeling rested and in an unusually good mood. He opened his eyes to see the most beautiful pair of green eyes looking back at him through sleepy, heavy lids.

"Good morning," Castor whispered.

Aedan blushed and smiled. He stretched forward and rested his lips against Castor's. "Good morning," he whispered back before kissing him. "Is it too late for you to change your mind about today?" he said with a small amount of hope.

Castor chuckled quietly. "Do not think I plan on going out today without coming back to you, my love."

Aedan smiled, but Castor could tell that it was not entirely real, as though he were forcing it. And he didn't even know that his mark wasn't working as well as it should, Castor thought. Knowing how much Aedan was going to worry regardless of how much Castor tried to soothe him, he decided to get up and get dressed. It was still before dawn, so he had some time to get ready.

Before he could pull his tunic over his head, Aedan jumped up. "Wait." He bolted to the wardrobe and retrieved a light, durable shirt. The dragonskin tunic that the Mac Lellan Clan had given him. "Wear this today."

"But she gave it to you," Castor responded.

"And now I am giving it to you!" Aedan said back somewhat force-fully. "I will be with you at the fight, so I will not be in any danger. Just wear it. For me."

His eyes were so round and misted that Castor could not find it in himself to argue. He slipped on the dragonskin, and it somehow man-aged to fit his body just as well as Aedan's despite their size difference. *The seeress* did *say it would do that,* Castor reminded himself.

"Thank you," Castor said. But then he remembered. "We should go check on Fiona—see if she is in better shape."

Aedan looked as though he had been slapped. "I cannot believe I forgot," he muttered to himself. "I am such a horrible brother."

"Do not worry yourself so much," Castor said. "It is not your fault."

It seemed as though Aedan suddenly realized something then. "You're right. It is *your* fault. *You* distracted me. With your *wiles.*"

"My *what?*"

Aedan laughed and quickly dressed himself before pulling Castor along behind him to Fiona's room.

She was still a little pale, Castor saw.

"She is not expelling anymore," Aria informed as she dutifully held a cloth to Fiona's forehead. "But she is still unwell."

"I just need more water and rest," Fiona muttered crossly. Then, she looked to Castor. "Will you forgive me if I miss your fight, Castor?"

Castor smiled. "Of course! Do not worry yourself over me; just stay and rest."

He looked to Aedan and saw that he seemed troubled.

"You are free to stay here with her," Castor said.

"What?" Fiona interjected. "Not a chance! Aedan, you are going to watch the love of your life defeat the Queen of Maecha. You will *not* stay here sitting uselessly! I will be *fine*. Just go!"

Aedan looked slightly embarrassed about having discussed his love life in front of Aria, a near-complete stranger, but he nodded. "Fine, but I swear on the Nine - "

"*I will be fine,*" Fiona enunciated each word, looking entirely frustrated.

"I will take excellent care of her," Aria said, though Castor was unsure how much that affected Aedan's decision.

Aedan grunted before leaning down and kissing Fiona's cheek lovingly. "I will see you when we return," he said.

"Good," she responded.

"I love you," he said as he and Castor turned to leave.

"Love you, too," she responded.

They made their way down the stairs and into the gathering room where Eos and Ophelia were already waiting, eating plates of sausages and hard eggs and fresh bread. There were two others set out for Castor and Aedan, the food still steaming.

Castor heard his stomach murmur approval as he sat down and swallowed his food in a matter of minutes.

As it often does before important events, the morning raced by, and soon it was time to walk out to the place where the challenge would be held. He met with Queen Aife in the courtyard of the castle and walked with her through the city past thousands of onlookers who lined the streets and cheered their march.

Aife had mentioned that the town criers would be notified of Castor's challenge so that the rest of the capital would be aware of the

PHANTOM FIRE | 303

potential change in leadership. Should any change be had, then the rest of the country would be informed.

They made their way through the entire city and out to the great burial mound that Castor had passed on his way into Letha a week before.

"This is where we will do battle," Aife told him as a crowd began to gather around the mound's base. She sighed as she looked mournfully at the mound, as though she were reliving some painful memory. "Are you sure you wish to do this? No one will shame you for changing your mind."

Castor shook his head. "I made a promise. I plan to fulfill that promise."

Aife nodded approvingly. "Very well. Follow me."

He trailed behind her up the side of the burial mound and stood on one end of the flattened top while she took the other side.

Crows began flocking to the nearby trees as though knowing what was soon to happen.

Aife and Castor crossed the distance to the center of the mound where they grasped each other's arms in a show of mutual respect before turning back and walking to their respective sides of the mound.

"Are you ready, Champion Vallas?" she called out.

Castor looked down the side of the mound where Aedan, Ophelia, and Eos stared on sharing the same encouraging looks. He gave them - his comrades and truest friends - his most confident smile and a short nod before returning Aife's strong gaze. "I am," he responded.

"Then," the Queen of Maecha said, readying her spear, "let us begin."

22

Rise and Fall

Castor expected Aife's fighting style to at least *somewhat* match her sister's. But where Branwyn was all speed and ferocity, Aife fought much more defensively, which made the fight take much longer than usual, because Castor was *also* accustomed to playing the defensive role.

They circled each other, neither wavering, neither initiating.

Castor eyed her spear. The blade was so sharp, a part of him wondered if the dragonskin on his chest would really be able to stop it if she were to thrust it into him. Even then, the dragonskin only covered so much of his body. There were plenty other ways she could kill him.

Finally, feeling anxious and impatient, Castor took a step in and called forth his mark, just to have it ready in case he got an opening. He felt it come up to the surface, though the flame was not as fierce as he had hoped it would be. Still, he had access to its powers, so he felt mildly confident that he would be able to do *something* at least.

He took another step forward - and Aife thrust out her spear directly at his head.

✦ . ⁺ . ✦ . ⁺ . ✦

After Aedan had left the room with Castor, Fiona had promptly fell asleep. She dreamed of sweet things. Of cakes and flowers and castles and servants. Of a world where her past did not haunt her. Where she

304

was free to be who she was and do what she wished without someone taking it from her.

But just as with most enjoyable things in her life, the dream was suddenly taken away by a strange sound that woke her from her wonderful sleep.

While being asleep, she had forgotten how ill she had felt, and upon waking, the uncomfortable, pulsing pain in her stomach was quick to remind her just how unforgiving it all was. She squinted her eyes open and searched the room for Aria, but the girl was not there. Her room, like the others in the guest quarters, was basically two rooms adjoined by an open archway that led to similarly sized room where the bathing tub was.

She tried peering through the archway, but she still could not see Aria, though the archway only gave her a limited view. She cleared her throat and said, "Aria, are you there?"

Silence.

She must be gone for lunch or tea, Fiona thought. Which was unfortunate because the chamber pot was all the way in the adjoined room, and Fiona was not entirely sure she could make it there on her own without crawling.

She told herself not to be dramatic and pushed herself out of bed. As she did, she realized she was still wearing that green dress from the day before. Had she really never taken it off since falling ill? She supposed she had not really had the energy for much since then, and the dress was actually quite comfortable. She shrugged and took a step forward, ignoring the rumbling pain in her stomach, but she stopped dead in her tracks.

There in the middle of the floor was a small pile of bloody organs atop two wings spread wide with feathers littered about.

Bas.

✦ . ⁺ . ✦ . ⁺ . ✦

Having trained to dodge arrows from Eos, Castor easily deflected her attack away.

"You are quick," Aife said. "I would expect no less from my sister's champion."

"She trained us well," Castor responded.

"Will you promise me one thing?" Aife asked him as they continued circling each other.

Castor nodded.

"If it is you who walks away victorious today," she began, "promise me that you will tell Bran that I love her and that I am sorry."

Castor's careful stride almost faltered, but he maintained composure. "I will."

There was something in the Queen's eyes that, for some reason, made Castor wonder if she even *wanted* to win.

Aife nodded back with a thankful smile.

Then, Castor lunged.

✦ ． ＋ ．✦． ＋ ．✦

Fiona's heart fell through the floor. She dropped to her knees next to her loyal falcon and cradled his tiny head in her palm. *Who could have done this?* Why *would anyone have done this?* Her mind was racing, but nothing could stop the tears from flowing. She had helped save this poor creature. Like her, he had been given a bad start, but they had worked together to keep each other safe.

And now he was *dead.* He seemed so much smaller now than he had before. She fondly remembered how he would puff out his chest to seem even bigger whenever he felt threatened or annoyed. He had saved her on more than one occasion, and she would never forget that.

A quick scraping sound shook her out of her thoughts. Her head jolted up to the archway, but she still saw nothing out of the ordinary. Uneasiness crept into her at the prospect of not being alone in the room. Her eyes crept to the door. She could easily slip out right now and find someone to help her, but what if it was Aria? Was she hurt?

She steeled herself as she pushed off the floor and stumbled as quietly as possible to the archway. Not seeing anything strange, she took a step through. Just as she did, she felt some kind of string snap against her ankle and heard the sudden, wrenching sound of some kind of mechanism working. She didn't even see the blade coming.

Aife easily dodged Castor's strike and stepped in, driving an elbow into his stomach.

While the dragonskin might protect him from her spear, it did nothing to block the blunt force of her elbow. He spun away, lifting his shield in time to deflect away an incoming strike. He followed up with his own thrust, pushing through the fresh bruise he felt growing on his stomach.

She dodged back, giving him enough time to regain his composure. But not too much time. She came back at him, but it was this style of fighting that he was more accustomed to defending against. He deflected her barrage of blows, maintaining his learned footwork, ensuring not to trip himself up. Only one strike came through his defenses, though it merely scraped off the dragonskin. A look of confusion flashed across Aife's face, but she said nothing.

He would definitely have to thank Aedan for loaning him that later.

Seeing an opportunity, he slapped her spear aside with his shield and lunged with his own spear just barely slicing open the fabric of her sleeve, drawing blood.

She leapt back, her eyebrow quirking up. "Impressive," she said with a smile.

She didn't know that he had just given himself another place to be able to use his mark on her. Her clothing nearly completely covered her after all, save for her neck and face. But now there was another opening right there on her right arm. He just needed to be able to make contact...

The trap Fiona had tripped sent a wide, sharp blade swinging around low to the ground. It connected with her ankles, and she fell straight to the floor, not even giving her time to catch herself with her hands.

Her whole body was numb for a moment as she tried to make sense of what had just happened. The cold of the stone floor was the first feeling that came to her once she began to regain her senses. It was ice on her face where she lay, but it was nothing compared to the inferno of fire that was her legs.

Choking out a gasp, she tried to push herself up, using her elbows and feet.

Only she couldn't.

Confusion slightly muddled the explosive pain as she turned over and looked to her feet. Her short legs stretched out from underneath the rucked-up green dress. She saw her thighs, her knees, her shins, but then ...

There was nothing past her shins. Nothing but blood gushing from savage stumps. She wanted to scream, but her voice would not come. She felt only the excruciating pain that permeated her entire body, crashing in horrible waves reaching out to every extremity.

She was in such terrible pain she barely noticed when someone dropped down from the rafters.

✦ . ＋ . ✦ . ＋ . ✦

Castor felt his mark burning on his chest, still not as hot as usual, but enough to where he knew he just needed to touch her.

He feinted with his spear and instead dove in with his left arm outstretched, but Aife was ready. She spun away and punished him with the back end of her spear in his ribs. He rolled away to give himself some distance, and she did not pursue him.

On the one hand, he should have known not to use Branwyn's tactics against Aife. Obviously, Aife would be expecting anything Branwyn taught him. On the other hand, why was she not attacking him while he was vulnerable? Was she *that* much of a defensive fighter that she would not take such an obvious opening? Or was she really giving him a chance to defeat her?

He couldn't wonder too much on that, though. She may be taking it easy on him, but she wouldn't give him an eternity to regain his footing - nor should she. He recovered as quickly as he could, feeling the burning pain of yet another bruise forming on his side.

He still wasn't sure if she wanted him to win or not, but he knew he needed to give it his all. He would never forgive himself if he was stopped from going back to Aedan.

Aedan. Mó krii.

Suddenly, his mark burned stronger on his chest. Strong enough that the fire began coursing through his own veins. He needed to win. For Aedan.

And he ran to Aife.

"Why would you cast me away?" Sai asked her as he squatted in front of her, hovering over her wounded legs. His question came out simply, almost as if he were asking about the weather.

The shock of seeing Sai again cut her words off. Her breath came out in rapid succession, not giving her a chance to even think of what to say. Then, suddenly, she remembered. That night in the Elderglas Forest with the nomad clan. She had forgotten before, but now she remembered. Sai had been there. He'd drugged her, and she had thought that it was all some foggy dream. But now she remembered.

It also dawned on her that he must have been the one who'd delivered the poisoned pastry. Clearly, he had the expertise. It was a perfect way to ensure she would be alone that day. Everyone else would be gone for Castor's challenge.

When she didn't answer immediately, his face twisted in rage, and he drove his fingers into the gory mess of her right ankle.

She cried out.

"*Answer me!*"

She whimpered as she tried to stomach the unbearable pain. "I … I told you," she stammered, her teeth clenched tighter than ever. Her words were interspersed between violent cries of agony. "I cannot accept what you have done and who you are."

He released his fingers from her wound. She did everything she could to steady her breathing, but her heart was racing too fast to catch up with.

"I do not believe you," he whispered. "Your brother made you say that, didn't he?"

"No!" she cried, hoping someone - *anyone* - would hear her screams and come help her. "He only told me what you did! And it is unforgivable."

He unsheathed a hidden dagger from the back of his waist. Fiona felt her eyes go wide at the sight of it. It was wickedly sharp with a blade as long as her forearm.

"You are right," Sai said gently. "It is unforgivable."

For a moment she thought it was all about to end. Her life cut short, but at least she would not be in pain anymore. But that is not what happened.

✦ . + . ✦ . + . ✦

Aife swung her spear wide, but Castor ducked under it easily, coming close enough to lay a hand on her. He reached out, but she drove the butt of her spear back towards his ribs again.

He was expecting that this time, though. In a flash, he managed to deflect it with his shield as he dropped the spear from his right hand to bring it up and around to the open wound on her arm.

Blasting the fire into her bloodstream, he reached out with the power in that instant and found the source - her heart. He let the fire consume it, but in its weakened state, the flame could not completely snuff out her life energy.

Instead, Aife dropped her spear and faltered back several steps, looking out of sorts. She fell to her knees and rested her head in her hands. The crows in the surrounding trees began to scream maddeningly.

"What - What sorcery is this?" she asked.

Feeling weary from the mark's power already, Castor struggled to maintain his footing. He did not fall, though.

"I am sorry for concealing this from you," he said, loud enough that those crowded below could hear. "I have been bestowed with a gift from the Allmother. She has given me power over the flesh and blood of others." He pulled down his dragonskin and revealed the glowing, fiery mark underneath. He was sure to let his mark be seen by as many of the people below as possible, while Aife became weaker and weaker.

Aife chuckled, her eyes glazing and unfocused. "So, the Allmother herself wishes this to pass as well?"

Castor did not respond as he retrieved his weapon.

"It is just as well," she went on anyway. "I have regretted my decision all these years." Then, for a moment, her eyes centered on Castor's. "You made me a promise," she said to him. "Will you honor it?"

Castor nodded. "Yes, Your Majesty. I will."

Aife smiled, satisfied. And without another word, she spread her arms wide, welcoming her fate.

And Castor brought down his spear.

Something seemed to pass over Sai's mind as he set his dagger on the floor just out of Fiona's reach and retrieved a bound book and quill from a pack hanging on his waist. He seemed to look around curiously for a moment muttering "Ink" to himself over and over before his eyes rested on Fiona.

He stabbed the quill deep into the bleeding flesh of Fiona's wound before using her blood to scribble something down in the book.

Fiona screamed, though it didn't seem to faze Sai in the slightest.

Seeing that he didn't care if she screamed, Fiona continued, calling out for anyone who might hear her. But no one was coming. "Aria!" she cried out. "Aria!"

Sai glanced over then. "Aria?" he repeated, his voice neutral. "Was that the servant girl?" He gestured over to the corner of the room as he turned back to scribble more in his book.

A deeper sense of dread filled Fiona's bones as she looked to where he had pointed. Sure enough, Aria was there, her throat cut, lying in a dark pool of her own blood. Her eyes were glassed over already. She didn't look as though she had been hurt any more than the single slice across her neck. At least she did not suffer long, Fiona thought - a small consolation for such a terrible thing.

Fiona felt the hopelessness begin to settle in even more then. Then, her eyes fell on the dagger just past her ankles. Sai was so busy writing in his journal, she thought she just might have a chance to grab the knife and at least hurt him for everything he had done.

She lunged forward, but Sai was too quick. A booted foot came blindingly fast, connecting sharply with her cheek. Her head cracked sideways, and she fell over to her side.

Sai sighed. "I didn't want to do that," he said, his voice unusually kind. He stooped down and lifted her head up gently by the back of her neck setting his journal down on the ground next to her. Her blood-shot eyes searched his calm, brown ones for any sort of humanity. But they were cold and empty. "You are so beautiful," he said.

He leaned down to kiss her, but she slapped and scratched at his face as hard as she could. The rage twisted his expression again as he dropped his knee down hard on her stomach. She coughed and choked, and he took both her wrists in his hands and slammed them into the stone floor above her head.

He bent down again, his mouth meeting hers as she struggled to push him off her, but he was too strong.

But Fiona wasn't the type of person to give up.

When his tongue found entrance into her mouth, she smashed her teeth down as hard as she could, feeling it sever from the rest of him. He released her and rolled off onto the floor, howling in pain.

Fiona spit out the bloodied chunk of flesh in her mouth, feeling a dark satisfaction of having hurt him. Of making him scream out like that in pain. She looked over at him as he writhed and wrinkled her lip in disgust.

She knew she couldn't run, so she did her best to crawl back through the archway towards the door that would lead to her escape.

But she heard Sai moving behind her, and she turned, seeing him rise from the stone floor and spit out a mouthful of blood onto the floor.

She twisted back and crawled - finally making it to the door. She reached up to push it open but was interrupted. A searing pain shot into her back, and her vision went white for a moment. She collapsed back down onto her chest, as the pain came again. And again. And again.

Still, with all the agony she felt, she did not want to give up here, not like this.

She forced herself to roll back over just in time to see Sai's manic face and a dripping dagger in his hand.

Then, the blade came down.

Watching Castor claim victory in the battle left Aedan feeling such a deep amount of comfort and relief. *Finally*, they were done. *Finally*, they were all safe.

From this point, he thought, as he ran up the mound to Castor's side, *everything will be all right.* They would live at Branwyn's side while she did all she could to better the country. And they would all be safe and cared for. *And Castor is alive.*

Aedan felt the same high as when he had won that first battle back in Albainn. A sound-numbing buzz filled his ears as he ran and lifted Castor in a spinning embrace. While probably not entirely appropriate, Aedan couldn't even pretend to care. *Castor did it. He's alive.* Aedan could tell himself that over and over, and it would feel just as wonderful and perfect as it did the first time.

He set Castor back down on his feet and kissed him there on the crest of the mound in front of all the clamor of the crowd below.

They were swept away to the White Raven where a hundred different people argued over who would buy their new champion a drink. The bard sang a song about the Odessan champion's victory over the Queen, establishing a new reign under the banished princess.

Aife's advisor, an elderly woman from the Sétanta Clan who watched over the battle and sat with them in the tavern, promised to have a ship sent to Endala to retrieve their new ruler. Satisfied, that everything was being taken care of, Aedan relaxed back in the chair there at the tavern with his hand firmly grasping Castor's.

After the party was over, Aedan, Castor, Ophelia, and Eos followed the Sétanta advisor back to the castle and into the keep where they discussed how their lives would be changed from here. Castor would have to stay there in the castle in one of the other structures along the wall in order to stand as their new Queen's champion, her most loyal knight, to serve her and defend her until her reign was over. The others were free to do as they pleased.

Ophelia mentioned potentially returning to Argos. After confused responses, she assured them all that she just wished to get closure with her father and that she would return to Letha afterwards. Eos asked if they could join her on her journey, and Aedan saw that she was more than happy to accept their offer.

When the advisor asked what Aedan's plans were, he said he would like to remain there in the castle with Castor and ask for a way to serve Branwyn alongside him. Castor assured him that, in the slight chance Branwyn did not approve for whatever reason, Castor would make it happen. Aedan believed him.

Then, the advisor asked if Aedan's sister was planning to join them in the castle as well.

Aedan cursed himself for forgetting to check on his sister as soon as they had returned to see if she had gotten any better. He had just been so caught up in Castor's victory and the party that it had slipped his mind. She was probably happy to have had the brief privacy, he told himself. She *did* seem annoyed at his constant hovering that morning.

Still, he couldn't help himself. He stood and said he would go check on her and inform her of the result of Castor's battle. "Do you want to come?" he asked Castor. "I am sure she will want to congratulate you."

Castor smiled and agreed. Eos and Ophelia said they would come too, and the advisor only smiled at the bonds of friendship that held the group together. "We can continue our plans at a later time," she said. "There is no rush without Queen Branwyn's presence anyway."

"Thank you, Matriarch," Aedan said to her before leading the group to the guest quarters.

PHANTOM FIRE | 315

The walk across the courtyard was beautiful - every step Aedan took filled him with such glee. He was practically bouncing. The world was just so much more wonderful when they were not in constant danger at every turn.

They entered the guest quarters and bounded up the stairs before stopping to knock on Fiona's closed door.

But she didn't answer.

"Fiona?" Aedan called out. "Are you decent?"

There was still no answer.

"She is probably resting," Castor said.

But Aedan saw Eos frown. "What is it?" he asked them.

"I do not think Fiona is in there," the half-elf said. "I cannot feel her energy."

Aedan frowned. Then, why was the door closed?

He creaked the door open slowly, peering through the opening. "Fiona?" he said, his low voice carrying through the room.

Then, all the strength left his legs. His knees wobbled, and Castor managed to catch him, but not before his body knocked the door open the rest of the way.

There in the middle of the cold stone floor was Fiona. But not as Aedan had ever seen her to be.

Her once flowing, red curls had been chopped off at the scalp, leaving bloodied patches of gore where there were chunks of skin missing. Her feet were gone entirely, and where they should have been were only vermillion stumps of bone and muscle. Her body itself was littered with a myriad of stab wounds. Aedan did not even know you could fit that many on one person. On one small, wonderful person.

He rushed to her side and fell next to his sister on his hands and knees. He picked up her lifeless body and held it to his chest as his howling cries filled the world.

Epilogue

When Branwyn had finally arrived in Letha two months after Castor's battle against Aife, everything seemed to speed up. There was a kind of coronation where she was formally given the title of "Queen" by the advisor. Castor was knighted as her champion there too in front of the hordes of Maechan citizens who had come to see their new Queen.

She fitted the role, Castor noticed. Though, he supposed it made sense. She'd grown up as a princess after all. She gave orders well and seemed to know how to speak to her advisor and her people despite her being gone for twenty years.

Occasionally, the thought would come to Castor if Aife really did deserve to die just so Branwyn could rule, but he knew that this was about more than just who deserved what. This was about the ruling of a nation. And nearly everyone seemed to be in agreement that Branwyn was the stronger ruler of the two. That Aife had to die was just the way things worked in Maecha, Castor would remind himself when those thoughts did resurface.

He did not break his promise to the fallen Queen either. He was sure to tell Branwyn of Aife's words final words to her sister. He almost thought that they might affect her, but Branwyn had only said, "Is that all?" in response.

Sometimes when he thought of his promise to Aife, his mind drifted back to that fight. If he really tried to remember it, he could have sworn that there was no way she had been giving it her all. He had only left that fight with a few bruises, and she was supposed to be even more skilled than Branwyn. It didn't make sense to him, but Aedan always reassured him that she didn't know about his power and that that is what saved him.

Despite all that, Branwyn had been extraordinarily grateful to Castor and his friends, promising them that they could have whatever they desired for helping her take the throne. When told of their plans, Branwyn told Ophelia and Eos that she would be sending twenty royal soldiers with them to escort them to the Roinn Mountains and back, which surprised Castor. She had never even *met* Ophelia or Eos, and she was granting them safe passage across the country just for having accompanied Castor on his journey.

When Aedan was asked about what he desired, he requested if there was any way he could work as a servant in the castle. He did not want to ask for too much, he had told Castor. Servitude in the Queen's castle was far more than any Ó Bháird could even dream of. But Branwyn rejected him.

"You will not be a servant in this castle," she had said. Castor had felt the hope leave his body then. Was being an Ó Bháird really so awful? "You will be a *sera* - one of my personal guards," she went on. "If you will accept, that is."

The color drained out of Aedan's face. "But ... But I am of Clan Ó Bháird," he responded. "An Ó Bháird cannot be a *sera*."

"And yet," Branwyn said, "here you are. Sera Aedan Ó Bháird."

It was a momentous occasion, apparently, Castor noticed. He thought it should have been obvious that Aedan could be any kind of knight - clans be damned. Still, it was good to know that they were going to be able to stay together in the castle.

Despite not having known Fiona very well, Branwyn had shown great compassion for their loss. She made Fiona an honorary *sera*, ensuring that her name would forever live on in the hearts of others.

Aedan had appreciated that a great deal, though that was not all he wanted for his sister. That day, those months ago, when they had first found her body, they had also found a bloodstained journal nearby. A bloodstained journal that belonged to Sai. Castor had read the latest entry in the journal that had been written in blood. It mentioned a promise that Sai was making to himself to get revenge on Fiona's brother for turning her against him.

With the knowledge that Fiona's murderer was still out there somewhere and might one day be coming back for him, Aedan wanted revenge more than anything. But with no leads as to his whereabouts, there was not much they could do but wait until something came to light.

There was also the issue with Castor's mark. Ever since the Ebonflow, the mark's power had begun to fade and become more difficult to call upon. Luckily, it was still effective enough to win him his fight with Aife, but every day it seemed as though his power continued to fade. He tried not to let it worry him too much, but the concern still nagged in the back of his mind most days.

Once things had begun to settle down, Aedan reminded Castor of something they had talked about on their journey. That the Empress of Odessa had been allegedly building an army and turning the Odessan people against Maecha. He reminded Castor that it was something they should probably bring up to her so that she could be made aware of it and hopefully send out diplomats to call an end to these vicious and untrue rumors about Maecha once and for all so that they could restore their international relationship.

But when Castor went to her and told her of all he had known of the Empress's actions, Branwyn did not send out diplomats. And Castor felt a deep sense of fear and foreboding at her simple response.

"If it is a war Odessa wants, it is a war they will get."

Acknowledgements

First, I'd like to give a special thanks to my dear friend Arcadian Barrett without whom this book would likely not be in front of you. I would also like to give a huge thanks to my mom, Carrie Teel, for reading this story in every stage of its life, helping me think of just the right word for an occasion, and for being a great support through the whole ordeal. Also, a big thank you to all my beta readers who helped make the book what it is. Finally, I'd like to thank *you* for picking this up and giving my book a chance.

Printed in the USA
CPSIA information can be obtained
at www.ICGtesting.com
JSHW022125190624
65066JS00006B/9